SUSAN SCHAEFER BERNARDO

Inspired

Inner Flower Child Books

LOS ANGELES

Publisher's Cataloging-In-Publication Data
(Prepared by The Donohue Group, Inc.)

Names: Bernardo, Susan Schaefer.
Title: Inspired / by Susan Schaefer Bernardo.
Description: Los Angeles, CA : Inner Flower Child Books, [2018] | Series: [The Firefly Tribe] ; [book 1] | Interest age level: Young adult.
Identifiers: ISBN 978-0-9711228-3-3 | ISBN 978-0-9711228-6-4 (ebook)
Subjects: LCSH: Teenage girls--Fiction. | Creative ability--Fiction. | Muses (Greek deities)--Fiction. | Stepfamilies--Fiction. | Menarche--Fiction. | Friendship--Fiction.
Classification: LCC PS3602.E76 I56 2017 (print) | LCC PS3602.E76 (ebook) | DDC 813/.6--dc23

Cover illustration by Courtenay Fletcher
Interior book design by Dog-ear Book Design
Author photo by Leslie Talley Photography

Inner Flower Child Books
LOS ANGELES

With love and gratitude to Jules Tanzer

This is the story of a girl

who forgot how to breathe,

and how life changed

once she remembered

ONE

I DON'T KNOW WHAT WOKE ME UP, THE NERVOUS CAT OR THE EERIE GLOW IN THE ROOM. MOO stood at the foot of the mattress, rigid and alert. He arched and hissed, backing up until he was practically on top of me. I batted his tail out of my face, sat up, and followed my cat's focused gaze across the room.

Light leaked around the frame of the door, a shimmering rectangle on the dark wall. I looked over at the clock where it sat atop the moving box that would be making do as a nightstand until my new furniture arrived.

Three o'clock in the morning.

"Go to sleep, Moo! It's just the hall light."

I dropped my head back to the pillow with a groan, exhausted after a long day hauling boxes from the cottage.

Something kept me from sinking back into dreamland. I remembered where I was—and that the door to the hallway was to my left, on the same side of the room as my bed. There wasn't a door across from me—just that enormous crate, delivered by a very strange, very gorgeous messenger late that afternoon.

He hadn't rung the front doorbell, just appeared outside the sliding door that led to the patio, wearing dark blue jeans and a white t-shirt, nothing unusual, but on him the standard clothes looked wrong somehow.

"Special delivery for Mistress Rocket Malone," he announced, gesturing to a wooden crate that was almost as tall as he was.

I let out a startled shriek when I saw a stranger standing at my door, and then tried to cover it with cool.

'Mistress'? I wondered.

"I'm Mizzzzz Malone," I said, drawing out the "z" in my most sophisticated voice. "Would you like me to sign for it?"

He tilted his head, confused. Thought hard for a second.

"Yes, yes, of course, you must sign for it. That's the expected custom in your world," he said.

With that odd statement, he whisked a gold clipboard and ostrich quill out of thin air and handed them to me with a flourish.

"What are you, an aspiring magician?" I joked. Welcome to Hollywood, I thought, where all the deliverymen and waiters are wanna-be actors.

Without responding, the deliveryman lifted the crate into my room like it weighed less than his feathered pen, and propped it against the wall.

I carefully signed on the dashed line in my most elegant cursive. I'd been practicing my signature all year, and I was particularly proud of the stylish loop at the tail. I handed it over to him, and studied the crate.

"Who sent this?" I asked, turning back to the messenger. But he had vanished without a word. Which was good, because I had no idea how much to tip, and even if I did know, I had no idea where to find my wallet in the clutter heap that was my new bedroom.

To be honest, I'd forgotten all about the delivery, because I'd been feverishly stuffing boxes at the old house most of the day. But now the mysterious package was lit up and keeping me from desperately-needed, probably futile, beauty sleep.

Letting out a full-body yawn, I slumped out of bed and squatted down next to the glowing wooden crate.

The words "Glass—Fragile" were printed on multiple sides, with odd writing just below. Greek? I recognized a couple of letters, "Ω"—the upside-down horseshoe of Omega, and "Π"—Pi, which everyone knows from geometry class. Pi are square, not round. Ha ha. Math humor.

Could it be something my mom had picked up for me on her honeymoon? She got married a couple of weeks ago, to this guy named Rick she's been dating for less than a year. He's actually her first husband, since my mom and real father never married. They were bohemians.

The newlyweds dumped me in England with my Nana while they went off to Mykonos for two weeks and had fun in the sun without me. Whatever, I could live with that. Once we got back to Los Angeles, though, we charged right onto phase three...merging into one big happy home. Rick's big home, to be specific, here in the Hollywood Hills. The "happy" is a matter of perspective.

I padded barefoot out to the laundry room where my mom stowed her toolbox. With a flathead screwdriver, I pried off the wooden lid. Peeling back layers of cotton padding and faded Greek newspapers, I found the source of the light—a tall, narrow mirror with silvered glass and a carved wooden frame that looked old. Antique old. Maybe even ancient. It had been covered in gold leaf at one point, but much of the gilt had flaked off, except for what remained in the etched Greek key design that bordered all four sides.

Embedded in the top center of the frame was a tarnished disk, about six inches in diameter, made out of some sort of metal. The disk shimmered and pulsed with a soft golden light that illuminated everything in the room.

A scene had been engraved into the disk, but thick green patina obscured the details. I grabbed a fuzzy pink sock off the floor to polish it up a little. Zap! A jolt tingled through my fingertips. I pulled my hand back with a start, dropping the sock.

Moo emitted a freaked-out mewl, like when the neighbor's Rottweiler got into our garden and chased him up onto the roof. I wasn't scared—curiosity had me in its clutches. Maybe the mirror was electric, like one of those bathroom gizmos where you can see your blackheads so magnified your skin resembles the meteor-pocked surface of the moon. I felt all around the wooden frame for some sort of switch. Nothing.

With the tip of my index finger, I explored the grooves in the disk. My skin tingled and the light pulsed more rapidly, as if responding to my touch. My finger felt magnetized to the metal surface, like an iron needle to the North Pole. Stuck. Placing my left hand against the disk, I pushed and pulled hard, trying to leverage my right finger free. That was a mistake. Now both my hands were held captive.

Light strobed the room now, getting brighter and brighter. Arms raised above my head, stuck to the mirror, I looked desperately around me for a way out. Moo leapt onto a stack of boxes, his arched back and erect tail casting spooky shadows on the wall behind my bed. The glass mirror began to cloud up. And when I say cloud, I don't mean it became milky or opaque. Actual clouds drifted out of the mirror, cool and wispy against my face. The hard surface of the mirror dissolved, leaving only the wooden frame, and me attached to the disk at the top. Behind the clouds, *inside* the mirror, voices murmured, distant at first but drawing closer to me. Peering into the fog, I perceived vague swirls of movement and color.

A woman spoke, urgency in her husky voice. "Is it done, Narcissus?"

"Yes, Clio," a man replied. I recognized his voice. The delivery-man. "The mirror is in place, as you requested. But, goddesses, I have a few ideas for a new portal, something other than the same old mirror. Perhaps a handheld device that warps time and space or—"

"Old?!" chimed another woman. "It's not old. It's classic. And you're the one who invented it in the first place!"

Narcissus spoke again, ticking off a list of names. "Plato, the Grimm Brothers, Lewis Carroll, JK Rowling, Agatha Christie, Sylvia Plath, Isaac Asimov… They all wove our mirrors into their stories. And that's just the writers—don't even get me started with visual artists—"

"It serves the purpose, Narcissus," interrupted another feminine voice, this one rich and sweet like warm honey. "But now, we must pre-pare ourselves to welcome our newest apprentice. Sisters, gather to me. Let us form the circle."

More voices rose in incomprehensible chatter, followed by the plucking of an unseen stringed instrument. The disk grew uncomfortably hot under my hands. What was I dealing with here? A coven of witches? Panicking, I braced my feet on the floor and strained my entire body backwards, using every pathetic little ounce of upper-body strength I had scraped together for those fitness tests in gym class. It didn't amount to much.

"Let go of me!" I shouted. Abruptly, the music and movement ceased. A woman spoke again.

"She is not yet ready."

The mirror went dark. My hands flew off the disk, and I went tum-bling back onto the carpeted floor, my head colliding with the edge of my metal mattress frame.

Everything went dark.

Two

RUMBLING...SHAKING...EARTHQUAKE! I STARTED TO DUCK AND COVER UNTIL MY SLEEPY brain registered that I was sprawled on the floor, and the quake's 'epicenter' was warm, furry and laying on my stomach. I stretched out my hand. A sandpapery kiss confirmed this wasn't a tremor, just a hungry cat purring for breakfast.

I gathered him in for a hug and started to stand up, but it felt like all the blood had drained from my head to my toes. I sat down, hard, on the mattress. The room swam in front of me. Touching the tender lump on the back of my head gingerly, I stared at the mirror. The night's events came spilling back into my conscious mind.

In the light of day, it all seemed so...silly. The mirror was tilted innocently against the wall, the black velvet bunched up at its top. A click-clacking at the sliding glass door drew my attention. The vertical blinds were rustling against the screen. I walked over slowly and pulled hand over hand on the long cord to open the vertical blinds. Squinting against the early morning light, shivering at the damp cool breeze, I stepped onto the patio and looked west. On a clear day, you could see the ocean from the edge of the patio, but with morning fog settled like a white blanket over the entire Westside, this hilltop felt like an island floating on a sea of down feathers.

Sounds drifted through the fog from neighboring houses and the busy city just beyond. I could hear the drone of leaf blowers, car engines revving, drivers honking in their impatience to get to work and start another day. No doubt there were a few giant plasma screens with surround sound speakers in this neighborhood, too.

A dream, then. Sleepwalking, too. That's all I had experienced the night before. And, why not? Everyone knows sleep deprivation can drive a person crazy. This was all just a reaction to jet lag, moving and sleeping in a weird new place, I told myself.

My mom tapped on the door and poked her head into my room, pulling me out of my trance.

"Rise and shine, Rocket," she said. "We need to get over to the cottage to pack up the final load. Rick already took the truck back over there."

Thirteen years and three hundred sixty-three days of my life bubble-wrapped, boxed and loaded onto a truck—and just like that, the cottage where I was born was about to become the place where I used to live.

"Moving sucks!" I told her not for the first time, as I rummaged through boxes looking for something to wear. I finally gave up and pulled on the same old shorts and t-shirt I'd worn the day before. "It's so not fair! Why couldn't Rick move into our house instead? Why are we the ones who had to move out?"

"Love, we've gone over and over this," she replied. "The cottage was perfect for two single girls, but it's simply too cramped for all of us now. Don't you remember how you were always moaning that your closet was smaller than your shoeboxes, and you hated sharing a bathroom with me? Now you have your very own bathroom and a closet practically as large as your bedroom in the cottage. And you know that Rick's company is downtown—the commute from the beach would be dismal."

"So, I have to commute from Hollywood to Venice for school instead? That doesn't make sense."

My mom hesitated. I could tell I was about to hear something I didn't want to hear. I was right.

"Umm, I've been meaning to speak to you about that. You know, Rick went to Hollywood High, just a few miles from here. He said they have a really good program. You could start fresh in the fall."

I couldn't believe I was hearing this. I stared at her in horror.

"Oh no, no, no. You promised I could go to VB High next year with Gillian. That was the deal. You said renting out the cottage would help cover the tuition!"

"Rocket, it's just an idea. You have two months of middle school and all summer to think about it. Now calm down or you're going to have an attack. Where's your inhaler?"

"In one of those," I said, pointing to the tower of boxes. She started rummaging through the box on top, sighing when she saw what a jumbled mess it was. She sat the first box on the floor, and was about to unpack a second when she spotted the mirror.

"Where'd this come from?" she asked.

I was surprised. "It's not from you? It was delivered yesterday, in that big crate. My name was on it."

"I think it's from Greece," I said, showing her the labels. "I figured you bought it on your honeymoon. Or maybe Yaya sent it?"

"Oh," my mom said, realization dawning. "I'll bet it's from Aunt Polly."

"Aunt Polly? The godmother I've seen twice in my life?" I asked, surprised.

My mother nodded. "It was the strangest thing. We ran into her outside the Acropolis. She told me she was sending you a little something for your fourteenth birthday."

"A little something usually means cash," I grumbled.

"It looks like an antique. Could be valuable. Be careful with it," said my mom. "And you need to write a nice thank-you note."

She looked at her watch. "We really need to get going, Rocket."

"I can't!" I wailed. The more I thought about moving, the tighter my chest got.

My mother reached down her hands and pulled me to a standing position. "Let's do some yoga poses for a minute, okay?"

She slid one foot up the inside of her thigh, balancing like a crane on her other leg. "Tree pose," she instructed. "You're stressed and jet-lagged...and you're focusing on all the negatives, instead of seeing the potential."

A bead of sweat appeared on my forehead as I wobbled on my right leg, trying to find my center of gravity. No use. I lurched to the side, my left foot landing with a thunk.

"Start with warrior pose," she suggested, moving smoothly into a lunge. "Stretch out your arm, like this. Come on, I said 'warrior,' not 'worrier,' pose!"

After a few moments of stretching and focusing on just my hand in front of me, instead of my whole looming future, my breathing slowed a little. My mom put her arm around my shoulders and gave me a squeeze.

"Come on. One more load, and we'll have everything moved out. Then we can grab cones at Rosie's. A last hurrah to the old neighborhood."

I shook my head. "There's nothing to hurrah about."

When we got to the cottage, Rick bounded over like a Labrador puppy and gave my mom a hug. "A couple hours and we will be locked, loaded and ready to roll," he announced. "Then it's three...two...one...blast-off!" he said to me, holding his hand up in the air expectantly.

"Wow—original," I commented, keeping my own hands tucked firmly inside the pockets of my gray hoodie.

"What, you've heard that one?" he asked with an extremely annoying wink. Honestly, if I had a dollar for every half-witted joke people have made about my name, I could afford to build an actual spacecraft and zoom off to Mars. Where I could form a colony consisting of two residents: me and Moo.

"Come on, Rocket, show a little enthusiasm," urged Rick. "This is a big day for Team Patrick!"

"I'd rather stay in the dugout if you don't mind," I muttered.

Between the space references and this whole "Team Patrick" thing, I'm constantly on the verge of barfing. My mother may have changed her last name, but mine is still Malone. Legally. And it's going to stay that way. Rocket Patrick does not roll off the tongue. It sounds like the name of an Irishman who's downed a few too many green beers, if you know what I mean. Hmm, that might explain how he got saddled with the name "Rick Patrick." Sounds more like a fast food breakfast sandwich, loaded with ham and extra cheese.

My real father was a glassblower, like my mother. Except he created actual art, and she makes tacky souvenirs to sell to the tourists who swarm Venice Beach 24/7/365. They met when he was teaching a workshop at my mother's college in York, England. When he died, a reporter in "Collector" magazine wrote: "The art glass world is shattered at the loss of its most vibrant craftsman, Gabriel Gonzaga." Get it? 'Shattered?' I was only four when he died, and I don't have any memories of him. My mom says he's responsible for my crazy name. It was his idea to name me after the thing she craved most while I was taking up space in her body. Once she got pregnant, it was "good-bye, bangers and mash"(which is Brit-speak for sausages and mashed potatoes) and "hello, vegetables." She jokingly calls it her "green period." Her favorite was a type of lettuce called "rocket." I guess I'm lucky she didn't use the American version and name me Arugula.

Living with a peculiar name can be tough. The first day of class, when the teachers call roll and get to "Rocket," they always look to the back of the room for a guy with a black t-shirt and shaggy skater hair. There's this moment of shocked silence when mousy me in the front raises her hand and mumbles "here." But I digress. Maybe the name thing didn't faze you. We live in an age when it's totally acceptable to name your helpless newborn Apple or Blanket, so why not a salad green?

My mom pulled some empty boxes out of the back of her car.

"Let me take those, beautiful," said Rick. "You know, that's why we're paying Nico and his son to help us, so you don't have to lift a finger."

I waited for my mom to snap back that she routinely lifts fifty-pound sacks of silica at work, but she just smiled and gave Rick a little kiss on the cheek. "You are such a lamb."

"Are you kidding me? Your biceps are bigger than Rick's," I exclaimed.

Rick ignored the insult. I swear he's eternally in a good mood, like a friendly robot. He never gets mad. Rick is what you'd call an average Joe, with a heaping tablespoon of eco-nerd thrown into the batter—he owns a solar energy company, drives a hybrid and is obsessive about recycling. It's not like he's a horrible monster or anything dramatic like that. I just don't know what my mom sees in him.

My mom and Rick gave each other cutesy amused glances, like I was a silly lapdog that just barked at the mailman or something. They do that all the time. It's unbearable. I shoved the white picket gate open, hoping it would clatter against the fence to show how irritated I was. Unfortunately, the gate got hung up—with perverse silence—on a for-lorn clump of purple lobelia. In their haste to transplant me, someone had also uprooted the flowers that edged our gravel walk. It wasn't the flowers' fault, so I stopped to tuck the little guys back into the soil.

Our front yard is tiny but packed with color, thanks to the cottage garden Nana and I planted a few springs ago. Los Angeles is so temperate you can pretty much grow whatever, whenever, but Nana lives in the Yorkshire Dales. She says that our endless sunshine makes people con-fused and lazy, and it's better to stick to a four-season schedule whether the weather cooperates or not. She sends seed packets to plant in April, and hand-knitted woolen scarves and sweaters in the fall, which is crazy, because September and October are scorching here—dry, windy and hot. While the rest of the country enjoys their autumn leaves turning red and orange, we Californians are praying that our hillsides don't spontaneously combust.

Nico and his son Hector came out of the house with a loaded dolly, carefully guiding it down a couple of wide planks set up as a temporary ramp. When he saw me, Nico waved his son off and squatted down without a word to help me. His big hands were almost as brown as the soil he was scooping up in them, and criss-crossed with a constellation of scars from years working at my mother's shop.

Once the plants were back in place, he gave me one of his kind smiles. "Rocket, cara mia, what is needed now is water," he said.

I grabbed my galvanized tin watering can and filled it up from the spigot at the side of the house. I offered the can to Nico, but he waved it away.

"This is for you to do," he told me.

Just then, Hector reappeared.

"Almost finished!" He said cheerfully, as he rolled the empty dolly back up the front steps. "One more load in the kitchen."

"And then we will drive the truck to your new home," Nico said. He stood up, patting my shoulder. If he noticed the tears trickling down my face and onto the ground, he was smart enough not to mention it.

I stood there and let all that water rain down on the little plants, until it soaked into the parched earth. It needed to travel deep to the roots so they could take hold again. When the can was empty, I made my way up the front steps, pausing to say good-bye to the daylilies and fat black bumblebees.

You know how honey soothes a sore throat? My front porch with its blue-painted planks and white wicker rockers feels like that, like a welcome mat inviting you into our cottage. I was born here—literally. My parents had a midwife who delivered me underwater in the bathtub. I hope they scrubbed it like crazy before I swam out, because from what my mom has told me, this place wasn't so charming when they got it. My mom says even the realtor who sold them the place had a hard time finding something nice to say about it, and a realtor's job is to make "a sow's ear sound like a silk purse." That's kind of like turning a lemon into lemonade, I guess.

It was all they could afford at the time—but since we've lived here, the neighborhood has gone from scary to trendy. Just over on Main Street, there are lots of restaurants, shops and galleries, including my mom's. It's gotten so popular it's hard to find a parking spot. These days, young artists can barely afford to rent a room around here. They call that gentrification.

I brushed my hand lightly over the leaded panes of the stained glass windows on either side of our green front door. I've walked by them every day for ten years, but it was like I was really seeing them for the first time. These were one of my dad's first-ever glass projects—a little rough, maybe, but you could already see his talent emerging. He made them when he was just fourteen, which is what I will be on Monday. His mother, the grandmother I call Yaya, gave them to us when she moved into a retirement home. They were a tribute to California, done in a classic Arts and Crafts style (that's with a capital "A" and "C"). Torrey pines form a bold silhouette in the foreground, against a backdrop of horizontal bands of ocean and turquoise sky. It's like a landscape painting made of glass.

Nana's thumb is green, but I guess you would say my mother's is rainbow-colored. The interior of the cottage is as colorful as those windows. She painted the walls in bright jewel tones—emerald green, ruby red, sapphire blue. The white wood trim makes it all juicy and sharp. Even the ceiling got special treatment—it's sky-blue and adorned with wispy hand-painted clouds. It's a tiny cottage—all that bold color should have made it feel even tinier, but somehow it had the opposite effect. It always makes me feel like I'm peering at the world from inside one of my mother's glass paperweights.

Stripped of artwork and clutter, the cottage looked lonely, like it knew we were abandoning it. Even the dust bunnies were being swept away by efficient Rosa, Rick's cleaning lady. She buzzed from room to room, polishing and scrubbing, bleaching and sweeping the house to an unfamiliar shine. My mom and Rick had decided to advertise it as a furnished rental. They decided that Rick's place has a different "aesthetic," and things like our rocking chairs and comfy overstuffed sofa wouldn't fit in there. Thinking about it made my chest tighten again, which set off my inner alarm bell. So I didn't linger in the living room. I headed straight for my bedroom door off the miniscule hallway.

I almost bumped into Rosa as she was coming out with her mop and wheeled bucket full of murky water. I know it sounds pathetic, but part of me resented the fact that even my dirt was no longer mine. Stop smirking. I already admitted it was pathetic.

As soon as Rosa was out the door, I shut it behind her. Naturally, this time the door closed with a bang. I felt guilty. Here she was slogging away to clean some spoiled brat's room—probably to earn money to feed her own hungry children in Guatemala or somewhere—while I was moaning about the fact that I had to move from one roof over my head to another, bigger roof over my head. I felt my lungs burn a little more.

My bedroom faced the street. Light streamed in from the big window, filtered by the wisteria vine that framed the front porch. Despite Rosa's efforts, a dark rectangle remained where my striped rug had kept the wood floor from fading. My mom had declared the rug too raggedy to leave for the tenants or to bring to the new house. It ended up in the dumpster along with piles of school papers, scarred toys and things that didn't make the cut for the garage sale. Out with the old, in with the new. Everything's disposable these days—even home sweet homes.

I sat on the bare planks, smack in the middle of the still-damp patch where my rug used to be, and tried to slow my breathing as I stared out into the green.

"Knock, knock." It was my mother, without her new better half for once. I seized my opportunity.

"Why can't we just remodel this house? We could add a second story. The people around here are more interesting," I said.

Rick poked his head into my room. "Interesting people?" he interjected. "Like that wino your mother found on the porch last month, sleeping it off in a pool of his own vomit?"

The first thing I planned to do at the new house was hang a "Keep Out" sign on my door. And install a padlock. And a motion detector.

"His name was Sam," I replied. "And it's better to see that real stuff instead of hiding a hundred miles away up in bubble-land."

"I'm sorry, Rocket, I didn't mean to be patronizing. We have lots of homeless people in Hollywood, too—you can make new friends," Rick said in a deceptively mild tone. I'd only known him a year, but I knew commando sarcasm when I heard it. "And you know what?" he continued. "I clocked it on the way down here. It's exactly 11.48 miles door-to-door. Substantially less than a hundred."

"Yeah, in actual miles. But in metaphorical miles, it's a hundred light years," I shot back. I knew I was being a melodramatic brat, but I didn't care. I turned to my mother with a silent plea for her to stand up for me, even though I knew it was futile. After all, just two weeks before, she'd stood in front of an altar and made taking his side legally binding.

"Look, we're all hot and tired, and we still have to unload the truck at the other end. If you're finished having your little funky time, I'd like to head over to Rick's house now. I mean *our* house," my mom said, in a ticked-off tone I was hearing from her more and more often.

"I'm staying here," I said, crossing my arms in front of my chest. It's funny—at school, I'll do anything to avoid confrontation, but at home with my mom? These days it's like an unstoppable chemical reaction, the kind that leads to a nuclear explosion.

Surprisingly, Rick defused the situation and agreed with me for once.

"She's lived here all her life, Josie. I'll tell you what—why don't we let Rocket hang here for a few more hours, while we meet Nico at the other end."

I looked at him, trying to figure out this new game. Mom still wasn't convinced. "Then we'll have to come all the way back down the hill just to get her."

"It's only 11.48 miles door-to-door," I chimed in, trying not to sound like too much of a smart-ass. "Or…I could lock up for you when Rosa's done and spend the night at Gillian's."

I could almost see their synapses firing as they made the connection: this would give them the house to themselves for a night. Rick smiled slightly. "That's a great plan, Rocket."

Newlyweds are so obvious.

As soon as they were out of sight, I moved out to the porch and texted my best friend Gillian.

9-1-1.

THREE

ELEVEN SECONDS LATER, GILLIAN WALTZED OUT THE FRONT DOOR OF THE HOUSE ACROSS THE
street. She stopped an oncoming car with an outstretched hand and an
irresistible smile. Sometimes, it bugs the heck out of me how easily she
can charm people, but having a best friend with that ability comes in
handy.

She paused at the "For Rent" sign staked in our front yard and feigned
karate kicks. "Want me to chop it down for you?" she asked.

I smiled in spite of myself. "Yeah, I do."

"Judy Garland went to Hollywood High," she said, once I filled her
in on the latest calamity.

"Wrong answer," I said.

She changed tracks instantly.

"Got it. Let's go back to my house and prepare the prosecution's
case," she said. "How could they be so cruel? Classic wicked stepfather
syndrome. I'm calling child protective services and reporting them for
psychological abuse."

Gillian's on the debate team—she lives for a good argument.

"Do you mind if we just sit here for awhile?" I asked.

I didn't need to say anything else—we'd been friends for so long we
were pretty adept at reading each other's body language. We sank into
our wicker chairs and rocked like old ladies, contemplating the awful-
ness of the situation.

After a little while, Gillian threw out the ultimate lure. "My mom
just made brownies."

"I'm supposed to lock up when Rosa's done," I replied.

"We'll come back in half an hour," she promised.

We let Rosa know I would just be across the street. It took a few minutes to get the message across. At first, I think she thought we wanted her to go clean Gillian's house too, because she looked really alarmed and started rattling off in Spanish "solamente *una* casa." I've had three years of Spanish in school, but I'm not really comfortable using it in the real world. I'm afraid I'll make a mistake and say something totally lame. Gillian just waded right in. With a few hand gestures and well-placed Spanish 101 vocabulary words, she had Rosa smiling and waving us along.

"La casa es muy lampina," I awkwardly blurted out as we left. Rosa gave me an odd look, and Gillian burst out laughing.

"What?" I whispered.

"You just told Rosa the house is very hairless," said Gillian.

"I meant to say clean," I said.

"Don't worry," replied Gillian, as she preceded me across the street. "Between your mom and you and Moo, she probably did have to sweep up a ton of hair."

Gillian's mom Megan bustled around us with all the sweetness and enthusiasm you'd expect from a pre-school teacher. When I was little, she was the mom we ran to when we needed our boo-boos cured with Barbie Band-Aids and lollipops. I could see by the usual mess on the kitchen table—her office, she liked to call it—that she was right in the middle of preparing for a week's worth of arts and crafts, but she stopped everything and offered her usual cure for the blues: a double dose of sugar. It's a cliché, but it's true…chocolate makes everything better.

After our infusion, we got down to business. Gillian sat down at her desk and swiveled to face me, yellow legal pad and pencil at the ready. There's nothing she enjoys more than putting things into "pro" and "con" columns.

"You be Josie and Rick, and I'll argue in defense of you continuing at VBHS."

I tried to sound like a total killjoy parent. "Rocket, with gas as expensive as it is these days, it would be better for you to go to a school closer to home next year."

"Mom, Rick, I beg to differ. Firstly—"

I couldn't help interrupting. "Is 'firstly' a real word?"

Gillian looked at me, her left eyebrow raised in polite disdain. She can project an entire range of emotions with those arched brown eyebrows of hers. "It is well-established that 'firstly' or 'first' can be used inter-changeably when enumerating a list. However, if you're more comfort-able with 'first off'?"

I nodded yes to her inquiring eyebrow. "And I don't think 'I beg to differ' really sounds like me either."

"Why don't we just get the basic argument down and then you can rewrite it in your own words, like the jocks do with the term papers Gary Grossman writes for them. All right, here we go—again… 'Mom, Rick, it's true that gas is expensive, but it is still cheaper than the therapy I would need if I lost all my friends.'"

I looked at her. "So, you're saying that if I go to a different high school, our friendship's over?"

Gillian shrugged. "I just don't think long distance relationships ever work out."

My mouth dropped open. "Long distance? It's less than twelve miles!"

Gillian continued on in a totally serious way. "Yeah, but firstly, in rush hour, it could take two hours to drive that. Secondly, neither of us is old enough to drive, and thirdly, public transportation in LA gener-ally sucks. If we lived in New York, then maybe…"

I was about to freak out when she started laughing so hard she almost fell off her chair.

"God, I wish I had a picture of your face right now," she said. "Keep that sense of fear and urgency in your voice when you talk to your mom."

Writing the list took a lot longer than I expected, mainly because my mind wouldn't focus on it. I kept thinking about what Gillian had said about long distance relationships. Even though she'd been joking, I worried that our friendship just wouldn't be the same once I moved. No more early morning walks on the beach or spontaneous stops at Rosie's on the way home from school. We'd have to plan our time together, schedule "play dates."

I had a sudden flash. "Hey, Gills. I know it's not summer yet but why don't we pull a slip from the BB Box?"

Gillian and I have a longstanding summer tradition. Some might think it's geeky, but our moms started it when we were little and we're still doing it. All year long, whenever there's an activity that appeals—a new beach hangout, an art technique, the latest cupcakery, a cool-looking bowling alley—whatever, no matter how big or small, we clip out the idea from the newspaper or write it down on a square of paper and pop it into the Boredom Buster Box. The box looks like one of those "mailboxes" you make on Valentine's Day in elementary school. In fact, that's what it started as. We have a stack of shoeboxes, each decorated according to our fancies that year, from My Little Pony to Harry Potter. Last year we paid blood red homage to our favorite vampire series. The only design rule is that we include the annoying quote our mothers drilled into our heads: "Only boring people get bored." I wrote it in a thought-bubble above one of the vampire's heads. (You probably guessed that the chick about to get her neck double-pierced had a thought-bubble that read: "I'm bored.")

I pulled the box off Gillian's bookshelf. It was already stuffed, since this year we hadn't had time to do much except study, study, study. People who think it's easy being a kid clearly haven't checked how much our backpacks weigh. In a generation or two, the human race is probably going to *de*volve back into walking on four legs, because we're so hunched over from the strain.

"I don't know," she said.

"You don't know what?"

"It's just, well, it seems kind of immature, right? I mean, decorating shoe boxes was fine when we were seven, but we're starting high school soon."

I looked at the shoebox and tried to see it the way Gillian was seeing it. Maybe she was right. After all, Mrs. Fletcher had just confirmed that I wasn't very good at art. Suddenly, I was embarrassed.

"So, what do *you* want to do together all summer?" I asked. "Just hang out and do nothing? I guess that would be cool. Just chilling. You could come over and swim in the pool, and I could come here so we can go to the beach."

"No, no. I'm not saying we shouldn't do stuff, but, you know, it wouldn't be such a bad thing if we invited other people. Some things are more fun with, with… a group."

"Exactly whom would you want to invite to join this proposed group?" I asked suspiciously.

She looked away, fiddling with the ends of her long hair. "Jasper said he would like to go on outings with us. We're, um, kind of dating."

"You started dating, and you didn't tell me? And you're dating a *jock*?"

"It just kind of happened while you were away."

Just then, Gillian's mom poked her head in. "Gillian, what time do you guys need to be at Carina's party?"

That was news to me.

"You're going to a party?" I asked Gillian. "At Carina's? I was only gone two weeks and your entire life changed and you didn't tell me?"

"It's totally not a big deal," Gillian hedged. "We ran into each other at the Promenade while you were on your trip. I'm sure she would have invited you if she'd known you'd be home in time."

"I'm sure she wouldn't have," I retorted. "I don't even register as a tremor on her Richter scale of popularity."

Carina was the queen of the diva clones, a pack of look-alike girls who ruled cool in our school. They spent every lunch break analyzing fashion magazines and trying to emulate the "what to wear" photos, no doubt right down to their designer skivvies.

Gillian kept trying to play it down. "She's not so bad. Anyway, it's just a stupid spa party with some girls from school. She's kind of picking me up soon."

"If it's so stupid, why are you going?"

A fancy-sounding car horn blared outside. Gillian's mom pulled open the kitchen curtain, and I saw a familiar limo out front.

Gillian's mother stepped into the quagmire. "Gillian, hon, why don't you just ask Carina if Rocket can come along? I'll bet there's room in that big car for one more."

Oh. My. God. I definitely didn't want to force myself along for the ride, like one of those suckerfish that hitchhike on sharks. Lampreys. That's what they're called. Even hanging out with the newlyweds was preferable to that.

Gillian looked imploringly at me. We both knew that asking Carina this favor would be social suicide. I took pity on her. After all, what was one silly little party compared to thirteen years of friendship?

"That's okay. Really," I said, to Gillian and her mom. "I have a lot of unpacking to do anyway, and I want Moo to have some time getting used to the new place. I'll see you at school on Monday."

Gillian looked grateful. Her mom gave me a hug.

"Two months until graduation, and you girls will have the whole summer to hang out and do each other's toenails."

She was wrong about that.

FOUR

MERCIFULLY, MY MOTHER DIDN'T SAY A WORD WHEN SHE PICKED ME UP, JUST TOOK ONE
look at my face and wisely left matters alone as we started the drive
back to Rick's house.

Rick lives off one of the canyon roads leading up to Mulholland
Drive, which twists and turns fifty-five miles along the crest of the Santa
Monica Mountains to form the great divide between the Westside and
the San Fernando Valley. The neighborhood was probably the go-to
scene way back when Elvis ruled the airwaves, but it seems a bit ick
these days. Marble fountains…fluted columns tacked tackily onto white
box houses…rows of Italian cypress trees marching across the hills in
geometric precision. So different from our sweet and funky cottage in
Venice Beach.

A few months after my mom started dating Rick, he figured out that
art was the key to her heart and bought her a framed print of "Nichols
Canyon" by David Hockney. My mom is gaga for Hockney. Maybe it's
because he was a Brit who came to California like she did, or maybe it's
the way his paintings jump off the canvas toward you. "Nichols Canyon"
is very Matisse in style. Broad, bright strokes, deceptively simple like
children's art—but I tried to recreate it once and didn't come close to
his perfect harmony of color and texture.

Rick's house looks and feels like an altogether different Hockney
painting: "The Collectors." If the word police only let me use one adjec-
tive to describe his place, I'd go with "flat." In my humble opinion, the
late 1960's were a low point in American architecture. My mother tried
to explain why Rick loves this place so much—something about mini-
malism and the play of light—but I just don't get it at all. The house
is shaped out of connected low white rectangles, like some kid made

the letter L out of giant shirt boxes. It's like a figure out of a geometry book, all sharp white angles and parallel lines, perched on the edge of a scrubby hillside. To top it off (pun intended), the house has a flat roof covered with white rocks, which leaks judging from the faint mildewy smell that pervades my room.

The back of the house is mostly glass, which I guess is kind of cool, opening to a concrete rectangle of a swimming pool and a view of the city. Both my room and the master suite face the pool, from opposite corners. In between, there's the kitchen, a dining room, a living room and the den, which Rick calls his playroom. There's a bigger bedroom near the master suite, but mine has the better location—as far away from the lovebirds as I could get.

Bigger is not necessarily better. Think about it—which would you rather eat? A generic, one-pound milk chocolate bar or a single Godiva truffle? Rick's house is like a Hershey's bar past its expiration date. Flavorless, divided into rectangular sections, unsatisfying no matter how much of it you stuff down your throat. The one saving grace is the pool. As soon as my mom and I got back to Rick's, I suited up in my tankini and headed out to the backyard.

Swimming in a pool is a completely different experience than swimming in the ocean. The ocean is exciting and unpredictable—the waves can knock you down but also give you the ride of your life. A pool is a known entity. You can see right down to the bottom, assuming you've balanced your chemicals correctly and it's not an algae swamp. Rick's is always crystal clear. He's scientifically-minded—that is to say, a bit of a geek. He used to be out there all the time with his little water-test kit, checking the levels, then he switched over to a saltwater system. Better for the environment.

The shock of arrowing into the deep end of a cold swimming pool helped shake off some of my growing-grumps, as Nana calls them. I tried to swim a lap completely underwater. Halfway across, it felt like my heart was going to pop right out of my chest, so I swift-kicked my way to the surface. I was frantically treading water, sucking in gulps of warm air, when I realized that Rick was standing there.

"A few more yards and you would have made it," he observed. I ignored him, dunking back under the water to slick my hair off my face.

My mom emerged from the house and made her way across the

rectangular concrete stepping stones set into the green lawn to Rick, wrapping her arms around him from behind and whispering into his ear. They were wearing the swimsuits they'd bought just for their honeymoon—board shorts for Rick, and a red one-piece on my mom—and they looked happy and relaxed. When Rick pointed to me in the pool, my mom released him and headed in my direction.

"I'll get the floats," said Rick, and walked over to a little cabana that housed the pool equipment. My mom sat down on the broad top step in the shallow end, inching her way into the pool.

"Just dive in and you'll get used to it faster," I called out. "Like ripping off a Band-Aid."

"I prefer the 'peel it off slowly and painfully' method, thank you," my mom retorted. "I am totally knackered. I could fall asleep right here."

I glided over next to her. "Wow, you ate well in Greece," I teased, patting her stomach.

"We did," my mom said, "but there's something else I want to tell you."

Before she could, Rick reappeared, carting two floating lounge chairs. He dropped one into the deep end and brought the other to the steps, holding it so my mother could climb in. She settled back with a contented sigh, pulled her wide brimmed hat over her face, and drifted off.

"I'm going to grab a beer," said Rick. "How about you, hon? Juice? Soda? Iced tea?"

"Mmmm, a glass of that peach iced tea sounds scrumptious," she answered, without lifting her hat.

Rick looked at me. "Are you feeling less cranky now?" he asked.

As soon as he asked the question, I remembered how miserable I'd been before the water temporarily washed the worries away.

"Not anymore," I snapped. He laughed and went into the house. I paddled around in the shallow end for a few minutes, but I'd lost the fun and couldn't get it back.

"I think I'll just go inside and take a nap," I said to my mother.

"You know the best way to beat jet lag is to force yourself to stay up and go to sleep at your normal bedtime. Why don't you just stay out here with us and relax? We'll float around and act like celebrities."

Rick came out with a tray of drinks and salted pretzels. He handed my mom her tea, then offered me a glass.

"I brought you an ice cold lemonade," he announced in a disgustingly chipper voice.

My mouth was watering. "I said I didn't want anything."

I toweled off and headed back into the house. My room was still bare bones. Just the new mattress and the stack of boxes that had come over with the last truckload. It was kind of depressing.

Lemonade and the pool suddenly seemed more tempting than dealing with the boxes, until I looked back out the window and saw my mom and Rick floating side by side. Rick had one foot stretched across the end of my mom's lounge chair, to keep them from drifting apart from each other. Forget that.

I scrounged through and found my old twin comforter wrapped around my nightstand lamp and shoved into a box. I was so tired all of a sudden, exhausted "to my very marrow," as Nana would say. After pulling the plastic vertical blinds shut with a clack, I swaddled myself in my old comforter and curled up on top of my bed. Just a teeny-tiny catnap with Moo wouldn't hurt.

When I came to, it was dark. I checked my phone and discovered it was four-thirty in the morning. Some little nap—I'd slept for eleven hours! My stomach rumbled, reminding me that the last thing I'd eaten was a brownie at Gillian's house.

I trundled down the dark hallway and through the living room to the kitchen, Moo tagging along at my heels. I'd been in Rick's house with my mom before, as a guest. I still felt like one. I rummaged through the cupboards until I spotted a package of English muffins. (There's no such thing in England, by the way ; the closest equivalent is called a crumpet). I pulled one apart and popped half down in Rick's retro aqua enamel toaster.

When it sprang up, I slathered it with peanut butter and took it to my room. Moo licked my sticky finger as I munched, gazing dolefully at my mountain of boxes. I wished I could just fall back asleep, but I was so wired that wasn't going to happen. Instead, I plugged my iPod into the speaker dock, selected a suitably energizing playlist, and tackled box number one, the wardrobe box. That one was easy. After I sliced through the sticky brown plastic tape, all I had to do was transfer the hanging clothes into my new closet. My shoes were jumbled in the bottom of the wardrobe box, so I tipped it upside down to get them out. I lined them up two by two on the closet floor. For fun, I dropped Moo into the empty box. He crouched down and leapt out vertically, like his legs were made of springs. It was good exercise for him, and entertaining for me, so I scooped him up and did it again. After the third time, he just gave me a half-lidded look of scorn and curled up at the bottom for a cozy nap.

The next box on the pile was marked "Rocket's bathroom." Although I'd never admit it to my mother, it was pretty cool having my own bathroom for the first time ever. It was basic—a sink, toilet and tub/shower combo job, tiled in a sickly shade of peach. Rick hadn't gotten around to remodeling this side of the house. The faucets were crusty and corroded—but there were three drawers in the vanity and a mirrored medicine cabinet on the wall, all for me. I placed my toothbrush and toothpaste in the top drawer. They looked pretty lonely there, so I moved them to the medicine cabinet. I spent half an hour deciding where everything should go before I was finally satisfied.

By now I was sick of unpacking. It was depressing. It made this move too real, too permanent. I shoved the rest of the boxes into the closet, except for a couple of boxes of books that I turned into a makeshift bedside table to hold my reading light. I perused my school yearbooks, and read some of my old journal entries (I couldn't believe I had ever had a crush on stupid Gary Grossman—he'd turned out to be such a jerk). By now, the sky had lightened, the horizon tinted pale pink like the inside of a seashell.

Rick and my mom emerged from the honeymoon suite and announced that they were headed to the flea market to take advantage of being up at the crack of dawn.

"The dawn cracked an hour ago," I informed them. "You'd think someone who makes a living doing solar would recognize the sun coming up."

"Close enough. We've got to save precious artifacts that other fools are too blind to appreciate. One man's junk is another man's…"

"…garbage." I completed.

"Come on, Rocket, throw on your sneakers," urged Rick.

I gestured to my laptop. "We have a field trip to the Getty Villa tomorrow and Mr. Horace assigned this extra credit report. I checked his homework website this morning."

"But aren't you getting an A++ in history already?" asked my mom.

"You can't be too careful," I said with a shrug. "I also have an art project due."

My mother seized on that last bit of information like terrier with a tug-of-war rope. I gave myself a mental smack on the forehead for not keeping it to myself.

"Oh, wonderful! What's the project? Have you started it?" she asked.

"We had to do a self-portrait. Mine's pretty much done."

"Can we see it?" asked Rick.

I reluctantly pulled up the assignment on my laptop screen. I had taken my seventh grade class photo, stripped out the color to make it black-and-white and then multiplied it so that the entire page was filled with a grid of miniature photos. My mother looked at it in silence for a moment.

"It's Andy Warhol-style. Like Campbell's soup cans."

"I see that," she said, examining the screen with a critical eye. "Nice."

"I tried drawing myself in charcoal, but it came out awful, so I ripped it up. I have to turn in something, or I might lose my A."

"All I said was 'it's nice,'" she answered.

"Yeah, but your voice was loaded like usual. You implied that I could do better. Well, I can't. I wasn't born creative like you and dad. I'm happy with this."

"Creativity is a muscle, Rocket," she said. "You need to exercise—"

My mom looked like she was about to get deeper into it with me, but Rick interrupted.

"Rocket, you are so very responsible to spend Sunday doing your homework. I want to grow up to be just like you someday. But in the meantime, your mom and I are blowing off work and unpacking. We're going shopping instead."

With a giggle, my mom linked her arm through Rick's, and the pair of them skipped off. Okay, they didn't actually skip, but close enough to be annoying.

FIVE

AFTER FINISHING MY REPORT, I SWAM A COUPLE OF LAZY LAPS IN THE POOL, HOPING TO SHAKE off my jet lag. I knew I would never push through it and get back on a normal schedule if I didn't force myself to stay awake. Unfortunately, a lounge chair under a giant canvas umbrella looked like a really inviting spot to rest my burning eyes for just a little bit.

"Rocket?" I heard my mother's voice as if she was talking to me through water. "Rocket? How long have you been out here? You're blistering!"

"I'm in the shade," I mumbled. But now that she mentioned it, I could feel my skin burning. My lips were as dry as driftwood.

"The sun must have shifted. It does that, you know," said my mother, exasperated.

"Actually, mom, the sun stays in place. The earth rotates."

My mother let out a snort as she snapped a point off a nearby aloe vera plant, stripped off the spiky skin and deftly oozed green slime onto my face. Instant relief. One thing about glassblowers—they really know how to handle burns.

"Rick and I thought we'd have a special birthday dinner for you tonight, since tomorrow's a school and work day. He ordered Indian food, your favorite."

"From Lotus?"

"No, from a local place."

My mom must have felt guilty about leaving me alone all day, because they'd tried to make the kitchen look all festive. Candles, the nice dishes, cloth napkins, even a little bouquet of gerbera daisies.

"Prepare to be amazed. My friend Scott said this place is terrific," Rick announced, once my mom and I had joined him at the dining room table. He opened the cardboard lid of a foil take-out container with a flourish. "First course, potato samosa."

"It smells delicious," said my mom. I wasn't inclined to be so generous.

I shook my head. "Sorry, Rick, there's just no way they can compete with Lotus." That was the place around the corner from our old house. My mom and I had been eating there for years. The owner, Ramachandar, treated us like royalty whenever we came in. He always folded my napkin into some exotic shape and brought us a complimentary papadum.

"Lotus will always hold a special place in my heart. It's where your mom and I went on our first date. However, they do not deliver to the Hollywood Hills," responded Rick.

"We do need a new local dive," agreed my mother.

"Lotus isn't a dive," I protested, as I grabbed a samosa and dipped a corner into mango chutney.

Rick cleared his throat. "Before we eat, I would like to make a toast."

I groaned. If I learned one thing at the wedding, it was that the Irish are extremely fond of making toasts.

Rick stood, raising his bottle of Guinness. My mom and I held up our water glasses. "May those that love us, love us. And those that don't love us, may God turn their hearts. And if He doesn't turn their hearts, may He turn their ankles, so we'll know them by their limping."

My mom laughed. I must have scowled. He smiled at me.

"I'm just teasing you, Rocket. Here's your real birthday toast: May you have all the happiness and luck that life can hold—And at the end of all your rainbows, may you find a pot of gold. Rocket, my girl, may you live as long as you want, and never want as long as you live."

He and my mom held up their glasses until I raised mine, and we clinked. Togetherness. Rah.

"Here goes," I said, taking a healthy bite. My mother nibbled the edge of hers. Rick looked at me and my mom, hopeful.

"Not bad," said my mother.

Rick's face fell. "Just not bad?" he asked.

"A little soggy, and the chutney is bitter," I explained.

Rick took an enormous bite, closing his eyes to concentrate.

"You're right," he said, heaving a huge, dramatic sigh. "I've ruined your birthday eve dinner! I'm not fit to live." He handed me his plastic knife. "Here—stab away. The world will be a better place without me in it."

I rolled my eyes. "Hilarious. I'm sure it doesn't totally suck," I commented, as I loaded up my plate with fragrant basmati rice, lentils, and chicken tikka masala. On top of my mountain of food, I poured raita, a cucumber yogurt sauce to give my tongue a cool and creamy break from all that spice.

"Did you hear that, Josie?" Rick asked my mom. "It doesn't totally suck! That's good, right?"

My mom didn't respond, just grimaced a little. She only had a couple of spoons of rice on her plate, so I waved a container under her nose.

"Look, Rick got your favorite, too!" I told her. "Saag paneer!"

Her face went green. She put out both hands to ward off the container of spinach and cheese.

"Not tonight—I'm just sticking to rice."

I stared at her in disbelief. "But it's your favorite! I'm the one who thinks it's disgusting."

"I'm just too hot to eat much tonight," she replied.

Rick shot to his feet. "I'll put on the A/C."

I laughed. "Hot? You don't get hot, Mom."

"They're predicting record heat this week," Rick commented. "There have already been a couple of brush fires up in the hills near Santa Clarita."

I looked at him. "My mom never gets hot. She works in front of a crucible all day. Maybe she's missing the ocean breezes, now that we live so far from the beach."

My mom looked at Rick for help.

"Hey, how about you open your birthday present now?" he said in this bright voice. I could tell when I was getting the runaround. But a present is a present.

With a wink to my mom, he went out of the room and came back carrying a big flat rectangle wrapped in brown paper. He set it down next to me.

Rick, getting all excited and pulling off the rest of the paper to show me his present, said "It's a reproduction of a really famous piece by LaBarge with that mid-century modern streamlined look."

"I saw one just like this at the mall."

Rick's face crumpled until he looked like a kid who had his balloon popped.

My mother narrowed her eyes at me. "Rocket, Rick went to a lot of trouble to pick out something special for your new room."

"I'm sorry, but I like the one from Aunt Polly better," I said. "I'm allowed to have an opinion, aren't I?"

"The least, and I mean the very least, you could do is say thank you," she said sharply.

Rick looked uncomfortable at the pressure she was applying. "It's okay, Josie. We can put this one in the nurser—"

He trailed off mid-word. I looked up from my dinner. Now my mother was glaring at him.

"The *nursery*?!" I looked at my mother, aghast. "You're not thinking of getting pregnant, are you? Are you kidding me? You just got married two weeks ago!"

My mother sighed. "This is not exactly how I pictured the evening going." She absent-mindedly reached for a forkful of saag paneer right out of the carton. As soon as she lifted the fork up to her face, she blanched, covered her mouth and pushed her chair back from the table in a hurry. "I'm going to be sick."

"Do you want me to come with you?" Rick called. She shook her head, practically sprinting out of the room, as white as the chunks of cheese in the dish.

It didn't take a math whiz to add things up. I turned on Rick. "Oh my god, she's *already* pregnant! I thought she was just getting fat, but she's having a baby!"

"Two, actually," said Rick. "We're having twins."

"Twins?! Would it have killed you to wear a condom? You grown-ups are always preaching on and on about abstinence and birth control. This is so irresponsible."

"Rocket, your mother and I were *trying* to conceive. We just thought it would take a little longer than this. She's thirty-six years old, and I just turned forty. We wanted to have kids before it was too late."

"She already has a kid, in case you haven't noticed!"

"That's not what I meant to say. Look, Rocket, this 'dad of a teen-age girl' gig is new to me. Sometimes I feel like I'm walking through a minefield—"

I cut him right off. "Well, you can just chill out, because you're not my dad, and you never will be. I'm really tired. Thanks for the mirror I don't need and the crappy Indian food. Maybe you should go check on your wife, and your children." And with that, I left him alone to clean up the mess from dinner.

SIX

THAT NIGHT I LAY IN BED AWAKE FOR THE LONGEST TIME, TRYING TO COAX MY BRAIN INTO turning off. It was quiet here compared to living at the beach, where we'd had neighbors within ten feet on three sides plus the continuous pulse of the ocean and traffic. Rick's house sat on a big lot, and the hillside behind us was uninhabited. At least, uninhabited by people. Rick said he'd seen raccoons and deer roaming around there, and an occasional coyote. I vowed to keep Moo indoors no matter what.

I fantasized what my life would have been like if my father hadn't died. Instead of settling down in Los Angeles, would we have traveled the world? I imagined us going to glamorous gallery openings, searching for inspiration in exotic places. My mother once told me he was a restless spirit who'd lived a tumultuous childhood, raised by older parents who kept moving between their two homelands, Colombia and Greece. When he was a teenager, they compromised and settled in Los Angeles. My grandfather died before I was even a glimmer, but 92-year-old Yaya Sophie was still kicking it up strong in her nursing home. She had even heated up the dance floor at Rick and Josie's wedding. I wondered what my father would think of Rick. Borrr-rrring.

Once my mom and Rick had their new babies, where would I fit into the picture? Free babysitter, I bet they were thinking.

The thoughts stung like a million mosquitoes trapped inside my brain. And that vision got me obsessing over how much my face itched and burned from the sun, despite the gooey layer of aloe vera gel I had reapplied. I turned on my reading lamp and reached for *A Little Princess.* Nana had given me this book and *The Secret Garden*, both by Frances Hodgson Burnett, when I was eight. Even then, the red cloth bindings were a little tattered and faded to a pinky salmon hue. The books had belonged first to Nana, then to my mother, before being entrusted to me. Someday, Nana hoped I would pass them on to a daughter of my own.

I've read *A Little Princess* all the way through nine times since the summer she gave the books to me. It's almost like eating macaroni and cheese, you know? Comfort food. It's the kind of book that takes me to my happy place. I opened to the first chapter, when Sara's father brings her to Miss Minchin's boarding school. After about five pages, my lids drooped, and I had trouble focusing on the words. The day had been long and exhausting, despite my mega-nap in the sun. The book slid from my sleep-slackened grasp. The muffled thump as it landed on the carpeted floor roused me enough to turn off my reading light, before I drifted into uneasy sleep with Moo curled into the crook of my knees.

I woke up to the sound of singing. My mother entered the room holding a blueberry muffin with a lit candle on it.

"For she's a jolly good fellow, for she's a jolly good fellow, for she's a jolly good fellow, that nobody can deny."

She put it in front of me. I drew in a breath to blow it out and expelled a huge yawn instead. "The holiday's over, sleepyhead!" she said. "Blow out your candle and throw on some clothes—you can eat the muffin on the way to school."

I looked past her, not very subtly.

"Rick already left for work. He's got a big installation on a warehouse roof in South Los Angeles."

She peered at me closely.

"You look exhausted. Do you want to spend the day in bed recuperating?" she asked.

"No, I've already missed a week. Besides, we have a field trip today, so it won't be too much stress." Ha. If I had known how wrong I was, I would have burrowed back under the duvet and stayed there—for the next seven years.

My mouth felt furry like I'd been eating unripe persimmons. I dove into the bathroom, loaded up my toothbrush with minty goodness and scrubbed away. I winced when I glanced up at the mirror and saw my blotchy sunburn and lanky hair, but there was no time. I'd forgotten to set out my clothes the night before, so it was a mad dash just to get dressed. I slid into the battered Land Rover next to my mom and we were off.

I wanted to tell her about the mirror. I mean, I knew it was all just a dream—the voices and the fog, the way I'd felt like my hands were glued to that disk. Still, it would have been nice to hear her dismiss it in her soothing voice. She'd always talked me down when I had nightmares about ghosts hiding out in my closet or under the bed. There was a barrier between my mom and me now, though. Like a gigantic concrete wall, too high to climb.

For the first few minutes of the drive, I ate my muffin in silence while my mother navigated the car through morning traffic. Getting down the hill was the easy part, but we soon learned that seven-thirty in the morning was not the best time to drive in Los Angeles. Talk about clogged arteries. After being stuck at the same light for about three cycles, my mom started to lose her British calm. Her accent thickened like it always did when she was upset or excited.

"What a bloody mess! I'll never understand why the hell they don't have roundabouts at these intersections. So much more civilized."

Once we were moving again, she glanced over at me. "I'm sorry you had to find out that way," she said, out of the blue.

"Find out what?" I asked. It took me a second to shift gears. "Oh, you mean about you being knocked up?"

My mother looked at me. I tensed, waiting for her angry reply. Unexpectedly, she laughed. "Knocked up? Rocket, you make it sound like I've been tramping it up at singles' bars." She dangled her wedding ring. "I am a respectable married lady."

"This time," I muttered.

She pointed to a thermos in the cup holder. "I brought you some orange juice."

I unscrewed the cap and took a sip, not looking at her as she spoke. "I know this has all been hard on you, honey. The marriage, the move— and now this." She ruefully patted her stomach. "It's a lot of changes. Big changes. We're all entitled to act a little crazy now and then. But you can't take it out on Rick. Give him a chance."

"I don't want to change schools, Mom," I said.

She sighed. "Well, let's see how it goes for the rest of the school year and then decide this summer. We'll get up extra early to commute together. I could use more time in the shop anyway—the Pasadena Expo is coming up in a couple of months."

She turned on the radio, and we settled back into silence. I was so tired.

"So do you think Gillian's decorated your locker?" my mom asked, startling me awake.

"Remember last year? The toy monkey that started banging cymbals as soon as I opened the door?" I smiled in spite of myself, remembering.

Gillian had started the tradition when we first got lockers in fifth grade. We decided it was smart to exchange locker combos for emergencies, like if one of us was sick and needed a book brought home. But then we started sneaking in a little surprise now and then, a funny comic strip, a fur-framed mirror. For birthdays, we went all out. Once, I actually removed her books and crammed in a bouquet of balloons, then taped four of those musical cards to the hinge side of the locker so that they all sounded off when she opened the door. A cacophony. It was a pain to cart her books to homeroom, but so worth it. I couldn't wait to see what she had in store for me today.

As we approached the front gate, I could tell the bell had already rung, because only a few kids were straggling up the front stairs. A couple of school buses were blocking the circular driveway, so my mom pulled over to the sidewalk in the red zone. I looked nervously around to make sure there were no tardy police anywhere. I hated being late, stuck at the mercy of traffic instead of just being able to hop on my bike and ride to school.

I decided a little birthday cheer would outweigh the embarrassment of walking into class last, so I made a quick detour to my locker.

I dialed in the combination and opened my locker millimeter by millimeter, on high alert for spring-loaded surprises. But nothing happened. No clapping monkey. No balloon animals. Not even streamers or a scrawled sticky note.

I trudged slowly down the corridor, trying to rearrange my features into nonchalance before pulling open the door to history class. The room was empty. My heart dropped. The field trip! I remembered the buses in front of school and flew back through the halls.

My teacher had just tucked his clipboard under his arm and started to board the bus. Ignoring the hooting from the bus windows, I trotted over and tapped him on the shoulder.

"Sorry I'm late, Mr. Horace," I said breathlessly.

Tragically, it wasn't Mr. Horace. It was my PE coach, Mr. Lennon, who frowned and checked his watch with an annoyed sigh when he saw me. He climbed back down the two steps, pulling his clipboard out from his armpit and making a big show of finding my name.

"Malone, Rocket. Present," he said. "Fashionably tardy today, I see."

Teachers have always liked me…except for this one. Of course, I don't particularly like him either—always blowing his whistle and trying to get us to jump higher, run faster, keep our backs straighter while doing push-ups for hours on end. In sixth grade, I dropped a fifteen-pound weight on his big toe, and he's had it in for me ever since. It was his own fault. I told him I wasn't strong enough, but he kept telling me I needed to increase the resistance or my muscles would atrophy.

Once up the steps, I hesitated next to the bored-looking driver, scanning the rows for Gillian. She was at the back—sitting next to Carina. Jasper was in the seat right across the aisle, leaning her way.

Mr. Lennon pointed to the lone empty bench, directly behind the driver. "Take a seat, Miss Malone."

I sat. He slid his considerable derriere next to me, wedging me toward the window.

Despite my discomfort, I was so tired that the rumbling of the bus soon had me drifting off to sleep. The squeals and laughter began to blend into a muted hum, an audio backdrop to my daydreams. I was starting to wish I'd listened to my mom and spent a day in bed, but I hadn't wanted to miss another day of school. Besides, a field trip was practically a free pass. No pressure. Just follow along, look interested. I could do that for a few hours, right? But my head, heavy as a beefsteak tomato on a slender vine, drooped toward my chest.

Bump. Bump. Bump. Cobblestones? I woke with a start, disoriented, until I realized we had arrived at our destination, the Getty Villa, a museum of Greek and Roman antiquities just north of Santa Monica. I'd been here a bunch of times with Gillian and our moms. The bus belched to a stop. Kids crammed the aisle, jockeying to be first out the door. I surreptitiously wiped a little drool off the corner of my lip, hoping nobody had seen. This day clearly was going to be a continuing disaster.

Mr. Lennon heaved himself up and faced the back of the bus. He let out a piercing blast on his whistle and waved his arms over his head like one of those guys at the airport.

"Sit down! All of you, get back in your seats THIS INSTANT," he thundered. "Nobody gets off this bus until I find our docent!"

Butts flopped back into seats as he swung off the bus. I was dozing off again, when something jabbed me in the back of the head and tangled up there. I reached back and discovered it was a paper airplane someone had fashioned out of the museum's glossy brochure. As I looked behind me to spot the perpetrator, Mr. Lennon heaved back onto the bus. He grabbed the paper airplane from my grasp with a glare.

"Field trips are a privilege, not a right, young lady. Anyone that steps out of line will find themselves waiting on the bus while the rest of us enjoy our day."

I burrowed deeper into my seat, wishing it would just swallow me whole.

"Our docent is ready for us," announced Mr. Lennon. "Starting from the *rear* of the bus, please exit your row in an orderly fashion and stand on the sidewalk."

As kids filed past me, I heard a familiar snicker from the row behind me. Gary Grossman. From the smug look on his face, it was pretty clear he was the real culprit.

"Surprise," he said.

"The only surprise here is that you know how to fold paper," I retorted. Actually, Gary's IQ is off the charts. The only thing he doesn't know is how to be a human being.

I forgot that Gary interprets any kind of response from a girl as an invitation.

"If we both get busted, we can spend the day alone on the bus together," he leered at me. "Maybe we can join the mile-high club."

How much more could this day suck? Gillian passed by just in time to hear his juvenile comment and rapped him on the head with her notebook. "We happen to be at sea level, Gross Boy."

I smiled at her gratefully. Maybe she had a good reason for not decorating my locker.

"Did you get to school late, too?" I whispered.

She shook her head. "No, we were early, why?"

We?

I was the last one off the bus, by which time some sort of silent ballet had choreographed everyone into perfect pairs leaving me solo. I took a deep breath and wedged myself in between Gillian and Carina. Cool and casual. Gillian was my best friend after all. She and I were the original "we."

Excited murmuring drew our attention to the front, where all eyes were focused on a woman descending the steps. She moved in a sultry glide I would never in a million years achieve, made all the more dramatic by the classical draped gown she was wearing. She was beautiful in a Mediterranean sort of way, with an aquiline nose and a tight coil of dark wavy hair.

"Good morning, my pupils. I am Calliope," she said. Her voice was somehow familiar, low and melodious, the accent hard to place. "I will be your guide as we explore the treasures of the Getty Villa. I know you're anxious to get started, so if you'll follow me, we will make our way to the main entrance."

"Do you think Calliope is her real name?" I wondered aloud, earning myself a "shush" from Mr. Lennon that froze me for a second. The class trundled around and past me, leaving me at the back of the bunch. Up ahead, Jasper pulled alongside Gillian and reached for her hand. I could hear her giggling as she leaned close into him. Carina had looped her arm into the crook of Brandon Geoff's. Ugh.

Calliope recited a few of the rules and regulations as we made our way up the steps of the villa...no eating, no drinking, no touching the artifacts. The last rule was accompanied by a secret little smile. I caught a glimpse of Calliope's toes peeking from beneath her gown. Her feet were bare! Odd dress code they had here, but I figured it was all part of the Getty's plan to bring history to life.

"The Getty Villa is modeled after the Villa of the Papyri in Herculaneum, one of the towns buried when Mount Vesuvius erupted in the year '79."

Our textbook has pictures of the archaeological site of Pompeii, which was buried on the same day as Herculaneum. It's like the town was frozen in time. The volcano lasted for two days, decimating the whole area. People were covered in ash and lava and mud and literally turned to stone where they crouched in corners, shielding their heads or huddled over their children. The volcano hadn't erupted in eight hundred years, so long that people forgot it was a volcano and just thought of it as a pretty mountain with particularly fertile soil. Imagine their horror when it started spewing out ash and lava one day.

As far as I know, there aren't any active or dormant volcanoes in the Palisades, so I couldn't explain the butterflies in my stomach as we walked uphill toward the museum. I just had a sense that something big was about to erupt. With my luck, it would be a spectacular zit on the tippity-tip of my peeling red nose.

Calliope continued to describe the museum as we walked past the outdoor amphitheater and entered the main entrance of the villa.

"The original Villa of the Papyri was owned by Julius Caesar's father-in-law. It was his country house, to escape the summer heat in Rome."

"Like celebrities fleeing to their mansions in the Hamptons when the asphalt starts smoking in Manhattan," I thought.

Someone behind me laughed, and I realized I had spoken out loud. Again. I swiveled my neck and eyed the kid behind me. I didn't recognize him. He definitely wasn't from our school. He was a year or two older and a head taller than I was. And kind of cute.

"Pay attention," he advised, pointing forward.

"What?" The nerve, I thought. I decided to tell him off. "I am paying attention. In fact, I happen to enjoy museums, and I'd like to listen to the docent if you don't m…"

SMACK. I walked into a column.

"To where you're walking," he finished his sentence, trying hard not to grin. "Are you okay?"

I nodded, mortified. Physically, I was fine. The damage to my ego was extensive.

"Hey, Space Cadet—did you leave your seeing eye dog at home?" needled Gary Grossman, who had somehow weaseled his way to my side. A few of the jocks snickered. Gary preened under their approval. The boy next to me pulled a notebook out of his back pocket and scribbled something in it.

My class had gathered in front of one of the larger-than-life statues that lined the inner courtyard of the villa. Calliope smiled at us.

"To you, this statue of the nymph Echo is in shades of white and gray—cold marble. But a woman posed for this statue once. She walked and talked and lived and breathed. And the sculpture itself was originally painted in vivid color—her lips scarlet, her hair midnight black and her gown in brilliant peacock blue."

"The draping is amazing," said Carina, her stuck-up attitude momentarily replaced by genuine interest. "I would love to see her in living color."

"Traces of pigment are still visible," replied Calliope. She gestured toward a smudge of blush on the lips, a faint smear of blue in the drapes of the carved fabric.

"Time has a way of making things in the physical world fade. But here at the Getty, scientists and historians and craftspeople have brought my," she paused, "that is the ancient world back to life."

Carina loitered by the statue for a moment to make a quick sketch, while the rest of the class moved on. As I filed past her, I saw her slink her hand toward the sculpture and dig her fingernail into one of the deep creases to see if she could scrape off some of the color. Then Brandon swung an arm around her waist and swept her back into the crowd.

Calliope led us through the outer garden toward a balustrade over-looking the ocean. "John Paul Getty chose to house his collection of artifacts here because this setting is so similar to the coast of Italy. Staring out at the Pacific from this terrace, it is easy to imagine that you are looking at the Mediterranean Sea. Let your senses be your guide—listen to the gentle splash of the water fountains, let your eyes feast upon the murals and mosaics throughout the villa, inhale the scents of spice and fruit from the nearby kitchen garden."

"Wow—Smell-o-Vision," snickered Gary, and once again the jocks laughed. Calliope frowned at him.

"Interesting," the boy murmured to himself, and wrote something else down in his notebook.

"Shouldn't you be joining your own school group?" I whispered to him.

"I'm home schooled," he answered. "Research project."

Our next stop was a tiny gallery of ancient glass, just off the main entrance hall.

"In the fall, the Getty is hosting a special exhibit on the ways modern artists are influenced and inspired by mythology," Calliope told us. "I'm curious. What thoughts come into your minds when you look at these little vessels?"

Carina piped up right away. "They'd make great perfume bottles."

The woman barely registered Carina's presence, dismissing her with a slight smile. She focused her dark eyes on me and waited. There was something so compelling about the way she looked at me, as if my answers mattered to her.

I looked back into the display case, trying to arrange the thoughts tumbling around my head into some sort of coherent order. Looking at the glass made me think of my dad, how he was linked in a long chain of artisans stretching back thousands of years.

"Do you see that little goblet there, and the tiny little bubbles trapped inside the glass?" I said, pointing at a delicate fluted glass that had once been a handful of sand. "The little bubbles form when small air pockets are trapped between gathers of molten glass from the crucible. That air has been trapped inside there for more than two thousand years, while the world around it has continued to move and change. It's amazing that this little goblet survived, intact."

Mystery boy chimed in. "Do you ever wonder what archaeologists will consider valuable when they dig up stuff two thousand years from now? I picture them excavating millions of plastic bags full of petrified dog poop, and theorizing that we worshipped dogs so much we preserved their feces."

I couldn't keep myself from laughing.

"Dude, in two thousand years, humans will be extinct," pronounced Gary, who had wandered too far into our personal space for my taste.

Calliope turned to him. "Such cynicism in one so young is disturbing," she commented. "Without hope and passion, the facial features soon putrefy youthful beauty into ugliness and decrepitude."

Leaving Gary with his mouth wide open like a fish, Calliope contemplated me for a long beat, before she gave a decisive nod, as if something about me satisfied her. She looked back at the little vessel. "It was one of Chariton's finest pieces. He would be pleased that it still draws the eye."

"You act like you knew him," I said.

Calliope grinned. "Let's just say I've been in this business for a long time."

Suddenly there was a commotion in the main hallway. I looked out and saw Mr. Lennon arguing with a little old lady.

"I'm telling you, we already have a docent," complained Mr. Lennon.

The old lady poked her finger in his chest. "And *I'm* telling *you*, we don't have anyone working here named Calliope. You were supposed to wait on your bus until I escorted you into the museum!" She shook a loaded basket of headsets in his face. "You don't have your name tags or headsets on!"

I looked back at Calliope, curious. She put a finger to her lips, her eyes sparkling. "It was a pleasure speaking to you, Rocket. Be sure to visit the Hall of Muses while you're here today. It's not on your school tour, but I think you would find it…inspiring."

SEVEN

MR. LENNON CLAPPED HIS HANDS AND BLEW HIS WHISTLE TO GET EVERYONE'S ATTENTION, earning him a shocked "shush" from the old lady. She frowned at him before addressing the class.

"I am Mrs. Plumbottom," she told us. "Apparently, there's been some confusion, but I will be leading your tour from this point."

Surprised, I looked around, but Calliope had vanished.

"Your class is supposed to be visiting the Hall of Athletes today," announced Mrs. Plumbottom.

Mr. Lennon perked up at that. "Maybe this field trip won't be a complete waste of time after all," he said.

"The Getty Villa is a world-renowned antiquities museum," Mrs. Plumbottom glared at him. "Before we begin touring, we will take a five-minute potty break." The word 'potty' made everyone crack up, naturally, but we dutifully filed into the bathroom.

When I came out of the stall, Gillian was washing her hands. I lathered up at the sink next to her. We regarded each other in the mirror.

"Hey, Gillian," I said, tentatively.

Gillian looked me over with a critical eye. "Are you okay?" she asked.

"Well, this isn't exactly the best bir—," I started to say.

"Because you look like crap!" she interrupted.

"I... I didn't have a chance to wash my hair this morning. I was up all night with the weirdest dreams, and then I overslept," I explained. I looked into the mirror. It reflected the usual depressing sight—unruly dirt-brown curls and eyes to match. Add my new scaly red skin, and I looked positively reptilian. I twisted my face into the most horrifying grimace I could muster.

"Oh, that's attractive," Gillian commented. "You know, if you do that too many times, your face will get stuck that way."

"Thanks, Grandma," I replied, starting to feel a smile blossom inside me.

"That's okay. We'll just get you started on a course of Botox. Nothing like an injection of botulism to smooth out all those teenage wrinkles."

I laughed, enjoying the return to our usual bantering. "Absolutely. And maybe I can cover my next break-out with lead white face paint and get demented like the Elizabethans?"

"You already are demented," she replied.

"Gillian, don't you just love this color?" Carina demanded, waving a tube of lip gloss and summoning Gillian to the vanity area adjacent to the lavatory. She puckered up and blew little fish-kisses with her camera-ready rosebuds.

"You could use a touch-up," she noted to Gillian. Gillian rooted through her purse and pulled out an identical silver tube. She applied it carefully and then handed it to me.

"Here, Rocket, you might as well have soft, succulent lips when they put you in the asylum."

I laughed and thought why not? I mean, that mysterious cute boy would probably never be interested in me, but a little lip gloss couldn't hurt, right? But before I even had the lid off, Carina stopped fluffing her hair in front of the mirror and freaked out.

"You can't wear that!" shrieked Carina, snatching it away as if it were kryptonite to my Supergirl.

What, was she afraid I had cooties or something?

Carina went on. "Your coloring is completely different from Gillian's!"

I looked at her in disbelief. "It's just lip gloss."

"That lip gloss was chosen for us by a professional make-up artist at my spa party," she retorted.

Gillian awkwardly rummaged through her bag and pulled out a different tube.

"Here, I have another one. How about Siren Red?" she said.

"Isn't that more appropriate for *Carina*?" I said, trying to lighten things up.

Carina looked at me blankly. I forged ahead. "You know—the Sirens. Mythological creatures who bewitched sailors?"

"I thought sirens were those flashing lights on top of ambulances and stuff," she replied.

"No, the siren is the loud wailing noise emergency vehicles make, derived from the fact that the sirens sat on their rock singing," I corrected. "Their songs would lure ships to the rocky shallows to capsize and perish."

Carina shook her head. "Who knows that sort of stuff anyway?" With a last lingering look at her Juicy Couture-clad butt in the mirror, she pulled Gillian out the door with her.

Umm, anyone who actually reads the books on the class reading list? I retorted loudly—inside my head. In reality, I kept my trap shut. The fact was that Carina—in the few short months she had been at our school—had somehow gravitated to the very center of our school's social web. Gillian and I had always existed—happily, I thought—on the fringes. But suddenly, Gillian seemed to be on the move, leaving me to dangle alone on a precarious thread.

I rejoined the class just in time to follow our new docent up a wide marble staircase to a gallery on the second floor. I casually looked around for the mysterious boy, but I didn't see him anywhere. I told myself I was glad when I didn't see him loitering around.

The jocks in the group perked up a little when they saw these displays were all about "Athletes in Competition." Brandon Geoff immediately struck a pose in front of a sculpture of a discus thrower.

"Look at me—I'm 'The Victorious Youth,'" he crowed. Carina seized the opportunity to move in closer and pat Brandon's biceps, managing to stroke his ego at the same time. "Ooh, they're as rock hard as that marble," she cooed.

The field trip went on like that for a while. The docent showed us a statuette of a musician playing a flute and told us that athletes had trained to live music.

Brandon snickered and looked at me.

"So you're saying there were band geeks back then, too?" he said. He and Jasper high-fived each other like total morons.

"I'm not even in the band," I retorted. "But your pal Gary here plays the tuba." Gary glared at me. I couldn't help myself, even though I knew he would retaliate. I could feel an asthma attack bearing down on me.

The docent frowned at the boys' antics, but Mr. Lennon let it go. I wasn't surprised, since in addition to teaching Phys. Ed., he also coached the football team. And the wrestling, swim and baseball teams.

Brandon looked around the room. "Dude, where are the football players? It's all track events."

"Football is a recent American invention. The ancient Greeks revered individual triumph. Victorious athletes in the five classic tests of skill—javelin, discus throwing, long jump, wrestling and footraces—brought great honor not just upon themselves but upon their village," replied the docent. "In fact, the pentathlon inspired our modern-day Olympics."

She stopped in front of a large pottery urn, painstakingly decorated with scenes of competition. "The victor at Olympia received a crown of olive branches, but the winner of the games in Athens was awarded an urn filled with olive oil."

Brandon chortled. "They gave them a jar full of oil? Seems kind of lame. Like, they're star athletes and now they're supposed to go home and cook up some spaghetti? I thought the women did that stuff."

Flustered, the docent launched into an explanation. "Olive oil was a prized commodity in those days."

I felt sorry for her, having to put up with morons like Brandon and Gary all day long. "Wasn't olive oil used for grooming, too, not just cooking?" I asked her, just to be polite. From the corner of my eye, I glimpsed that strange kid again, lurking on the other side of the room.

"That's right, young lady. I can see someone has done her homework!" the docent enthused.

"Modern day bodybuilders still grease up before a big competition," commented Mr. Lennon, looking intrigued despite himself.

"I think Little Miss Dictionary here used olive oil to wash her hair this morning," snickered Gary. He gave my limp ponytail a tug then made a big show of wiping his hands on his jeans. Brandon snorted and gave him a thumbs-up. Gary puffed up so much he almost popped, while I tried to shrink myself to microscopic proportions.

"It's totally rude to call attention to someone's bad hair day, Gary," scolded Carina, adding fuel to an already blazing fire. "You should apologize to Rocket."

The docent gave us a few minutes to wander the room. No sooner did she have her back turned than Gary Grossman sidled over to a little device in the corner of the room. It looked like a seismograph. I watched him suspiciously. He looked both ways to make sure the coast was clear of guards and other grown-ups then with a thumbs-up to Brandon and

Tony, he leaned in and breathed on it hard. The needle went haywire. He puffed one more time and walked away, just as the device started bleeping a loud alarm. Mrs. Plumbottom and the security guard raced around the room, practically knocking me down in their haste to find the source of the noise.

Gary was smirking next to me.

"It's a hygrometer," he whispered, as if I cared. "A device for measuring the relative humidity of the room. The moisture in my breath is about seven hundred percent higher than the ambient climate, so it set off the alarm. Genius, huh?"

The alarm went off. Mrs. Plumbottom talked to the security guard in a hushed whisper. Gary snickered. Actually, he giggled. Like a girl. Mrs. Plumbottom's head whipped around at us. At me.

"You, the one with the greasy ponytail," she said. "Do you know anything about this?"

Shaking my head no and tying to blend back into the walls, I struggled to get my breathing under control. I would now be forever known as the "girl with the greasy ponytail." Fan-freaking-tastic. With a mumbled "excuse me," I ran out of the room—and promptly ran into the boy.

"Don't you have a paper on Greek history to research?" I wheezed the words out with difficulty.

"Actually, I'm doing an analysis of middle school social hierarchy, and I got exactly what I needed in there," he said happily, tapping his notebook. "I figured out a great title, too: "The Nerd in the Herd.""

The Nerd in the Herd? That was the last straw. My eyes already felt like a toad's, bulging out of their sockets, and now even a complete stranger had concluded after thirty minutes of observations that I was a total loser. I fled down the marble stairs, seeking a place where I could be alone.

EIGHT

EVERYWHERE I TURNED, THERE WAS ANOTHER SCHOOL GROUP OR CLUSTER OF JAPANESE tourists. I ducked into a little gallery, smaller than my bedroom, but quiet and empty. I sank down onto a marble bench, closed my eyes and focused inward to slow my erratic breathing. In a few minutes, I was calm enough to survey my surroundings. A domed ceiling arched overhead like a timbale, one of those fancy custard molds they're always using on cooking shows. Along two walls, panels made of translucent alabaster let in golden dappled light, framing four smallish statues on individual pedestals. Being in that room felt like sitting in one of my wicker rocking chairs. Home.

A uniformed security guard strolled in from an adjacent gallery, eying me with suspicion. I walked over to the statue closest to me, making a big show of reading the informational placard at its base.

Muse
Roman, from Cremna, about A.D. 200
Marble, pigment and gold

Each of the nine Muses, daughters of Jupiter (king of the gods, known as Zeus in Greek mythology), presided over and inspired a specific branch of the arts and sciences. In fact, the word "museum" denotes an institution filled with their presence. The clothing and pose of this figure identify her as Euterpe (Muse of music) who is usually shown holding the aulos (double pipes).

I couldn't really see how clothing could help identify them, since they were all essentially wearing your basic classical toga style draping, but whatever. I was willing to take the museum's word for it.

I moved on to the next one. The guard must have decided I was a model citizen, because he tipped his head to me before continuing on his rounds.

Muse
Roman, from Cremna, about A.D. 200
Marble, pigment and gold

The four Muses in this gallery all have traces of pigment on their eyes and lips, indicating that the statues were once brightly painted. Particles of gold leaf remain in the crevices of their hair, which was originally fully gilded. This figure's pose and garments identify her as Clio (Muse of history).

Another Muse? Had I somehow ended up in the room our mysterious tour guide had recommended?

I looked up at the face of Clio. She had not made it through the years unscathed. Chunks of marble were missing from around the base, both arms had broken off, and her nose looked like she'd been swimming with piranhas. Must have been a long and difficult journey from Rome to California. Of course, I should look so good after eighteen hundred years.

"Nice nose," I muttered, and moved on to the third statue.

Muse
Roman, from Cremna, about A.D. 200
Marble, pigment and gold

The drapery and leaning pose of this figure identify her as Polyhymnia (Muse of mime).

Seriously? The Muse of *mime*? I took a closer look. This Muse's clothing did look a little different. She had her sheet wrapped tightly around her and was huddled into it, her hands clutching the draping up under her chin, as if she were trying to keep warm on a chilly day. It reminded me of my godmother Polly, who was never without her white silk shawl.

She let me play with it once when I was little. I remembered that day. How could I forget?

Polly arrived at our house soon after my father died, bringing an oasis of calm to the confusion and chaos that pervaded our house. All I remember from the funeral is her singing—beautifully haunting hymns that sounded like they were coming from the lips of an angel. This impression was heightened by the fact that she was wearing her trademark white, while all the other adults looked scary and somber in black. My Nana even found a stiff black dress for me to wear. It was wool and I can still remember how stiff and itchy it felt on my skin.

After the service, Polly took my hand and led me away from all the weeping adults, including my mother, who seemed to have lost her smile forever. Polly played in the garden with me, letting me drape her white shawl over my hair like a veil and pretend to be a bride. She picked a few lilies from the garden and fashioned a bouquet for me, humming a wedding march in her entrancing voice. Later, we swaddled one of my dolls in it, and Polly sang the most beautiful lullabies, in English and an unfamiliar language that I assume was Greek.

I hadn't seen her since that day, but I smiled, thinking of it so clearly, and let my eyes drift up to the face of the statue.

I couldn't believe what was in front of me. Couldn't believe *who* was in front of me.

"Aunt Polly?" I gasped, staring in shock at the statue. It was an exact likeness of my Aunt Polly—her delicate features, youthful smile, curly hair restrained in a ponytail. But this statue had been carved almost two thousand years ago. I looked wildly around and realized with a start that the fourth statue bore a strong resemblance to our renegade fake docent from the morning—the one who had suggested I check out this very Hall of Muses, in fact. What was happening here? Was I going nuts?

The folds of Polyhymnia's gown fluttered, which was impossible since she was carved out of marble. She leaned down to greet me with a familiar laughing glint in her eye, which was also impossible. Extremely, supremely impossible.

"Hello, dear Rocket. Are you enjoying your excursion to the Getty?" she said with her marble lips.

I tried to talk myself down. "Get a grip, Rocket. It's your imagination. You didn't—sleep—well—last—night." But all the self-talk in the world could not get my breathing under control, and I soon found myself gasping again. I couldn't catch my breath.

I sank to the floor, right in the middle of the gallery, wheezing and feeling the room spin around me. I upended my tote bag, frantically searching for my inhaler. Aunt Polly took one look at me and stepped down from her pedestal in a swirl of skirts, expanding and solidifying until she was one hundred percent real, living, breathing Aunt Polly— fully intact, no missing chips or limbs, and as young and vibrant as she had been ten years before at the funeral. She riffled delicately through the pile on the floor, extracting the glass atomizer from the tumble of books, bagged lunch and other school detritus. She held the bottle in her palm, carefully, ignoring my outstretched hand.

"I remember this! Your father was such a clever man," she admired. She turned to the other statues. "Come down and look at this, sisters."

One by one, the others transformed from stone into flesh. Clio stepped down from her pedestal, a contented smile on her face. "Well, Melpomene should be pleased that Narcissus developed another portal for us, although it's a pity that her statue is missing from the collection," she pronounced. She surveyed the room with a critical eye. "Hmmm. A little too public for my tastes. Let's redirect the tourists, shall we?"

With that statement, she closed her eyes and lifted her hands palm upward toward the ceiling, chanting softly in a foreign tongue. The room filled with a familiar fog, which drifted out to the edges of the room and up along the walls, sealing the doorways. Once that was accomplished to her satisfaction, she took the bottle from Polly's hand, holding it up to the light to study the delicate etching in the ruby red glass. She squeezed the old-fashioned bulb on the bottle, leaned into the spritz. A smile of appreciation lit her face. "Mmm, smells like home."

"Lovely glasswork, isn't it?" Polly commented. "And so cunning. It looks just like a perfume bottle, doesn't it, Euterpe?" Yet another Muse— Calliope—had joined our little circle. Before Clio could pass my precious bottle along for more show and tell, I snatched it from her hand and aimed a cool puff into my open mouth, closing my eyes in sheer relief as it traveled to my constricted lungs. Instantly, I could feel the vessels relaxing and opening, allowing oxygen back into my bloodstream.

Polly looked at me with gentle concern. "Are you all right, Rocket?"

"I'll be fine, now that I've taken my asthma medication," I replied, waving the glass bottle. The four Muses looked at each other and burst into laughter.

I was a little irritated. "Asthma can be a life-threatening condition."

"In Greek, 'asthma' just means 'short breath.' They've told you it's some sort of sickness?" questioned Clio. "And that bottle contains the cure?"

"It's how her father explained it when she was a little girl," Polly explained to the other Muses.

I was confused by their reaction. "I've had stress-induced asthma since I was a little girl. My father made this bottle for me as an inhaler."

Clio stepped forward. "Polyhymnia, although this is most entertaining, we don't have much time for chit-chat."

"This is crazy. Where is that guard?" I looked around wildly for a way out.

"As you know, it is time for you to begin your apprenticeship," continued Clio.

"What apprenticeship? Aunt Polly, what is going on here? Am I having some sort of breakdown? Or is this like a big practical joke maybe?" I asked hopefully. "A new reality television show for kids."

"You activated the mirror!" said Clio.

"I didn't 'activate' anything. At least, not on purpose." I couldn't believe I was having this conversation. With mythical beings. Maybe I had already passed out from the asthma attack and was hallucinating.

"You've just celebrated your fourteenth birthday, correct?" Clio seemed very surprised. "Your mother should have explained this to you years ago."

She looked over at Polly, who had taken a sudden interest in examining the floor. "Polyhymnia? Do you know something about this?"

Polly explained, contrite. "Josie was just so heartbroken when Gabriel died. I just gave her the tiniest little drop of Lethe water to ease her suffering."

"You erased the mother's memory?" exclaimed Clio. "Polly!"

Clio closed her eyes and took a few deep breaths. Her lips moved as if she were counting to ten…in Greek. Finally, she opened them and turned back to Polly.

Clio folded her arms across her chest and looked at Aunt Polly. "Polyhymnia, you created this mess, and this time, you can fix it. Why don't you explain to Rocket why we are here?"

Aunt Polly looked a little sheepish. She took a deep breath. "Rocket, I'm not really your aunt...I'm actually your great-great grandmother."

Euterpe smirked. "Add about two dozen more greats."

Polly ignored her and continued speaking to me. "You've probably gathered that my sisters and I are Muses."

"I thought there were nine of you," I said, suspiciously. "I only count four."

"There are only four muse statues in this room. We have certain limitations on how we can manifest in the mortal world," explained Clio. "You'll meet our other sisters when you enter the mirror tonight."

"When I what?"

Polly stepped forward and took my hands. "You see, Rocket, dear, many, many years ago, I fell in love with a mortal. Zeus allowed me to follow my passion, but in return for this privilege, all the firstborn descendants of my union must serve the Muses for seven years."

"So, you're saying that because you had a fling with a human a thousand years ago, I have to be your slave now?"

"Not a slave, dear. An apprentice. Very different. It's a wonderful opportunity."

Aunt Polly beamed at me, as if she expected me to jump up in sheer joy.

"And if I say no?" I asked.

Polly's face fell. I felt a twinge of guilt, as if I'd disappointed her.

Euterpe turned to Clio. "Maybe Father is right. The mortals of this world have become too distracted by their gadgets and their television and, and, their hip-hop. The mere mention of an honest day's work and they run for the..."

I held up my hand, a little irritated at the assumption. Clio read my mind and spoke up.

"She didn't say no. She only asked what would happen *if* she said no."

I nodded, glad that someone understood me. And she seemed to be the one leading this pack.

"Personally, I rather like hip-hop," said Aunt Polly, in her sweet, soothing voice. "Such a fun dance beat!"

Euterpe snorted. "*You* like *every*thing."

Clio laid a hand on Polyhymnia's. "The truth is, Rocket, we're not exactly sure what will happen to us if we don't keep up our end of the bargain. Zeus can be very creative with his punishments."

Aunt Polly appeared distressed.

"Zeus?" I asked. "The King of the Gods?"

"And also our father," answered Clio. "Our mother is Mnemosyne, the goddess of memory."

"What sort of punishment are we talking here?" I asked.

"Hmmm. Let's see," said Polyhymnia tentatively. "Well, Father once turned Apollo into a mortal and made him serve a king…"

"That's not so bad," I said.

"He's always turning people into trees, or shooting them down with lightning bolts when they betray him or break their oaths."

Euterpe interjected. "Don't forget what he did to Prometheus."

Polly shuddered and pulled her shawl more tightly around herself, like a security blanket. I was beginning to wish I remembered more of my sixth grade mythology unit.

"Remind me again who Prometheus is?" I asked.

"He stole fire to give to the humans. Without him, you still wouldn't be able to boil water, let alone blow glass. To punish his audacity, Zeus bound him to a rock and sent an eagle to peck at his liver every night."

Clio wrapped her arm around her sister Polly and gave her a squeeze. She fixed me with a stern eye. "But we know you won't let something like that happen to Polyhymnia. And yourself."

I could see that I really didn't have a choice. Not only did I love Aunt Polly, I also loved having my liver intact.

"Fine, I'll do it," I said grudgingly. "But I have to say, your father sounds like kind of a jerk."

Euterpe chimed in. "Oh, no, he's a sweetheart really. We sing his praises all the time."

"That's the reason he had us—to sing his praises," added Clio. She smiled briefly. "We'll start your training tonight."

Polly patted my cheek. "Don't you worry, Rocket dear. Being a muse is in your blood. I'm sure it will come naturally to you." Euterpe let out a noise that was somewhere between a laugh and a snort.

As they turned to go, I thought of something that had been troubling me.

"Aunt Polly? I mean, Polyhymnia, or whatever your name is?" I asked.

"Aunt Polly is fine. What is it, Rocket?"

"Why did you all laugh about my asthma medication?"

She smiled and touched my cheek softly. "Since you haven't yet completed your muse training, every so often your body needs a little whiff of godsbreath in order to overcome your mortal fears and thrive. A diluted version of this is in the bottle." She pursed her lips and blew softly toward my face, as if she were blowing me a kiss.

Surprised, I drew in a breath and caught the kiss full into my lungs. It felt like I was inhaling a piece of a cloud, infused with an autumn sunset, pink and gold. I'd always thought of air as nothingness, just gases and a hint of smog...but this, this air was so rich with love and joy and possibility that it almost made me weep. In the space of a heartbeat, ideas and images flooded into my consciousness faster than I could process them, every synapse in my brain firing more rapidly than teens playing laser tag.

The Muses drifted back into their statues, like genies being sucked like vapor back into magic lanterns. Clio paused, turning back to me.

"Rocket? One important rule. You must write down everything that happens. In this," she said, a golden-bound book materializing in her hands. She tucked it into my backpack on the floor, touched my cheek with a soft finger, and then leapt into her statue as delicately as a ballerina. I sank back down to the floor in a daze, laying my head against the marble mosaic and staring up at the intricately molded ceiling. I had a sudden urge to write a poem about it. I closed my eyes and began trying out rhymes in my head. Ceiling, feeling, wheeling, reeling.

After I don't know how long, I began to come back to myself, slowly, like I was swimming to the surface through mud. Something brushed my face. I opened my eyes, and blinked them shut again in confusion when I realized that mystery boy's concerned face was so close to mine that his shaggy hair tickled my forehead.

NINE

I THOUGHT I WAS HAVING ANOTHER HALLUCINATION, SOME SORT OF FANTASTIC DREAM. The boy leaned in even closer, and his lips met mine. Then he blew two quick puffs of air right into me, pinched my nose shut, tilted my head back and awkwardly stuck a finger into my mouth, fishing around like he was looking for gum.

I gagged and bolted up off the floor.

"Eww," I exclaimed. "Get your hand out of my mouth!"

He fell back in shock, yanking his hand out so fast I thought he was going to take one of my tonsils with him.

"For your information, I was starting CPR. Step one: sweep airways to make sure there are no blockages," he said defensively.

"Step one is to see if the victim needs help by tapping them on the shoulder and asking! Where did you learn CPR? MASH reruns? Nobody does blind finger sweeps these days, it's totally obsolete," I told him. "A simple 'Rocket, are you okay?' would have sufficed."

He stared up at me like I'd grown an extra head. "Pardon me for trying to save your life!"

After a beat, he asked a question I've heard before.

"Is your name really Rocket?"

I narrowed my eyes at him. "Yes. What's it to you? And why are you following me anyway? Why don't you go find some other loser to harass?"

The boy looked confused, as if I were a rabbit that had suddenly turned into the wolf.

I pressed my attack, getting myself nice and lathered up. "Look, I get it. I am a nerd. I wear glasses. I like museums. I have asthma. And now I'm starting to see things that don't exist. Just leave me alone."

His clouded expression cleared.

"Oh wait, are you talking about my research paper? I didn't mean you. I meant the little dirtbag trying to suck up to the jocks by picking on you," he explained. "Garrett or Gregory, something like that. I'm Ryan, by the way."

He stuck out his hand.

Reflexively, I shook hands with him.

"Are you talking about Gary?" I asked. "Gary Grossman?"

"Yeah, him," said Ryan. "Not you. You know, I must have walked by this gallery twenty times when I was looking for you. I just didn't see the door. Isn't that weird?"

Weird? Weird didn't begin to describe my current situation. I looked over at the statue of Polyhymnia. It, she, winked at me.

I shut my eyes hard to block out the sight and flopped back down with a groan. "Please. Leave. Me. Alone." I repeated.

Alone was not what I got. The next voice I heard came from the doorway and belonged to our docent, Mrs. Plumbottom—and it was more of a shriek.

"What in the world is going on here?" she exclaimed. "Mr. Lennon, is that one of your students lying down in the middle of the Hall of Muses?!"

Before I knew it, my entire class had tromped into the gallery and mobbed around me, immediately re-triggering my asthma attack. Short breaths.

Mr. Lennon elbowed everyone aside in his blustering way. "Back up, back up, people. You're smothering the poor girl," he commanded. "You there. What happened?"

Mystery boy's voice: "I saw her lying on the floor. I did some CPR, and she's breathing okay. She was awake a minute ago."

Way to make it sound like you saved my life, I thought.

Next I heard Gillian's voice. "She gets really bad asthma attacks. Somebody, find her inhaler…it's a pretty little bottle…yeah, yeah…that's it."

Mr. Lennon spoke up again. "Did you know that one out of six Olympic athletes suffers from asthma?" Yes, because he lectured me and the entire class about that every single time I had trouble breathing and had to sit on the bench in PE, as if my inability to run a four-minute mile was a personal affront to him.

"Was she unconscious?" demanded Mrs. Plumbottom. "Somebody call 911 right away. Wait, I'll call security on my walkie-talkie."

Gillian shoved the bottle under my nose and before I knew it, I'd inhaled another big puff of godsbreath. I got all floaty again, but this time I gritted my teeth through it and opened my eyes so nobody else decided to 'save' me by sticking their fist down my throat.

The next hour was completely mortifying. Mrs. Plumbottom fluttered around, feeling my forehead and telling people to get me water and cold compresses. Mr. Lennon refused to let me ride home on the bus and insisted on calling my mom. Rick happened to be doing an installation in the neighborhood, so she sent him to fetch me and bring me back to the shop. Gillian offered to stay with me, but it was against school policy, so I was forced to lie down alone on a little cot in the security office until Rick came and collected me.

In the car on the ride home, Rick kept glancing over at me, acting all concerned.

"That was a doozy, huh?" he asked. "How often do you get attacks like this?"

I snorted. "Trust me. I've never had one quite like this."

"Should I take you right to the doctor?" he asked.

I shook my head. "I'm fine now. Just a little tired. And I'm starting to think I need a different kind of doctor." A psychiatrist perhaps, I thought to myself.

"How was the museum?"

I stared at him. "Not to be rude, but do we have to make small talk right now? It's been a long, crappy day."

In silence, Rick leaned over and flipped on the radio, flicking through the channels until he got to a news report. Something about forest fires in the foothills outside Los Angeles. I didn't pay much attention, just stared out the window and tried not to think about anything, which is pretty much impossible. Isn't thinking about not thinking actually a form of thinking?

Rick found a parking spot in front of my mom's shop. His cell phone rang, so I hopped out and entered my mom's studio through the gallery at the front. Little brass bells tinkled as I walked in, and my mother's latest sales clerk looked up from the register with a practiced smile. I could tell the instant she recognized me as her boss' daughter—the same instant I remembered her name. Laelia. My mom always advertised at the career center at the local arts college, so she got a steady stream of hip wanna-be artists. They usually lasted a few months, before minimum wage and boredom took the polish off ringing up sales and wiping off fingerprints.

Laelia gave me a wink from across the room, subtly nodding her spiky-haired head at a couple of tourists browsing at the rear of the store. I eyed them as they picked up this and that—checking the prices of paperweights, cobalt blue tumblers, glass beaded jewelry. They'd probably end up buying one of the inexpensive sun catchers in the front window display, taking it home to hang in the kitchen as a reminder of their big trip to California. My money was on the dolphin.

Yep. Laelia rang them up, pattering away cheerfully as she wrapped their souvenir in tissue paper and carefully boxed it. Once they were out the door, she pulled out a cloth and started erasing their trail. Cleaning out the glass was my least favorite thing.

"I told my mom she should post 'Do Not Touch' signs, but she refused."

Leilia looked over at me. "I don't mind. Sometimes people need to hold art in their hands to feel the connection to it."

"That's what my mom said."

"Plus, the price tags are all on the bottom!"

Rick came in with a jingle, looking pleased with himself.

"I've got to get back to work—some of the panels aren't fitting cor-rectly and my foreman is panicking. But I just got off the phone with someone who is very interested in renting the cottage. He wants to see the inside. Rocket, tell Josie to head over there after work and show the guy around, okay? Here's his phone number. I told him it would be about five o'clock."

He handed me a scrawled number on a scrap of newspaper and took off before I could respond.

I poked my head into the back to see what my mom was working on. That part of the building isn't pretty like the store in front—it's all about function rather than form. A glassworking studio—or hot shop, as the professionals call it—is not a glamorous place. Everything, not just the door, is utilitarian—gray concrete floors, cinder block walls, exposed metal ductwork.

One side of the shop held the crucible, a ceramic vat inside a super-hot furnace where the silica mix was heated to liquid glass. Alongside stood two smaller furnaces—the glory hole and the rod-warmer. That side of the room was *hot*. Really hot. I never needed to be reminded to stay away from the crucible when I was a little kid—from a few feet away, your body just knows it's a bad idea to loiter there. You know those hair dryers they have at salons, the big plexiglass bubbles that set curls and sizzle highlights to perfection? If they get over 140 degrees Fahrenheit, they can blister your scalp. The crucible is two thousand degrees.

My mom waved hello when she saw me, then pointed to the phone she had stuck up to her ear. I stretched out on the beat-up sofa in the office end of the hot shop. Nico was hard at work with his back to me as he prepared to start a new piece. With practiced dexterity, he pulled a blowing rod from the pipe-warming oven, like he was selecting a javelin. He slid open the furnace door, revealing what looked like the surface of the sun—all glowing orange like lava. He started spinning the gathering rod in his hand even before the point slid into the vat. When he pulled the rod back out, nimbly rotating it all the while, a lump of glowing glass was stuck to the end. Picture a giant red cotton swab, fit for the devil's ear.

Nico slid the furnace door closed and turned away from the crucible. I could see he was wearing his safety goggles. They were essential in a glass shop—to shield the eyeballs from the searing heat and potential shards if something shattered. Nico paused to give me a quick thumbs-up and grin, but there was no time for a break just yet. He had to keep that rod spinning continuously, rotating it all the time to keep the piece centered.

Working quickly, in rhythm to the Latin rhythms blasting out of the shop's old boombox, Nico moved to the bench and sat down. It was a complicated little dance, maneuvering his body into the seat and laying his rod across metal rests extending out on either side of him, all while taking care not to touch the red-hot working end of the rod. Once seated, he used his left hand to keep rolling the rod back and forth as he reached down with his right hand to grab a wooden tool from the bucket of water by his feet. He slipped the ladle-like end over the blob of glass, using it to shape a sphere. With sharp tweezers, he poked several depressions into the glass. He gathered a second layer of glass in the crucible. The dents would become air pockets, tiny bubbles between the layers just like the ancient glasswork in the museum.

"I just saw some glass in the Getty that was two thousand years old," I called out.

Nico looked over at me briefly. "Hey, Rocket. Not that much has changed in glassblowing since then, huh?"

Glass cools and hardens quickly, so he took the rod to the glory hole for a quick reheat so he could keep shaping it. The glory hole is even hotter than the crucible. He stepped over to the marver, the heatproof work table where he had already laid out an array of emerald green and cobalt blue frit. Frit is what they call little chips of colored glass. They look like nothing much, but they can be used to embellish clear glass in the most amazing ways.

He rolled the hot glass bubble into the chunks of colored glass like he was rolling a Russian teacake in powdered sugar. Another pop into the glory hole, and the frit was melded to the piece.

Now Nico puffed into the cool end of the hollow rod. A slow bubble formed in the hot glass at the other end. With deft spinning and shaping and a few more puffs, a vase began to emerge, rapidly becoming defined in Nico's skilled hand. It was true—a lot of the tools and techniques glass artisans use today are just like the ones in ancient Rome.

My mom finally got off the phone and came over to give me a hug. She pulled back and looked at me.

"You should be in bed," she exclaimed. "I'm feeling pretty beat myself." She rubbed the small of her back, arching it a bit as if to relieve pressure. She looked at the big art-glass clock on the wall. One of my father's pieces. "I've got about another hour here to wrap up. Do you think you could just veg on the sofa for a bit? Do you want me to make you a nice hot bowl of soup?"

"I hate soup," I answered.

"I know," she replied. "But it seems like the sort of thing a concerned mother should offer a daughter who's not feeling well."

I didn't tell my mom about what had happened at the museum. I was afraid she would race me off to the nearest mental hospital and leave me there for a long time. Instead, I relayed Rick's message about the potential tenant.

She brightened. "Oh good. We can pop over there on our way home. It shouldn't take too long. You don't mind, do you?"

"Of course I mind," I said, "but it's not like I have a choice."

TEN

WE DROVE THE SHORT DISTANCE TO THE COTTAGE INSTEAD OF WALKING (LIKE TRUE
Angelenos, my mom commented). That happy feeling of being back in
my 'hood where I belonged evaporated as soon as I saw that big "For
Rent" sign planted in our front yard. Worse yet, a big gas-guzzling tank
of a car was parked in front, with the big hairy driver leaning against
it, smoking and ranting away at some poor schmuck on the other end
of his cellphone. Ugh. I just couldn't picture that guy in our cottage.

When he saw us, he barked a "later, dude" into the phone, then
dropped his cigarette on the ground and crushed it out with the most
pretentious cowboy boot I had ever seen, black leather dripping with
silver studs.

My mom eyed the hot mess on the sidewalk. "This is a non-smoking
rental," she told him.

"If I like the place, I'll quit," he said, in a loud coarse voice, laughing
like a gorilla at his own joke. When my mom opened the door to the
cottage, he muscled his way past her and moved right to the center of
the room. Without speaking, he did a slow pivot, taking it all in, while
he stroked his beard into a black hairy triangle of a goatee. I don't know
what I expected. Applause, maybe. Not what he actually said.

"God, it's like a paint store exploded in here. Every wall is a different color."

There was an awkward silence. "I suppose we could have it repainted
in a more-neutral color," my mother offered. "I just thought renters
would prefer an authentic, colorful Venice Beach experience."

"I like black," the man said. "Doesn't show dirt so much, and shows off
my art collection better. But maybe I could live with the circus theme."

He tromped around the rest of the house, opening and shutting cabinets, peering into closets, all the while nodding and muttering snide little remarks under his breath. I felt like Attila the Hun was invading us. Finally, he turned to my mom.

"I'll take it," he said. "It's small, but the location is right." He pulled out his wallet and started peeling off hundred dollar bills.

My mom was flabbergasted. "Oh, well…" she hedged. "First, we need you to fill out a rental application."

"Why don't I just pay cash for six months up front?" he said, practically thrusting a wad of bills in my mother's face.

"My husband insists on running a credit check, too," she replied. For once, I was grateful Rick was such a stickler for detail. My mom ushered the man out, pulled an application from her purse, and gave the man instructions for faxing it back to the shop. He peeled off in his monster machine like he was on his way to world domination.

I turned to my mother in horror. "No way," I said. "That man absolutely, positively cannot live in our house."

"Rocket, beggars can't be choosers," she said, "but I promise, I'll review his application very thoroughly. And he did say he collected art, so maybe he's not so bad."

Once we settled into the car, I flipped on the radio. A "breaking news" report came on—more hype about the drought conditions and the fire that had started raging out of control in the foothills northeast of Los Angeles. I was about to switch channels when my mom stopped me.

"Wait, did they say the fire's moving toward Sun Valley? That's where Bethie lives."

"Bethie?" I queried.

"Beth Mathews—my friend who creates the windchimes we sell in the shop? I'm sure you've met her before. That's strange—she dropped off an order this morning and didn't say a word about the fires."

"It's probably not a big deal," I said. "Remember 'Carmageddon'?"

"True," she agreed. "A drop of rain and the news calls it Millenial Stormwatch. I'm sure she's fine or she would have mentioned it. I'll call and check in with her later."

When we got back to Rick's house, I avoided the mirror for as long as possible. Instead of retreating to my room, I did my homework at the kitchen table. Rosa bustled around me, checking on something amazing-smelling in the oven. Enchiladas.

I checked and re-checked my geometry homework, but eventually I ran out of ways to stall. Then Rick got home from work, and he and my mom started peppering me with questions about how I was feeling. I just didn't want to deal with the interrogation.

I closed my bedroom door behind me, wishing again that I had that padlock. I walked over to the mirror and cautiously pulled back the black velvet, without touching the mirror itself. It was pulsing with light again, streaking the room. I had it all figured out, though. If I didn't touch the disk at the top, I wouldn't "activate" it. Which was good, because I still hadn't decided what to do about the whole Muse thing. For now, I was going to stall.

My cell phone buzzed in my pocket, and I jumped, letting out a high-pitched little shriek. Moo ran into the closet. By now, I was feeling like one of those dim-witted girls in a horror film. I looked at the display on my phone. Gillian. After a couple of rings, I picked up.

"I forgot your birthday," she said.

"Whatever. It's fine," I replied, trying to sound nonchalant. I guess I failed in that, or maybe it's just that Gillian has known me long enough to read my body language even when she can't see me.

"I'm sorry," she repeated. "What? Do you need it in writing?"

"Maybe," I said.

She hung up on me. Three seconds later, I got a text message: "I'm sorry."

I called her back.

"So spill. Tell me all about the mystery boy who saved your life," she demanded. "He looked better than one of my mom's brownies."

"Not possible," I laughed. And just like that, we fell back on track.

"Hey, do you want to hang out this weekend?" she asked "Carina and I are meeting up at the mall on Saturday afternoon."

"Oh. Maybe we could do something with just the two of us?" I asked.

"Carina's nicer than you think, Rocket," protested Gillian. "You'd totally like her if you gave her a chance."

"I just don't have her passion for fashion," I retorted.

"Well, come over early and you and I'll have time to do something first," said Gillian.

ELEVEN

THE REST OF THE SCHOOL WEEK PASSED IN A BLUR. MIDTERMS WERE COMING UP, AND THEY were especially important this semester. I had a perfect grade point average. All I needed to do was maintain that for this final semester to make class valedictorian.

I was confident of my grades in all the core subjects: algebra, chemistry, history, literature. Success was simply a matter of learning and memorizing the material and regurgitating it back to the teachers in whatever form they mandated. Multiple choice tests and pop quizzes were easy enough, as long as I studied. I didn't find it much harder to turn out a structured essay or a detailed book report. Call me Hermione, or teacher's pet, or whatever, but I really like school, and it likes me back. Even in PE with Mr. Lennon, I was getting an A, because I showed up, wore my uniform and tried to do what he told us. It wasn't my fault that I sucked at sports.

No, it was my elective that had me worried. Visual Arts. I had requested computer skills or French, but the office made a mistake on my schedule and there was no changing it. Don't get me wrong. I appreciate art and artists—I'd be an ungrateful daughter if I didn't. Looking at my father's glasswork, visiting museums and galleries on Venice Boulevard—it could be cool. Even checking out the latest creations on the bulletin board outside the school arts room gave me a needed boost as I walked to PE every morning. But I'm not an artist or performer myself. I've tried to explain that to the art teacher, Mrs. Fletcher, but she doesn't get it. She truly believes that every person on the planet is creative.

Mrs. Fletcher *always* dresses originally. She loves combing thrift stores for things to transform into gypsy-bright wearable art and prides herself on never repeating the same outfit twice, not even a pair of earrings.

This leads to some unusual fashion choices: today, for instance, she was wearing a long t-shirt dress hand-painted with a design of vining leaves, accessorized with big purple grapes dangling from her earlobes. Not plastic ones, but actual grapes that she pulled out of her vintage Scooby Doo lunch box and skewered onto hoops just as we were filing into class.

While I'd been in Europe, the class had begun the pottery unit. We gathered around the head table, and Mrs. Fletcher taught us how to cut a disk for the base, roll out coils and use them to form a cylinder.

"I'll be calling you up individually during class today for your portfolio reviews," she reminded us before sending us back to our worktables.

"Carina, can you help Rocket get clay and show her how to wedge it before she starts the coil project?"

Great.

"Sure, Mrs. Fletcher," said Carina with a pleasant smile. A smile I didn't trust in the least.

Carina pulled a wire through one of the big blocks of clay on the back table and efficiently cut off a lump.

"That's about a pound," she said. "Now you try it."

My lump was a little wobbly, but Carina moved right onto the next step.

"That's good. Now we wedge the clay to get the air bubbles out. Otherwise the heat expands those bubbles and they explode, like tiny little bombs explode. If you're not careful, you could destroy everything in the kiln," said Carina.

"No pressure or anything, huh?" I joked.

Carina laughed. "It's kind of like kneading dough for bread," she said, showing me how to push the clay against the hard surface of the table. Then she dropped the lump into my hand. "Your turn."

After I got the hang of it, she went back to her spot. I shoved the clay back and forth wondering why Carina was being so nice. Maybe she didn't want to reveal her true colors in front of a teacher. Or maybe she had one of those split personalities, and the nice one was running the show today. I'd just have to stay alert.

Making coils was much harder than it looked when Mrs. Fletcher did it. My first few were all uneven—sausage-fat in some sections and pencil thin in others. I mushed the clay back into a ball, wedged it and tried again. This time, the coil was more even, but it cracked apart when

I lifted it up to put it on the base. I looked around. Most of the other kids were already building their pots. Michelle Li had efficiently turned out a series of tiny symmetrical coils and assembled them into a perfect teapot—now she was making perfect little cups to match.

Jasper the jock, Gillian's new flame, had a vase about six inches tall already. Of course, his coils were about two inches think, and he just kept spraying them with water and shoving them together without any regard for symmetry. I had a sudden vision of him making them with the magical feet Gillian had mooned on and on about. Carina, sandwiched in between Jason and Brandon, was managing to flirt with both of them and still nonchalantly roll out and assemble flawless coils. Nobody else seemed to be on the verge of tears like I was.

Mrs. Fletcher walked around the class, admiring people's handiwork, stopping here or there to comment.

"Class, these are looking be-you-tea-full," she said. "But let's not forget to throw a little wabi-sabi into the mix."

Wabi-sabi? Had I missed an ingredient somewhere? Maybe that was why my coils were falling apart, and the rest of the class had it together. I raised my hand, and Mrs. Fletcher made her way over to my workstation.

"What is it, Rocket?" she asked. "Need some help?"

"I didn't get any wabi-sabi," I told her. "You told us to throw a little wabi-sabi into the mix, but I think mine is missing." I threw Carina a suspicious glance, wondering if Carina had tried to sabotage me.

Mrs. Fletcher laughed. "Oh! Wabi-sabi's not a thing. It's a Japanese philosophy," she said. "It's about seeing the beauty in the fact that things are impermanent and imperfect by nature. Many talented Japanese artists deliberately make pieces simple and rustic, or add a flaw to an otherwise perfect piece in order to capture the spirit of wabi-sabi."

I looked down at my mess of coils.

"I don't think I'll have to add any flaws," I said.

Mrs. Fletcher looked at me sympathetically. "Show me how you're doing it."

She watched me destroy another ball of clay. "Hmmm. Your left hand and right hand are working in opposition. Try rolling with just your left hand until you get the rhythm."

She picked up a ball of clay and demonstrated the technique again, right there at my table. "Less pressure. Lighten up and have fun with it. But first, step into my office, so we can review your portfolio. Spritz your clay with water and put some plastic over it for a moment so it doesn't dry out."

Mrs. Fletcher's "office" was just a back corner of the room that she had sectioned off with folding screens to make an artsy cubicle. The panels were covered in layer upon layer of art posters, gallery show announcements and magazine clippings. Ceiling high bookshelves in two corners dripped with art reference books, art pieces, jars of paint brushes and the like. But her desk—a large black drafting table like you'd see in an architect's office—held just one thing, my portfolio. Making it had been our first homework assignment: two sheets of black poster board duct-taped on three sides and labeled with our names.

Mrs. Fletcher had not given us individual grades on any of our work all semester. She had simply collected the assignments and made a note in her grade book on whether or not we turned them in on time. I had asked her how I was doing on several occasions, but she'd evaded all my inquiries. Now was the mid-term moment of reckoning.

"I've looked through all of your work," she said, pulling a stack from my folder. "Now I want you to tell me something about it."

"I know I'm not very creative," I said defensively, "but I followed the rubrics you gave us exactly."

"Rubrics, schmubricks," answered Mrs. Fletcher. "The school board makes me hand those out, no matter how often I protest that you can't force creativity into a grid. That's for the editing phase—the creating phase needs to be left alone."

She tapped my self-portrait. "Tell me why you decided to do your self-portrait in the style of Andy Warhol."

"I, ummm, really like pop art and that repetition thing?" I responded.

Mrs. Fletcher looked steadily at me, waiting for more. I decided to go with honesty.

"I tried other stuff, but it wasn't very good. So I did it like the sample you showed us in class."

Mrs. Fletcher sighed. "That's the problem, Rocket. You keep coloring inside *my* lines, when what I want is for you to look inside yourself and show me the world through your own eyes."

She flipped through the stack of art.

"In each one of these assignments, you obeyed the letter of the law.

But you ignored the spirit of the law. How can I explain?" She thought for a moment, eyes closed. Opening them, she snapped her fingers. "Here's an example. I grew up in an Orthodox Jewish household. The Torah told us to cover our heads in the presence of God…meaning to show humility when we went to temple. But my mother and her friends, instead of wearing veils or hats, covered their heads with wigs, which they spent hours selecting and styling. Technically, they met the requirement, but they failed to honor its deeper intention. Do you see?"

She carefully put all of my work back into the portfolio.

"So. Here we are. Like it or not, the powers-that-be insist that I assign you a grade for this class. All of your assignments have been turned in on time, and as you said, you satisfied all the rubrics." She turned over the sheet of paper, and there at the top of the page, in bright green ink, was a letter I had never seen before on ANY of my papers: 'B.'

"A 'B'? You're giving me a 'B'?" I felt this buzzing in my head, like my brain had shriveled and a swarm of bees had settled into the hollow space between my ears. I suddenly felt nauseous and chilled. My chest started to contract. I reached for the inhaler around my neck, forgetting that I hadn't worn it since the freaky museum incident.

I wheezed, clutching my chest. Mrs. Fletcher looked alarmed. She grabbed a brown bag from the shelf, dumped out a bunch of cotton balls, and shoved it on my face.

"Deep breaths. Slow. Slow. It's just a letter on a piece of paper, Rocket. It doesn't define you. Besides, this is just your mid-term review. If you nail the final presentation, you can still pull up your grade if it's that important to you," she said in a kind voice. "Why don't you sit here for a moment while I check to see how everyone is doing with their coils?"

I nodded blindly, taking another rusty breath and swallowing my tears. I had to choke back a bitter laugh. The Muses wanted me to inspire people? I couldn't even get an A in art.

Twelve

IT WAS TOUGH SLEEPING WITH THAT STUPID MIRROR DOING ITS USUAL GLOWING AND pulsing. Saturday morning found me glazed over, perusing my closet in despair, looking for the perfect outfit to hang out with Gillian and maybe, possibly, perhaps, going to the mall with Carina. It was hopeless. I settled for my usual weekend uniform—faded baggy jeans and a black t-shirt.

Just in case we went to the beach, I stuck my swimsuit and a towel into a tote bag. No chance I would ever borrow a suit from Gillian. She's way more comfortable in her own skin than I am, and her bikinis are so tiny they could double as postage stamps. You know that old song "Itsy-Bitsy-Teenie-Weenie-Yellow-Polka-Dot-Bikini"? Make it hot pink paisley and you've got the picture. I brushed my teeth, ran a comb through my hair and slid my feet into a pair of tattered sneakers. Gillian says I make a terrible girl, but, really, what's the point of trying when you have such limited assets? I'd long ago realized that I wasn't going to win any beauty contests. Remembering my breakdown in art, I slipped the inhaler over my head. I didn't care if it was the placebo effect, or some otherworldly oxygen, I needed it. Besides, I liked the way the art glass looked against my black shirt.

At breakfast, my mom informed me that she had decided to rent our cottage to Mr. Revolto. His credit check had passed with flying colors, and his references, including one from an art gallery in Manhattan, were all glowing. And since there were no other offers, she was going to let him have it.

"I just want to get it done," she said. "Cross one thing off the endless list."

I couldn't believe it. When she said it was time to go to Gillian's, I got into the car, but I didn't speak to her, for the entire drive. She kept trying to get me to engage, but I blocked her just like I ignored the mirror, staring out at the window instead.

As soon as we arrived, I jumped out, slammed the door and stomped over to Gillian's.

The first words out of her mouth didn't make me feel any better.

"Look what Jasper gave me," she squealed, extending her wrist and flashing a shiny bracelet.

"It's magnetic," she told me, toying with the long beaded strand wrapped several times around her arm. "It can be a necklace or a bracelet or an anklet. Isn't it amazing?"

"I can't believe you are actually dating Jasper the Jock."

"Don't call him that. He's really nice. And smart," responded Gillian.

"Wait," I said. "Didn't your godmother get you one just like that for your birthday last year? She did! You thought it was too gimmicky and re-gifted it to the class holiday swap," I reminded her.

"Oh wow. Do you think this is the same one? That's so romantic, that Jasper saved it for me," she breathed. Her eyes went all round and unfocused again. "Wait until Carina hears about this!"

The rest of the morning was pretty much like that. Gillian blathered on about how romantic it was that Jason had given her some piece of junky jewelry she hadn't wanted in the first place. And I got to hear in nauseating detail about his eyes, his muscles, and weirdest of all, more about his perfect feet.

It was actually a relief when she glanced at the clock and realized it was time to go to the mall with Carina.

"So, are we taking the bus or riding our bikes?" I asked her.

"She's picking us up. We're going to Rodeo Drive in Beverly Hills. Didn't I tell you? That's where Carina usually shops."

"We're going in the stretch?" I said, disbelieving.

"It's not a stretch, it's just a standard-sized limousine."

Suddenly Gillian was an expert on luxury vehicles, had a boyfriend and shopped in Beverly Hills. Things were not good.

Still, surreal as it seemed, even I had to admit it was cool when the elegant black car came cruising down our little street and stopped in front of Gillian's house, mercifully obscuring the sight of my mother taking down the "For Rent" sign and stowing it in her trunk. The chauffeur came around the front of the car. He was a good-looking guy, about the same age as Rick. He was in a very relaxed-looking uniform—a black jacket and white dress shirt over a pair of jeans, plus a black cap and dark sunglasses. He opened the door with a flourish. I managed to slide into the car without cracking my head on the roof. Carina was relaxing in the back, elegantly dressed in a patterned wrap skirt and brown silk camisole.

I tried to act all nonchalant like Carina and Gillian, but I was drinking in every detail—the buttery leather upholstery, sparkling crystal decanters, a plasma television screen peeking out from behind a discreet mahogany panel.

"What exactly do your parents do?" I asked. In the months that she had been at our school, nobody had figured it out as far as I knew.

Carina cast a little glance up toward the chauffeur. With a touch of a button on a remote, she closed the glass partition between the driver's seat and us. She put a finger on her lips. I leaned in close to hear her.

"I'm not at liberty to say."

"Oh. I understand," I said. But I didn't, not really. What kid was 'not at liberty' to mention what her parents did for a living? My imagination went a little wild. Famous movie stars? Drug lords? Mafia? Deposed royalty on exile from some exotic, war-torn foreign land? I was leaning toward the latter, since every so often, I detected a hint of an accent in Carina's cultured voice.

The glass partition slid open. The chauffeur turned his head and gave us a grin.

"Hope you don't mind. The air's not working up front. This way it can circulate."

"Maybe you could open a window up front, James," suggested Carina.

"Oh, I think I'll just leave the partition open. Don't you worry about me, Miss Carina."

There was something a little ironic in the way he said it. I wondered if Carina was a difficult client. Carina turned her back on him with an annoyed huff.

"Would you like some orange juice?" she asked, flashing her pearly whites. "The housekeeper squeezed it this morning."

"Sure, that sounds great," I said. "Lovely."

"You can pour. The decanter is on ice next to you. I'll have a glass, too. And Gillian would like one as well."

"Gillian doesn't like juice."

"She'll love this," Carina said confidently.

"Sounds delicious," said Gillian agreeably.

I felt a bit like Cinderella doing my stepsister's bidding, but what the heck, I was thirsty. And I love fresh-squeezed orange juice. I carefully took the stopper out of the crystal decanter and poured.

I was a little nervous about spilling, but the limo glided as smoothly as if it were waltzing on a polished dance floor, sliding so slowly as we approached stoplights that you could barely feel the transition between coming and going. All too soon, we had arrived in Beverly Hills. James came around to open the door for us. He stopped Carina with a touch on the arm as she emerged from the car.

"Shall I meet you here in two hours, Miss Carina?"

"Three," she replied.

"You'll recall we have an evening engagement?" he said.

She sighed, a little exasperated. "Fine. Two hours. Thank you, James."

I caught an expression on James' face that I wasn't quite sure how to interpret. Sadness or hurt, maybe. Carina hadn't exactly been rude, but maybe it was hard being in service to a fourteen-year-old and not being able to say what you really felt.

A few tourists had stopped on the sidewalk, eager to catch a glimpse of us, thinking we might be celebrities. I was self-conscious, but Carina handled it with aplomb, breezing past the gawkers into a designer boutique. Gillian followed Carina, and I followed Gillian, trailing behind a few yards.

The saleslady gave us each a quick but thorough scrutiny then directed her attention to Carina. I was suddenly, painfully aware of my cheap t-shirt and grubby shoes.

"Good morning. Are you looking for anything in particular?" she asked.

"Yes, I heard the new Misanthrope line is available," Carina drawled in a semi-bored way.

The saleswoman lit up and hustled Carina across the store to a rack. Carina flipped through the hangers efficiently, pulling several items out and handing them off to be hung in a dressing room.

"Do you guys see anything you like?" she called over to us.

"The exit sign," I muttered.

Gillian laughed. "It's not that bad."

"Seriously, this is not where we fit, Gills," I replied. "Carina is in a different league than us."

"Oh, relax. I know she can come off as snooty and privileged, but she has a really nice side once you get to know her. I think she's kind of lonely."

"Lonely? She's the most popular girl in school. She's rich and gorgeous. Why would you think lonely?" I exclaimed.

"Just a feeling," said Gillian, idly browsing through the sparsely-hung racks. "Have you ever noticed that the more expensive the store, the fewer items they actually put on display?"

"We should try on something," she announced. She pulled out a butterfly-sleeved shirt in dazzling shades of peacock and magenta.

"This would look amazing on you, Rocket," she said.

I checked the price tag and almost gagged. "Two hundred dollars for an amped-up t-shirt?"

The saleswoman magically appeared at my side and plucked the shirt from my fingertips. "Shall I show you to a dressing room?"

Helplessly, I followed her.

The curtain of the dressing room next to mine was pulled shut, but I could see Carina's polished pink toenails peeping out underneath it.

I decided to make an effort. Maybe Gillian was right, and Carina was shy or something.

"Hello," I called in a friendly voice through the upholstered wall that separated us, as I undressed.

"Hello," she said back to me.

I stripped down to the training bra that my grandmother had forced on me in England, and pulled the butterfly shirt over my head, cautious not to snag it on anything. I didn't want to invoke the "you break it, you buy it" rule.

I stepped out of the dressing room to look at myself in the three-way mirror. It actually looked good. Could it be possible? The way the fabric draped actually made me look like I had curves. I started calculating in my head just how many hours of babysitting it would take to replenish my college fund if I secretly raided it to buy the shirt. I was about to ask Carina for her opinion, when I heard her talking out loud to herself.

"No, I don't want it," I could hear Carina's voice, protesting, as if she was trying to talk herself out of something.

"Want it," she repeated to herself, in a more insistent voice.

"Want me to help you make up make up your mind?" I joked, pushing open the curtain to her dressing room.

She immediately snapped back at me. "Make up your mind."

I flinched at her tone. As I let the curtain drop, I noticed she was holding a small pair of nail scissors in her hand.

I tugged my own shirt back on and hurried out of the dressing room.

"Let's go," I said to Gillian. "She's mean, and we can't afford any of this anyway."

"What happened?" asked Gillian.

"I don't want to talk about it. Let's just take the bus home, please?"

Gillian froze. I turned around and Carina was standing there.

"You guys planning to ditch me?" she said. Her stone cold freaky voice was gone. Now she sounded a little hurt.

"Rocket was, not me," said Gillian hastily.

Great. Instead of taking the bus with me, she had thrown me under it.

"That's pretty rude, Rocket. I've gone out of my way to include you today, for Gillian's sake."

"Gillian and I have been best friends since we were toddlers! You can't just buy her and bundle her away in a shopping bag with the other things you want. Gillian, can we please stop playing dress-up and go home?"

The three of us stood there for a charged moment. Gillian looked so torn. Carina gave me a look full of sympathy, like she was some sort of nurse or therapist.

"Oh, Rocket, I think I know what this insecurity is all about. You have abandonment issues because of your dad killing himself when you were little."

I froze. How did she know about that?

Slowly, painfully, like my neck had rusted stuck, I turned from Carina, and looked Gillian in the eyes. I saw a stranger I couldn't trust anymore.

Without so much as a garbled good-bye, I fled the store to find my own way home.

Thirteen

THE SIDEWALKS OF DOWNTOWN BEVERLY HILLS WERE CROWDED WITH SHOPPERS AND THE usual assortment of gawkers. I blundered my way to a bus stop on Santa Monica Boulevard. Two transfers brought me to the intersection of Laurel Canyon and Sunset. I started the long uphill walk to Rick's house. One foot after the other. I'd had the counseling. I'd read the books. I knew I shouldn't take my father's death personally. My father didn't abandon me. But, he wasn't coming back. That was a fact. A fact my once-upon-a-time best friend had told Carina.

No. Don't think about Gillian. Don't think about my father. No.

I focused on my feet, desperate for the sanctuary of my room, where Moo would be waiting for me.

Moo. A safe place for my brain to burrow.

When I was nine, I begged my mother for a puppy. She said they were too much work. I wheedled for months, until she partly relented and said I could get a kitten. There was a pet store right down the street with a huddle of adorable ginger fluff balls, but my mom said no way was she paying for a cat. She grew up on a farm in England, and there were just always tons of cats around the barn.

We took a trip to the animal shelter. The cat room was lined from floor to ceiling with cages full of every kind of cat imaginable, from babies to resigned-looking adults. It was heartbreaking. I wanted to take them all home with me. A few meowed loudly, sticking their paws through the cages to get my attention. There was one kitten that was a total stand-out. He was glossy black with white "tuxedo" markings—white chin, chest and paws—like he was dressed for a gala affair. He rolled over and batted at my finger when I stuck it through the bars and then kissed me with his rough little tongue. I fell in love at first sight, turned to my mom and said, "I want him!" She looked for his tag on the outside of the cage, but it was missing.

Just then, one of the shelter attendants came into the room, holding a tag, followed by a teenage girl and her dad.

"This little guy, right?" the attendant said, pointing to "my" kitten. The teenager nodded, smiling, and the attendant unlatched the cage and pulled him out, handing him to her. My heart withered and dropped somewhere into my stomach. But after they left, prize in hand, my mother noticed a second kitten, curled up at the back of the cage, a tiny ball of white fluff with black ears and spots that looked more like a balled-up fur sock than a cat.

"How about that one, there?" she asked. "Or we can come back another day."

It was hard to adjust my expectations, but I also knew with my mom that a kitten in hand was best, because "another day" might be months later.

"Fine," I agreed reluctantly.

Maybe that other cat was fabulous…I'll never know. But, I'll tell you this: I was the lucky one that day. Moo (I named him that, because my mother and I thought his markings looked just like a spotted calf) is the world's best cat. As soon as the attendant pulled him out of the cage and handed him to me, he reached his little paws out and stretched them up against my neck. Then he gave out the sweetest little mewl, nuzzling under my chin. I know they say dogs are a man's best friend, but for little girls, nothing beats a kitten. Except maybe a pony.

I finally arrived at the house, huffing and puffing. Rick's car was there, but I didn't feel like answering a lot of questions, so I let myself in with my house key. When I got to my room, I couldn't find Moo anywhere. I noticed that my sliding door was ajar a few inches, enough for a determined cat to escape. Just then, Rick appeared in the doorway with his toolbox.

"Oh, hey, Rocket," he said with a smile. "I was just about to fix the track on your door, so it doesn't stick so much."

"You let my cat out!" I said.

"What?" Rick replied, bewildered. "Are you sure he's not in the house somewhere?"

"My bedroom door was closed—and this one was open."

Rick remained frustratingly Zen-like when I yelled at him. Moo was out there, lost in unfamiliar territory, in coyote country. Missing, presumed eaten. Catastrophe.

"Look, don't panic. He's probably just out exploring the neighborhood," Rick advised, in a placating sort of voice that made me wish we were on the phone—so I could hang up on him.

"Moo is a cat, Rocket," continued Rick. "It's in his nature to want to go out. It's instinctive. Carpet-wrapped poles and feathers on a stick just don't compare with real tree trunks and live birds."

"Aren't you the one who warned me about coyotes?" I demanded. "Not to mention German shepherds, pit bulls and teenaged drivers."

"Why don't you grab a fork and a can of his food, and we'll look for him together?" he suggested.

So there we were, banging the fork against the tin can and making whispery whistle sounds. Rick "meowed" a lot, which I would have found cute, if I weren't so angry. We searched every shrub, even hiking a few hundred yards down the dirt trail that led into the Santa Monica Mountains at the end of the cul-de-sac. All I could think about was predators lurking around every bend.

Soon it was too dark to see our feet on the path in front of us. Rick turned to me.

"Look, it's getting late. I'm sure your cat is fine—he's probably out there chasing rats and enjoying his adventure. We're not going to find him unless he wants us to find him, which will happen when he gets tired of hunting and wants a real meal."

Sleeping that night was an impossible dream. The stupid mirror glowed and fogged up the room again. I grabbed my comforter and was about to chuck it over the mirror when I heard mewling coming from behind the mist.

Moo. Inside the mirror. I didn't have a choice.

Muscles tensed, I stepped in, expecting to tumble down a hole like Alice into Wonderland. But, it was as simple as stepping through my sliding door and out onto the patio. The ground beneath my bare feet was dry and rocky, like the canyon path I had been on earlier that day. It was night here, too, but night like I had never seen it before. On trips to the Griffith Observatory, I had heard about light pollution—street lamps and houselights dimming our view of the heavens. Here, the sky was purely sky, the moon low and bright against black velvet. A million billion stars glittered as if the gods had sown the universe with vast handfuls of diamond dust. Somewhere close, I could hear the crash of surf. I stepped forward, only to retreat hastily once I realized I was on a narrow mountain path, exposed to a sheer drop on one side.

Starlight danced upon water far below me, illuminating jagged rocks and the foamy spray of waves that I could hear battering the shore. A warm breeze was blowing, like a Santa Ana wind off the desert, laden with fiery potential. Something brushed against my legs, and I jumped a mile high before realizing it was Moo. I crouched down and he arched and purred, butting his head into my palm in his familiar way.

"Moo, where have you been? Come on, let's go home. I'll give you a whole can of tuna," I promised, gathering him into my arms.

Moo stiffened like the wild panther he was at heart, breaking my hold on him and springing down to the ground. He trotted a few steps away, then turned and looked at me expectantly. He followed a path up and away into a dark wood, and soon he was out of sight. I ran after him.

Despite years of barefoot beach walks, my soles flinched as I climbed the rugged terrain. I looked behind me, at the rocky plateau below. The outline of the mirror through which I had entered still shimmered, suspended a few inches off the ground by invisible forces. It grew fainter the farther I climbed. If I went on, I might never find my way back again.

My brain tried every argument it had to persuade me to take the safe path.

That dratted cat got himself into this mess—let him find his way back. I can go home, snuggle back into my bed, I thought.

Up ahead, where the path forked, stood a lone figure, shrouded in a voluminous silvery cloak and holding a torch aloft in each hand. My train of thought came to a crashing halt...and so did my feet.

A raspy voice issued from inside the deep folds of the hood of the cloak.

"The Dark and the Light are ever entwined. Remember this at every crossroads, young Rocket."

She shuffled forward in an awkward way. I took a step back.

"You know my name. I don't know yours." I said, trying to sound more confident than I actually was.

"I am one and yet I am three. I am Hekate, goddess of women and the dark moon, and I stand at the crossroads of the three paths," said Hekate. "Past, present, future."

She let fall her cape, revealing herself. Or selves, to be more accurate. I could see now what she meant by the "one, yet three." She was formed like Siamese triplets standing back-to-back, conjoined at the sides, their faces looking out like a prism. Three bodies in one being, representing three stages of life…young, middle-aged, ancient.

"I am Hekate-the-Crone," continued the ancient one. Her dark eyes, glittering with wisdom, were deeply sunken into her wrinkled face. Her gnarled hands, spotted with age, trembled as she held the torches.

"I am Hekate-the-Maiden," said the young Hekate, twisting her long, slender neck to peer over the crone's right shoulder. She was a beautiful girl about my age, with flowing hair and a mischievous smile.

The third Hekate looked steadily at me from over the crone's other shoulder. Her hair was drawn back in a practical braid, and she looked solid and reassuring. Noting the crone's unsteady hands, she kindly took hold of the torch closest to her and held it aloft.

"I am Hekate-the-Mother. What is it you seek, Rocket?" she asked in a soothing voice. "How may we serve you?"

"I just want my cat back," I said, "so we can leave."

"So soon?" said the Maiden, surprised. "Don't you want to stay and explore Mount Helikon?"

"It's late and it's dark and I want to go home," I said.

Only…where was home? The world I knew was crumbling wall by wall, and I needed… something. Maybe it was this.

Hekate-the-Maiden took the other torch from the crone and waved it down along the path behind them.

"You needn't ever be afraid of the dark, Rocket," she said. "Muses carry such a bright light within them."

I let myself be curious, like the cat, and took a single step into the dark wood. And another. I looked behind me, and could no longer see Hekate. I could not see the mirror. The path narrowed as trees closed in on either side of me, gnarled and ancient oaks swathed in a dense tangle of vines that blocked the starlight and even the vivid moon. My eyes were useless in the sudden and total darkness. I reached for my inhaler, fighting down claustrophobic panic.

Stop. Think. I forced myself to take slow deep breaths of the sweet air.

I wished I had Gillian next to me. I kept thinking of the research project we'd done on Hellen Keller. We blindfolded ourselves and spent an entire weekend bumping into walls with our hands outstretched, trying to navigate our way to the bathroom and the kitchen. Pouring and eating cereal without being able to see is tricky. We dropped a few bowls, and I tripped over Moo when he tried to lap up the spilled milk. Gillian stayed calm and found the towel without cheating and taking off the scarf around her eyes. She was good to have around in a crisis. Then I remembered I never wanted to see her again.

Gillian wasn't here. But I was. I kept my body still, allowing other senses to take center stage. A step to my left encountered the subtle crunch of forest floor, a springy cushion of fallen leaves and twigs. The same was true a few steps to my right. I brought myself back to the center of the path again and hesitantly scuffled forward, using the stony texture to guide my feet inch by inch along the path. After a few steps, I stopped and listened. The forest was alive with noises—chirps and squeaks and odd rustlings.

As my eyes adjusted, I could see tiny sparks of light here and there. Fireflies. Some people call them lightning bugs, or glow worms. We don't have fireflies in Los Angeles, but they were so familiar. I knew I had seen them once, had chased and caught them between my cupped hands when I was little. A memory teased at me, as elusive as the fireflies themselves.

The random nature sounds infusing the air around me were coalescing into something rhythmic, something harmonious. At first, it was just a happy murmur and then suddenly more. Music. A yearning rose in me, and I stumbled forward, arms outstretched, seeking the source of that unearthly flute and the accompanying voices. The path curved out of the wood and into a clearing where that crescent moon and dense field of stars bathed the earth in cool blue light.

The Muses were there, nine sisters weaving a joyful chain through the meadow. Some held instruments—I recognized Euterpe by her aulos, the double pipes, and her easy laugh. Clio looked carefree, younger than when I had met her in the museum. And Polly was wearing the smile that I remembered from my holidays with her—a smile so loving it swallowed you in and forced you to smile back, no matter how grumpy you were.

When I stepped out of the woods, the Muses looked up with joy, and skipped toward me, chattering excitedly.

"Welcome to Mount Helikon," Calliope said. "Are you ready to dance with us?"

I hesitated, looking down at my scruffy jeans, completely out of place in this classical setting. I felt that same self-conscious angst that strikes me at school dances, where I end up spending most of my time warming the metal folding chairs around the perimeter of the dance floor or making awkward conversation with the other geeks over the pounding techno-rock. I actually, secretly love dancing. In my room, with my own music blasting or my headphones on, I am a dancing queen. When I'm expected to shake my booty for the whole world to see, though, I'm about as a groovy as a mailbox.

But this music…and the moonlight…I needed to dance, wanted it as much as I had ever wanted anything in my life. Polly smiled and grabbed my hand, tugging me into the Muse version of a conga line.

"I don't know the steps," I said to her, resisting the pull.

She leaned in closer, to hear me over the music.

"I don't know the steps!" I repeated, more loudly.

A muse with a hand drum whirled around me, pounding out a rhythm. Tom-tom, tom-tom-tom. Terpsichore. I recognized her from my research.

"Your spirit knows what to do. Let it be your guide," she urged. "Try closing your eyes."

"I think I'll just sit and watch, instead," I said and pulled away.

Terpsichore didn't try to convince me. She just kept moving her feet and beating the drum. Most of her long silky hair had escaped from its intricate knot and was flying free around her face as she spun a circle, her eyes closed, her head thrown back.

I sat on the fringe, watching. They were beautiful, dancing and singing and playing their instruments for what seemed like hours. Each had her own style. Clio was all stately elegance. Polly alternated between quiet gliding and playful pirouettes. Euterpe high stepped herself into a sweaty frenzy. I was mesmerized, watching them come together then twirl off into their own dances as the music moved them. Eventually, the pace slowed. Erato, whom I recognized by her stringed lyre, strummed a sweet little closing tune. All of the Muses stopped where they were in the meadow, bowed their heads and listened.

"Sisters, let us form the closing circle," instructed Calliope, once the last note had stopped vibrating in the air.

The Muses gathered. Clio and Polyhymnia left a space between them, reaching out to me. I took their hands—and my place in the circle.

Here I was, through a mirror and into a meadow, holding hands with a circle of ancient Greek goddesses. Growing up in Venice Beach, California, I'd seen a lot of New Age stuff. My mother's shop was parked between a Tarot-card reader and a store that sold healing crystals and essential oils. Gillian and I had tried our hand at goddess worship once or twice, lighting candles and weaving flowers for Gaia. This? This was different.

"Let us offer our names, and a word for how we feel in this moment," said Clio.

One by one, the Muses offered their name and a word. Gratitude. Joy. Mystery. Polyhymnia's word was celebration. Then, it was my turn. Polly gently squeezed my hand.

"My name is Rocket, but not like the space kind," I said, in a rush to get it done. "Um, and my word is confusion." The Muses laughed.

"No, really," I said. "What exactly does a Muse do?"

Another Muse I hadn't met yet stepped forward. "I am Urania. My domains are astronomy and universal love. Perhaps I can explain it to you in more scientific terms."

Urania pulled a golden wand from out of her robes. As she waved it, diagrams appeared in the air, like the world's coolest PowerPoint presentation. "You know that energy travels in waves, yes?" She sketched out a series of long rolling lines.

"Like light and sound waves?" I said, a little hesitantly, thinking of my science textbook.

"Exactly! Light from distant stars, sound, even the gravitational pull of the moon acting upon the tides. Mortals have learned much about the invisible forces that govern the universe." She smiled at me indulgently, as if I were a dog who had learned how to roll over on command.

I basked in the praise, feeling like such a clever mortal, until one of the Muses burst my bubble.

"All those gadgets—your satellites and your cellphones and your televisions—produce billions and trillions of light and sound waves. They're killing the only waves that truly matter," she groused.

"Melpomene is the Muse of tragedy," whispered Polly to me with a wink. "She does tend to dwell on the dark side."

"I heard that, Polyhymnia," Melpomene said in an aggrieved voice. "And for your information, without shadows, we could never fully appreciate the light."

"So it may be. Still, 'killing' is too harsh a term, Melpomene," chided Clio. "Muting, perhaps, or smothering. And let us not forget, some of these devices have the power to amplify creativity waves and extend them to the masses."

Urania looked grave. "Perhaps a few do. But many others cancel each other out."

"Wait, wait," I interrupted. "Did you say 'creativity waves'?"

"Yes, I was getting to that before I was interrupted," said Urania calmly. "Creativity is the source of life—the most important wave of all, the one that underlies the universe itself. Yet, so far, it has not found its way into your science textbooks."

With a few more rapid swishes of her wand, Urania sketched in the air.

"Every living thing receives and transmits creative waves—each blade of grass, each stone, and each creature, whether it walks the earth, swims in the sea or flies through the air."

"Stones aren't living things," I interrupted.

Euterpe let out one of her infectious giggles. Urania just smiled and continued on in a calm voice. She reminded me a lot of my sixth grade math teacher, Mrs. Hinkley.

A stone appeared in her right hand, a walnut in her left. "Everything in the universe has energy. Energy cannot be lost or gained, simply transferred. If you hold this stone in your hands and then raise your hands high above your head, you transfer your energy to the stone—and it becomes filled with potential. Release the stone and you can use that energy—as a weapon, or as a tool."

She threw the stone down onto the walnut. Crack! The walnut shell opened.

"If that stone's alive, it's going to need an aspirin," I muttered. Euterpe smiled. Polyhymnia shushed me. Urania just continued her lesson without missing a beat, handing me the sweet nutmeat.

"As Muses, we gather creative energies, amplify them, and send them back into the Universe. We hear the music and we sing it. We feel the beat of happy hearts and we dance it."

Another Muse stepped forward, holding a smiling mask in front of her face. She fanned it to the side, revealing her own grin behind it.

"Put simply, Rocket, we're here to celebrate. To get the party started, you might say. I'm Thalia, the Muse of comedy."

Polly smiled at Thalia, and stepped forward with her hands cupped. She opened them to reveal a single firefly. "We see the little spark, and we reflect it, until it shines bright enough to light the dark."

The firefly twinkled out of her hands. I watched it flit above my head until it merged with Urania's diagrams and the glittering stars in the night sky. My eyelids felt heavy.

Polly stroked my hair with a mother's love. "Sweet child, now you must sleep. Dreams are like ambrosia to Muses. Let them nourish you tonight and prepare you for the work that starts tomorrow."

All around me, the Muses were finding themselves places to rest. Clio reclined on a chaise lounge as elegant as her own frame. Urania drew herself a golden hammock between two slender trees. Euterpe simply settled down onto a patch of sweet clover. Polly snapped her fingers. The mirror materialized in front of us, right there in the meadow. Through it, I could see my bed—and me, already asleep. I turned to Polly, startled.

"I think you would call this excursion an 'out-of-body' experience," she explained. "Your spirit danced with us, while your physical body stayed in bed, in a resting state. You'll learn more about it during your training."

"Wait!" Calliope came running up to us, breathless, clutching the golden journal that I had left behind in the museum. She thrust it into my hands. "Take this with you, Rocket! It's one of the few things that can travel with you between your home and the astral world."

"Bring it with you whenever you visit Mount Helikon," advised Polly. "It will be useful."

She took my shoulders and turned me around. Gently but firmly, she pushed me into the mirror. It felt like stepping into a vertical wall of clear water, cool and fluid against my skin. But when I emerged into my room, I was perfectly dry. Moo was curled up at the foot of the bed, watching me with a languid eye as if to say, "What took you so long?" And, as easily as if I were sliding into my favorite flannel pajamas, I slipped back into my body and fell fast asleep.

Fourteen

AT A TOTALLY RIDICULOUSLY EARLY HOUR, MY MOTHER RAPPED ON THE DOOR AND POKED HER way in, without waiting.

"Hop to it, Cinderella," she ordered. "We're going on a rescue mission and you need to be ready in fifteen minutes." She didn't wait for my reply, just dropped the bomb and fled the scene.

I groaned a lot, but complied, pulling on a pair of jeans and a sweatshirt. Curious despite myself, within the allotted time I plopped down at the kitchen table. I expected to be groggy from the night before, but instead I felt refreshed. Energized. Rick set a bowl of oatmeal and a glass of orange juice in front of me.

"Eat fast," he said. "Your mom's on a mission.".

"What's the emergency?" I asked, shoveling brown sugar into my bowl.

"We finally got in touch with her friend Bethie. That big forest fire across the valley swept right through her neighborhood, and they had to evacuate. She and her son have been sleeping at a Red Cross shelter. Your mom offered to go pick them up."

"And do what with them?" I asked.

"Well, we'll just have to bring them back here, I guess," said my mom, bustling in with stacks of clothes in her arms. "Poor thing is in total shock. Bethie can sleep in your room, and you and her son can bunk down in the spare room, I guess. I'll dig up the air mattresses."

"I wish you hadn't rented the cottage to Mr. Revolto," I grumbled. "Then they could go there, and I wouldn't have to give up my room."

The phone rang. My mom picked it up, listened in silence for a moment, then exclaimed, "You're kidding!"

She clicked to end the call and looked at me. "That was the FBI. Mr.

Revolto was just arrested for fraud, thanks to the background check we did. We once again have a vacant, furnished house. And you're right, that's the perfect solution for Bethie and Ryan."

Quite a coincidence. Almost a "deus ex machina" ending, I thought, remembering how in Greek plays, the gods always swooped down from the heavens to resolve a crisis. Hmmmm. I wondered.

We drove to the high school doubling as an evacuation shelter. The parking lot was overflowing, so we parked down the street and trudged back with our arms full of blankets and bags of stuff my mom had decided to donate. Even though we were several miles from the fire, the air hung hot and heavy with smoke, making it hard to breathe. A fine layer of ash had settled over everything like grimy snow, giving the area a shabby Christmas feeling.

A security officer stopped us as we crossed the parking lot. "You folks evacuees? This shelter's full, but the rec center in Sunland still has a few spaces."

"Actually, we're here to see friends… and we brought extra blankets and clothes for whoever needs," my mom answered.

"I have to ask you to sign in, then." He held out a clipboard and a pen. "Sorry to be suspicious, but we had some vandalism here last night." He gestured toward the parking lot. A couple of smashed car windows had been hastily covered with cardboard and duct tape.

"You're kidding!" Rick exclaimed.

The guard shook his head mournfully. "I'm afraid not. These folks fled the fire with all their valuables in their cars. Someone broke in and took what little they had left."

He directed us to the gymnasium. Inside, the floor had been covered with blue plastic tarps and lined wall to wall with cots, which were covered in a hodge-podge of Red Cross-issue gray blankets, sleeping bags and kids' fleece throws. Some cots were occupied, even though it was the middle of the day. A woman in ash-streaked sweatpants gazed at a sleeping infant cradled in her arms, her face equal parts despair and wonder. An elderly couple scooted their cots side by side, so they could hold hands.

At the far end of the gym, about a dozen or so people were gathered in a semi-circle, their eyes glued to a television news report of the fire. On the floor near them, little kids were stretched out and scribbling in coloring books. My mom scanned the room. Her eyes lit up when she saw Bethie at one end of a long plastic folding table, the kind you keep in the garage and set up when extra people come over for Thanksgiving. At the other end of the table, a teenaged boy was helping an old man work on a big jigsaw puzzle.

"There's Bethie," my mom exclaimed.

At the sound, the boy turned and caught me staring. I knew him— the home-schooled kid from the field trip to the Getty, the one who had given me mouth-to-mouth. I felt my neck and face flush—and knew I had just turned a really unattractive shade of red, the way I always do when I'm embarrassed.

My mom ran over and hunkered down beside Bethie, opened her arms wide and folded her up into a big hug. They poised there, rocking slightly for a long time. I'd met Bethie before at my mom's shop when she was dropping off an order of windchimes, but I'd never seen her in such disarray. Her mane of curly brown hair was flattened on one side, and she was wearing clothes that didn't fit quite right. Rick and I stood there awkwardly.

Rick cleared his throat and stuck out his hand to the boy.

"You must be Ryan," he said. The boy nodded and shook hands with Rick. Rick pulled me forward.

"This is Rocket," he said.

I took the coward's way out. "Hi, nice to meet you," I said, acting as if we were total strangers. Which, I thought to myself defensively, we kind of were. I mean one little lip-lock didn't make us best friends. Ryan didn't react at all. He seemed a little out of it. Numb.

Bethie put her arm around her son. "Ryan has just been a blessing through all of this," she said, giving his shoulders a squeeze and aiming a kiss at the top of his head. "If it weren't for him, I don't think I'd be here today."

Ryan flinched, his muscles tightening against her embrace. Bethie sighed then laid her hand on the forearm of the elderly man next to him.

"This is our neighbor, Mr. Lombard," said Bethie, in a bolstering sort of voice.

Mr. Lombard ignored us, staring at the puzzle in dismay.

"The last piece is missing! Who would put out a puzzle with pieces missing!" He pounded his fist on the table. "It's a crime, that's what it is!"

Heads turned in our direction at the commotion. Mr. Lombard's face was screwed up with rage. A little bit of spit foamed at the corner of his mouth from all his ranting. I couldn't believe he was getting frustrated over such a minor thing.

"I'm sure it's here somewhere, Mr. Lombard," said Bethie in a patient voice.

She leaned toward us and whispered. "He lost his wife last spring, and his mobile home just went up like a firecracker..." She looked at him with a pitying glance.

Oh. Well, that would explain it, I thought, feeling like a jerk. Spotting a bit of orange under the old man's chair, I crouched down just when Ryan did. We clonked heads so hard my eyes watered. As I rubbed my forehead, I looked apologetically up into his eyes, and it was like I was hit in the head a second time. You know that cliché: the eyes are the windows to the soul. Looking into his eyes again... suddenly the phrase made sense. Brown with gold and green flecks—hazel was the word, I guess, but it was something behind the eyes that I recognized.

Ryan took the puzzle piece from my limp hand. "Look what we've found, Ike," he said. "I think this might be the last piece of that clownfish."

The old man carefully fitted the puzzle piece into the empty space, the last orange bit in a colorful scene of tropical fish. He gently ran his hands over the completed puzzle, as tenderly as if he were smoothing a blanket over a sleeping child.

"Livvy and I went snorkeling down in the Caribbean once," he said, calm now. "Back before I became an old fart. Cozumel, that's where we went. You could see right down to the bottom, fifteen, twenty feet. The water was that clear."

He stared at the puzzle. "Livvy loved jigsaw puzzles."

"Your son Edmund is going to be here just as soon as he can," Bethie said. "He is just going to love seeing that puzzle all finished."

She stood up awkwardly, reaching for a pair of crutches to support her weight. "I have to sign some forms before we leave, and say good-bye. The people from the Red Cross have been so wonderful. Really, I don't know what we would have done..." she trailed off.

She reminded me of a butterfly, all flittery. A butterfly with a damaged wing.

"You take your time, Bethie," Rick said, in a kind voice, before turning to my mom. "Hon, why don't I go with Bethie in her car? You and the kids can meet us at the cottage."

"I want to go with my mom," said Ryan, a little belligerently, as if he were prepared to defend his ground.

Rick gave him a quick squeeze on the shoulder. "Of course," he said. "Rocket and I will help you carry your things out, and we'll be on our way."

My mom and I rode the entire way back in silence. I was so overwhelmed by it all, I didn't even want the added stimulus of listening to music.

We pulled in front of the cottage one after the other. Rick ushered in Bethie and Ryan. "You all go in and check out your new digs. It won't take me long at all to bring in your stuff."

There was an awkward silence as we reflected on the reason Ryan and Bethie Mathews' remaining possessions would take a pitifully short amount of time to unload.

Bethie forced a smile. "I can hear the ocean. Living here for a few weeks will be such a treat, won't it, Ryan? Like a beach vacation."

Ryan didn't answer. He just looked around.

My mom nudged me. "Rocket, why don't you give Ryan the grand tour? Bethie, how about you and I have a cup of tea while I tell you about the house?"

Bethie nodded gratefully and headed with my mom to the back of the house toward the kitchen, leaving me standing there with Ryan.

"Umm, so. The grand tour," I mumbled. "Well, we are standing in the living room. That little hallway over there leads to the bedrooms. My bedroom, I mean, your bedroom, is through that door to the right. The other bedroom is to the left."

I gestured to the open door in the middle. "And that is the –"

"Wait, wait—don't tell me…" Ryan interrupted, walking into the small space. "Hmmm, sink, toilet, bathtub—is this the garage?"

"Sarcasm is the lowest form of humor," I muttered, feeling like a dope.

"I always thought fart jokes ranked lower than sarcasm," he replied.

"So, Sherlock, clearly you've deduced that this is the bathroom. The one and only bathroom," I replied. "On with the tour."

I pointed to the bedroom door. Ryan followed me in and did a slow circle, checking out his new digs. It didn't take long—it was a small room.

"It's kind of boring," I mumbled.

"No, it's good," he said. "Simple." He sat down on the bed and looked out the window.

"That's a wisteria vine," I offered. "Outside the window."

Ryan didn't respond. I couldn't stop. I kept chattering out of sheer nervousness.

"My Nana and I once went to see the world's largest wisteria vine. It's in Altadena, about an hour from here. It covers a whole acre and they have a festival and everything."

Ryan looked at me blankly. "I should go find my mom and see if she needs help," he said.

He moved for the door, I moved to get out of his way, and we engaged in one of those embarrassing two-steps. I stopped, let him pass then trailed after him into the living room just in time to see Gillian and Carina at the front door, bearing a plate of brownies. If people were flowers, Gillian would be a daffodil—bright, sunny and the first one to poke her nose up in the spring. Carina's a hothouse type, like an orchid, maybe. Me, I'm the brown mushroom. Not even a flower…just a fungus.

Gillian did a double take when she saw Ryan.

"Wait a minute, I know you! You're Rocket's mystery lifesaver from the Getty!"

Oops, I thought, my face burning. I acted all surprised. "Oh, that's right. Although, I wouldn't say he saved my life, exactly," I protested.

"Close enough," scolded Gillian. "Hey, Rocket, where are your manners? Aren't you going to introduce us? Never mind, I'll do it myself."

"Hello and welcome to the neighborhood. I'm Gillian, and this is Carina. These brownies are for you."

She thrust the plate at Ryan. He took one.

"You just happened to be baking today?" I asked.

"Actually, your mom called my mom a couple of hours ago and asked if we could get some basics, you know, food and stuff," answered Gillian.

She pointed outside. Sure enough, her mom was out front handing off a couple bags of groceries to Rick. "Chocolate is one of the most important items on the food pyramid."

"Good," Ryan managed to reply through a mouthful of fudge. Gillian extended the plate to me. I shook my head. Ryan took seconds.

"Well, since you're here, you can help us unload stuff, I guess," I said, trying to take the reins again. "Many hands make light work."

Oh my god, did I just say that? I groaned inwardly. I sounded like a nineteenth-century school marm.

"Yes, ma'am, Miss Mayberry," said Gillian, saluting me. I stomped past her and headed out to the curb.

Carina carried in a duffel bag, babbling away to Ryan and me as if we'd all been friends for life—as if the scene at that boutique had never even happened. I was beginning to think she had some sort of split personality.

"Gillian just showed me this awesome ice cream place around the corner, on the way to the beach. Have you been to the beach yet?" she said.

"I've been to the beach before, but not here," said Ryan. "We just got here."

"Oh, of course," said Gillian. "That's so awful."

Carina set the duffel down on his bed. "Did you know the outside pocket on your duffel bag is falling off?"

"Bummer," Ryan said, examining the bag.

"I could fix it for you," offered Carina. "I love to sew. I have a machine at home, but all I need for this is a needle and thread."

"I don't think I have any," replied Ryan.

"That's okay. I'll bring some next time I'm here."

Next time? She was planning on repeat visits? I was about to go in and say something—I don't know what, but it was going to be clever and cutting and brilliant—and show Carina that I was a force to be reckoned with. A force with which to be reckoned. Even in a verbal battle, I had no intention of forgetting my grammar. English was my best subject. School marm, remember? But before I crafted my retort, Rick popped in, as oblivious to the tension in the room as everyone else.

"Hey, Rocket, time to say adios to your friends," he said. "Josie's looking a little tired. I want to get her home so she can put her feet up. And Bethie and Ryan probably want some quiet time to settle in, too."

"We'll take good care of them," promised Carina, smiling at me as she put an arm around Ryan and gave him a friendly squeeze.

Gillian nodded. "We've totally got this."

That's what I was afraid of. Even more than I fear dangling prepositions.

FIFTEEN

AS IT TURNED OUT, I DIDN'T HAVE TIME TO WORRY ABOUT RYAN MATHEWS FOR THE NEXT
couple of weeks. The end of the school year was bearing down like a
tidal wave, flooding me with term papers and final exams and anxiety
about where I would be attending high school in the fall. One night, after a marathon session outputting an eight-page essay on the decline of
the Roman Empire, I fell asleep at my desk before I finished my math
homework.

When the mirror pulsed its invitation, I startled awake. A thin strand
of drool dribbled onto my geometry book as I lifted my head. Ugh. I
wiped it off with the sleeve of my sweatshirt and looked at my clock. I
stomped through the mirror, ready to confront the muses for once again
waking me up in the middle of the night.

I emerged on the other side of the mirror, right near the same cliff
I'd emerged by the first time. The landscape wasn't spooky or starlit this
time. The sun shone down warm and bright on a grassy bluff overlooking the calm sea.

"Do you know what time it is?" I demanded once I got to Polly, who
was lying on her back looking up at a cloud drifting by. A young woman
in an old-fashioned navy dress was lying next to her, eyes closed, seem-
ingly asleep.

"What time *is* it, dear?" she asked absent-mindedly. "And does it
matter?"

"It's three o'clock in the morning! School starts in a few hours!"

"It's a beautiful spring morning here," said Polly. "A unanimous deci-
sion made by all nine of us. And Emily here."

"Emily?" I asked. I looked at the woman next to Polly more closely.
Her dark hair was pulled back and parted severely in the middle, and

she wore a grosgrain ribbon around her neck, and pinned in an "X" at her throat. "Emily Dickinson?"

"It's a pleasure to meet you," said Emily, neither confirming nor denying that she was the famous poet.

"Would you like to join us?" Polly touched the grass between them. "We're working, but we don't mind company."

There were no instruments, or books, or tools of any kind near either woman.

"Working?" I asked. "What sort of work?"

She gave me a look of vague surprise, as if the answer should have been obvious.

"Oh, we're daydreaming, of course. And wool-gathering, although I haven't decided what I want to knit together just yet."

She pointed a lazy finger at the sky. "Don't you think that cloud resembles one of those flying machines...what do you call them again? On Earth?"

"An airplane?"

"Yes, that's it. An air plane!" she said, drawing out the compound word with delight. "A *wedge* for cutting through the air. So clever."

I looked back up at the sky. Her cloud was moving closer. "I think that might be an *actual* airplane."

Polly scrambled to her feet, shading her eyes with her hand to get a better view. "Oh, it's Amelia! How lovely! She hasn't been here in such a long time."

"Amelia?" I had a sneaking suspicion. Polly confirmed it.

"Yes, Amelia Earhart, the aviatrix—do you know her?" asked Polly.

"I know *of* her," I said. "From history books. She lived a long time ago. Her plane went missing about a hundred years ago."

Polly wasn't paying attention to me. She was too focused on Amelia Earhart's approach. "Oh! I do believe Amelia's brought friends!"

I looked up and blinked in surprise, then rubbed my eyes and looked again. Yep. Two men sporting large feathery wings were gliding in lazy loops around Amelia's plane, keeping a safe distance from the propellers.

Polly waved her arms vigorously until one of the winged men spotted her. He signaled to Amelia and the other man, and all three adjusted their course until they were flying right toward us. Soon they were close enough that I could see Amelia's face. She looked calm and controlled in her snug leather helmet and white silk scarf. As she buzzed by us, she dipped one wing down in greeting and gave us a jaunty salute from her open cockpit.

After blowing her a big kiss, Polly turned to me, eyes sparkling. "Isn't she marvelous?"

Emily gave a decisive nod. "Simply remarkable."

Amelia leveled out her plane and continued flying across the island. The men with wings, however, headed in for a landing, circling lower and lower until they were practically on top of us. The older of the two—a cross-looking man with a white beard—set down easily on a flat stretch of grass about fifty feet away from us. He removed the wings, which were attached with a clever harness, and was setting all of his equipment down in a neat pile when the second, younger man bobbled his landing and ended up collapsing in a heap on top of him, scattering feathers everywhere. Polly ran to the accident site.

"Is that Daedalus? And his son Icarus?" I asked, dashing behind her.

Emily followed at a more sedate pace, hampered by her long skirts and laced ankle boots.

Polly threw me a glance. "You've been reading up on all of us. You are half right—the older one is indeed Daedalus, but I do believe his companion with the bruises on his bum and his ego is our friend Narcissus."

The old man groaned as Polly and I helped him to his feet. He dusted off his toga and examined a bent feather on one of his wings. "You need to work on your precision, Narcissus."

Narcissus! I recognized him—he was the deliveryman who had brought me the mirror! Laughing, he untangled himself from his harness and leaned back on his elbows to look up at the sky.

"Look, here comes Icks," he said, pointing.

A third winged man whizzed into sight. He didn't glide—he zoomed. Angling his wings to catch each updraft and downdraft, he skimmed low along the water, and then shot upwards like a missile straight toward the sun.

Daedalus shook his head with a sigh. Polly dropped down on the grass next to Narcissus, and the two of them made themselves comfortable to enjoy the show.

Emily stood a few yards away from us, rapt at the sight, one hand fingering the crossed ribbon at her neck, the other hand shading her brow.

Polly pointed to the flying marvel. "*That's* Icarus."

I couldn't believe everyone was just sitting there so calmly. "Somebody should stop him! He's flying too high!"

"He's fine," said Daedalus gruffly, his voice filled with fatherly pride. "Watch what that boy can do."

"But…won't his wings fall apart if he gets too close to the sun?" I said.

"Genius here sorted that out for us," Daedalus said, reaching down to cuff Narcissus gently on the head. "He's developed a wax that becomes heatproof and water-resistant once exposed to solar rays. Not to mention stronger and lighter weight than titanium."

Narcissus blushed. "It was a simple matter of tinkering with the formula and adding a couple of new ingredients. You'd have figured it out yourself if you'd had more time before your escape from the Labyrinth."

"Thanks to you, my boy can fly as close to the sun as he wants or skim the sea like a pelican without fear of losing his feathers. I'm grateful."

"It was Urania's idea, really," said Narcissus, humbly. "She's a gifted engineer."

Emily tilted her head, as if she heard a distant sound.

"Alas, Mother's bell calls me downstairs," she said with a deep sigh. "My escape to Mount Helikon comes to an end, despite my flying attitude."

She looked up once more at Icarus, and then wistfully at the wings that Daedalus and Narcissus had discarded on the ground. At first I thought it was my imagination, but she seemed to be turning paler, transparent.

"Thank you, my dears—I, for one, have gathered wool in many colors here today. Perhaps a skein grand enough to knit a rainbow."

Her words drifted away on a breeze, just as her body faded until all that was left of her was a shimmering ray of sunlight.

I stared at the spot where Emily had been standing.

"Don't worry, Rocket," said Polly. "You'll see her again, I'm sure. Emily escapes to Mount Helikon quite frequently."

She took Daedalus by the arm. "Deddy, dear, you must be parched after flying in the sun. Won't you come share some mead with me in the meadow? Or we could conjure up your favorite! Pineapple juice."

She turned toward me. "Rocket, you and Narcissus can linger here as long as you'd like. Perhaps do a little sketching in your journal, if that appeals. Or stare at the clouds, and keep a lookout for more flying machines. They're scattered across the sky like rose petals today!"

The air on Mount Helikon was having its usual effect by now, so I just lay back on the grass as Polly had suggested and dreamily watched the clouds. Narcissus noticed me squinting in the bright sunlight. He pulled off his sunglasses. They looked like the kind motorcycle cops wear—gold metal frames with a double bridge across the nose and mirrored lenses, of course.

"Here, try these on," he said. "I've been meaning to give you a pair."

"Thanks," I said. I reached for them, but he didn't let go. Staring into the reflective surface, he started adjusting his hair, his eyes becoming glassy and unfocused.

"Hello? Earth to the Acropolis?" I asked.

Narcissus shook his head, coming out of his trance. He looked down at the glasses in his hands. He seemed surprised to see he was still holding them.

"Oh, sorry, lost in thought."

"Geez, no wonder your name is synonymous with self-absorption," I muttered. "Is there any mirror you can resist?"

"Excuse me?" Narcissus demanded.

"You ignored that girl Echo, because you were too busy staring at your own reflection."

"That is such a crock! For your information, I was staring into that pond, because I was thinking," he said indignantly.

"Uh-huh," I said. "Thinking about how hot you are?"

"You shouldn't believe every myth you read, Rocket," he told me. There was an edge to his voice.

"So, what really happened?"

"There was this glade in the woods near my home in Greece where I used to like to go to think when I was a mortal youth," he began.

"Wait, a minute. You were a mortal?" I asked. "So, how did you get to be immortal?"

"Stop interrupting and I'll tell you. When I'm inventing stuff, I need it to be quiet, you know? And this place I went was perfect—a little pond surrounded by trees, far away from all the hustle and bustle of the village where I lived. One day, I'm sitting there, alone as usual, enjoying the quiet and thinking about how I can see a reflection of trees and clouds and my face, and I started wondering if other surfaces could achieve the same effect—when all of a sudden someone throws a big rock into the water. Splash. So I call, 'Who's there?' and I hear, 'Who's there?' repeated in this annoying girlie voice."

"Girlie voice?"

"Sorry, but yeah. I was frustrated, because she interrupted my train of thought. So, I politely said, 'Please, go away,' and then she says it back to me! 'Go away, go away!' Over and over. How was I to know she had some sort of cursed speech defect? I just thought she was mocking me in a very ill-mannered way."

"So then what happened?"

"Well, once Hera and Zeus got involved, the whole thing got blown out of proportion. Artemis turned me into a flower for a while to teach me a lesson. After I was back to myself again, I said, 'Sorry,' to Echo. And then she said, 'Sorry'." He gave me a wink.

I laughed. "What else could she say?"

"On the up side, while I was stuck in flower form, I had nothing to do but meditate on that pond, with no distractions except for the occasional honey bee or butterfly. That's when it dawned on me how to create the first mirror by polishing a piece of metal. The one above your portal is an early prototype."

"Cool," I commented.

"Yeah, cool. Plus, I can transport through narcissi now, which is a nice little bonus come springtime. And eventually, Zeus restored me to my form, this incredible, gorgeous form you see before you."

"Vanity! I knew it!" I said.

"Kidding," he said.

"But how did you get to be immortal?"

"Oh, the Muses talked it up and inspired some ancient bards to write down the story, and I was immortalized in word and song. And here I am. You know how that goes."

He pointed to the glasses in my hand. "So, aren't you going to try your new specs on? They're my latest invention. I call them Sparktacles."

"Sparktacles? No offense, Narcissus, but these things are really ugly."

He looked hurt, so I put them on. I looked around. "Trees, clouds, sky, crazy guy zipping around with wings. Everything looks perfectly normal. For this place."

"Try them back on earth. They'll help you see more clearly," Narcissus told me. "It's important. I don't want to scare you but, well, something or someone began deliberately canceling out creativity waves, right around the time you started your apprenticeship. At first, it was just a trickle, but now it's serious. The Muses are quite worried, even if they don't show it. Keep your heart open."

I corrected him. "You mean, 'Keep my *eyes* open.'"

He touched his hand to his chest. "You'll feel it here first if something is off. Your eyes can deceive you. These glasses mitigate that, but an open heart's your best defense."

Sixteen

THE MORE TIME I SPENT WITH THE MUSES, THE MORE OUT OF PLACE I FELT IN MIDDLE SCHOOL. I was secretly beginning to enjoy, even depend upon my time in Mount Helikon. Muse training didn't deplete me in the same way that regular school sometimes did—on the contrary, it felt like an extended, beautiful dream. Maybe it was the super-enriched air swirling around the Muses' creative sanctuary, or maybe it was the way the Muses immersed themselves in pleasure. Whatever the reason, I liked it, although I still couldn't believe it was the most efficient, productive use of my time. The very concept of "time" barely registered with Polly and her sisters. I never knew if it would be day or night when I stepped through that mirror. There were no clocks or calendars, no schedule, no bells ringing to hurry us from one class to another.

We spent hours reclining on the grass, staring up at clouds drifting across blue sky or silvered moon. We rambled the meadows and the hills, gathering wildflowers and pausing to sketch creatures that caught our eye. The only rule was that we keep our golden journals and quills at hand, to write down any ideas that popped into our heads.

Middle school had become a pretty lonely place. The divide between Gillian and me reminded me of the Grand Canyon. Our moms had taken us there for winter break a few years back, and I pictured it now, so deep and wide it seemed an entire ocean couldn't fill it up. Now, she was on one side, and I was on the other. There were so many things I wanted to tell her, but my words couldn't span the gap. I filled pages and pages of my golden journal with poems and pictures.

I felt lost at home these days, too. Rick and my mom spent all the time looking at each other like ice cream cones, when they weren't busy preparing for the arrival of the dynamic duo. In the car on the way to school one morning, my mom handed me a picture, a fuzzy black and white image from an ultrasound, which is kind of like an x-ray that uses sound waves. With a little effort, I could make out two little strings of dots topped by blurred white circles. My mom said they were the babies' spines and heads.

As I walked up the front steps, I thought about showing the picture to Gillian, how we would make jokes about how maybe my mom wasn't really pregnant and had just swallowed a jar of marbles. I looked up, and there she was, across the hallway, putting books into her locker. 12-24-33. I still knew her combination. I had joked that it sounded like my body measurements. A perfect pear.

I decided what the heck? It was ridiculous that I hadn't even told Gillian about the babies yet. Somehow it hadn't come up in conversation on that horrible shopping excursion with Carina. But just as I was reaching out to hand her the picture, Gary Grossman swooped in and grabbed it out of my hand.

"What's that?" he asked loudly, the only volume he seemed to have.

Gary's shrill voice stopped an entire corridor of kids like a traffic light. I didn't know what to do. I was so shocked at the unexpected attack. My face flamed up.

"My mother is pregnant, you jerk," I finally sputtered, snatching back the photo. "This is a picture of my new baby brothers."

Gary snickered. "I hope the sequel's better than the original."

Gillian looked at me, her mouth wide open. "Josie is pregnant? When did that happen?

"I found out the night before my birthday and I keep forgetting to tell you."

"You're going to have twin baby brothers, and you didn't think to tell me?"

"You're not someone I can trust with a secret these days," I said bitterly. We stared at each other across the corridor.

"Cat fight. Yes!" Gary egged us on.

Gillian and I looked at him in mutual disgust. "Shut it, Grossboy," we said simultaneously.

Just as something between us started to soften, Carina appeared. She opened her locker and squealed when a balloon and teddy bear popped out. She threw her arms around Gillian.

"You are the best friend ever," she said. Gillian looked at me uncomfortably.

I felt my shell harden again. I crumpled the photo in one hand, grabbed the books I needed for homework that night and slammed my locker shut with a bang. As I was fumbling to shove the picture deep into my bulging backpack, my hand made contact with the sunglasses Narcissus had given me. Sparktacles. Really? I clutched them tight and stumbled to the relative safety of the girls' bathroom. At least it would be a Grossman-free zone.

I took off my regular glasses, slid on the new ones. They fit perfectly. I looked like a dork, but at least my eyes were now hidden behind big mirrored lenses.

As I was staring into the mirror, willing myself not to cry, a girl came in softly humming a tune to herself. I recognized her. Ella Welch. She was a sixth grader, with such a spectacular voice that she was the first one ever to be bumped up to the eighth grade choir. When I looked at her, the Sparktacles sort of shivered on my face, as if they were excited. I caught a flash of hot pink light radiating out from Ella's center, just over her lungs. She disappeared into a stall.

Thinking the glasses might be dirty, I pulled them off and held them up to the fluorescent lights. No smudges or blobs of gum or anything like that—they were as clean as they could be. I ran them under the sink, just to be sure, and dried them carefully on the soft underside of my hoodie.

When Ella came out, I gave her a once over with my bare eyes. She didn't look like a musical prodigy, just an average girl with straight brown hair and a shy smile. I put the Sparktacles back on—and yep, there was that pink glow again. It spiraled up her neck and out through her lips. It was so beautiful I was mesmerized.

Ella caught me staring at her and smiled nervously. She checked herself in the mirror and looked down at her white choir blouse. The pink glow receded, dropping out of her throat and contracting into a little glowing ball about the size of a marble down by her belly button.

"Do I have something on my face?" she asked awkwardly, trying to see her back in the mirror. "Or on my shirt?"

"No, no," I said. "You look great. Sorry, I was just thinking about other stuff."

I gave her a little half-wave as she fled the bathroom.

Curious to see how other people looked through the specs, I kept them on for the rest of the day. Before long, it dawned on me that the sunspecs created a kind of map of someone's talents or passions. When I aimed my view at Harry Knox, the star of our school's track team, the glow was brightest around his legs and feet. A lot of the jocks had glows like that: dancing orange flames streaked all around our star quarterback's hands, and Gillian's crush, Jasper, had brilliant blue streaks fizzing around his muscular arms and shoulders.

Some people just had a little light flickering in their guts or around their hearts, no bigger than the flame of a birthday candle. You could see in their body posture how they tried to protect it, hunched over their middle sections, as if afraid the slightest breeze would snuff it out.

The sunspecs quickly became an addiction for me. I couldn't help myself—it was so beautiful to see the lights dancing and shimmering, expanding at times to whirl up and out into space, and then condensing and contracting back into their physical bodies. I wanted to figure out why, and how, the lights worked—what made them expand, what made them shrink. I kept thinking of a trip we'd taken to the science center when I was a child: I had stood mesmerized for hours in an exhibit on electricity, touching my fingers to the glass wall so that the currents arced toward me like miniature lightning storms. But wearing sunglasses day and night, and sometimes in class, sends up red flags.

Mr. Lennon was the first teacher to express his "concern." He flat out told me that wearing sunglasses in PE class was rude. I told him that I had tried to switch to contact lenses but had an allergic reaction, which left my eyes sensitive to light. That shut him up, and left me free to wear them for at least a few more days.

In history class, where he was still serving as a substitute for Mr. Horace, I noticed that Mr. Lennon's light dimmed to barely a glow. He just went through the motions of teaching the class, writing the assignments on the board, making us read, quelling any sort of dialogue that happened to evolve. But when he was coaching, Mr. Lennon lit up like the scoreboard at the sports arena downtown. Some of the kids in the class did too—hoisting themselves up a rope or kicking a ball into a goal made them light up inside the way music sparked something inside Ella Welch.

It made me wonder about my other teachers.

I realized that my favorite teachers had lights as bright as anyone's.

They lit up when the class was having a particularly intense discussion or when a student did an exceptional job on a presentation. When I finished reading my essay on *The Bell Jar* by Sylvia Plath, I thought the radiance off my English teacher Mrs. Michaels would give me a sunburn.

Not surprisingly, Mrs. Fletcher glowed with rainbow intensity all over her whole body, whatever she was doing. In fact, everyone's lights seemed brighter during her art classes, with one giant exception. Carina.

Carina's flame didn't shrink and expand organically like the others. One minute, it beamed scarlet bright like the lip gloss she preferred. But in a heartbeat, it would be gone. Not smaller. Out. Like a switch had been turned off, or a lead blanket had been dropped over her head. More troubling was the way other people's lights started to flicker and dim in her presence, like a black hole was trying to inhale them. I made a mental note to ask Narcissus about it the next time I saw him.

SEVENTEEN

POLYHYMNIA WASN'T THE ONLY MUSE WHO HAD SUCCUMBED TO TEMPTATION WITH A mortal, because there were eight more girls my age beginning their apprenticeships—one for each Muse. Add in the girls in the years above us, and that made a total of sixty-three apprentices from places across the globe. Alums visited Mount Helikon frequently, too, to check in with their former mentors. Right now, Urania and Polyhymnia were strolling around the rustic reflecting pool, deep in conversation with a girl I thought I recognized.

I gazed at the variety of outfits around me—kilts and sarongs to grass skirts and burkas. There were only a few apprentices clad in jeans like me.

"I feel like I stepped into the fashion segment at a Miss Universe pageant," I murmured to the Irish apprentice who was sitting next to me. "And I'm about to get voted off."

Brigit was a little sprite of a thing with a delicate pointy face and a tangle of dark-red curls. She looked like Thumbelina, flitting from here to there like a magical woodland creature. I loved the way she danced, all her energy in her flying feet, while the top half of her body stayed smooth and controlled.

Brigit looked at me blankly. "Sure, and what's the Miss Universe Pageant?" she asked in her lilting voice.

"You know, the beauty contest, on television," I replied. "Don't they have that in Ireland?"

"Tell-vision?" she replied, even more confused. "Is that like a gazing crystal?"

Something dawned on me. Polly had mentioned that the apprentices came from different countries—maybe…

"Brigit, what year is it for you, back in the real world?" I asked. Polyhymnia, Urania and the girl strolling with them had just reached us.

"Bravissima, Rocket, you have discovered one of the many wonders of Mount Helikon!" said the girl, giving a little clap before Brigit even answered my question. She was so familiar. Where had I seen her before?

"In this ethereal world, we can come together not just from any place, but from any period in time," Urania explained.

"And still we all understand each other perfectly," said Dani slowly.

"Yes, that's right. You can speak fluently with the muses from every culture when you are here," explained Polyhymnia. "Everything you say is communicated to them exactly as you feel it in your heart, perfectly."

It was true, I realized with a start. I had talked with girls from all over the planet, felt a close connection with them—without ever needing a translator.

"I just assumed everyone was speaking fluent English," I said, realizing how self-absorbed that sounded.

"Here on Mount Helikon, everyone remembers the universal language," said Urania. "Without even trying."

"Are there no boys who can speak this language?" asked Dani, in her soft voice. Dani was from Bali. I didn't know much about her home country, but looking at her made me think of lush rice fields, swaying coconut palms, and white sand beaches. She was like an exotic version of Gillian, charming and fearless.

As Dani gestured with her hands at the multitude of girls and women around us, a dozen bangles on her slender wrists tinkled like bells. I realized with a twinge that she was right. She had noticed something that I hadn't. Our entire class, if you could call it that, was female. I hadn't really gotten to know the other first year apprentices yet, just their names and exotic faces: Magdalena from South America, Samira from Egypt, Astrid from Norway, Ayumu from Japan, Galina from Russia, and Kanoni from Tanzania, in Africa.

Except for Narcissus and Apollo, or the occasional visitor from the material world, there were no boys here.

"Dani's right. Didn't you guys ever have any male offspring?" I asked Polly.

Polyhymnia replied, selecting her words carefully. "Our female descendants typically have stronger powers of intuition and a certain fluidity of spirit that allows them to move more easily between the earthly and astral planes than boys. Take Laelia here."

"Laelia! I do know you," I blurted out. "You work in my mother's shop! But your hair is different here."

I was used to seeing her with short green spikes. Here, she had wavy black hair falling almost to her hips. She gave me an impish smile.

"I was wondering when you'd figure it out, soul sister," she said.

"Laelia is in her final year of apprenticeship with us," said Polyhymnia. "She dances a wicked tarantella. You should ask her to show you sometime."

Thalia, the curvy Muse of Comedy, shimmied in from the edge of the circle, winding her hips in a sinuous figure eight like a belly dancer. "All muses are wicked dancers. More in touch with the connection between spirit and body."

Thalia paused for a beat in front of her apprentice Magdalena, trying to pull the solid earthy-looking girl from South America into the dance. Magdalena recoiled reflexively, shaking her head. She ducked her chin down and withdrew into herself like a tortoise, pulling her knees up into her chest, wrapping them with her solid brown arms. We couldn't see her eyes now, just her straight black hair pulled tight into two braids tied off with red string. It was a defensive body posture I knew quite well myself—as clear as a neon sign flashing the word NO.

"Perhaps it's better without boys here," said Dani, looking at Magdalena thoughtfully. "Safer."

"That is sometimes true," said Polyhymnia, smiling gently. "But through the years, there have been notable exceptions to that rule."

There was a mysterious edge to her voice, like she knew something that I didn't. Which was true, of course. She was an immortal Muse, after all, with eons of experience under her golden corded belt.

The sky began to rumble. Polly looked up with a sigh, counting off the bolts of lightning as they crackled across the suddenly dark sky.

"One...and...two...and...three," she said, with another sigh. "I'm afraid that's the end of our discussion session this afternoon, darlings. Father needs us."

"Wants," corrected Thalia. "Father Zeus is perfectly capable of conquering the heavens one thunderbolt at a time all by his lonesome. He just enjoys making us drop everything and hightail it to Mount Olympus, so we can all proclaim his general fabulousness in perpetuity throughout the known universe."

"Thalia!" said Polly, scandalized. "He might hear you!"

Polly looked around nervously, as if the God of Gods might just pop out from behind a laurel tree at any moment.

"It would serve him right," said Thalia. "I was having the loveliest dream about a donkey who falls in love with a mermaid. Now instead of dreaming deeper into that, I've got to write an homage to a stubborn ass who chases after every female on land or sea."

Polyhymnia turned to us. "Don't let Thalia's words distress you, dear ones. We are all very grateful to Zeus. It's true—he does demand a fair amount of epic poetry about his heroic deeds and achievements, but—"

Thalia cut her off with a snort. "You forgot to mention the victory marches and the tribute dances and the three-act plays and the eloquent inscriptions on every single one of the monuments mortals erect in his honor. Not to mention the actual monuments—sculptures and parthenons and elaborate mosaic floors."

"Muses have to tile floors and build parthenons?" I asked, confused.

"We don't do the actual construction," Polly reassured me.

"You don't think the ideas for those things pop out of people's foreheads like Athena, do you?" exclaimed Thalia. "We have to whisper ideas to them while they sleep, or when all those bewildered artists come lurking around Mount Helikon, trying to ferret out a little inspiration for their patriotic monuments and battle hymns."

"Inspiration which we happily provide," said Calliope, who had entered the meadow just in time to hear Thalia's rant. "I, for one, think it a privilege to honor Father's remarkable achievements. Paying homage to heroes—whether they be mortal or immortal—allows others to be inspired and elevated by their triumphs."

"Yes, we must sing for our supper," said Thalia. "We'd best be on our way before Zeus comes here looking for us."

At these words, Thalia's apprentice Magdalena stiffened up more than ever.

"Would he hurt you?" Magdalena asked in a low voice.

Thalia squatted down and gave Magdalena a fierce hug, taking her by surprise. Magdalena looked too stunned to move.

"This is your safe haven, Magdalena," said Thalia. "As long as you need protection, you may stay here. And, to tell the truth, Zeus hasn't stepped foot on Mount Helikon in a very long time."

"Why not?" I asked.

"Because to find Mount Helikon, you first have to recognize that you are a little bit lost," said Thalia. "And even if he were hopelessly wandering in circles for years on end, Zeus would refuse to admit it. Because then—he might have to stop and ask for directions."

She erupted into a fit of belly giggles at her own wit, just as the rest of the Muses arrived in a flurry.

"Where's our ride?" asked Melpomene, Thalia's not-so-identical-twin. "Haven't you sent for your boyfriend, Thalia?"

Calliope beamed at us as she explained. "Lovely, clever Thalia has bewitched Apollo, the Sun God."

"Ah, but now that handsome devil is in love with Urania, too," said Thalia, giving her more serious, scientifically-minded sister a hug. "Talk about solar flares! The poor fool's so besotted he doesn't know which way to point his chariot!"

As if on cue, Apollo arrived in a golden chariot pulled by four fiery steeds, a sight so beautiful and brilliant that it hurt to look directly at him. Apollo gazed back and forth between Thalia and Urania with complete adoration, stretching out his hand in their direction. Urania clasped it with a solemn smile and allowed Apollo to pull her into the chariot. While he helped Urania settle onto the gleaming bench, Thalia bounced up and sat on his right, flashing him a dazzling smile. The other sisters followed, arranging themselves in the back of the chariot. Apollo looked dazed but happy as he sat there in his driver's seat, lost to the beauty all around him.

Thalia picked up the reins Apollo had let fall from his grasp, leaned down from her high perch, and spoke to us in a stage whisper.

"THAT, my girls, is the very definition of 'bemused,'" Thalia chortled. "Today's vocabulary lesson for you!"

She let out a peal of laughter so luminous that it was easy to see why the Sun God himself had been enchanted by her, then turned her attention to getting the chariot aloft and on its way to Mount Olympus.

We admired the horses as they sprang into the air like flames, licking the sky.

"Aren't they beautiful?" asked Laelia. "Of course, Pegasus is a lot easier to ride than the Sun Steeds."

"Pegasus?" I asked. "*The* Pegasus?"

"Yes, yes. The winged white horse of myth and legend," she said. "He's been grazing in the southern meadow all day. I'll introduce you if you'd like."

Brigit and Dani asked if they could join, and Laelia smiled and linked her arms in theirs. I gathered up my journal and quill.

"Shouldn't we be working or something?" I asked. "While the Muses are gone?"

"Remember your E's," said Laelia, in a sing-song voice.

"Explore...Experience...Emote...Express... is the Muse's path to true success," Brigit and Dani sang back to her, dutifully repeating the ditty we had learned just that morning.

"Egads, Exhausting," I muttered.

"Effervescent," retorted Brigit good-naturedly.

"Ethereal and endlessly enjoyable," added Dani.

"Excruciating," I said.

Brigit erupted into a fit of giggles, and soon we were all laughing and feeling as light as the lavender-scented breeze blowing sweetly in our faces.

I had never been to the southern pasture, and I wasn't sure I would ever find my way there again without Laelia guiding me. She wove us through shrubbery, vaulted over fallen logs and boulders, and finally parted the branches of a willow tree. I caught my breath as I stepped through the fall of feathery leaves and spotted Pegasus for the first time.

He was more beautiful than I ever could have imagined, larger than any horse I had ever seen on Earth. His coat was whiter than snow, and it sparked in the sunlight, iridescent, as he grazed on sweet bunch grasses and dandelion leaves. There was no fence around the field. What would be the point? With his powerful wings, there could be no imprisoning him.

"Athena brought Pegasus to the Muses when he was just a colt," Laelia told us. "It was love at first sight, for all of them."

I pulled out my journal and began sketching and scribbling notes as Laelia told us the story of Pegasus.

"At that time, the young Muses were pouring forth ideas and visions so abundantly that Mount Helikon began to expand, like a balloon," said

Laelia, who emphasized every sentence with exuberant hand gestures. "Zeus feared that the entire region would shatter, or perhaps become untethered and float away into the stratosphere. He sent the newborn colt to distract the sisters and relieve the pressure. Little Pegasus was so happy to meet the Muses that he flapped his little white wings, and flew for the very first time."

Pegasus nickered and nodded his head, clearly enjoying this story about his babyhood. Laelia smiled at him, and patted him on the neck.

"He was just a baby then," she continued. "Unsteady on his feet, and very clumsy with his unskilled wings, fluttering and tumbling this way and that. Wherever his hooves struck the earth, springs bubbled up, spilling out water that inspires anyone who drinks it. The most important of these is called Hippocrene, which means 'Horse's Fountain,' and there's also Aganippe and a few others."

"The Hippocrene spring feeds the reflecting pool, doesn't it?" I asked. Laelia nodded. I wondered if one of Pegasus' springs also fed the pond where Narcissus did his inventing.

"It's hard to imagine him as a wee colt," said Brigit, who had swung herself up into an oak tree to get a better view. "He's a spectacular brute, and doesn't he know it!"

Pegasus rippled the muscles of his flanks, and tossed his mane, as if he knew we were admiring him.

"You've actually ridden him?" I asked Laelia, trying not to sound too doubting.

"Many times. Would you like to try?" There was a mischievous glint in Laelia's eyes, but curiosity overcame my fear. I nodded.

"You'll have to win his trust first, and prove to him that you are worthy," she said. "Here—offer him some ambrosia."

Out of nowhere, Laelia produced a golden bowl loaded with fruit salad…which the Muses made exactly like Gillian's mom. Marshmallows, shredded coconut, canned pineapple and whipped cream.

I approached Pegasus slowly, with my head bowed and the bowl extended in front of me like an offering, trying my best to appear humble and worthy of his attention. He trotted away with a harumph. Laelia called over to me.

"I forgot to tell you. You also have to sing to him," she said.

"I'm not much of a singer," I told her.

She shrugged. "Singing is the only way he'll let you ride him."

Feeling a little silly, I walked once more toward Pegasus while warbling an off-key version of "Row, Row, Row Your Boat." At the first note, Pegasus lifted his head expectantly, regarding me with his lovely, liquid brown eyes, but before I finished the first line, he lost interest and dropped his head to munch another mouthful of grass. I edged closer to him. He whinnied in an annoyed tone and flew out of my reach. I kept singing, but Pegasus stayed stubbornly on the far side of the pasture, tossing his mane in a dismissive sort of way and presenting me with his big white rump. I knew when I wasn't wanted.

I went back to Laelia. "I have the world's worst singing voice," I told her. "I guess I'm not worthy enough to ride Pegasus."

"It's not how you sing," she said. "It's *what* you sing that matters to Pegasus."

Brigit persisted, following him and talking the whole while in a cooing sort of voice.

"Come here, my beauty. Brigit won't hurt you. How could I hurt a great beastie like you?" she said.

"Come back here, you winged wanker, you!" Brigit called after him. Laelia laughed.

Dani stepped up. "Maybe he prefers traditional Balinese music," she said. "I'll try Jangi Janger, it's a sweet little song all the little girls learn in my village."

She launched into a playful tune, but before she even got past the first verse, Pegasus stomped his front hoof, shook his head in a frustrated way, and galloped even further across the pasture.

Brigit took the bowl of ambrosia out of Dani's arms and shoved it into Magdalena's.

"Maybe you'll be the lucky one," she said.

Much to my surprise, Magdalena accepted the bowl and stepped forward to try her hand at taming Pegasus.

"Ave Maria…Ave Maria…Maria."

Magdalena's clear voice pierced the dusky air, as she passionately sang the timeless Catholic hymn in Latin, looking up at the sky instead of at the horse. It gave me goosebumps, listening to her, her pleading voice so full of heartbreak. Pegasus swung his great silken head in Magdalena's direction, ears pricked and attentive until the very last note had faded, as if he too appreciated the beauty she was offering him. But when she walked across the meadow and tentatively touched his mane, he galloped off. A decisive no.

Magdalena shrugged and walked back to where we stood.

"So...he doesn't like sacred hymns, Irish ballads, Balinese children's music or American classics. What kind of music does he like?" I asked Laeila.

"That you'll have to discover for yourself," she said.

I was about to press for more clues, when a fanfare of pipes and the rippling melody of a lyre rang out across the mountain. The Muses were back.

Apollo brought his golden chariot in for a haphazard landing, still distracted by the Muses surrounding him.

Laelia pointed to an older bearded man in a toga, who was ensconced in the back of the chariot with the Muses. He exited the chariot and gallantly assisted the Muses down, one by one, while Apollo saw to unharnessing the Sun Steeds.

"Oh, brilliant! They've brought Homer with them!" said Laelia. "He's awesome."

"We have more special guests arriving in a few moments," Polly told me in an excited whisper. "It's going to be a spectacular night!"

"Sisters, apprentices—please make yourselves comfortable as quickly as possible," instructed Calliope, gesturing to cushions which had been arranged on the natural grassy amphitheater. We were soon joined by other audience members, some of the residents—river and wood nymphs who lived in Mount Helikon year-round.

"Oh, look at the darling cherubs," said Brigit. She pointed above us, where a dozen or so sweet little winged angels hovered, peering shyly down from their fluffy cloud-beds.

"They're not cherubs, they're called 'putti,'" said Laelia, waggling a warning finger at them. "They look innocent, but they get up to a lot of mischief with those miniature bows and arrows. You've probably heard of Cupid? He's their ringleader."

When Narcissus materialized with a golden podium, Calliope linked her arm into Homer's and pulled him toward it.

"It is with great pleasure that I welcome our dear friend Homer, a masterful scribe who has captured our stories with such zeal," she said to all of us seated in the audience. "He shall serve as Master of Ceremonies tonight."

"Thank you, my dear Calliope," said Homer, bowing to her. "I am but a humble servant to you and your sisters. My words are mere moonlight on the sea of your brilliance. Yet it would give me great pleasure to share them with you, by means of introducing tonight's very special performance."

Calliope bowed in return, gracefully surrendering the stage to him. With great solemnity, Homer pulled a scroll from a leather pouch at his waist. He unfurled it and began to read:

"I sing of Artemis, whose shafts are of gold, who cheers on the hounds, the pure maiden, shooter of stags, who delights in archery, own sister to Apollo with the golden sword. Over the shadowy hills and windy peaks she draws her golden bow, rejoicing in the chase, and sends out grievous shafts. The tops of the high mountains tremble and the tangled wood echoes awesomely with the outcry of beasts: earthquakes and the sea also where fishes shoal. But the goddess with a bold heart turns every way destroying the race of wild beasts: and when she is satisfied and has cheered her heart, this huntress who delights in arrows slackens her supple bow and goes to the great house of her dear brother Phoebus Apollo, to the rich land of Delphi, there to order the lovely dance of the Muses and Graces. There she hangs up her curved bow and her arrows, and heads and leads the dances, gracefully arrayed, while all they utter their heavenly voice, singing how neat-ankled Leto bear children supreme among the immortals both in thought and in deed."

Applause broke out as Homer concluded his speech.

"I am humbled by your generous reception," he said, blushing modestly.

Homer gave another deep bow. "And now…I give you Artemis and her warrior-huntresses!" he exclaimed.

Everyone leapt to their feet as Artemis entered the meadow, accompanied by another dramatic clarion call from Clio. Several Muses and an orchestra of apprentices played lyres and pipes, as Artemis led her troupe through a complicated sequence of impossibly high leaps and acrobatics. They looked fierce but joyful at the same time. Serene in their strength.

"Who *are* they?" I whispered to Polly, who was sitting at my side, as mesmerized by the performance as I was.

"To you, she is the goddess Artemis, sister of Apollo, just as Homer described," she replied. "She's lecturing tonight after the dance."

Goddesses as guest speakers. Classic. "What do you mean when you say 'to you'?" I asked.

"Remember…each of the apprentices sees us through the veil of her own culture," said Polly. "Magdalena sees warrior angels and saints… and, through a veil, she is also beginning to see us as ancient spirits revered by her lost tribe. Brigit sees the faeries and goddesses of Celtic legends. Dani sees us as the Apsara, and others worshipped in the Hindu faith. The surface changes, but the essence is eternal and immutable."

"I'll have to get my dictionary out later," I told her. "I don't want to miss this!"

Once the music stopped, and the thundering applause dwindled into silence, Artemis gestured for us all to form a circle. Hands clasped together and raised high, we walked together toward the center until we were brought into the dance equivalent of a huddle. Artemis looked at us with stern dignity.

"Apprentices, listen to my counsel," she instructed. "There is a time of great change approaching. Your light must be strong enough to fight the rising tide of darkness. You must wax and shine like Mother Moon."

"Wax and shine—sounds like an ad for a car wash," I whispered to Dani, who was sitting in lotus position next to me. She giggled.

Artemis' eyes shot over to me like lasers. "This amuses you?"

I gave the tiniest hint of a nod. Artemis returned a grim smile.

"Good. Muses derive their strength from joy and laughter, from delighting the senses and the spirit. But do not deceive yourself: your purpose is still to serve as warriors. Train well, Rocket, if you want to blaze a path to the stars."

Seriously? Even the immortals couldn't resist making lame references to my name?

Just then, Narcissus materialized next to the podium.

"Ready for me to put this away?" he said. When he realized that Artemis was still there, at the center of the huddle, his face went white.

"Trample on any hearts today, Narcissus?" called out Artemis in a voice as sharp and cold as diamonds. "Maybe you need to stop and smell the flowers. Or *become* one again."

She turned to her warrior handmaidens, and they let out obedient hurrahs. The air suddenly grew thick with tension. The Muses looked alarmed. Clio stepped forward with a laurel wreath.

"Courageous Artemis," she said, offering the wreath to Artemis. "Thank you for your wisdom today. We dare not part you and your sisters from your beloved hunt for one more second."

Artemis seemed somewhat appeased. She signaled her attendants and they leapt back into formation with the grace of gazelles. Narcissus tried to blend into the background with all of his might—an impossible task for a mortal almost as handsome as Apollo.

He froze as she directed a final warning at him. "Remember the fate of Actaeon."

"What was that about?" I asked him once Artemis had melted into the forest.

"Artemis isn't a fan. Let's just leave it at that for now," he said. "I've gotta run."

EIGHTEEN

I WAS RUNNING THROUGH THE FOREST WITH ARTEMIS AND HER TRIBE OF FEMALE WARRIORS, alongside a herd of sleek deer. We raced between the trees, through dappled meadows, leaping over fallen trunks, full of joy at the strength and grace of our own bodies. We entered a dark part of the woods, and Artemis slowed. The air was dank and heavy with some foul, rotting odor, not the healthy compost smell of crumbling leaves, but one of death and decay. Something violent had happened here. From the corner of my eye, I saw Magdalena running. She stumbled and fell to the ground, her eyes wide with fear. I reached out a hand to help her up, and she clutched my shoulder—

The dream slipped out of my grasp. I opened my eyes, and realized my mother was shaking my shoulder, trying to rouse me. I really, really, really needed to get that padlock installed on my door.

"Go away!" I moaned, still half in the woods, and worried about Magdalena. "I'm a teenager. We're nocturnal."

"Right, I guess I missed that bit in the comprehensive instruction manual they gave me when you were born."

"I'm not making it up, you know. My Circadian rhythms or something are upside down. I'm supposed to sleep until noon."

"That'll have to wait until summer vacation. Bethie just heard that she can finally visit their house to retrieve stuff—and we are going to help," she said.

"Wait, it's Friday," I realized out loud. "I have school!" I said, pulling my pillow over my head. "Can't you and Rick go without me?"

"Rick's in Palmdale all day. And sometimes, life is the best classroom," she said. She swatted me with a pillow then opened the blinds wide to let in the sun. "I'm happy to write the school a note to that effect. Hurry, Bethie and Ryan will be here in a few minutes."

And before I knew it, I'd been hustled into clothes then the back seat of the SUV with Ryan. He looked just as dazed and cranky as I was. We both retreated to our corners.

The fireman had warned us what to expect, but hearing and seeing are very different senses. As we wound our way up the canyon road, everyone got really quiet. The scorched hillside looked like a lunar landscape. Charred tree trunks stretched their blackened limbs up toward a painfully blue sky. It was surreal—that one day there could be homes, with people in them cooking dinner and watching television and tucking their kids into bed…and the next day, it was gone in a puff of smoke. Like the Big Bad Wolf and those unprepared pigs.

"There, turn right into that driveway with the stone mailbox," directed Beth.

Ryan and Beth got out of the car first and stood on the driveway, looking at the remains of their house. A few skeletal walls stood here and there, and the brick chimney rose like a lone sentry in one corner. Mostly, there were just piles of blackened rubble. Bethie reached out to give Ryan's hand a squeeze. He shook it off and walked away from her.

She turned to us with a big, false smile. "Okay, we knew it would be bad. This is what we expected. Let's see what we can salvage."

My mom passed out rubber gloves, masks and goggles. I put mine on. She handed me an extra set of gear and a couple of rakes and pointed me in the direction of Ryan.

"Mom," I said. "I think he just wants to be left alone."

"He needs a friend, Rocket," my mom said gently but firmly. "And, there's work to be done here."

I walked over to where Ryan was kicking in what was left of one of the interior walls. Clouds of ash filled the air, and I was grateful for my mask.

"You look like ridiculous," he said.

"What? Haven't you seen this month's issue of Vogue? This is the latest fashion craze," I said in a haughty voice, striking a pose with my long yellow gloves.

"Carina and Gillian have nothing on you," he replied, smiling a little.

Where there was a smile, there was hope, so I plunged ahead with my lame comedy. "You, too, can achieve dork high style," I said, thrusting the bundle of gear towards him. "So, where is…was…your room?"

Ryan grimaced and pointed to a corner of the house indistinguishable from the rest of the wreckage. He tugged the gloves and mask on but shoved the goggles into his back pocket. He took one of the rakes from me and strode off. I tagged at his heels, not sure what to say next.

We picked through the debris in silence. Everything was gray and mostly unrecognizable. I uncovered a metal coin bank in the shape of an old Model-T car and held it out to him, excited.

"My grandfather's," he said curtly. He brushed it off and placed it carefully into the plastic "keep" bin my mother set near us. After an hour, we found a few more things for the bin—a couple of crispy-fried framed photos, an old Little League trophy, stuff like that. It was hard to play the cheerleader every time I found some pathetic-looking object I could identify.

All of a sudden, Ryan made a sort of choking sound, and I looked up to see if he was okay. He had uncovered an aquarium, half-melted and laying on its side.

"Were there fish in it?" I asked, horrified. He nodded. His jaw clenched, as if he were trying to stop his emotions rising like bile.

He picked his rake up over his head and smashed it into the teetering wall. The rake's teeth caught in the wood. He couldn't yank it out, so he let go of the handle and kicked the wall with tremendous energy over and over until it fell down with a crash.

"I need to get out of here," he said, and walked off without waiting for me.

I surveyed the wreckage then looked skyward, as if a Muse might be floating in the sky above us.

"This seriously sucks," I said out loud. "Are you guys watching this? You want to tell me how in the world I'm supposed to inspire people when crap like this happens?"

As soon as the words left my lips, a breeze lifted the ashes in a little swirl about ten feet away from me. Choosing to believe it was a sign, I walked over and began wrenching away chunks of burnt timber, until I reached twisted metal. Ryan's bed frame? Protruding from underneath was the edge of a black case. Holding my breath, I pulled the case free of the rubble around it. It was a guitar case, miraculously still intact. I brushed off as much of the ash as I could and hurried to find Ryan.

I spotted him down the hill, about a hundred yards from the wreckage. He was in an area that looked like it had been painstakingly terraced, with retaining walls patch-worked together out of bricks, stone and chunks of recycled concrete. Maybe it had been a vegetable garden, but now it was just raw black like the rest of the landscape. On a lonely little circle of gravel in the center, there stood a stone statue of Saint Francis, a sparrow perched on his outstretched arm.

"I found something!" I called out to him.

Ryan didn't even turn around. "Fan-freaking-tastic. What is it this time? A warped golf club? Another melted soccer trophy from when I was six? No, thanks," he said, bitterly.

I stood my ground. With a sigh, he turned around. When he saw the case I was holding, he let out a laugh that was more like an angry bark.

"Just perfect. The one thing I wanted to go up in flames," he said.

Not the reaction I'd expected.

"It was under the bed," I replied. "At least, I think it was your bed. I thought you'd be happy. It's like a miracle."

I held it out to him again, but he refused to take it. He let out another of those unhappy laughs. "Umm, I guess I'll just go put it in the car then."

"You do that," he said and turned away from me again.

I trudged back up the hill. From a distance, I saw my mother bouncing and twisting, like she was having some sort of seizure. I started to run, worried that something else had happened. Closer in, I could hear old rock music pulsing from the car stereo. My mother was dancing, her hands supporting her growing belly bump. When she lifted her hands to pump them in the air with the beat, I could see ashen handprints streaked all over her t-shirt.

Bethie was sitting in the front seat, giggling at my mother's antics. I clutched the guitar case in front of me like a shield, not sure what to do next. My mother took one look at my face and poured a cup of icy lemonade from a big thermos. I gulped it down, letting it cleanse my mouth of bitter smoke.

Bethie stopped smiling and swore when she saw what I was holding.

"Language!" said my mother, in a reflexive way.

"Oops, sorry," Bethie exclaimed, crestfallen, clapping a dirty-gloved hand to her mouth.

Now ash was streaked all over Bethie's face. My mother started laughing, pulling down the window visor, so Bethie could get a look at herself in the mirror.

"I look like a second-rate clown. You know what? I retract the 'sorry.'"

Bethie leaned out of the car and unleashed a long, loud string of swear words. There were some I knew and a few that sounded like French or Italian.

"Take that!" she shouted up at the sky, like she was talking to God. "I mean, seriously? Who do You think You're dealing with here? Job from the Old Testament?"

"You tell Her, Beth," said my mom.

The two of them laughed and high-fived each other like teen jocks, and the hysterical laughter bubbled up again. I stared at them like they were a pair of lunatics.

"If I didn't laugh, I would cry all the time," explained Bethie. She looked at the guitar case and her smile disappeared.

"It was under the bed," I said. "Ryan didn't seem too happy to see it either."

I looked at her. "I haven't opened it."

She hesitated. Moved her head up and down slowly, just a fraction of an inch. My mother moved next to her, for support. I sank down to my knees, setting the case down on the gravel at her feet. With some difficulty, I pried open the nicked and charred clasp, lifted the lid, and there it was. Intact. Perfect. Whole. Gleaming. All three of us released a breath audibly, one we didn't even realize we had been holding.

I looked up at Bethie. She was holding out her arms. I released the guitar from its velcro restraints and set it in her lap. She pulled it in gingerly to her chest, running her hand over the smooth wood. Then she closed her eyes against the tears that were streaming again and handed it back to me.

"It was the guitar Evie learned to play on. She gave it to Ryan after she started getting gigs and bought a fancier new one, promised him that when he got good enough, she'd make him part of her band."

"Who's Evie?" I asked.

Bethie stiffened. My mom put an arm around her and gave her an encouraging squeeze.

"Evie is...was...IS my daughter," said Bethie. "She died in that car accident four years ago, the one that did this." Bethie pointed at her fake leg.

Sometimes, I wish I weren't so curious.

"Ryan practiced all the time," continued Bethie. "He used to write little songs for her to sing—it was so cute. But after the accident, I was in the hospital for a long time. Ben—that's Ryan's dad—couldn't take the guilt and took off to go find himself. Without him and Evie... well, when it was just Ryan and me, we didn't feel much like singing anymore."

She smiled at me. "Why don't you just put that in the trunk for now, sweetie?"

I carefully stowed the guitar. After that, everyone lost the taste for scavenging. The hopeful energy had flown. I shoved our tools and salvaged boxes of charred bits and pieces into the trunk. My mother lifted in a crate of broken china and twisted silverware that Bethie had gathered.

Ryan came back to the car when we were almost finished loading. Without speaking, he got into the backseat and put on his headphones. He closed his eyes and I understood, without him saying, that he needed a cone of silence, however fragile, in which to recompose himself.

Nineteen

Bethie and my mom vanished into the cottage for tea the minute we got back. Ryan and I were standing on the sidewalk in awkward silence when Gillian and Carina came tripping across the street. The two of them were wearing adorable little summer dresses, all bright and breezy and girlie. Me? I looked like the smudgy filth at the bottom of a barbecue grill.

"Ryan! You're home! We have something for you," exclaimed Gillian. She handed him a hot pink flier. I read it over his shoulder.

"A beach party? That sounds kind of fun," I said tentatively.

"Oh," said Carina. "Gillian didn't think you'd be interested."

Gillian looked embarrassed.

"I like the beach," I protested.

"But you don't really like parties," said Gillian, a little apologetically. "You're more into school and stuff, and just doing things with one person."

And that person used to be her, I thought, hurt. "Well, maybe I've changed," I said. "Maybe I like parties more than school now."

"You?! The empress of enrichment? The queen bee of the spell-a-thon? The academic decathlete?" said Gillian.

Okay, I know I'm smart, but did she have to make me sound like a complete social reject? I'm not trying to brag here, just the opposite. According to the experts, I am gifted and talented, but as far as I can tell, that doesn't mean I have an actual aptitude for anything except maybe taking IQ tests and getting good grades. Figuring out how to complete a pattern of prime numbers or making a shape with toothpicks is all well and good, but it doesn't exactly set you on a career path. And it doesn't guarantee popularity either. Obviously.

"What's so bad about being smart?" asked Ryan. "Why can't someone be smart and still like a good party? You know, Rocket and I have had a really long day. We're on our way to the beach."

Maybe it was mean-spirited of me, but I kind of liked the way he shut them down. Gillian wouldn't let go of the issue though. She had her debate hat on and she wasn't going to take it off without a fight.

"But, Rocket, there's going to be dancing at the party. Don't you remember the seventh grade Sadie Hawkins dance? And the Spring Fling? You'll be miserable."

"If I want to be miserable, that's my choice," I said heatedly.

Carina intervened, rolling her eyes. "Fine, whatever. You're both invited. It's the day after graduation. Come on, Gillian. We have to deliver the rest of the invitations."

The pair of them took off on their beach bikes. Gillian didn't even look back.

Ryan set the flyer on the porch step and put a rock on top so it didn't blow away. Then he started walking down the sidewalk toward the ocean. I hurried to catch up with him.

"You really want to go to the beach right now? Like this?" I said, looking down at my filthy clothes.

"Yep."

"Don't we need our swimsuits? And towels? I usually bring a water bottle and a book or something, too."

"Nope."

"So we're just going to, what? Jump in with our clothes on?"

"Yep."

"Oh." I hung back, unsure what to do.

Ryan kept striding toward the beach. I was tired, and hot, and suddenly nothing in the world appealed more than being washed clean in the Pacific Ocean. So, I followed him. He kicked off his shoes as soon as we hit the sand. My shoes were too disgusting to touch, so I wedged them off by using the toes of my opposite foot. I peeled off my sooty, stinky socks that way, too, but it was hard to keep my balance. When I wobbled and windmilled my arms, one of my hands accidentally landed on Ryan's back.

He stood perfectly still, like a rock wall supporting me, and soon my feet were deliciously bare. Something sparked inside me, and I just went with it. Sprinting across the sand, I tossed back a dare over my shoulder.

"Last one in is a rotten egg!"

Ryan caught up to me within a few yards, and we ran flat-out the rest of the way together, not slowing down a bit when we reached the waves. I dove right into the first one, emerging on the other side slick and wet like a sea lion. Exhilarated, I let the next big wave propel me toward the shore, riding out in front of it with my arms outstretched. Ryan followed suit. We repeated that a few times, until we could bob around in the calmer deep water past the swells. I floated on my back, letting the buoyant saltwater cradle me, enjoying the sun on my face. When we finally emerged out of the water, we sat together in the hot sand, which clung to us like cinnamon on churros. I was too tired to care. It had been an intense day, and my eyelids were doing their drooping thing.

The sun was, too, dipping down to the horizon. But that was false perspective, an optical illusion—the sun wasn't really moving. We were sitting on a planet that was rotating away from it. Good night, sun, see you tomorrow, I thought. I was just about to let myself slide into oblivion when Ryan spoke.

"Every time I see that guitar, it makes me think of my sister, and how crappy life can be. I'm tired of being that 'poor, poor kid from the Mathews family' suffering through all the tragedies. Here, nobody knows me and I just, just want to be...just want to..."

"...be?" I finished for him. "You just want to be. Period."

"Yeah. Just be."

"But the things that happened to you, you don't need to be ashamed about them," I argued.

"I'm not ashamed. I'm just sad. And I'm sick of being sad."

We sat together staring at the sun as it sank into the ocean, tinting the clouds shades of raspberries and orange juice. Ryan didn't say anything else. He just kept scooping up handfuls of sand and letting the grains spill through his fist into a soft, shifting mountain. I did the same, enjoying the feel of the warm sand, thinking idly about the magic of sand melting into glass. And the fact that I had not needed my inhaler once, even though I had been running and swimming. I confess, I was thinking a lot about Ryan, too. I liked the look of his fingers, long and strong, squared off at the end, his nails not chewed to shreds like mine. Our hands synchronized their sand-shifting without me even trying, and I found myself wondering how his fingers would feel entwined in mine. Most of all, though, I was thinking about how much I wanted to help him find his way back to music. I couldn't wait to get back to Muse training to learn how.

TWENTY

AFTER THE USUAL OPENING CIRCLE AND DANCING IN THE MEADOW, URANIA TOOK US TO
a rocky outcropping for a special lesson. She led us up a flight of weathered stepping stones set into a grassy hillside. At the crest was a circle
of nine towering pillars that resembled arms trying to pull themselves
up to the night sky. She beckoned for us to each head toward a pillar.

I looked around at the other first-year apprentices, not sure how to
react. Brigit winked at me and plopped down. Dani followed, gracefully
settling herself onto the luxuriant grass, tucking the loose ends of her
sarong neatly around her bare feet. Magdalena's face betrayed no emotion, but her clenched fists made me wonder if she might be even more
nervous than I was. One by one, we arranged ourselves as Urania had
instructed, lying down on the grass with our heads pointing toward the
standing stone in the center. We looked like spokes on a human wheel.

Urania nodded with satisfaction.

"Beautiful," she said. "You have all grown so much in such a short
time! This evening, we are going to work on a vital skill that I usually
don't teach until the third year: astral projection. Can anyone tell us
what that is?"

I couldn't help myself. I raised my hand.

"The night of the dance—you called it an out-of-body experience," I
said, before she even called on me.

"Yes, that is one way of looking at it," she said. "Anyone else?"

"'Astro' means having to do with the stars, right? Like in astronomy
and astrology?" offered Brigit.

"It's related, certainly, but a little more complex than that."

Urania drew out her golden conducting wand and sketched pictures
and words in mid-air, like she had for my impromptu lesson on wave

theory. A few scrolling motions and boom! A golden human form hovered above us. With a couple of quick flicks, she copied the first form, enlarged it slightly. She colored the second figure opalescent silver, translucent so that stars sparkled through it.

"In addition to your physical body, the corpus, you have what is called an 'astral' body. The astral body has many names, such as the diamond body, the soul vessel, the emotional-thought body and the dream body. Dani, in the Hindu faith, you might know it as the linga sarira. The physical body is elemental. It is made up of the earth itself. Without the astral body, it would be animate but not conscious, not aware."

"We look totally the same here as we do in a mirror. Does that mean that the physical body we're in determines the shape of our astral body?" I said.

"Good question, Rocket," Urania replied. "It's actually the other way around. Your astral body is your higher self, and it makes a conscious choice where and when it will spend its time here on earth. The physical body provides a vehicle for your ethereal body to experience the physical world."

"But when we're here, I still feel like myself," I said. "Not only do I look like myself, I can feel the pillar against my head, and the grass under my fingers."

"This place exists entirely in the astral plane," she said simply. "You each create the reality you see here. You are capable of doing the same in the embodied world—but that takes many years, even lifetimes, of practice."

"That brings me back to our topic," she continued. "Astral projection: the process of consciously separating your astral body from your physical body, and projecting or sending it somewhere else. The astral body can travel unencumbered in the astral plane, gliding easily on the creativity waves, which permeate all that is. Eventually, you won't need the mirror or the assisting power of these stones. You'll be able to move effortlessly, at will, to any place and any time—past, present and future—from your bed. You already do it in your dreams unconsciously, but you will be able to control the ability and use it to fulfill your higher purpose."

Urania beckoned her sisters to come into the stone circle.

"I've asked each of your Muses to help in the training," she told us.

Polly knelt down by my head and gently positioned her left hand over my forehead and her right hand over my heart. She murmured instructions softly to me.

"The easiest way to begin is with a familiar place your spirit loves and knows very well. Paint yourself a clear mental picture. Try to remember specific sensory details—not just how it looked, but how it smelled, the textures, the sounds, and most importantly, the feelings it stirred inside you."

Tentatively, I closed my eyes and visualized my Nana's knot garden in England. She had inherited it along with the stone farmhouse where she and my grandfather lived, and where she raised my mom. I tried to recall the view of it from the second floor guest room where I stayed whenever I visited—the intricate geometric pattern, formed with hedges of glossy boxwood, the whole garden enclosed within a stone wall to shield it from harsh Yorkshire winters. I opened my eyes. Nope, I was still lying next to my pillar. I sat up, shaking my head.

"I don't think I can do it," I told her.

Polly squeezed my hand. "This is very advanced work…but Hekate came to us yesterday with a premonition. I cannot say more, just that it is very, very important that you learn how to do this, Rocket. And that I know that you are capable of it."

Sighing, I laid my head back down. Polly moved her hands to my heart and forehead.

"Let's try activating your pineal gland," she said. "And this time, I want you to remember to use all of your senses, not just sight," coaxed Polly.

Gentle lyre music filled the air, soothing me into a more relaxed state. Other senses…hmmm. I closed my eyes and thought about the herbs that flourished in my grandmother's garden: rosemary, lavender, sage, thyme, and peppermint, and a bunch more whose names I'd forgotten. I remembered my grandmother's cat Imelda, how she liked to weave between my ankles, mewling to be picked up, and the low whoof-whoofing howl of her old basset hound Barney. As the scents and sounds and textures wafted into memory, I opened my eyes, and I was standing in the garden.

My grandmother was kneeling beside one of the beds a few yards from me. Instead of the wide-brimmed straw hat I was used to seeing her wear, she had on the blue Dodgers baseball cap we'd bought for her on her trip to California. She was crazy about American baseball. She was clipping long stems of lavender, which she bundled into wands each year with ribbon.

I ran over to her. Only it felt more like gliding. I was insubstantial, weightless.

"Nana!" I said, reaching out to hug her. But my arms slipped right through her, and she didn't even look up. It was as if I wasn't there.

I dropped my arms to my sides, saddened that my grandmother couldn't see me. But then, something amazing happened. Barney looked right at me, his tail thumping, and gave a soft happy bark of recognition. I believed he could see me. A slight glimmer rose from my grandmother's body, like a shadow but made of sparkly light. It moved a little toward me in recognition. I could sense joy rising from it—and touching it felt just like one of Nana's hugs.

The tinkling of a bell brought me back to the stone circle. Polly was sitting by my side. I was crying.

"It was so beautiful," I sobbed. "I'm so happy."

Polly handed me a white silk handkerchief. "Happy tears! You're making it rain somewhere."

I wiped my eyes. "Did I do all right?"

"You managed that perfectly!" she beamed at me. "Your grandmother's astral body is tethered to her physical form very strongly, but it recognized you and came out to say hello. Some people call it an aura. Your grandmother has a very bright, loving spirit, like you."

I looked around. All of the apprentices were being helped to their feet by their Muses. Magdalena looked glum, more troubled than I had ever seen her.

The Muses hustled us off for our dance session. The mood was particularly joyful and celebratory, although Magdalena stayed in her usual funk, huddled in conversation with Clio and Melpomene. She left the dance early.

That night, when I slipped back through the mirror, there was an e-mail waiting from my grandmother. She said she'd been thinking about me while puttering in the garden that morning and had just mailed a package of lavender wands to hang in my new closet. A little belated housewarming gift.

We practiced astral projection several times at the stone circle over the next week. I hung out in Gillian's room, but she was always mooning up at the ceiling, or sending cutesy text messages to Jasper, or both— simultaneously. I visited my old room once, but Ryan was nowhere to be found. It made me sad to visit those places, so I returned to Nana's again and again, to watch her knitting and puttering about in the garden. Each time, her aura enveloped me like a cozy shawl, as happy to see me as Barney and Imelda were.

Brigit wasn't so lucky. She was upset, because she hadn't once been able to connect with another spirit.

"I project myself out there but then I can't get myself upright," she confided in her lilting Irish voice, which so reminded me of Rick's family. "I just hover about an inch above the ground, with my nose in the carpet. Maybe it's because I'm a stomach sleeper?"

I laughed. "You'll get it eventually. And hey, maybe you'll discover lost jewels or something someone's dropped on the ground."

"More likely fleas," she said, squinching her nose in dismay. "Wish I had it conquered like you do. You're probably ready to go off inspiring people in their sleep." She looked around. "Where do you suppose Magdalena's gone off to, then? She missed yesterday's session, too."

"I don't know. I was wondering the same thing."

But I couldn't spare too much time wondering about Magdalena, because my own worries were looming. All systems were go for me to become valedictorian... except the wild card. Art.

Mrs. Fletcher had assigned something deceptively simple for our final project. Each student had to create a flower, using any media we wanted, as long as the flower represented something about our lives or our personalities. To go along with it, we were supposed to express ourselves through creative writing, dance or music.

I was prepared. I'd completely departed from Mrs. Fletcher's samples and gone my own way. Throwing my inhibitions to the wind, I had created a mixed media spectacular. My flower rocked. I was finally going to be a maverick, a renegade, a style maven. (Okay, maybe Gary Grossman had a point when he called me a walking thesaurus last year).

I wasn't sure how my art had even happened. It seemed like all the events of the weekend—the visit to Ryan's house, our impromptu swim, learning to astral project—had catalyzed something within me, and the art project had been a way of expressing it all in tangible form. I'd also downloaded a ton of scribblings and ideas into the golden journal. Polly was going to have quite a challenge deciphering and responding to these entries!

I alternated between euphoria and terror as class approached. Would Mrs. Fletcher love my project? What if it wasn't as good as I thought it was? I was so focused on that question that it took me awhile to realize something was weird about school. The hallways were subdued, quiet, a little dull. Everyone seemed to be wearing the same colors, ranging from charcoal gray to black. It felt like I'd stepped into a monochrome painting.

History class I couldn't tell much of a difference, because Mr. Lennon had always discouraged any sort of dialogue in class. Per usual, he droned and we took notes on chapters I had already read ahead, undercover, months ago out of sheer boredom.

But in English, usually my favorite class, I could tell something was off from the moment we walked into the room. Mrs. Michaels seemed asleep at the wheel, her voice as flat as the old-fashioned chalkboard she had insisted on keeping when all the other teachers switched to high tech. She always said that the softness of chalk on slate made her feel connected to a long chain of teachers and that it was important to retain a little of the romance that made literature so magical.

Today, the blackboard was obscured by a pull-down movie screen. Mrs. Michaels turned on the overhead projector and a poem, "I carry your heart with me" by e.e. cummings, flashed onto the screen. I anticipated Mrs. Michaels engaging us in a lively discussion about what it meant, but instead she asked us to copy out the poem, making sure to correct all of the grammatical errors.

I raised my hand. "What do you mean by 'grammatical errors'?"

Mrs. Michaels looked at me blankly. "Please don't ask questions."

I looked around the room. All of the other students already had their heads bent over their papers, their mechanical pencils and black ballpoints replacing e.e. cummings' distinctive style with the appropriate capital letters and punctuation…dotting i's and crossing t's in unison, as if it were a military drill. Even wacky Sara Chambers had forsaken her usual purple pen in favor of plain black ink. I looked back at Mrs. Michaels.

"Umm. I know e.e. cummings really well," I said, carefully trying to tell the truth without actually revealing that I'd been part of an awesome poetry workshop he and Maya Angelou had led on Mount Helikon. "Unconventional punctuation and grammar were intentional choices, not mistakes."

"Just do the assignment like I asked," she said in that dead voice.

I stopped arguing and did as I was told, trying not to think about how "double e" (my nickname for ee cummings) would feel if he knew what we were doing. I figured I could write a few extra poems in Muse school and make up for it, kind of like extra credit to balance out getting a bad grade on a test.

PE seemed like more of the same—sit-ups and jumping jacks followed by boring drills. Even the jocks, who usually gloried in displaying their superior skills, just did as they were told without their customary bravado. And at lunch, the cafeteria was strangely silent. It felt like somebody had hit the mute button on the whole school.

After the world's most painfully boring day, I was actually looking forward to Mrs. Fletcher's art class. I finally felt I was tapping into my artistic side, like a proper apprentice muse. But I started to get worried when I saw how she had updated the display case outside her room. Instead of the diverse array of thought-provoking art pieces, which had always both inspired and intimidated me, I was shocked to discover her tacking up military rows of identical flowers assembled from colored sheet foam and pipe cleaners. There was room for one more flower. Mine. I was about to just shake it off—maybe it was a political statement or something, when Mrs. Fletcher came out in the hall. She was wearing a simple button-up blouse, a plain black skirt, and pumps. She looked like every other teacher at the school—sensible. It was all wrong.

"Rocket," she said in a dull voice. "Don't you just love these beautiful flowers?"

At that exact moment, Carina sauntered up beside us. "*Love* these beautiful flowers," she repeated, shooting us a plastic smile.

"Carina gets all the credit," said Mrs. Fletcher, looking at her. She was praising with her words, but her voice was still oddly atonal, like a bad computerized customer service rep. "It was her brilliant idea. All of the students did them in class yesterday."

"But I thought the assignment was to create a flower that expressed your originality," I said, confused. "I worked on my project all weekend."

"Oh, that wasn't necessary. Not at all. I have materials for you to make one just like this."

"Just like this," seconded Carina, as if I had asked for her opinion.

Mrs. Fletcher turned her attention away from me, and silently held the door open for the rest of the students. They filed in methodically, without any bustling or banter, and sat down to work at their desks, where materials to complete paint-by-number pictures had already been laid out for us. Nobody protested or deviated from the assignment. It was eerie, like the art room had been co-opted as an assembly line.

I followed Mrs. Fletcher into her little cubicle. I pulled my flower out of the bag, carefully unwrapped it from its protective tissue paper, and set it in front of her.

From papier-mache and recycled copper wire I'd pilfered from Rick, I had created a lotus rising out of a pond. I'd decorated it with tissue and metallic paints, and then, in a stroke of what I considered inspired genius, I'd combed through my journal and found words and phrases to copy out in calligraphy and used a decoupage technique I'd found online to stick my words right onto each petal of the flower.

"Look, Mrs. Fletcher. I even wrote a found-poem to go with my flower," I said, trying not to jump up and down like an overly-excited puppy.

She barely glanced at it, before looking at me with those flat eyes.

"If you want an A in my class," said Mrs. Fletcher, "you'll have to do it again, like the others."

I'd like to say that I took the high road. But at the time, I didn't realize what I was giving away. All I saw was a simple obstacle between me and my dream of valedictorian, an obstacle I could overcome just by biting my tongue and copying the sample. It was something I'd been doing all year, after all, so why should it suddenly make my skin itch? I accepted the stack of foam Mrs. Fletcher handed me, and tried not to flinch when I saw her crumple my beautiful lotus and toss it in the trash can. When Carina flashed me a maliciously triumphant smile, I looked away. Eyes on the prize, I thought to myself.

Twenty-One

TIME TUMBLED FORWARD. BEFORE I KNEW IT, GRADUATION DAY ARRIVED, AND ANOTHER chapter of my life lurched to an end. My mom and Rick were embarrassingly proud of me, waving and whooping like total groupies when I walked on stage to give my speech. I'd been working on it for the better part of the year, just in case. It was a solid speech, full of humble gratitude toward the teachers who had set me on my path and wise words for my fellow classmates. Follow your dreams and work hard to achieve your goals, whatever they might be. I used all the tricks I had learned watching Gillian practice for debates: I spoke slowly and deliberately, injected enthusiasm into my voice, frequently paused to make eye contact with the audience. I should have felt triumphant, but instead, I just felt…hollow.

A sea of zombie eyes looked back at me from the audience, or was I just imagining things because I was nervous? After I finished speaking, Principal Silviria awkwardly shook my hand and motioned me off the stage. I resumed my seat in alphabetical order, wedged between Ethan Mackey and Wanda Nathanson, two kids I hardly knew after three years of school together. I surreptitiously slipped the Sparktacles on while walking back to my seat, but they didn't seem to be working anymore. Gone were the bright color bursts I had seen swirling up from the jocks, the artists, the drama team. The closer people sat to Carina, the more charcoal they appeared through the specs. Here and there, I saw a few limp wisps of color, mostly whizzing around the heads of younger siblings who'd been dragged along for the ceremony.

It seemed like I was caught in a bad dream. Here we were, the entire eighth grade decked out in matching polyester blue robes and snappy mortar boards, filing up onstage to collect our diplomas while the seventh grade band performed "Pomp and Circumstance" with robotic perfection. I felt disconnected, not just from my classmates but from myself. Who was I? Where did I fit? What was my purpose, my dream?

A few months ago, I had been so sure I knew where I was going. Graduate from middle school, have the best summer of my life, move on to VBHS with Gillian in the fall. But now, I was adrift from my best friend, trying to find my own way to somewhere. One minute I was on top of the world, the next I felt like that guy Atlas, struggling to support the weight of it.

I watched Gillian and her mom get into Carina's limo. They were going with Brandon and Jasper's families to some swanky restaurant in the Marina. I wasn't invited. James the chauffeur helped them all in with a courteous smile, but I noticed he dropped it like a plastic mask the instant he shut the car door behind them.

Rick and Josie took me to lunch at Lotus. Ramachandar bustled around, treating me like a princess. He folded my napkin into the shape of a lotus blossom, and I thought about my flower in art class, how it had hit the bottom of the trash can with a soft thump. It made me feel sick. Not even my delicious mango lassi could erase the sour taste that lingered in my mouth. Maybe I *had* sold out in order to become valedictorian.

But then I remembered: I was an apprentice Muse. I did have a purpose, to inspire others. Artemis, warrior goddess, had told me to be strong. Tonight was the graduation beach party. Another chance to shine. Maybe I could figure out what was happening to the kids at my school. Was it just end of the year burnout, or something more insidious?

And maybe, just maybe, Gillian would see what she had lost.

I attacked my curry with new enthusiasm.

I usually love parties on the beach. Since I could remember, Gillian's mom and mine had been the queens of impromptu summer gatherings, and Gillian and I their party princesses. A few simple phone calls, and voila. Celebration. At our moms' parties, day just slid into night, people coming and going in an easy sort of flow. Gillian and I were put to work gathering shells for sandcastles or driftwood for bonfires. The food was never fancy—a potluck of salads or sandwiches, corn on the cob, fresh bread, and whatever fruit caught their eye at the farmer's market that week. Simple and delicious. No tables or chairs, just colorful cotton blankets on the sand. Often someone would bring music—a guitar, or a set of bongo drums, accompanied by the steady pounding of the waves.

This was my first evening party on the beach with just kids from my school, though, and I wasn't sure what to expect. It didn't matter, though, because I had a perfect plan that would make the whole night magical, not just for me but for everyone there. Rick and my mom were headed up the coast for a romantic night in Santa Barbara to celebrate yet another ridiculous anniversary (I think this time it was one year since they had declared their love for each other). I had told them I would be spending the night at Gillian's after the party. Anxious to get on the road, they dropped me in front of Gillian's, which worked perfectly for my intentions. My mom didn't even get out of the car—just told me to say hi to Gillian's mom and that she'd call her in the morning. I waved them off. The truth was Gillian and I still weren't speaking, so she hadn't actually invited me yet. I hoped she would.

I still couldn't believe that a friendship could just end like a movie... minus the end credits. I wanted things back the way they had been. Civilization B.C. Before Carina. Before Gillian started to hate me and shut me out for no apparent reason.

Once the car was out of sight, I walked across the street to the cottage to put my semi-nefarious scheme into action. I had deliberately arrived an hour after the party start time, so Ryan should already have left, but I rang the bell just in case. Nobody answered, so I went to step two. Breaking and entering, I didn't actually have to break anything to enter, though, because I had a hidden key, tucked up underneath one of the rocking chairs. My heart was beating double time.

"It's still your house, Rocket," I reassured myself.

But it didn't feel true. The Mathews family didn't have many personal possessions, but already the house felt more theirs than mine. A navy blue hoodie was slung over the back of the sofa. A used teabag and an unfamiliar pink mug rested in one of our old chipped saucers on the end table. Signs of life. Someone else's life.

There was no time to worry. I had a surprise to spring on Ryan that had popped into my head when I remembered the beach parties of my childhood. What better time to learn to love his guitar again than tonight, gathered around a bonfire with me and a circle of new friends?

It would be perfect. We could all sing songs, and Ryan would rediscover his love of music. He would be inspired. And I would get an A-plus on my first assignment for the Muses, assuming Ryan actually was my first client. It annoyed me to no end that Polly wouldn't come out with it directly, instead of just telling me to trust my intuition.

The case was still shoved under his bed, as I had hoped. I slid it free then opened it to make sure the guitar was in it. Yep. I stroked the gleaming blonde wood with a delicate finger, traced the delicate scrolling pattern inlaid in a darker wood around the circular opening. I itched to experiment with the knobs connected to the strings at the top of the handle, but stopped, afraid I would damage something. I wished I knew more about guitars. I plucked a string. It sounded like a chicken squawking. Clearly, I could add guitar to the long list of examples of my complete lack of talent. Sighing, I snapped the lid back down and set out for the beach.

Have you ever tried lugging a guitar case—plus a stuffed-to-the-brim tote bag—three blocks, on soft sand? It's a complete drag. It seemed like every teenager in the county had descended upon Venice Beach, and gathered around fire rings spaced up and down the shoreline for miles. The sun hung low over the horizon, about to set. So when I finally located the right party, I should have been thrilled to sink onto the beach and relax with my classmates.

I wasn't. A fearful voice inside me whispered, "It's not too late to go home." From about twenty feet away, I could see that I was dressed all wrong. That *I* was all wrong. I didn't fit into this group. The jocks. The fashionistas. The inevitable Gary Grossman. The voice grew louder, paralyzing me there in the soft sand. I gave myself a pep talk as I trudged the last few feet. I had a job to do. Maybe I wasn't exactly the most popular kid on the planet, but being their valedictorian had to count for something, right?

Once I was close to the circle, I gave an awkward wave to nobody in particular. Ryan was off to the side, tossing a Frisbee with Gillian and Jasper. They hadn't seen me yet, and I wasn't sure what kind of reception I would get.

"Where to sit?" I mumbled to myself, like I usually do when I'm nervous.

"Sit," someone immediately piped up in response.

I looked around to see who had spoken. Carina was sitting on the periphery of the party, patting the sand beside her.

"I can sit here?" I asked, surprised she was even talking to me.

"Here," she said.

Weird. I set down the guitar case and my heavy tote.

"I brought a blanket if you want to share," I offered.

"Share," she agreed. It was strange the way she just kept repeating what I said, but I was grateful to be included and didn't question it.

Carina always looked pretty, but tonight she looked different, very dramatic and otherworldly. There was something about her that reminded me of the Muses—her flawless golden skin maybe, or her glossy hair, which seemed darker tonight, like a raven's wing. It flowed into perfect waves down her back, casually sexy, with a few strands caught up in a little silver hair clip shaped like a knot. She was wearing a sophisticated silk sarong that made her look like a cover model. As usual, I felt like a complete schlump next to her. But tonight, I was determined not to let it distract me from my goals.

I rummaged through my tote bag to find the blanket. It was one of my favorites from my mom's beach party collection, a batik cotton print swirled in blues and greens. I spread it out, and Carina and I arranged ourselves on it. I started pulling some other things out of the bag—my water bottle, a plastic bag full of cookies, a container of cheese sandwiches.

"Geez, Jetpack, are you moving in?" hollered Gary Grossman from across the circle, where he had set himself up as the drinks' master of the evening.

"Moving in," agreed Carina.

"It's just a blanket and a few things for the party," I said, defensively.

"Party!" said Carina.

Weird. We sat there for a few minutes in silence, just watching the scene. Tons of the cool kids from school were at the party, sitting on the sand or standing around munching on snacks and gabbing. I was suddenly filled with an intense longing to let myself blend into the flock. It buzzed under my skin like hives, leaving me irritable and itchy.

"Do you want to go over and play frisbee with Gillian and Ryan?" I asked.

"Ryan," said Carina. Her face looked friendly again.

She rose to her feet fluidly, the silk wrap falling in a perfect drape down to her calves. I scrambled up with a little less grace. Carina took the lead, and as we made our way through the crowd of kids, they parted before her like peasants before an empress, and me her handmaiden, reveling in the reflected glory. As we walked together across the sand, I decided to take a chance.

"I think I like Ryan," I confided.

"*I* like Ryan," said Carina, in a nonchalant tone.

I stopped and stared at her. If Carina, with her perfect hair and pedicured toes, wanted to dig her claws into Ryan, what chance did I stand?

Before I could formulate a reply, Ryan spotted us. He walked over, holding the frisbee.

"Hey, Ryan," I said, awkwardly, casting a sideways glance at Carina.

"Hey, Ryan," echoed Carina. Only when she spoke, it sounded like purring.

"Rocket!" he said. "You made it."

Ryan seemed happy to see me, which gave me a shred of hope. Gillian, on the other hand, ignored me completely. Without even looking at me, she handed off the Frisbee to Carina.

"Jasper and I are going to walk to the snack shack for some fries," she announced.

"Fries?" queried Carina, in that mocking little voice of hers.

Gillian squirmed and backtracked. "Actually, Jasper wants the fries. I'm just going to get a salad or maybe just water."

"Water," Carina said, and she smiled. Only it was more of a sneer, and I could see Gillian wither a little under it. She looked happy to be escaping with Jasper.

Conversation came to a halt, with me caught between Ryan and Carina. Thankfully, Brandon Marks arrived with a couple other football players I recognized. They surrounded Carina in an adoring huddle. I seized my opportunity.

"Wanna toss it around some more?" I asked, gesturing to the frisbee in Ryan's hands.

"Sure," he said, and off we went. Carina stared me down in a mean little way over Brandon's shoulder, but I ignored her.

Pretty soon, it grew too dark to play. Ryan and I meandered back to the group, chatting like old pals.

"I have a surprise for you," I told him as we approached the blanket. His eyes lit on the bag of cookies. "Chocolate chip?"

"Not those," I replied. I pointed to the guitar. His whole body clenched.

I tried to fill the silence with an explanation. "You can play the guitar, and we can all sing with you around the fire," I said, coming to a stuttering halt when I saw the fury in his eyes.

"I don't get why you had to push. Can't you just relax and let be?" he said.

"I just wanted to help."

"It was a stupid idea. It's not even practical. How do you expect me to play in the dark, on a guitar, which hasn't been tuned since, since—"

"Since your sister died?" I said back to him. Loudly.

Ryan rocked back on his heels, looking at me in shock. I realized I had just blurted out his secret in front of everybody.

Into the uncomfortable silence plunged the ever-inappropriate Gary Grossman. "You had a sister that died? Dude, that totally blows."

"Yes, Gary, it totally blows," agreed Ryan. He was looking straight at me when he said it. "I'm so out of here. Where's my hoodie?"

"I think you left it on the sofa in the living room," I offered, without thinking. He stared at me.

"Of course, you broke into my room to get the guitar, didn't you?"

I didn't answer. I couldn't.

"You know what? It's yours. You love this guitar so much, why don't *you* learn how to play it?" said Ryan, thrusting it into my hands and storming off.

"I just thought—I just thought you'd be inspired and it would be really cool," I called out after him in a rush.

"Really cool," sneered Carina.

Angry at myself and the way my perfect plan was spinning out of control, I directed all of my rage at Carina.

"For Pete's sake, Carina, stop repeating everything I say in that mean little voice of yours. Who do you think you are, anyway? Everyone's all impressed, but nobody has ever been to your mysterious mansion. For all we know, your dad's just the chauffeur and your clothes are shoplifted," I ranted, thinking back on how suspicious her behavior had been that day we went shopping on Rodeo Drive.

Carina's face wavered in front of me, like one of those holographic images that changes with your angle. For an instant, the arrogant mask dissolved away, leaving a face that was hurt, vulnerable, and entirely human. Had I inadvertently exposed her secret, too? I wondered.

Carina's face hardened again. Someone laughed, and deliberately, coldly, she echoed the laugh, wielding sound like a weapon. Like sharks scenting blood, the other kids—including Gillian—jeered at me. Carina hung back, her eyes glinting eerily. Desperate to leave, I stumbled away from them all and began gathering my belongings. My bag had been kicked over into the sand. I stepped on the bag of cookies and felt them crumble under my feet. I hadn't even tasted one.

I spotted familiar mirrored lenses picking up the flicker of firelight. Despite the dark, I put on the sunspecs, driven by a niggling little voice deep inside me. Intuition. I looked closer, still huddled over my things and trying not to call her attention. As I had seen in art class, Carina's spark was masked. I could just make out a dark shadow anchored to her—but with enough free rein to wave a spectral hand into the chests of those around her, pinching out their creative sparks, too. Was this Carina's own spirit, or something else that had attached itself to her?

As I was trying to figure it out, Gary Grossman sidled up next to me and handed me a can.

"Here," he said. "Have a soda."

Touched that he was actually being nice for a change, I took a sip. And promptly spit it out when I realized the can did not contain the beverage I was expecting.

"What?" I sputtered.

"Look, guys, Rocket's foaming at the mouth," mocked Gary. "I put dish soap in her drink."

I spit the disgusting mess out as best as I was able, then wiped my mouth roughly with the edge of the picnic blanket, before shoving it into my tote bag. I slung the tote and the guitar case over my shoulder and started weaving my way out of the party, attempting not to step onto any of the kids sprawled round me. I brushed past Gillian. I stopped, looked her in the eye.

"Why?" I said.

"Oh, Rocket. You always think you're so special. The golden child. But everything's different now. You're the only one who doesn't see that," she said. And she turned away, too. Gary sidled up to me.

"Hey. It was just a joke," he said, after looking around to make sure nobody was watching him speak to the pariah.

"Maybe I deserved it," I said, thinking of the pain on Ryan's face. "You know, I screwed up, but at least my intention was to help someone. To do something good. Maybe you should use your evil genius for good one of these days, Gary. Your IQ is off the charts—why don't you come up with a cure for cancer or something instead of acting like a tumor?"

Wet-faced, I stumbled down the beach and headed toward Main Street. My feet plodded a dull rhythm on the concrete sidewalk. Home. Home. Home. All I wanted was to crawl into my bed and pull the covers up over my head, and burrow in for a long, long time. Maybe I could just stay in bed until my teen years were over, or at least until the Muses gave up and released me from this stupid apprenticeship.

Without thinking, I found myself in front of the cottage. Crap. Could I be any more of an idiot? When would my brain and body figure out what my heart already knew? This was not my home now.

I needed somewhere to sleep. Clearly, spending the night at Gillian's was out. Rick and Josie were a hundred miles away by now, and I shuddered at the thought of taking the bus across town at night and walking through Hollywood. Then I remembered something. My mom was forever losing keys, so she kept one to the hot shop on the same ring as the cottage spare key.

I thought about leaving the guitar case on Ryan's doorstep, before my arms ripped out at the shoulder sockets. But then he would know I had been back there and I'd been embarrassed enough for one night. Besides, I was afraid he would do something stupid and impulsive like throw it in the trash—and it was too valuable to me for that. Someday, I knew it would be valuable to him again, too. So I trudged back to Main Street, which had transitioned into a hip night time scene. Light and music spilled from dozens of trendy bistros and cafes. I navigated through the crowd clumsily, suddenly hyper-aware of the looks I was getting as I went by—a slightly chubby, mousy teen out by herself at night.

The extra few blocks down Main Street to my mom's shop had never seemed so long, or so scary. During the day, this area felt bohemian. At night, it bordered on dangerous. Fewer tourists and professionals— more homeless people. A white kid with dirty dreadlocks and tattered clothes gazed at me with his hollow eyes, listlessly raising a ripped piece of cardboard with just one word on it. "Hungry."

I hurried past him, anxious to put distance between us. But I stopped a few yards down the sidewalk. I dug through my tote bag until I found what I wanted and walked back to him.

"These cookies are kind of messed up, but they should taste okay," I told him.

He looked up at me, blank at first. It took a few moments for him to realize I was offering him something. I got the feeling that he was so used to people just walking by that his hope had gotten frozen. He set down the sign slowly and reached up to take the food from my hands.

"The sandwiches are cheese. I hope you're not like lactose-intolerant or anything," I said, trying to coax a smile from him.

He shook his head. "Thanks," he said.

"You're welcome," I said. "Good luck." And then I continued on my way. The tote bag felt lighter, easier to carry.

My little happy bubble lasted until I got to the alley behind the shop, and its depressing abandoned air. The only thing alive and kicking was a rat that skittered past me through the shadows, no doubt on its way to a dinner party in the overflowing trash bins of the nearby delicatessen. The motion detector my mom had installed a few years back didn't work at first, even when I waved my arms over my head. I started wondering if it was me or my weightless, formless astral self standing there. Just when I was about to give up, it flashed on, bathing the doorway in just enough eerie flat light for me to find the keyhole.

I had never been in the shop alone. I was used to a beehive buzzing with activity. Now the gas kilns had cooled, and Nico's old school boom box was silent. Leaving the lights on, I set down the guitar case and my tote. I curled up on the old sofa and closed my eyes. Sleep didn't come. My thoughts circled round and round like goldfish in a too-small bowl. Water, I needed water. I got up, filled a chipped cobalt blue glass from the cooler and downed it in a gulp. A few drops trickled down my chin. I drank down another, fast, and managed to inhale some of it. I coughed, trying to catch my breath and panic washed over me, a tsunami filling my lungs and drowning out all rational thought. What if I died here, alone? Maybe that would be best for everybody since I was such a complete loser.

I sensed that I was working myself into a complete state of frenzy, but I felt powerless to stop it. I reflexively reached for my inhaler. But as I clutched it in my palm, my anxiety changed into anger.

I wasn't sure where it was directed. At Carina, and the way she mocked me and made me feel like a loser? At my father who had made this beautiful bottle, right before he decided to stop playing the game of life? Or maybe at the Muses who set me an impossible task, one which I had no idea how to complete? At my mother and Rick, who loved each other and those stupid babies more than they loved me? The more I tried to figure out why I was angry, the more enraged I got. Angry at everything and everyone. I looked down at the bottle again, squeezed my fingers until I could feel the flowers etched into it cutting into my palm. And then I chucked it as hard as I could across the room. The bottle struck the metal door of the kiln, where it exploded and rained onto the floor like glass confetti. Wisps of godsbreath drifted up, up and away.

Something in me splintered, too. I grabbed a box of tissues and crumpled back down on the sofa, blubbering and wailing like a toddler. I blew stretchy oodles of snot into tissue after tissue, wadding them up and dropping them on the floor until I had used them all up. Only then did I fall into sleep…and immediately felt myself fly.

Astral projection felt natural to me now. I could feel the moment I separated from my body, just like I was one of those wisps of godsbreath escaping the bottle. Pure energy and lightness, no container to keep me from expanding, except the one I imagined for myself.

But this time something was different. Instead of thrusting myself out toward a destination, it felt like I was being pulled backwards by an invisible string that went through the center of my back and attached to my belly button. An umbilical cord. When the tugging sensation ended, I found myself in exactly the same spot. In the hot shop. But everything looked subtly different. The sofa wasn't quite so beaten-up. There were different magazines and catalogs on my mother's desk. The industrial shelving Nico had installed two summers before was missing. Instead of the usual music, a song called "Ripple" by the Grateful Dead blared through the boom box. (I recognized the tune, because my mom played it on an endless loop once a year on the anniversary of my dad's death, while she poured herself a goblet of red wine and sat on the floor of the kitchen crying. She always waited until she thought I was asleep.)

A little girl, about three or four years old, sat on a high stool at one of the work tables, fingering through a bowl of frit, looking for something. She appeared fuzzy to me, out of focus. This was odd, because I could see my mother quite clearly sitting at her workbench, using delicate calipers to shape opaque white glass. She looked young and cheerful sitting there, I thought. The trip to Santa Barbara must have been good for her.

The little girl spoke up. "Mummy, there isn't any white."

"Oh, I just used the last of it to make a tail," my mom called over to her. "Can you use yellow instead?"

"No, I need white. I made crowns for Hekate with emeralds and sapphires and rubies. Now Artemis wants one, too. But hers needs to be silvery white, like the moon."

"What's this about a crown?" boomed a man's voice.

The little girl and I turned our heads toward the door at exactly the same moment.

"Daddy!" we both said, although not in harmony. Her voice was a squeal of pure joy—mine hesitant and full of disbelief.

The man made a beeline for the little girl, ignoring me completely. That's when realization dawned: that little girl was me. I had astral projected myself into the past. I darted over to the desk—and saw that the magazines were dated ten years ago. I shook my head and turned my attention back to the little girl. No matter how I squinted and strained, her edges remained blurred and obscured. But then, we never really see ourselves as we are in the flesh, do we? Not completely—we just glimpse pieces, reflections in mirrors and still ponds, home movies and photographs.

"I need white, but Mummy used it all," the little girl confided in him. "And there's not a single piece in the scraps bowl."

"Ah, your mother is doing very important work right now, conjuring wings out of sand, and we mustn't disturb her," my father said in a stage whisper. "But if my firefly princess needs jewels for a crown, then jewels she shall have! I asked Nico to order another jar of white. Let's check the cupboard and see if it arrived, shall we?"

He picked up the little girl and carried her over to one of the metal cabinets. I knew what was in there, since sometimes after school I helped my mom inventory supplies. At that age, the cupboards at the shop felt like magical treasure chests. Frit of every color was packed densely in big jars so that it was hard to tell what color they were unless you read the label, or held pieces up to a bright light, so they would shine like jewels. Little me began to do just that now, a pint-sized professional completely absorbed in her mission of finding the pieces of glass she needed.

I had a sudden memory of hours spent marveling at how the glorious true colors of raw glass could be concealed then revealed, like dull gray stones at the beach when you got them wet. At that age, I spent all my time at the shop with my parents. It terrified my Nana to no end. She was afraid I would fall into the crucible and end up scarred beyond recognition or have my eyes gouged out by flying shards of glass. I could see, in fuzzy focus, that the little girl version of me was wearing child-sized safety goggles. Those goggles were still hanging around the shop somewhere.

Little me was jabbering to my—our—dad, spinning an elaborate fairy tale which involved all the colors of frit in the cabinet. Something about flying to the moon and dancing there with stars made from golden fire and drinking water from a magic spring. How confidently she spun stories out of the air like they were strands of cotton candy being swirled onto a paper cone.

Within minutes, she found white frit and filled a little metal bucket with it. She put two big rainbow handfuls of frit in another container.

"Ready to be a magician?" asked my dad.

"Like you and Mummy!" she said, jumping up and clapping a little. "Are you going to help me make the crown for Artemis?"

"Eventually," he smiled down at her. At me. "But first and foremost, we are going to create a glass bottle just for you."

"Ohh. With a genie inside?" she asked eagerly. "So I can get three wishes? My first wish is for a sister!"

My father smiled down again. "No genie, I'm afraid. We are going to fill the bottle with enchanted air," he told her. "I want you to remember something, Rocket. You are already more powerful than any genie ever could be. You can make all your own wishes come true, just by breathing them into being."

He tweaked her nose and scooped her up, carrying her toward the marver table across the room. I tried to follow, to watch the bottle being created, but my spirit wouldn't budge. It stayed tethered to the sofa. I felt myself sinking backwards, like gravity was pulling me back into my poor exhausted body.

When I woke up, the first thing I saw was Nico, delicately sweeping the fragments of my inhaler bottle into a dustpan. I started to cry.

Nico came right over and sat down on the sofa next to me, lifting my chin in his big, scarred paw.

"You don't have to give me the details," he said. "I raised two teenagers. Things happen. You're testing your wings, seeing how far from the nest you can fly. I just need to know if you are safe and whole."

I didn't know what to tell him so I just nodded.

"Good," he said. "You can give the details to your mother and Rick when they get here."

"You called them?" I said, horrified.

"No. You're going to do that. But not just yet."

I started weeping again. I pointed to the dustpan, still in his hand. The remnants of my beautiful bottle lay there in shards, intermixed with dust and debris.

"My bottle, I smashed it. I was so mad…."

"We will save all of these pieces," he said. "When you are ready, I will teach you how to make a new one."

"It won't be the same."

"No, it won't be the same. It will be stronger, because the new story and the old one will live together in it. Find yourself something for breakfast. You'll need your strength when you call Josie and Rick."

I scrounged around the metal storage cabinet that served as a pantry, grabbing a banana and some graham crackers. I sat at the desk, munching and morosely staring at the dreaded phone, wondering what kind of trouble was headed my way.

After putting the fragments of glass into a clean mason jar, Nico pointed to the guitar case on the floor.

"Do you play?" he asked.

"Huh?" I asked.

"The guitar—do you play?" he repeated.

"I wish," I said. "It belongs to a friend. At least, he was sort of a friend. Now he hates me."

Nico picked up the case and set it on the work bench. He looked at me.

"Would your friend mind if I took a look?" he asked.

I shrugged. "He told me to keep it."

Nico pulled the guitar out of its case. He examined it carefully.

"This is a beautiful guitar," he said. "It's a classical acoustic, built by a Spanish luthier, I would guess."

Seeing my blank look, he expanded. "A luthier is a craftsman who makes stringed instruments...lutes, guitars, mandolins, violins."

He turned it over and looked at the back.

"The inlay, the back and sides are made of rosewood. Indian rosewood, I think. The hardwood is what gives the guitar its volume. The top is softer, maybe from an ash tree."

"Six strings...and you play with both hands, just like a piano, which is a stringed instrument, too, of course, but not as portable." He grinned at me.

"You sound like a master guitarist," I said.

"I'm a glassblower, but I love good guitar music. I grew up listening to some of my cousins play in a salsa band and spent a lot of hours wishing I had their talent for music. Truth, I used to waste a lot of time worrying I wasn't good enough and wishing I could master every thing I touched. Your father was like that, too, always searching, searching to find his next best thing. He taught me many things, your father."

Nico strummed the guitar, listening and fiddling with the knobs to tune it as he talked.

"I've learned it's impossible to walk down more than one road at the same time, at least not if you're trying to get somewhere in particular," he said. "Gabriel was what they call a Renaissance man. He was a passable chef, played a little piano, a little guitar, and a little chess, could paint reasonably well. Did you know he even taught himself to juggle on a unicycle? His greatest gift and passion was glassblowing."

Nico strummed a few more chords on the guitar, then paused, looking thoughtful. "No, that's not true. Actually, now that I think about it—his greatest passion was for passionate people. He surrounded himself with them."

He put the guitar in my hands.

"So you wish to learn the guitar. Maybe that will turn out to be your passion. Maybe it won't. But learning a little won't hurt you. Wherever life takes you, it's a good thing to make a little music along the way."

So the Muses had been trying to teach me. Nico showed me the basics of how a guitar worked, how to tune it, how to play a couple of basic chords.

"Now, I have my own work to do," he said. "And you have a phone call to make."

Turns out I didn't have to make the call. My mother had already been in touch with Gillian's mom, realized I hadn't spent the night there, and driven back to Los Angeles in a panic trying to find me. She came storming into the hot shop, and the temperature rose about a hundred degrees. You know how that goes. And then your basic grounding for life. Me crying. Relieved hugs and kisses, alternating with speeches about being more responsible. More grounding for life. More hugs.

After ten minutes watching us ride the emotional rollercoaster, Rick stepped in to slow things down in his practical way.

"I think Rocket has learned a valuable lesson here, Josie. She can start to work off her sentence by doing some time in the shop today. You need to rest."

My mother opened her mouth, prepared to continue arguing with him. He looked pointedly at her belly, and she reconsidered.

"Fine," she said. "Nico will tell you what to do. You report to Nico; he reports to me. No mooning around, you have to work." She looked at Rick. "And I will sit on the sofa with my feet up and have a nice cup of tea."

She went and sat on the sofa. "Herbal tea. I think there's some ginger and lemongrass by the kettle."

Rick looked at her blankly for a moment before jumping up. "Oh, right. I'm on it."

Nico immediately put me to work unpacking the new shipment of colored glass stock. It was a relief to be a robot for a while, just opening the boxes and efficiently putting things where they belonged. I'd had a lot of practice recently at unpacking boxes. Nico and my mom run a pretty tight ship, but there was still a little tidying up to be done. I got a damp rag and wiped down the shelves. I retyped some of the shelf labels. I opened more boxes.

One box did not contain raw materials—it was full of finished glass sun catchers. I went to go ask my mom where they belonged, but she had dozed off on the sofa.

"What are these?" I asked Nico, who was sitting at the work bench shaping a vase with calipers.

He glanced up from his work and frowned when he saw what I was holding. "Your mother sent off some of her designs to a manufacturer in China," he replied.

"These are *factory-made* reproductions?" I asked.

I could tell he wasn't too happy about it, but being Nico, he took the high road and kept his tone neutral. "Yes. They cost about half as much as making one in the shop."

I studied one. "But they're not handmade."

"She feels like most tourists won't know the difference, or wouldn't care even if they did. In fact, I think she said it was your idea."

"What?" And then I remembered. I *had* said something like that to her, about a year before. I had knocked down one of the sun catchers at the cottage, and when she got upset, I made some snarky comment about how I could get something just like it at the Dollar Store.

"I didn't think she ever actually listens to my opinions," I complained.

I looked down at the box. "Look, let's stick this somewhere she won't find it for awhile. She's pretty distracted these days. It shouldn't be too hard."

Nico looked at me with a flash of approval and helped me shove the box to the back of a little-used cabinet.

At the end of the day, my back hurt from all the lifting and stacking and sweeping and mopping. I made the mistake of telling my mom and Rick that, as we were driving back to Rick's house.

"Get used to it," she said, "because you still have a ways to go before you're in the clear from last night's little stunt."

Twenty-two

JUST WHEN I WAS THINKING THAT THINGS COULDN'T GET ANY WORSE, THEY DID. RICK decided to practice his parenting skills.

"Rocket, given recent events, your mom and I don't think it's healthy for you to mope around the house when we have our date night."

I looked at him in horror. "You're not going to make me go on your date night, are you? Eww!"

"Of course not!" Rick looked as repulsed as I did at the mere thought. "When I was your age…" he began.

I cut him off at the pass. "You walked to school in a snowstorm? Bare foot? With Abraham Lincoln?"

He tried to hold his tone even, but he was clearly irritated. "No…but I did have a summer job."

"Carrying water from the well? Polishing muskets?"

Rick groaned. "You know, the old age thing has really gotten out of hand. I was not born during colonial times."

"Next you'll be telling me that forty is the new fourteen."

He sighed. "This must be why babies are born without the ability to speak. Because their parents would smother them with a pillow before they reached their teen years. Here's the deal. The Rowans, our neighbors down the street, are looking for an occasional summer babysitter."

He held out a flyer and continued. "I know them. They're nice people. Two kids. Robbie is two, maybe three, and the big sister, Amelia, just finished kindergarten."

"I know what you're up to. You just want me to get some practice, so you can have a free nanny when the twins are born."

"Marla's expecting you tonight at five-thirty," he replied, implacable.

"Five bucks an hour to start. She wanted to pay you seven, but I told her to see how it goes first and give you a raise if she thought you deserved it."

"You negotiated her *down*?" I said in disbelief. "Gee, thanks."

"If you've got a better way of earning enough money to pay the bill for that cellphone of yours, let me know," he retorted. "Would you rather we hired a babysitter for *you*, or do you want to take this opportunity to show us how responsible you can be?"

I walked over to my makeshift desk and grabbed my copy of the same flyer. I waggled it under his nose.

"For your information, I was planning on calling her myself," I told him. "I babysat last summer. I even took one of those first aid classes. I'm not the loser you think I am."

"I don't think you're a loser. You're just new to the neighborhood, and I'm helping you line up gigs. And keeping you safe at the same time. I'm sure that after one evening with Robbie and Amelia in your competent hands, Marla'll jump you right up to seven, which is good for me, because then my ten percent commission will increase from fifty to seventy cents an hour."

At my look, he laughed. "Just kidding. About the commission, that is. Marla's a doll."

That's how I found myself at the Rowans' house on the first Saturday night of my summer vacation. Of course, it's not like I had any invitations to decline. I was a social pariah at this point. The Rowans lived in a house just as obnoxious as the rest of the neighborhood. From the front, it looked like a single story, but when she opened the door and led me into the foyer, I saw a staircase leading down to a second level. Marla was in fact a doll, as Rick had promised. Not like a Barbie, all plastic and busty, but in an American Girl way, golden blonde with intelligent brown eyes, wearing jeans and a grubby t-shirt.

"You must be Rocket! Welcome to the neighborhood!"

She led me through the living room and into the kitchen, explaining that the house was upside down, because of the slope: the dining and living areas and master bedroom were on the top floor, with the kids' rooms and a den downstairs. The spacious kitchen looked like a recent remodel, straight out of a home magazine. Warm cherry cabinets above granite counters, beige stone floors with a cozy-looking braided rug and a large island that doubled as the kitchen table, if the swivel stools and left-over dinner dishes were any indication.

Marla interspersed factoids about the kids ("Robbie doesn't eat anything yellow") with a million and six chit-chatty questions ("So, how do you like your new neighborhood?"), all while showing me where to find the fridge ("The only problem with stainless steel is that you can't use magnets so I have to tape the kids' stuff on it"), carrots and secret stash of homemade oatmeal cookies ("just one before bed, with ice cream or a glass of milk"). She scribbled her cell phone number on a piece of paper and stuck it on the fridge, with tape.

"I meant to type up everything for you, but it's just been one of those days, and I still need to get ready. Kasper, that's my husband, has a screening tonight, and I'm meeting him there. It's casual, but not this casual," she laughed, gesturing to the stain on her shirt. "Spaghetti-o's were on the dinner menu today."

"I didn't know anybody still ate those!" I blurted out.

Marla grimaced. "I know, totally toxic. A good mother would have them eating tofu and seven-grain crackers and bean sprouts."

She actually looked a little worried for a moment then she shrugged. "But you know what? They had broccoli with their spaghetti-o's, so I'm not an entirely lost cause. Come on, I'll introduce you to my little junk food junkies."

Walking downstairs was like leaving grown-up land and entering a toy store that had just exploded. The ruler of this domain was clearly the grubby little boy chattering to himself as he propelled wooden trains around the world he'd created in the middle of the den floor. Track went off in every direction, never quite meeting up, but the disjointed layout didn't faze him in the least. He just gave his engines flying powers and lifted them over the gaps or crashed them into abysses with a toddler's gleeful disregard for lives and property damage.

Robbie looked at me and got right down to the important stuff. "Do you play trains?" he asked. It was a test, and both Marla and I knew it.

"Well," I said. "Playing trains is definitely on my fun list, right up there with Hot Wheels, Legos and hide-and-go-seek. But you probably don't like any of those things."

"I do!" he replied indignantly. Reverse psychology works beautifully with small boys. He handed me a green train. "You can be Percy."

I looked up at Marla, then back at Robbie. "You know what? First let me meet your sister, then I will be back to play trains with you."

Marla looked a little embarrassed. "Um, Amelia's already in bed."

I was surprised. "Is she sick?"

Pipsqueak piped up. "Ame-wia doesn't like babysitters."

Marla rolled her eyes. "Whenever she has a babysitter, she just goes to bed early. Avoidance behavior. I'll show you where the bedrooms are, just so you can check in on her once in awhile, but she'll probably sleep the whole time you're here."

"Then wake you up at five o'clock in the morning?"

Marla laughed. "Exactly!" She led me down a narrow hallway, pausing at an open door. I took one look at the race car bed, the collection of Hot Wheels cars and the dinosaur mural. "Ummm...let me guess. Robbie's room?"

She laughed. "Right first time. You know, when I was in college, I was a budding feminist and completely convinced that boys and girls were the same, just programmed differently by society as they grew up. Then I had one of each, and let me tell you, they were different before they even got out of the uterus. Robbie's jammies are on the bed. Lights out by eight o'clock for him. Brush teeth and story first, at seven-thirty."

We moved down the hallway. Amelia's room was pretty easy to spot, given the wooden sign on the door that spelled out 'Amelia' in pink flowers. Inside, it was dark, except for a nightlight, also in the shape of a flower, which cast a pink glow on the dolls and stuffed animals heaped on a frilly canopy bed.

"She's in there somewhere," whispered Marla.

I tiptoed closer to the bed. I could just make out a slender form burrowed into the blankets and a jumble of brunette curls on the pillow. I gave Marla a thumbs-up.

Back in the hallway, Marla eased the door shut and turned back to me. "Well, this cuts your workload in half, I guess."

"What does she do when she has a babysitter during the daytime?" I whispered, curious.

"Buries her nose in a book, or draws pictures, or takes a long nap," Marla whispered back. "Okay, I'll show you how to work the alarm, then I've got to get dressed and on my way."

After she left, I played with Robbie. I made him my buddy for life by squirting whip cream on his cookie and giving him an extra blast right out of the can into his mouth. After he was tucked in bed, I settled onto the sofa. Nothing on television caught my attention, so I flipped it off. The sofa was incredibly comfortable. Too comfortable. I found my eyes closing. Without warning, without any effort, my astral self launched. Destination unknown.

I found myself in my old bedroom. Ryan was sitting on the floor in the center of the ghostly imprint left by my missing rug, holding a photograph. Hovering closer, I saw it was a picture of his family, when they were still healthy and whole. His sister was pretty, with long brown hair and a mischievous smile. In one hand, she held her guitar. Her other hand was behind Ryan's head making bunny ears. Ryan was a few years younger, intently hunched over a set of bongo drums. Standing behind Ryan were his mom and a handsome man with shaggy brown hair, who had his arm looped around her shoulders. They were looking into the camera and laughing. I wondered where Ryan had gotten the photo—salvaged from the internet maybe or sent by a family friend to replace all that he had lost.

Tentatively, even though I knew he could not feel my touch, I reached out toward Ryan's shoulder. His aura instantly expanded toward me, steely blue and so full of icy-cold pain that I reflexively pulled back to shield myself. Tears streamed down Ryan's face. I felt helpless.

Above me, golden script began to unfurl. Musical notes and lyrics. Was I supposed to sing to him? I wondered.

YES! formed in giant capital letters in front of me, and a golden lyre and an aulos floated in space, playing the opening chords to a song I recognized immediately: "While My Guitar Gently Weeps" by the Beatles. I took a deep breath, released it, and settled myself behind Ryan. I knew he couldn't see, feel or hear me, but I still felt self-conscious wrapping my arms around his icy cold spirit body. I took another calming breath, laid my head on his back, and began singing softly.

I look at you all, see the love that's there sleeping
While my guitar gently weeps
I look at the floor and see it needs sweeping
Still my guitar gently weeps

And as I sang, a faint lustrous blue shape joined the aulos—Evie, cross-legged on the floor, a ghostly guitar in her lap, long brown hair tucked behind her ear. Delicately, she strummed the chords and harmonized with me.

I look at the world and I notice it's turning
While my guitar gently weeps
With every mistake we must surely be learning
While my guitar gently weeps…

By the time we reached the "oh oh oh" part of the chorus and the instruments trailed into silence, the energy in the room felt different. Warmer. Not as shivery. Ryan's tears had slowed to a gentle rain instead of a torrent. Intuitively, I knew that his astral body, his spirit, had been comforted by the music, even though his physical body could not even hear it. Evie set down her shimmer of guitar and moved in close to sit in front of him. She reached for my hands, and the two of us formed a circle with our arms around him.

Love planted itself inside me like a seed, sending down thready golden roots and sprouting up green tendrils. It wasn't directed at Ryan, not specifically, or Evie. It was larger than that. I had a glimpse of how it might blossom, unfold like an enormous golden flower, or even a blooming vine dripping with radiant, scented blossoms that extended in all directions as far as the eye could see. This love I felt could be like the wisteria vine I had visited with my grandmother, pulling the world together in a dense tangle of light and love.

And it all became too much for me. I pulled away from Ryan abruptly, started pacing the floor. Agitated. It was too much responsibility, too much power; too many things could go wrong; people could get hurt or start to hate me if I made mistakes… maybe they could even die… Snap. Polly was there holding my hand, tugging it, lifting me up and out through the window…and soon the faint glow of manmade lights paled in the face of the moon and the stars as we whizzed into the cosmos, past comets and meteor showers and supernovas, stars being birthed and stars dying…and dropped with a thud into the Muses' meadow, where naturally, joyful music was being made. Polly touched my head gently.

"You need to dance," she said simply. She spun away in a series of graceful pirouettes and left me there in a heap, trembling.

A gentle finger tapping at my shoulder brought me back into the present, although at first it seemed like a continuation of my astral travels. I opened one eye and found myself staring into pools of blue. Pulled myself into focus, I connected the dots. A little girl. Pink satin nightgown dotted with tulips.

"You're Rocket," she said. "The babysitter."

"I *am* Rocket," I agreed. "Are you Amelia?"

She nodded. "I dreamed about you."

"You did?" I asked, still a little muddled. "What did you dream?"

"You were hugging a boy, and singing to him, and then you were flying through outer space with a lady in a white nightgown. And then, you fell onto a lawn where lots of people were dancing and singing and playing funny instruments. And the lady that flew you there said you needed to dance."

"That's quite a dream," I said.

She nodded again, very seriously. "So I brought this."

Amelia lifted a little stereo up where I could see it. It was pink, of course, with sparkly heart stickers covering most of its surface. She set it on the coffee table, her finger poised above the 'play' button.

"I like to dance, too," she said in a hopeful voice.

I smiled at her. "Not too loud—we don't want to wake up your brother."

After so much intense astral work, it felt surprisingly good to be back in my physical body. Every sensation felt brand new, vibrant. Pounding my bare feet on the hardwood floor, burrowing my toes into the plush rug in front of the fireplace, feeling the muscles in my arms and shoulders and back and legs all working together to help me dance, in a way I had never truly appreciated.

When Amelia's parents came back, they were surprised to see us doing eggbeaters and giggling together. Amelia went running to her father and he picked her up and swung her so high that she squealed.

Marla introduced us. "Kasper, meet Rocket, the miracle worker."

"Nice to meet you, Miracle Worker," said Kasper, extending a hand to me. "I'll let Marla settle up with you while I waltz Cinderella off to her room and see if I can magically transform her into Sleeping Beauty."

Amelia flashed me a joyful smile as her dad twirled her out of the room. Marla flashed a smile equally bright.

"Rick said five dollars an hour, but honey, you are worth every bit of seven," she exclaimed. "I can't believe you were able to bond with Amelia like this, in one night!"

She followed me out and watched until I was safely home. We waved at each other from our front doors.

Twenty-three

THAT NIGHT DURING A BREAK IN MY MUSE TRAINING, I TOLD POLLY ABOUT MY CONVERSATION with Amelia. She wasn't in the least surprised.

"I love to visit the minds of children," exclaimed Polly. "Such delight! Very young children don't need assistance from muses. They are natural receptors and amplifiers of all the creative energy buzzing around them. Children live without limits."

"Over the years, they begin to doubt themselves or to compare themselves to those around them. Suddenly it's all green grass and blue skies, colored inside the lines, and not a purple tree or blue cow in sight for most of them," noted Polly. "Amelia is in the danger zone. That's why she goes to sleep so early. She feels safest and happiest in her dreams."

Living without limits. I wondered what that would feel like. On Mount Helikon, I could stretch and twist and twirl with ease. No limits, except my imagination. I could fly, climb, run in my astral form, which was to say, whatever form I chose for myself. But when I was on my side of the mirror, my body refused to cooperate in the same way. I had only taken one dance class in my life, and let me tell you, that had been a complete disaster. Getting your fingers stepped on by eleven second-grade girls wearing tap shoes *really* hurts. And I had always avoided competitive sports like soccer or swimming, because I was afraid they would trigger my asthma attacks and leave me gasping on the ground like a floppy fish. I was happier competing in the classroom.

I told all this to Polly.

"Rocket, your limitations exist only in your own mind. Only you have the power to release yourself."

"You sound like my gym teacher," I grumbled. Polly was an immortal goddess. She couldn't possibly know how hard it was being a fourteen-year-old girl in the real world. An orphan. Well, a half-orphan anyway. A friendless, half-orphan teenager.

I couldn't sleep after that, couldn't shake the foul mood brewing in me. In the kitchen, my mom was sitting at the table with a how-to-raise-babies book, which didn't cheer me up at all. I stormed over to the pantry. "Where's the granola?"

"We're out," replied my mother, irritatingly calm. "How about some eggs? Or a piece of toast?"

"I don't want toast or eggs. I want cereal!" I whined.

"You and Gillian still fighting?" she asked.

How did she always do that? My mom saw right through me. I slumped down in the chair across from hers and dropped my chin onto my folded arms. "Everybody hates me."

"I don't hate you. And it sounds like Robbie and Amelia like you, too. Marla already called Rick to rave about you."

"Great, my new best friend is a five-year-old," I said, sarcastically. "We can do each other's nails and talk about boys together."

My mom reached over and stroked my hair. "You know what? I could really use your help in the shop this summer a couple days a week."

"Sounds super fun," I said, unable to get my voice out of bitter mode.

"You did a great job last week, even if it was just to redeem yourself after The Incident. Nico and I both appreciated it. It pays eight dollars an hour," she said. She looked at me expectantly. "If we leave now, we can grab Stan's Doughnuts on the way. I've been craving one for weeks."

"I thought you craved salads when you were pregnant with me."

She shrugged and patted her stomach, where my future half-siblings were no doubt high-fiving each other in anticipation of the sugar rush to come. "That was you. Your siblings just sent in an order for designer doughnuts—specifically, peanut butter-chocolate chip."

I reached out a hand, wanting to touch my mom's belly, then pulled it back. I just wasn't ready to play adoring big sister. I didn't know if I ever would be. My mom looked disappointed, but she didn't force me, just sat there for a moment and gave her belly a little rub, like she was making a wish on the Buddha. She put on her Mary Poppins face—calm and cheerful and positively British. Unflappable.

As we neared Westwood, my mom and I started chanting our mantra: "car-ma, car-ma," and for once, it worked—a metered spot opened up right in front of the doughnut shop. If I lived walking distance to this place, I would weigh a thousand pounds. The aroma wafted out onto the street, luring in customers of every kind from half a block away. I could practically SEE the doughnut aroma rising above its competition and pointing the way.

My mother's nose was twitching, too—in a way that made me nervous. As we passed the alley behind the doughnut shop, someone opened a dumpster to chuck in a bag of garbage. My mother stopped and thrust her purse at me. Gagging, she darted into the alley. I could hear her puking behind the dumpster. Ewww.

I didn't know what to do. I ran into Stan's and got a cup of water and stack of napkins. I cautiously approached—the closer I got to the dumpster, the more I felt like vomiting myself. My mother reached for the water gratefully, like a child. It was so weird, my mother never got sick. Her hearty Yorkshire constitution was in direct contrast to my own.

"It's the hormones," she explained. "My sense of smell is especially acute. It happened when I was pregnant with you too, just not quite so soon and not so severe."

"Lovely," I replied. "Do you still want doughnuts?"

She grimaced. "Later. I just need to rest in the car a minute. With the windows closed." She fished out some cash from her purse and handed it to me. "Better get two dozen. Between you and Rick and Nico and the boys, they'll disappear."

I got into line, behind scruffy UCLA students, suited businesspeople and harried-looking assistants, all of them talking into mobile phones while they pointed to this tray and that, driving the girl behind the counter near to crazy. When it was my turn, I ordered with military precision. Six banana peanut butter, four raspberry-filled, four peanut butter chocolate chip, four custard-filled, four plain glazed, and two lemon-filled. The last two I ordered on pure reflex, realizing only after the clerk put them in the box that Gillian was the only one who ate them. But it was too late to change my order. Within a minute, the sale was rung up, the change given. I grabbed the box and headed back out to the car.

My mom was leaning back, eyes shut, both hands curled protectively around her belly. She sat up when I tapped on the window. After another sip of water, she revved up the engine, pulling into traffic with her usual capable navigation. Between traffic and the stop at the dough-nut place, it took us almost an hour to travel the twelve miles. My mom pulled into her parking spot in the alley behind her shop, turned off the engine and collapsed back in her seat. She looked at the clock. It was close to ten already.

We walked into the hot shop from the back through the roll-up steel garage door, which makes it easy to move in bags of glass mix and ship out the finished products. Like I said, the back of the shop is functional, not pretty. All the beauty goes into the glass itself.

"I'm going to freshen up a little," my mom told me. She headed for the bathroom in the office area, between the hot shop and the front store. I settled down with a doughnut and watched Nico work. After a few minutes, my mom came out of the bathroom looking less like death-on-a-stick. She slipped on her work apron before pulling a doughnut from the box. We raised our doughnuts together as if they were champagne glasses, clinking them together in our usual ritual.

"Toast," I proclaimed.

"Toast," my mother said, "wishes it were a doughnut."

My mother closed her eyes in ecstasy as she savored one sticky sweet mouthful, then she set her doughnut down on a napkin and went over to check in with Nico. Laelia came in from the front, carrying a footed blue glass bowl streaked with orange and red in a whimsical sea star design. She stopped when she saw that Nico and my mom were at a critical stage.

"I can't read the writing on this price tag," she whispered to me.

I held out the box from Stan's. She hesitated. I could almost see her inner calorie counter doing the math. Then she set down the bowl and grabbed a peanut butter chocolate chip, munching into it with gusto.

"Good for you!" I reassured her.

"Good—yes," she replied. "Good for me? Not. I'll have to run my dog an extra hour on the beach tomorrow." She waved her doughnut toward the work in progress right in front of us. "Ohh, I love this part. The big reveal."

Nico was at the end of the blowing process on his vase, and my mother had moved into position. She was wearing heat-proof gloves—just picture a pair of extra-strength oven mitts—ready to receive the vase. Nico gave a sharp rap with the calipers at the end of the rod, and the percussion caused the piece to break off cleanly. But somehow, my mom fumbled the catch. The vase slipped from her grasp and tumbled to the floor, shattering as it hit the polished concrete.

I turned to Laelia, unable to resist saying the classic glassblowing joke hot on my tongue.

"You know what they call that, don't you? A floor model."

But Laelia wasn't laughing.

My eyes shot back to my mom. She was hunched over in pain, clutching her belly. Nico dropped the calipers on the workbench and rolled the hot iron rod safely out of the way. He put his arms around my mom, supporting her.

"I just need to sit down for a few minutes," she said, biting the words out with a gasp. Her face was stark white again. Nico spoke to her soothingly, as if she were a small, scared child.

"It's okay, Josefina. It will be all right. I know you want to sit, but here there is broken glass. Put your arms around my neck, and I will carry you to the sofa."

She nodded, her eyes big and round, a sheen of sweat on her pale face. Nico picked her up in his muscled, tattooed arms with infinite tenderness. I waited, not knowing what to do. Patiently, Nico held my mother and turned to me.

"Rocket, niña, clear the books and boxes off the sofa, please?" he requested.

It was a relief to have something practical to do. I raced across the room to the office area and piled everything onto the floor, clearing it just in time for Nico to set my mom down gently. She curled onto her side, her knees tucked up. Fetal position.

"Laelia, por favor, call the ambulance. And then call Señor Rick and tell him to meet us at the hospital."

"Oh, I don't need an ambulance or the hospital," my mom argued. "I'll be fine. I just need to rest for a bit."

Laelia hesitated, her hand hovering over the phone on the office desk. She looked to Nico for guidance. He waved her on then turned his attention back to my mother.

Nico smiled at her. "You must go to the hospital, Josefina, for the doctor to see you and the babies."

He gently patted her stomach with his big hand, scarred from years of working with hot glass. "They will be fine, no worries."

I wasn't allowed in the ambulance, so Nico took me in his car. We left Laelia in charge of the store and gave her instructions for shutting everything in the hot shop. When we got there, Rick was already in the emergency room next to my mother's stretcher, holding her hand as the paramedics wheeled her up to the maternity floor. Nico sat with me in the waiting room, doing his best to keep me calm. He scrounged through his pockets for change and bought us a bag of potato chips from the vending machine.

Rick finally came out. "They're keeping her overnight to run some tests," he said, slumping into a chair across from me. "She probably just needs to take it easy for awhile. I called Rosa—she's going to stay at the house tonight with you. Nico will take you home."

"I want to stay here!" I protested, but Rick shook his head.

"Please, Rocket," he said. "I'll call you when we're on the way home."

I barely slept that night, even though Rick called me a few hours later to say that my mom was doing well and they'd be home first thing in the morning. As soon as I heard the garage open, I rushed the door like a quarterback. Rick was helping my mother from the car. I elbowed him out of the way and put my arm around my mother to help her up the little step out of the garage and into the house. He didn't say a word, just went ahead and held the door open for us.

"I'm fine, Rocket, I feel much better now," my mom said. But she didn't look fine. She looked tired, pale, her lips drawn tight in pain.

"A week lounging around and catnapping is exactly what the doctor ordered," my mom announced. "That and a few iron pills."

She walked slowly toward the master bedroom, holding Rick's arm for support. I ran ahead and fluffed up her pillows and pulled back the comforter, while Rick helped her change into clean pajamas.

"You can go back to work if you want. I've got this covered," I told him. But I couldn't shake him. After bringing her a mountain of magazines and books, he settled himself onto his side of the bed with his laptop computer and briefcase. I hunkered down on the floor with my homework.

For the next couple of days, she mostly just slept. When she was awake, she spent her time trying not to cry in front of me. I cornered Rick to ask what was really going on.

"Look, I probably should let Josie be the one to tell you about this," he said. I stared him down.

"Well, it's kind of freaky," he told me, sighing. "They did another, more detailed ultrasound. The doctors think that your mom was actually pregnant with triplets, but one of them wasn't thriving, and got absorbed back into her body. The net result is that she not only has a lot of extra hormones swimming around in her system, she might have some complications with the placenta."

I sat for a moment to digest this. Triplets? And one of them gone before we even realized it had been there. I couldn't wrap my head around it. "What do you mean, absorbed?"

"The doctor says it happens sometimes with multiples. The body can't sustain all those fetuses, so one just sort of withers away. They call it a 'vanishing twin.' If she stays on bedrest, she probably won't have any other complications."

"Probably?" I asked.

"Well, this kind of thing usually happens earlier in the pregnancy, so they want to keep a close eye on her."

Rick patted my shoulder awkwardly. "She'll be fine. The hardest part is going to be getting her to stay in bed. Taking it easy is not Josie's style."

Twenty-four

BY DAY FOUR, MY MOM WAS AS RESTLESS AS A CAGED TIGER AND HAD CLAWS JUST ABOUT as sharp. "Stop hovering over me like news choppers at a traffic pile-up," she snapped. "I'm perfectly healthy."

"In a week, we'll see Doctor Merkle again, and let her decide," said Rick, firmly.

I was secretly impressed that he stood up to her like that. I asked her if she wanted another glass of milk or some herbal tea. She gritted out a "no" through clenched teeth.

"How about orange juice, honey?" asked Rick. "Does that sound good?"

My mother slammed her book down in disgust. "I don't want any more milk. Or orange juice. Or tea. Or cinnamon toast. Or another magazine. Or a back rub. What would really make me happy is if you two got out of the house and did something fun. Away from here."

"Like what?" Rick and I said simultaneously.

She flipped through her datebook, the one I had thoughtfully placed on her nightstand.

"A-ha! Perfect!" she announced, jabbing her finger on an entry. "Today's that Tree People native plant thing-y at Malibu Creek State Park. Rocket can go with you."

"I already called Jeff and told him that we had a family emergency," replied Rick.

"Me lying in bed reading magazines is not a family emergency. Rocket, put on jeans or old trousers and a shirt with long sleeves. Oh, and wear your ratty red tennis shoes, the ones I said you should throw out but which I know are hidden in the back of your closet. It starts at ten."

"Yippeee," I muttered.

"Oh, and don't forget sunscreen. And the floppy hat Nana gave you for gardening. And a water bottle." She clapped her hands like an Arabian sheik. "Go, go!"

"Bossing us around sure seems to make you happy," drawled Rick. He stubbornly planted himself on the bed next to her. "Josie-doll, I am NOT leaving you here by yourself. I'll go putter around in another room, but I'm just not comfortable…"

The doorbell rang. My mother clapped her hand to her head.

"Oh, didn't I tell you? Bethie said she was going to stop by. Rocket, go let her in."

"What convenient timing," drawled Rick.

Bethie gave me a big hug as she came into the house. Ryan was right behind her, although I could barely see him. He was carrying an enormous mass of mop-headed hydrangeas and he looked like some crazy flower creature.

"Are those from our garden?" I asked, pointing at the flowers.

"Yep. She told me to bring them when she called me this morning," said Bethie.

"Wait. *She* called *you*?" I asked.

"You and Ryan catch up—I'll find the way," Bethie said hastily, taking the flowers from Ryan and making a quick exit.

Ryan hung back, too cool for school. I let him in anyway, though I was beginning to suspect I was just the victim of a master manipulation.

"You're still angry with me," I said. No use beating around the bush.

"I'm not angry, I'm indifferent," he replied.

"Being indifferent is like being bored," I retorted. "A complete waste of time."

He frowned at me. He started to talk, and I could see his mouth move, but suddenly it was as if I had lost the ability to hear. He really had beautiful lips, even when they were all scrunched in a straight line like they were now. I had a flashback of him giving me mouth-to-mouth and wished I'd been less panicked so I could have appreciated it more. At the rate my love life was shaping up, that had probably been my one and only chance to lock lips with a boy before college. Assuming it even happened in college.

Rick entered the room. "Did I hear someone say they were bored? Not for long. We are off to save the universe from invasion, since my wife has decided that she would rather spend the day with anyone other than me and Rocket. Ryan, your mom is going to stay here for a few hours, and she has decreed you to be my slave for the day."

He eyed Ryan's jeans, t-shirt and scruffy sneakers.

"Hmmm, you're in pretty good shape. I'll grab a long-sleeved shirt and gloves for you, and we'll be on the way. Rocket, better get a move on and change out of your pjs."

No! I looked down with horror. Yep, I was still wearing my hot pink happy face boxers and an old Space Mountain t-shirt. I looked up to see Ryan smiling.

"Why is it that the one thing guaranteed to make you smile is me being humiliated?" I said. It came out more like a snarl, actually.

He laughed. "Space Mountain is my favorite roller coaster. And I think your boxers are kind of cute."

"Ha ha. I'll get you a pair for your birthday," I muttered, my face flaming as I fled to my bedroom to change.

Twenty minutes later, we pulled into the graveled lot, and parked alongside a bunch of other cars. At the head of the main trail, a group of people holding gardening implements and backpacks had gathered.

Rick hopped out of the car and opened up the hatchback of his Prius. He pulled on a pair of well-worn leather work gloves and pointed to two more pairs in the trunk.

"Glove up, grab tools and a water bottle," he said. "This is thirsty work."

Ryan grabbed a pickaxe and I went for a shovel. We trudged over to the group. A uniformed park ranger broke off in mid-sentence when he saw us. With his thick bushy beard and eyebrows, he looked like a smiling brown bear.

"Well, hey howdy hey—it's Rick Patrick. Didn't think you were going to make it, my friend," he exclaimed. He and Rick slapped each other on the back, and then the bear turned toward us. "Who's this with you?"

"This is my daughter, Rocket. Rocket—this is Jeff Jamieson—the best park ranger and naturalist in the Santa Monica Mountains."

I was shaking Jeff's hand, but I was staring at Rick. "My daughter?" I wasn't sure how I felt about that. A little mad, but also a little something else I couldn't figure out.

Jeff engulfed my hand in his giant paw and gave it a hearty shake.

"Good to meet you, Rocket. Your dad's a great guy. We met doing a big conservation project in South America back in our college days."

"Rick's not my real dad. He's my stepfather. He and my mom just got married a couple of months ago," I blurted out.

There was an awkward silence. Jeff still had hold of my hand and was trying to figure out a response. Ryan elbowed me in the ribs then stuck out his hand to Jeff.

"I'm Ryan Mathews, nice to meet you."

Jeff let go of my hand and shook Ryan's. "Any relation to Ben Mathews?" he said.

I could see Rick subtly shaking his head, trying to warn Jeff, but Jeff missed the hint. "No way! How is that old son of a gun? How come you didn't drag his lazy butt out here this morning? I remember he was pretty handy at digging latrines when we were in Santiago!"

He stepped back and examined Ryan intently. "You look a lot like him, especially around the eyes. How's your old man?"

"I don't know. I haven't seen him in two years," replied Ryan.

"Oh."

It was clear Jeff didn't know how to respond. He looked helplessly at Rick. Rick just shrugged his shoulders. Jeff regained his composure.

"Well, it's always a pleasure to have some new hands on board—hope you don't mind a few blisters. The restoration site where we'll be working today is about a fifteen-minute hike."

He led the way across the asphalt access road toward a dirt trailhead. It was gorgeous, like a scene out of an old Western film—rolling hillsides studded with gnarled old oak trees and the darker green live oaks. The sky was clear blue heaven with just a few wisps of white. The sun was beating down, but we were close enough to the ocean to catch a cooling breeze now and then. Jeff pointed things out along the way, like a clump of yellow sticky monkey flower and the deliciously herbal-smelling purple sagebrush that adorned the sunny slopes. We crossed over a creek on a footbridge, and paused for a moment to look at the water tumbling over the rocks below. Downstream, the creek widened over gravelly shallows. A black bird with scarlet shoulder feathers lifted up from the reeds alongside the gravelly bank.

"What's that bird called?" I asked Jeff, pointing. "The black bird with the red wings?"

"That's an easy one," he laughed. "It's a red-winged blackbird. Keep your eyes peeled. If we're really lucky, we might spot a red-tailed hawk or even a golden eagle."

A choir of birds chattered and chirped from every direction. We moved forward once again, the path getting narrower as we moved into a less-traveled trail. Eventually we reached an open stretch of meadow that was aglow in lemony-yellow blossoms.

"Gorgeous wildflowers," I commented.

Jeff sighed. "Yeah, they're pretty, all right. Pretty invasive. And pretty flammable when they shrivel in the summer heat. Our goal today is to remove all of these mustard plants and a couple other noxious weeds like euphorbia before they go to seed, dry up and increase the fuel load during fire season. We've already marked off the boundaries of the restoration area with stakes and plastic ties." He pointed these out to us. "It's important that you stay inside the perimeter. Once the site is cleared, we'll prep it to plant native bunch grasses and wildflowers."

He turned to an older woman sporting long gray braids and a tie-dyed peace sign shirt. "Sally, did you bring the burlap?"

Sally removed the bulging knapsack from her back and pulled out several large sheets of burlap.

"Right. So we'll divvy these up and spread out around the meadow. Lay 'em flat then pile 'em high. You can cut the weeds to the ground then dig out the roots. Sometimes you can pull the whole plant up with a good yank, but that's rough on the back. Rick will show you how it's done."

Rick got his shovel into position and looked around at the group. "The ground is really dry, so you need to put your whole weight into it," he said, matching words to actions.

"It helps if you dig in from all sides of the plant. Try to cut off the big taproot, then it's easy to pull them up. If it won't budge, go back at it with the shovel, or cut the roots with your pruners."

He leaned down and grabbed the mustard plant and chucked it onto the burlap, which Sally had laid out next to him.

"Awesome," Jeff commented. "If you're in doubt, give a holler. All right, pair up and spread out. Rick, why don't you help me? There's a nasty little patch of pampas grass I want to dig out before it spreads farther."

"Ryan, Rocket—you think you get the general idea?" asked Rick. "I can stick with you for a few more minutes if you want."

"We can handle it," said Ryan.

"It's not rocket science," said Jeff, with a wink. I gave him a half-hearted smile.

Ryan and I worked in silence for a few minutes. Then we both spoke up at the same time. With the exact same words.

"I'm sorry—" "I'm sorry—"

We both stopped and looked at each other.

"Um, you first," he said.

I blurted it out hyper-speed. "I'm sorry I brought your guitar to the beach. You said you didn't want to play and I should have respected that." I sucked in a deep breath.

"I'm sorry I was so rude," replied Ryan. "You kind of hit a nerve."

That done, we set to work. The silence felt lighter now, friendlier—not heavy with the weight of words unspoken. Square foot by square foot, we dug out the unwanted plants. Jeff and Rick came by to check on us.

"Awesome. You guys have quite a pile there," Jeff praised us. "I know it seems counter-intuitive to pull up perfectly healthy plants, but it's part of returning our wild lands back to a healthy balance. Do you guys know the story of how this flower got here?"

Ryan and I shook our heads.

"The story goes that Father Junipero Serra brought the seeds from Spain when he was trying to establish Catholicism here in the late 1700s. The padres dispersed seeds as they rode between the missions, marking out a golden trail."

"El Camino Real," noted Ryan.

"That's right—the Royal Road," agreed Jeff.

"These wildflowers have been here for hundreds of years, and you still consider them non-native?" I asked.

Jeff nodded. "Yup. Sure, they're well-adapted to live in this climate, so they spread like wildfire. But our own native plants evolved over millions of years in conjunction with local wildlife species. Lots of local birds and other animals are endangered because they've lost important forage and habitat thanks to invaders like these."

"I know just how those critters feel," joked Rick. "My bachelor pad has been taken over by a couple of domineering English women."

I knew he was joking, but his comment pushed my buttons.

"I didn't have much of a choice," I snapped back.

Jeff chuckled. "We're all here now," he said in a peaceable voice. "I guess the trick is to learn to live together, fix what we can like we're doing here today, and make sustainable choices so we don't do any more damage in the future. Rick, wanna haul a load back to the truck with me? We need to empty a few of these tarps."

"Sure," replied Rick. He bundled up the corners of our burlap and slung it over his back. "I'll be right back."

After they left, Ryan shot me a disgusted look.

"What?" I said defensively. "What did I do wrong now?"

"I don't see why you have to be so rude to Rick," he muttered.

"Rude?"

"You know you were."

"He's the one who married my mother and turned my life upside down," I said.

"Whatever. I just don't think you should be so harsh on him. He WANTS to do stuff with you. You should, I don't know, treasure that, not blow him off all the time."

"Back off," I yelled at him. "It's not like you're perfect." I said.

Ryan turned his back to me and pulled on his headphones. He got back to work, ignoring me.

"You can't just check out of a fight like that!" I yelled at him. Nothing.

So I yanked the headphones off his head and put them on mine.

"What are you listening to all the time?" I demanded. I couldn't hear a thing. I yanked the player out of his pocket. The screen was blank. No songs, no playlists. Nothing. It wasn't even turned on.

"The Sound of Silence," I cracked. "Why don't you just leave the headphones off and enjoy the sounds of birds?"

"Because then I'd have to listen to *you*," he retorted, grabbing the earbuds and shoving them back in his ears. We spent the rest of the day in silence. Horrible, awkward, painful silence.

When I got home, I let my mom have it.

"Stop trying to run my life," I glared at her, arms crossed.

"All right, I confess. I just didn't want you moping around friendless all summer, and I thought you and Ryan might hit it off. He seems like a very nice boy."

"He's a total jerk."

"Cut him some slack, Rocket. He's had it tough the last few years."

At Muse School that night, I consulted Polly. "I know he's in pain. I want to help him, but all we seem to do is fight. He makes me crazy," I complained. "I'm not even sure he's the person I'm supposed to be inspiring, since you people won't tell me ANYthing. Maybe he's right, maybe I'm the one who's got the problems."

"Oh, Rocket, of course you've got problems," Polly said with a smile. "That's why your spirit chose to be born into the world in that body—to give yourself a particular set of challenges to overcome. But don't worry, your wings are developing nicely. You'll be flying in no time."

Veering off the path, Polly selected two small brown leaves from the masses heaped on the forest floor, placing one in each of her palms. She crouched next to the stream and beckoned me alongside her. The leaf in her right hand she blew into the stream. It danced atop the ripples, bobbing like a tiny boat navigating past boulders, until it was caught in a swift current and carried out of sight.

"Where has that leaf gone?" she asked me.

I shrugged my shoulders. "I don't know—maybe all the way to the ocean?" She waited, watching me.

I pondered, warming to the topic. "It could get swallowed by a fish. Or stuck in wet sand for a couple million years until it turns into a fossil."

Polyhymnia opened her other hand to reveal the other leaf, which she had crumbled into confetti.

"That leaf's journey is over before it begins," I said.

"Not at all," she replied. "This leaf is just as important as the one that traveled down river. It will decay into essence—and be absorbed into new life."

She took me by the shoulders and stared deeply into my eyes. I'd noticed all the Muses had a tendency to do that—as if they were trying to imprint messages into my retinas. It was uncomfortable, since like most Americans, I'm fond of my personal space. But I was getting used to it.

"To create art, to compose music, to write a poem—is to take a journey, Rocket. Sometimes creativity is fast, thrilling, tumultuous. Sometimes ideas need to germinate in the dark, slowly. You cannot prescribe a creator's path, nor predict whom they will touch and inspire in the future."

"I don't get it. What's my job, then?"

"Your task is to stir the air, to provide the zephyr wind, which will blow them along their path, wherever that may lead them."

With that, she filled my hand with the leaf fragments. I brought my cupped hand up to my lips, and gave a little puff. The bits of leaf stirred slightly in my hand.

"You have to believe in the possibilities, Rocket," admonished Polyhymnia. "That's why the world needs muses. We're the believers."

I tried again, breathing in a great lungful of air and exhaling with all my might. The leaves scattered, swirling all around me, and a wind blew up out of nowhere—or maybe out of me. More leaves showered from the trees above and eddied up from the ground below. I jumped back in surprise.

Polly laughed out loud, twirling in a circle with her arms outstretched, as light as one of the spinning leaves.

"Yes! A blocked artist is like a fire in a room with no windows. A fire needs oxygen to burn. Your job is to create the window and blow the breath of inspiration into it."

"Sound, light, energy—and creativity—are all invisible forces, but we know they're there by how things react to them. The moon's gravity pulls the tides. Ryan's sister died, but her creative spirit, her energy, her love—still dances and sings. That energy surrounds Ryan, but he can't receive it."

I must have looked confused.

"It's like he's being pushed and pulled by two opposing forces: the end result is stasis, going nowhere. Light can inspire you, and so can darkness. But in his case, grief and joy have canceled each other out. He needs to touch each feeling one at a time."

"Sappho once said: 'There is no place for grief in a house which serves the Muse,'" said Polyhymnia. "And it's true that a heart filled with music is as buoyant as one of these leaves. But if we acknowledge our grief, let it out into the light and look at it—it can inspire poetry just as purely as joy."

"I guess I just have to work harder, until I get it right," I said stoically. "Nana always says that genius is one percent inspiration and ninety-nine percent perspiration."

"Actually, dear, it was Tommy Edison who said something along those lines," she said. "Such a hard worker. And almost as clever as Nikolai Tesla."

I sighed. "Better get my nose back to the grindstone, then, I guess."

"Another Nana saying?" asked Polly.

I nodded.

"Well…Nana and Tommy are right. It often requires hard work to accomplish brilliant things," said Polly, as we emerged from the woods and entered the meadow, which was filled as usual with music and muses. "But perspiring can be achieved multiple ways, and *my* favorite is dancing."

Polly grabbed me by both hands and spun us around until we were both dizzy. We collapsed in a fit of giggles on the green grass.

"You know what else little Tommy Edison said?" asked Polly, lying on her back and watching the clouds drift into shapes. "I never did a day's work in my whole life. It was all fun."

"It's summer vacation, Rocket," she advised. "Feed your joy. Amuse yourself." She gave me a wink and a nudge. "Get it? A-muse yourself? Because you're a Muse."

"I got it, Aunt Polly, I got it."

"Go play, Rocket. You used to know how to do that, just as well as Amelia."

Twenty-Five

Feed my joy. I kept thinking about what Polly had said and wondering how I was supposed to do that. Between my job at the hot shop and babysitting Amelia and Robbie three afternoons a week, I didn't have much free time these days. I thought of summers past, how I'd spent them having adventures with Gillian. The next time I babysat Amelia and Robbie, I brought the Boredom Buster Box with me.

"What's in the box?" asked Amelia. "New shoes?"

"Nope. Wishes," I said. "We are going to write down all the fun things we want to do together on little pieces of paper and put them in the box."

"Why is it covered with vampires?" asked Amelia. "Vampires are gross."

"Gillian and I were really into vampire books last year," I said.

"Who's Gillian?" asked Robbie.

"She's my best friend," I said then corrected myself. "Was. She was my best friend. We started this when we were about your age."

"Where's Gillian now?"

"She thinks she's too old for wishes, I guess."

"I hope I never get that old," said Amelia, wistfully.

"We can make our own box if you don't like this one," I told her.

I expected Amelia to cover the box with pink hearts and flowers, but she had a new passion: monkeys. Robbie approved the jungle theme. We spent an hour that afternoon decorating and thinking up ideas to put in the box.

"Does it have to be places to go?" asked Amelia. "Or could it be learning how to do stuff, like blow bubbles with bubble gum?"

"I guess it could, Amelia," I said, thinking about it. "It absolutely could."

We followed the one golden rule of the Boredom Buster Box: whatever we pulled from the box, we had to accomplish that day. We found treasure, buried a time capsule, planted pumpkin seeds, and made marshmallow treats dipped in chocolate and sprinkles. I taught Amelia how to tie her shoes and to ride a bike without the training wheels. Robbie taught us how to be invisible in superhero capes. We hunted for lizards and made a volcano out of baking soda and vinegar. We all learned how to keep our balance in tree pose.

We even went to Mars. "Jump on my back, Robbie," I said. "I'm a Rocket."

Amelia wore a green dress and painted her face and tickled us when we landed, apparently an age-old Martian greeting.

On hot afternoons, we practiced our swimming together in Rick's pool. Robbie paddled around with his little water wings. Amelia could already swim like a fish.

"I think you might be part-mermaid, Amelia," I told her.

"Maybe. I'm going to be a marine biologist when I grow up, so I can figure out where blue whales go to birth their calves. Did you know that blue whales have veins so big you can swim through them?" she said, before diving into an underwater handstand.

I didn't believe her, so she made me look it up later. It's true! We printed out a picture of blue whales and added whale-watching to the boredom buster box.

Twice a week, Rick dropped me off to work in the hot shop with Nico and Laelia. I swept and mopped the floors, inventoried stock, and sorted the mail to bring home to my mom. I spent hours cleaning fingerprints off glass. Whenever we had a little free time, Nico would give me lessons on the guitar. I bought myself a couple of beginner books from the music shop down the street. I was getting pretty good.

When Laelia took her break, I manned the cash register and rang up sales. One Tuesday, a girl I recognized came into the shop. She gave me a quick shy smile then started browsing the shelves. It took me a minute to place her.

"Ella, right? From the school choir?" I asked.

"Oh, hello. You're Rocket Malone, right? Valedictorian and all that. You work here?"

"It's my mom's shop," I said. "I'm helping her out this summer. She's pregnant and has to stay in bed."

"Oh," she replied. She looked at me. "Is she going to be okay?"

"Yeah. No. I don't know," I said. I changed the subject, clamping down the tears, which welled up whenever I thought too hard about it. "You've got an amazing voice. How did you learn to sing?"

"I've loved singing ever since I can remember," she said. "I listen to songs and sing them over and over, until I can do them just right. Then I take them apart, mix it up and make it my own. I have a really good voice teacher, too. He's taught me a lot about controlling my breath. Exhaling with intention."

"I never thought about it that way," I said. It was funny, I had spent so much time with actual Muses and godsbreath on Mount Helikon, but one little sentence from someone in my world changed my whole perspective.

"It's true—you take in air and then, depending on how you relax your larynx and adjust your tongue and the position of your mouth, the sound changes. Like this."

She began to sing, right there in the shop. Trilling a high note, dropping down into deep breathy oh-oh-ohs then taking it back up into the stratosphere. She kept a hand on her chest to show me how she was breathing.

"That's so cool! I wish I could do that!"

"You totally can," she said. "Follow my lead."

She sang a note. I tried, but all I could muster was a tight little "arg" of a noise. I laughed and shook my head.

"Try again," she urged. "But this time, you go first. Just open your mouth and let any sound come out. Do you ever do yoga? Try an "ohhhhmmmmm."

I gave it another shot, slightly better.

"Take another breath, open your mouth wider and let it just vibrate in your chest."

There was something really satisfying about hearing my own voice resonate in the shop. On my next "ohm," Ella joined in, harmonizing her voice with mine and then lifting us up until I felt like we were on Mount Helikon. The air in the room shimmered, as Ella held her final note for an impossibly long moment.

Laelia walked back in and smiled at the two of us. "Careful, you're going to shatter all the goblets in here!"

The goblets stayed intact, even after Laelia added her lovely voice to ours. I helped Ella pick out a beautiful red one as a gift for her music teacher, which was why she'd come into the shop in the first place.

The next day, I didn't work in the shop. Marla needed me for the whole afternoon and evening while she and her husband went to a big awards show. The kids started fighting with each other, even before their parents walked out the door. Amelia, usually so happy and content to sit at the table and do art, was clingy and demanding. I wasn't feeling so hot myself. My stomach hurt and I was ultra-crabby.

In desperation, I turned to The Boredom Buster Box. I let Robbie pull a wish, which of course made Amelia jealous. "He can't even read!" she shrieked.

"Fine, you read it for him," I said. Amelia yanked the slip of paper out her brother's hands, which set him crying.

"Go for a nature hike."

I groaned. I was too tired to go for a hike. All I wanted to do was curl up on the sofa.

"How about we watch a nature movie instead?" I said.

"But Rocket, you said we always had to do what the box tells us," said Robbie.

"Sometimes, the box doesn't know what it's doing," I said.

I turned on the television. For an hour, they sat there like little zombies on the couch, while I did my best potato imitation. It made me more cranky, not less.

"Okay, time for some fresh air," I said, trying to sound peppier than I felt.

In typical kid fashion, now that I actually wanted them to go on a hike, they had changed their minds. "I don't want to go," whined Amelia.

"We are going to explore the trails in the canyon behind us, like it or not," I ordered. "First, we need to pack a survival bag. What should we put in it?"

Gradually, they got into the spirit of it. We stuffed a backpack with chips, apples, and cookies. I set Amelia to work at the kitchen sink filling a thermos with water, while I put orange juice in another. Robbie handed me a couple of miner's flashlights—the kind you strap to your head.

"Huh," I said. "I think we're going to be home before it gets dark, Robbie."

"Yeah, but maybe we'll find a cave," said Amelia, "with bats. And tarantulas. And snakes." Robbie's eyes got really big. Amelia went in for the kill. "Big giant pythons that eat little boys."

Robbie started crying again. I rushed them out of the door, reassuring Robbie that there were no pythons slithering around the Hollywood Hills

The hike went south fast. The kids complained about every little thing. Amelia fell down and skinned her knee, and when I went to clean it, I accidentally poured orange juice all over her leg instead of water. I didn't have the energy to look for lizards or point out interesting plants. At the first available flat area, I stopped and let the kids dive into the snacks. I dove deeper than either of them, devouring a giant bag of potato chips and a pack of cookies. It made me feel sick, but I couldn't seem to stop. I was super cranky and tired. All I wanted to do was crawl into bed.

To top it all off, Amelia convinced me to stop and smell the sagebrush—and I was promptly attacked by a swarm of bees. I brushed them frantically out of my hair and face, but one stung me right on the forehead. Amelia was freaking out, and I figured she'd been stung too. I didn't know what to do. Panicked, I picked up Amelia and carried her back to Rick's house. Poor little Robbie clung to the back of my shirt the whole walk home, which slowed me down considerably. She was still screaming when we got to the front door.

"Amelia, stop it!" I snapped at her. "You're breaking my eardrums and you're acting like a bigger baby than Robbie. Big girls don't cry like this. Suck it up!"

That clammed her up, but I felt like a jerk when I saw her eyes.

"I'm not a big baby," said Robbie in a quiet little voice that made me feel even more like a monster.

"We need back-up," I muttered. "My house."

I let myself in through the front door. Rick took one look at Amelia and relieved me of my burden, murmuring sweet nothings to her. After determining that Amelia was just scared, not stung, he sat the little ones down at the kitchen table with popsicles.

He examined my face. "Hold on one sec," he said. "I know just the thing." He went right to the kitchen cabinets and pulled down a spice bottle.

"Meat tenderizer," he said, sprinkling some onto a wet paper towel and pressing it to my head. "Takes down swelling."

"Go, wash your face, take a rest," he said. "Oh wait, you need one of these. Green is your favorite, right?"

He rummaged through the popsicle box in the freezer and pulled one out. "Voila!" he said. "That completes the bee sting cure, as learned from my own mother."

My mom was sitting in bed reading a magazine.

"How are the dynamic duo?" she asked. The kids loved my mother and were fascinated by her British accent. Robbie had a little crush on her and was convinced she was related to Sir Topham Hatt, the train conductor in his favorite storybooks.

"I can't do this," I said. "I can't make it through this day."

"What's so dreadful?" she said.

"Besides the giant bee sting on my head?" I said, sarcastically. "My stomach hurts, my back hurts, little kids have been climbing on me all day, Amelia and Robbie hate me. I don't want to talk about it, I just want to crawl into bed and sleep for a hundred years. Can't Rosa watch them?"

"Rocket, watching the kids is your responsibility, not Rosa's. Why don't you sit and play games with them or something? Or maybe take them swimming."

I could feel my eyes welling with tears as I wondered how I would get through four more hours. I pulled it together and somehow managed. I took them back to their house. Amelia retreated to her room without a word. Robbie went and played with his toys. Neither of them wanted to speak to me, and frankly, I didn't care.

By the time Marla came home, I was completely exhausted. She wanted to chat about my day, but I was too zoned out to hear anything she said. My stomach and back hurt worse than ever.

That night, I was in no mood for Muse School. I was there anyway. Clio droned on about the significance of bees.

"Bees are powerful symbols," she said. "Where bees are found, wisdom, the honey of our lives, is always close at hand."

She sent a pointed look in my direction. "And bees die when they sting. The Muses' way is to inspire others with loving-kindness and joyful example, not with fear or anger."

The lesson didn't end there. Terpsichore was teaching a special dance to go with Clio's bee theme.

"The apprentices will play the role of female worker bees," she said, handing us yellow and black striped tunics with filmy wings attached to the backs of them. "And the Muses will be flowers. We also have a very special guest musician tonight."

Terpsichore strummed the equivalent of a drum roll on her harp. An old man in an antiquated-looking black suit appeared out of nowhere.

"Ladies, it is my great privilege to introduce the legendary composer Nikolai Rimsky-Korsakov, who will play 'Flight of the Bumblebee' from his opera The Tale of Tsar Saltan."

She looked expectantly at the composer, who looked quizzically back at her.

"Oh, yes, you need a piano!"

A gleaming, black-lacquered grand piano floated down from the clouds and wafted gently to the stage, followed by a padded bench. After some knuckle-stretching and keyboard warm-ups, the composer tucked his long grey beard into his shirt front and launched into a lively performance. His fingers flew over the keys in a dizzying blur.

Terpsichore motioned for us to start buzzing around. "Bees, quickly, begin by flying to a flower. Sip nectar into your special honey stomach."

I ran over to Polly, who handed me a golden straw and a cup of peach nectar. I took a sip but I was too tired to get into the role.

"This is just silly," I told Brigit, in what I thought was a discreet whisper, as we were flying back to our "hive" to deliver the nectar. But I'd forgotten that Muses are so attuned to breath that they can detect the slightest shift in air currents. It makes them amazing musicians, but also means they have an annoying capacity for hearing remarks you didn't want them to hear. Brigit made a beeline for a "flower" across the meadow.

"Silly? And what is wrong with being silly? Rocket, when will you realize that ecstatic dance is not frivolity? It is an essential part of your Muse training!"

"It's dancing!" I said. "Dancing is a *recreational* activity. It's not exactly productive."

Terpsichore smiled at me triumphantly, like a cat that was about to pounce on an elusive mouse. "Exactly! Dancing IS recreational...but in the fullest sense of the word, not just the diluted half-meaning you've learned. The first syllable of the word isn't "rec;" it is "re"—meaning "again." Re-creational. Ecstatic dance allows us to access joy, to release our barriers to the source of creativity. When we open our hearts and minds in dance, we are able to integrate our physical and spiritual selves in order to align with our spirit's highest purpose. It's a gift that will serve you well in the coming days."

Her speech just flowed over me. I was so tired, so cranky, I snapped.

"You know what would serve me well? Sleep."

Polyhymnia glided over like a beautiful white mother swan to her cygnet's rescue. She put a protective arm around my shoulders and spoke firmly to her sister. "Terpsichore, I think Rocket has had enough training for today."

Terpsichore protested. "But...our next act is pollination!"

Polly gave her a warning look.

Terpsichore sighed. "It's important to trust your body wisdom, Rocket. If you need to rest, you're excused. When it is time to dance and sing like the muse you are, you will know."

TWENTY-SIX

ASTRAL PROJECTING BACK INTO MY SLEEPING BODY WASN'T THE USUAL COMFORTING experience. I hurt all over. I wasn't surprised by the throbbing in my head where the bee had stung me, but I didn't understand why my back and belly ached so much, until I saw the smears of rusty brownish red on my sheets and my underwear. Suddenly, I put the pieces together. I knew what this meant, thanks to our sex ed class in fifth grade. And sixth. And seventh. I even had a "Welcome to Womanhood" kit with free maxi pad samples under my sink. Gillian had gotten her period two years ago, and I had started to think mine would never come. It was kind of a relief to know I was normal.

But as I stuck the bulky pad inside my underpants, I started blubbering. I didn't want to feel like this every month for the rest of my life. It was barely dawn, but I couldn't sleep, so I made a covert trip to the laundry room. I dumped in detergent and was aiming a bottle of spot remover at my sheets and pajamas when Rick flipped off the light switch.

"Hey! I'm in here," I protested. He flipped it back on.

"Sorry, just saving electricity. What are you doing?" he asked. He spotted the stains. "Oh. Ummmm. Oh. Okay. Umm."

The inevitable awkward silence followed.

Rick cleared his throat. "So, cold water is what you use for bloodstains. And better for the environment. And, um, congratulations on becoming a young woman, Rocket."

"Oh my god. Yaaacck! Please, just shut up!" I shrieked.

I slammed down the lid of the washing machine and ran back to my room, where I buried myself under the covers and tried to forget the whole horrible thing.

Later that day, my mom texted me in to have The Talk. Rick slipped past me and out the door. I avoided eye contact.

"Rocket, Rick told me your period started today," she said, with her usual lack of squeamishness.

I groaned. "Ewwwww, god, you guys *talked* about it? That's totally humiliating."

"I know you know all the technical stuff already from school and me blathering on about it. I sent Rick out to buy supplies for you, which was a total act of heroism on his part. Everything you need is in the bathroom."

She hesitated. "Just so you know…He went to the co-op…and bought you a reusable menstrual cup," she said.

I shuddered and groaned again.

"There are directions on the package, but if you need more help or advice, just ask me. I know it will seem weird, but it makes sense in the long run. Very eco-friendly."

"Girls are cursed!" I grumbled. "For the next forty years, I have to deal with cramps and blood. It's disgusting. My body has turned on me."

My mom smiled. "You know what Nana once told me? Periods are a bloody miracle. Without them, she wouldn't have had me, and I wouldn't have had you, and these babies wouldn't have the perfect place to ripen inside of me now. Someday, you might have children—or you might choose not to…but the power women have in their wombs is a blessing, not a curse."

She gently patted my stomach. "You probably have cramps and feel rotten?"

I nodded.

"There are some surprises for you in my bathroom, not just the dreaded supplies."

I hauled myself off the bed and slogged into the bathroom, where I was…shocked. It looked like Valentine's Day in there. Pink, red and white rose petals floated on the surface of a steaming bath. Candles were burning all around the edge, and a fluffy pink towel was placed on a stool nearby.

"I sent Rick off to play soccer with his buddies for a few hours," my mom yelled. "I suspect they will really just hole up in a pub somewhere and watch a match on television. You can lock the door and stay in there as long as you like. It's something Yaya did for me once, after you were born. I remembered it in my dreams last night. Isn't that funny? It made me feel like a goddess, which is how you deserve to feel today. Divinely feminine."

I dipped in a toe—the water was Goldilocks temperature. Not too hot, not too cold. Just right. So I sank into it and just sat there, eyes closed. The hot water enveloped me, dissolving away some of my aches and pains. I perked up a bit and started toying with the rose petals, so soft and delicate I wanted to brush them against my cheeks and inhale their sweet fragrance. I lifted up my foot, admiring the way the wet petals clung to my skin and transformed me into some sort of fairy princess. How beautiful this skin was. I turned the faucet with my toes to add more hot water. My leg was tanned, not pale and doughy anymore, the muscles lean and defined from the swimming and exercising I had been doing. It was as if the fuzzy edges of me were coming into focus, as if an invisible artist were shading and contouring and adding little details to bring me to life. Maybe I wouldn't remain an ugly duckling after all. Maybe there was a chance I was a swan.

I stayed in there for a long time, luxuriating in all of my senses, letting myself be cradled in warm water, gently stirring the flower petals with my fingers and toes. I took careful sips from the glass mug my mother had left for me—honey-sweet ginger and lemongrass tea. Only when my skin started to wrinkle did I emerge like a mermaid onto a rock. A siren. I felt better. Calmer. Soft but strong.

I toweled off. My red flannel pajamas and clean undies were on the bathroom counter, next to the fluffy pink towel. I wasn't ready for a menstrual cup yet. There didn't seem to be that much blood anyway, so I just stuck a cotton pad into my undies. It felt bulky and weird. My whole body felt somehow mysterious to me, like I'd crossed the border into a foreign land.

Once I was dressed in the pajamas, I went out and sat on the bed next to my mom, suddenly feeling shy. She grabbed the hairbrush on her nightstand and began brushing my hair. It reminded me of sleepovers I'd had with Gillian, when we'd spend hours styling each other's hair into elaborate French braids.

"I wish I could call Gillian and tell her about this," I said.

My mother just kept brushing until the tightness in my shoulders melted.

"Bed rest rocks," I said.

"Once a month maybe. Not for months on end," she said. "But it's definitely more fun with you here."

After a long, lazy break reading trashy romances and watching old movies with my mom, I went back to my side of the house to catch up with my journal writing. I didn't have many words this time—still it seemed like something I wanted to remember. I doodled, sketching pictures of the bathtub, overflowing with flowers. I scribbled a few snippets around the margins.

When the mirror lit up, I was ready and waiting. In the absence of Gillian, I had made new friends. I wanted to tell Dani, Brigit and Magdalena about what had happened that day. But I didn't have to tell them—the Muses knew, even before I did, about my moon cycles…and they had planted the seed for the flower bath in my mother's dreams. I could tell something was up as soon as I broke through the woods into the meadow. Like Rick and my mom, the Muses were always celebrating something—summer solstice, a new star being born, a first kiss—and a ceremony was about to take place. Instead of the usual dancing, the Muses and apprentices had formed a circle. Artemis and her huntresses were there, too. Each held a white candle. Polyhymnia guided me down a spiral path of red petals to a golden divan near the reflecting pool. A single red candle stood on a pillar behind it. I didn't know what to expect, but my stomach was filled with happy butterflies.

Dani stepped forward and presented me with a glittering wooden box. I lifted the lid and she tipped the opened chest forward, spilling the most glorious fabric I had ever seen into my lap. It was a red sari of gossamer silk, softer than the rose petals in my bath, scrolled in pure gold thread on the edges with a pattern of waves and dolphins. In a flash, Dani wrapped the sari around me, tucking and draping and knotting like a professional. Then she kissed me on each cheek, and bowed over her clasped hands with a simple "Namaste."

"Namaste," I said back to her in thanks.

"You're gorgeous," she whispered into my ear.

Dani gracefully melted back into the circle, and Magdalena stepped forward, somber as always, but her eyes full of love and wisdom gained through sorrows I could not imagine. She extended a handwoven basket made of green palm leaves, which contained a glittering rainbow of rocks and crystals.

"I bring you pieces of Gaia, Mother Earth, because your time of bleeding reminds you that from the earth your body is created, and to earth, it will return. In your body, you have trace amounts of all of these things—iron, copper, calcium, salt. Replenish your body with minerals, nourish it always, so that it can serve as a strong vessel for your spirit."

I took the basket from her and held it tight against my belly.

Brigit came next. From one of her apron pockets, she pulled a simple twig, about eight inches long. "Rocket, this is a wand taken from a living birch tree and carved with symbols from the ancient Ogham tree language. It will bring you good fortune and a connection with nature." She handed me the wand. "Blessings of the Green Woman and the faery folk upon you."

I was about to thank her, but she held up her hand.

"I have another gift," she said, pulling a small earthenware jug from yet another apron pocket. "This vessel contains water from a sacred well. May the goddess of the river, Danu, flow love and joy into your life, and may your tears be as raindrops, which help good things grow."

I waited.

"That's it," she whispered. "Ye thank me now."

I laughed and gave her a big hug. She fairly skipped back to the circle.

Artemis stepped forward, raised her right arm toward the full moon, and placed her left hand on the crown of my head.

"I call upon the powers of the moon, she who holds sway over the tides of this planet and also the tides within your body. Rocket, my sister, may you embrace both the ebb and the flow of your life. Blessings upon your ability to create, your power to translate Source and quicken it into new life to inspire those around you with your passion and beauty and grace."

She summoned one of her warriors and took from her a red velvet cushion. On the cushion rested a beautiful chain of fine silver and diamonds with a gleaming charm in the shape of a crescent moon at its center. Artemis carefully clasped it around my neck, holding me with her intense gaze as she spoke again.

"This pendant represents the gifts that come to you with the onset of your monthly bleeding. Wisdom from the deep knowledge of your unity with the moon and the cycles of nature. Strength because the crescent is also the shape of my bow, which I use not to incite violence but to protect the vulnerable and innocent from those who would harm them."

She winked at me before returning to her place in the circle with her usual decisive stride.

The Muses came forward in turn to present me with beautiful charms for my necklace. A golden ballet slipper from Terpsichore, a filigreed aulos from Euterpe, tragedy and comedy masks from Melpomene and Thalia, a tiny golden tablet from Calliope and even tinier silver book from Clio, a cupid's heart from Erato, and my favorite, a miniscule globe full of sky and star from Urania, who had taught me so much about my astral body.

Polyhymnia stepped forward and added one last charm to my necklace, a tiny silver firefly whose body blinked on and off with a little golden light.

"Why a firefly?" I asked. She just smiled mysteriously then turned me to face the water, where my reflection glowed brightly.

"Rocket, these beautiful garments and gifts exist only in the astral world, but their lack of physical substance actually makes them more permanent, more enduring. They are manifestations of pure, creative energy. Objects in the physical world are easily destroyed or lost, but these gifts are yours to keep forever. The most important thing to remember is this vision you see of yourself: beautiful, strong, beloved. Worthy of receiving the gifts that have been bestowed on you, simply by being yourself."

The Muses got out their instruments and began to sing. A few of Artemis' warrior women sat and pounded out a steady beat on skin drums; others pounded it out on the earth with their feet. Soon the air was filled with music.

The drums echoed in my beating heart, my hips swayed, and I was whirling and shaking and stomping, weaving the meadow with all my sisters. Watching each other, not judging, just appreciating each other for what we brought to the dance. I have no idea how long the Muses played. Time ceased to matter; perhaps, it even ceased to exist. But gradually, the tempo slowed, giving my heart and breath a chance to rest. Maybe it sounds dorky, but I felt like my body had become one with the trees swaying in the breeze, my arms graceful branches reaching toward the rising sun in a physical prayer. Finally, I understood what the Muses had been telling me about the power of dance.

As I looked into the reflecting pool, I saw a single lotus flower rising from the muck, breaking the surface of the water and unfolding in the tender morning light.

The next day, once my cramps had subsided, I went over to apologize to the kids. I brought the guitar. Robbie seemed his usual happy self, more interested in his trains than he was in my guitar-playing. But I had some work to do to repair my friendship with Amelia.

"I don't want you to babysit me anymore," said Amelia, not looking at me.

"That would make me sad," I said. "I really like spending time with you, and we still have so many boredom-busting things to do together."

Nothing. She pulled away.

"I'm sorry I was grumpy. I didn't feel good yesterday, but I should have been nicer to you," I said softly. "Is it okay if I practice my guitar here for awhile?"

Amelia didn't answer or even look at me, but she settled down crisscross applesauce, and I could tell she was listening.

I played for a little while, getting absorbed in the music. I still wasn't a professional, but I was getting better.

"I missed a lot of notes," I said.

"It doesn't matter. You smile the whole time you play," said Amelia.

"Do you remember the boy in the dream?" I asked her. Amelia nodded. "This guitar belonged to his sister. She died, and now he's sad."

"Music will make him happy again," said Amelia. "You should give him a concert."

I set the guitar down and she climbed into my lap for a big hug. I could tell I was forgiven.

"Hmmm. I'd like to perform for a bigger audience," I agreed. "But I need someone non-critical. Preferably someone who can't hear all that well."

"Gammy says I'm better than Barry Manilow," Robbie piped up from the train table.

"My great-grandmother has a hearing aid, but she doesn't like to wear it." Amelia looked at me. "She lives in a home full of old people. We go sing there sometimes."

Of course. It was time to pay a visit to my Yaya Sophie. The next day I had free from both babysitting and the hot shop, I would visit her nursing home.

I created a colorful pot of flowers to take to her. I had already placed an inch of gravel at the bottom of the pot then filled it about two-thirds of the way up with potting soil. I was fiddling with various combinations of plants—lobelia, petunias, ivy—to see which looked best when Rick came out.

"Wow, that's really pretty," he said. "You have a knack with color."

"Thanks," I mumbled.

"Your mom's still sleeping. She had a rough night. I made pancakes—are you hungry?" he asked. I nodded. "I'll fix you a plate. Wash your hands and meet me in the kitchen."

By the time I was satisfied with the flowers, Rick was halfway through a mountain of pancakes, which he had drowned in a lake of syrup. I reached for the milk carton.

"Hallelujah," Rick said suddenly, almost causing me to spill the milk. "They've extended the rebates."

"Rebates?" I asked.

He looked up at me, startled, like he had forgotten I even lived in the house, then launched into an explanation I wasn't all that interested in hearing.

"Rebates for solar power. If it's cheap and it's easy, then we can sell more. A lot of people say they want to save the environment—but only if it doesn't cost them anything."

"Like everybody wants to have a perfect body, but they don't want to eat right or exercise," I commented.

"Exactly!" Rick mumbled through a forkful of pancakes. "Solar power can't get cheaper until there's enough demand for it, and they can mass-produce it on a grand scale. Kind of a catch-22."

I saw where he was going. "So, the government rebates are sort of like an incentive to get people to try it out?"

"Yeah, and then they tell two friends, and they tell two friends, et cetera. But you still need pioneers to lead the way. Sort of like an Olympic torchbearer, you know? Or, or—what did they call those guys who led settlers to the west?" He scratched his head. "Trailblazers! Without trail-blazers, nothing would ever change. We'd all just keep spinning around in our comfort zones until the planet imploded."

With a snap and a crackle, Rick popped behind his newspaper again. I thought about that as I slowly chewed on my pancakes. Trailblazer. That was kind of my job description, wasn't it?

"Thanks for breakfast," I said once I'd finished.

Rick set the paper down and looked at me. "Wait. There's something I want to talk to you about, Rocket" he said. His face looked serious.

"What? Am I in trouble?" I asked.

"No, no. Nothing bad." He paused, trying to gather his thoughts. "I've been talking to your mom. And she said it was okay for me to ask you this. I'd like to adopt you, officially. I know I'm not your real father, but I would like to be your legal father."

"What's happening? Is there a chance my mom could die because of these babies?" I asked.

"No. Well, yeah. Eventually, we all die. But I don't think her time is up anytime soon. That's not why I'm bringing this up now."

Rick paused again and then resumed speaking, slowly, choosing each word as if it were part of a recipe that he wanted to get perfect.

"Now just seems like the right time to tell you that I would like us all to be a family. One family. I don't ever want you to think that you're an afterthought. Because you're not. I think you're pretty amazing."

I was stunned. "Me? You think I'm amazing?"

Rick smiled. "Yeah, I do. Do you really find that so surprising? You're smart, and loyal, and you have a wicked sense of humor. And a really huge heart."

"Thanks," I mumbled, embarrassed.

"You're welcome," he said. "Listen, you don't have to answer right away. And if you decide against it, I'll still be proud to be your friend."

Rick helped me carry everything into the lobby, where Yaya Sophie was already waiting for us. Only Yaya could simultaneously pull off elegant and flamboyant. As usual, she was dressed to perfection like an elegant gypsy in swingy bolero pants, a vibrant silk blouse and chunky jewelry. Her hair, once black, now silvery gray, waved around her face in a riot of curls that she could never quite tame. She grabbed me with a surprisingly tight hug for someone her age. I sank into it, loving the smell of her familiar perfume.

Rick handed her the pot of flowers with aplomb, giving me all the credit. He kissed us each on the cheek before heading off to work.

"So beautiful! Did you put them together yourself?" Yaya said, admiring the flowers. "You always did have an unerring eye for color."

I started to deny it then stopped myself.

"Thank you. I'm sorry I haven't been here to see you much this summer," I said instead.

"Nonsense, no apologies needed," said Yaya. "I know you love me. And I am going to put these right here in the lobby so everybody can enjoy them."

She placed them on the reception desk with a smile for the secretary then grabbed my hands.

"I told everyone to gather in the community room for the show," she announced.

"'Everyone'? What do you mean?" I asked, starting to panic. "I just came to play for you, Yaya! I'm not really ready for a stage debut."

Yaya gave me a thorough once-over, which made me squirm. "You are perfect," she pronounced. "The dancing has been good for you."

It was true. All those days dancing and swimming and doing yoga— not to mention lugging bags of silica and giving piggyback rides to Robbie and Amelia—were melting away my pudge, revealing a new shape. I preened.

Then, I wondered how Yaya knew I'd been dancing. "Wait—" I started to ask.

Yaya Sophie didn't let me finish. She just gestured for me to pick up the guitar case, linked her arm in mine, and away we went. By the time we got to the community room, I was so nervous I could barely see straight. It was a large multi-purpose sort of room with a scarred black-and-white checkered linoleum floor and bland decor. Yaya and I played checkers in here sometimes. Dozens of seniors were sitting around tables, playing cards and doing puzzles. A few of the women were bent over their needlework or knitting, clucking away like hens.

Yaya Sophie let out an exasperated sigh. "This is how they prepare for a special guest performance?"

I tried to tell her that it was fine, that I would be happy to slip into a corner and play, hoping nobody even noticed me. But she was in what my mother always called "Sergeant Sophie mode," bustling around and handing down orders. In a few minutes, despite the fact that some of her soldiers needed walkers and wheelchairs, the tables had been pushed back and the chairs lined up into proper rows facing a makeshift stage. A single chair, music stand and a microphone dominated a set of risers next to the piano.

While Yaya ushered everyone into seats, I set the guitar case on the floor and opened it. I put my sheet music up on the stand. I thought I would have butterflies fluttering up a storm inside me, but instead I was calm. Happy, even. I slid the guitar strap over my head and settled onto the edge of the chair. I wasn't a pro, but the guitar felt like a friend.

I tried tuning the guitar like Nico had taught me, adjusting the knobs and strumming each individual note. I really didn't have much of an ear for it, but I got close enough. I looked up at my audience. Really looked at them. They were just people, waiting for me to entertain them.

Just as I was about to begin, the double doors clattered open and in walked Ryan followed by a familiar old man. Ike. I recognized him from the Red Cross shelter. I froze, my pick poised over the strings. Ryan hadn't seen me yet. He had his hands full with Ike.

"I don't see why we can't just put this puzzle together in my room, blast it," grumbled Ike. He came to a dead stop when he realized the room was full—and that every single face was turned in his direction.

Yaya gestured for me to wait and hurried over to the door, singing out a greeting.

"Mr. Lombard, we are so glad you could make it for the concert."

I felt a little sorry for him. He protested, of course, moving to head back to his room, but he didn't stand a chance. With a little shuffling, Aunt Sophie maneuvered him and Ryan to front row center seats. And that's when Ryan looked up and realized I was there.

The butterflies showed up then. I wasn't scared to perform. It was more about the proximity to Ryan. And those eyes of his. And the fact that I was holding his sister's guitar, and even though he had told me to keep it and learn to play it myself, I knew he hadn't really meant it. Soon it would be time to give it back.

Yaya came up next to me, adjusting my mike.

"Look for the synchronicities," she whispered in my ear. "There are no coincidences in this world."

And with that, she tipped over the mike stand, sending it crashing to the floor. She made it look like an accident, but I knew better.

Yaya looked out into the audience, directly at Ryan. "Young man, could you please come up here and help my granddaughter? You can hold the microphone for her."

I shot my grandmother an exasperated look. Now what? My simple desire to practice my guitar skills had turned into a giant production.

Without a word, Ryan walked over, took the microphone from Yaya and held it a couple feet from the guitar with a bored look.

"Sorry to be such a pain," I said, a little sarcastically. He didn't even look at me.

I opened up my book of beginner guitar songs to the one I'd been practicing with Nico.

As soon as I strummed the first chord, I felt her arrive. Ryan's sister, Evie. I couldn't see her, because I wasn't wearing the sun specs. But I could sense her presence, her warm happy glow as she heard her cherished guitar being played. I could sense Ryan felt something, too. His right hand was clenching the mike, but he was playing air guitar with his left.

"You're not quite in tune," he whispered.

I smiled. "Close enough," I said and continued on with my simple songs.

When I was done, Yaya led the crowd in a standing ovation, which meant a lot, considering how difficult it was for many of them to stand. I slipped the strap over my head, but instead of putting the guitar back in its case, I handed it to Ryan.

"Here, hold this," I said.

And like that, the guitar was back where it belonged, with Ryan.

I gave Yaya a discreet thumbs up. She didn't miss a beat.

"Oh, how wonderful," she said. "Everyone, please sit, this young man is going to play for us, too."

Ryan sat for a moment, just holding the guitar.

I was afraid that once again he was going to push it right back at me and walk off stage. "You don't have to play. But maybe you could tune it for me?"

He nodded and took the guitar pick out of my hand. Spent a few painfully long moments fiddling with the knobs, strumming and listening and adjusting. I felt Evie beaming like sunlight next to us. I realized I was holding my breath…and just when I remembered to exhale, Ryan began to play.

And, oh, how he could coax magic from that guitar. I remembered what Nico had said, about how my father had liked to learn enough about a craft to appreciate a maestro when he saw one…and Ryan was clearly a gifted musician. His fingers flew over the strings, creating complicated chords that I could appreciate even more now that I'd had a few lessons. One melody blended into another and on into the next—a melody of songs that he clearly loved and knew by heart.

I think he would have played for hours if one of the seniors hadn't succumbed to a fit of coughing. Even with that, it took a minute for Ryan to register the noise. He glanced up, a little dazed, like a space creature that wasn't quite sure how it had landed on this planet.

Music was in his blood. And being a Muse was in mine. Yaya had gotten to her feet and was leading the audience in applause so loud even folks on the top floor with their hearing aids turned off could probably hear it. As if a veil had fallen away from my eyes, I saw her clearly. I suddenly realized…being a muse didn't come to me through my mother. My father must have been the Muse, and before him, his mother. Yaya.

I had so many questions to ask her.

But they would have to wait, because next Yaya got a little old man named Floyd to play the piano. He launched into some fifties music, and pretty soon, more than a few seniors were pushing chairs out of the way to make room for rocking and rolling, twisting and shouting. Age might have slowed them down, but not even orthopedic shoes were keeping them from kicking up their heels.

Ryan pulled the guitar strap off his head and tried to give it back to me. I crossed my arms across my chest, refusing to accept it.

"Evie wants you to have it," I said. "It belongs in your family. But if I get one of my own, do you think you could give me some lessons?"

Ryan ignored my question and blurted out one of his own. "What do you mean 'Evie wants me to have it'?"

Before I could answer him, Yaya pulled us into the dance. "It's called the Stroll. Ladies on the left, and gentlemen on the right."

Two lines formed. Ike the puzzle king revealed his smooth side, as he elegantly sashayed down the center with Yaya on his arm. Before we could blink, Ryan and I were expected to strut our stuff.

"Focus on the dancing," I asked. I lifted his arm up, twirled under it, and made us look good.

Ryan followed my lead, looking a little frustrated, as we had to part and get back in our separate lines. There were more old ladies than men, and they all clucked to be paired with Ryan as the song went on and on. When it ended, he bowed to his last partner before dropping his smile and approaching me with determination. Yaya bustled over to the rescue.

"I need to sit down for a bit, Rocket dear," she said. "Would you care for a cup of tea in my apartment? Young man, you don't mind if I steal my granddaughter away, do you? I believe Mr. Lombard is eager to begin that puzzle with you."

Like Ryan ever had a choice.

As soon as we were out of his line of sight, Yaya murmured to me. "Rocket, dear, it's best if you retain a measure of mystery. Don't give away all of our trade secrets."

By the time we got to her room, Yaya's spunk had sputtered. After setting the electric kettle to boil in her compact kitchenette, she moved to a cabinet, emerging with a stack of golden journals identical to my own, just more tattered around the edges.

"I've been waiting a long time to give you these," she said, putting them into my arms. Relieved of her burden, she sank into a plush armchair and hooked herself up to a tank of oxygen. Happy to have something to focus on beside the alarming sight of my grandmother attaching tubes to her nose, I plunked down on the purple velvet chaise lounge and set the books on the coffee table in front of me.

"Your father would want you to have them," she said.

"He was the apprentice Muse," I said.

"Your father was an apprentice Muse, yes."

"I thought it was my mom," I said. "And that she'd forgotten because of the Lethe water."

Yaya smiled like she knew something I didn't. "Maybe everybody's got a little bit of muse in them."

I browsed through the journals. My father's artwork and scribbles leapt out at me, including the initial sketches for the stained glass windows in the cottage.

"I wish I were an artist like him," I said.

"Why would you want to be an artist like him, when you can be an artist like yourself instead?" she asked me.

She leaned forward and gave my nose a gentle tweak. "When Gabriel was fourteen, he wanted to be a pro-basketball player. He spent hours practicing after school, shooting and dribbling. Unfortunately, his genetics in this lifetime didn't favor height, and he didn't make the junior varsity team."

I laughed.

"He took an art class instead," she finished. "And poured all that passion for the game into something new."

"There's still an old basketball hoop hanging outside the shop," I remembered.

"Well, he didn't stop playing just because he couldn't be the best. That would be silly."

Her laugh ended in a strangled gasping sound. I rose, panicked, but she held up a hand to indicate that she had it under control. She fiddled with the tank. Closing her eyes, she focused on her breathing, until it settled back into a slow rhythm.

"Oxygen," she told me. "Not quite the same rush as godsbreath, but when your lungs are starting to give out, modern technology comes in handy for us mortals."

The kettle chirped.

"Can you do the tea for us, honey?" she asked, her eyes still closed. "Everything is already set out on the tray."

"I'm an expert tea maker now," I replied, moving into the kitchen. "I've been making tea for my mother all summer."

I scooped tea leaves into the mesh ball, dangled it into the pot, and poured in the boiling water. I peeked into the pink pastry box on the counter and was happy to see my favorite dessert nestled in white waxed paper. I set two pieces onto a china plate and added it to the tray then carried the whole thing out and set it on the coffee table, being careful not to spill on the journals.

While the tea steeped, I stood beside Yaya, petting her shoulder and looking at her collection of photos and artwork. They covered the walls from floor to ceiling, all matted and displayed in mahogany frames of various sizes.

"Your mother helped me arrange that wall when I moved in here," said Yaya.

"Rick brought that one when he visited last month," she said, pointing to a framed photo of me and my mom on her wedding day. "A very nice man, that Rick. Devoted to family."

I wondered if Rick had given Ryan the photos to replace the ones he lost in the fire. It wouldn't surprise me, I realized. We sat for a time drinking in our tea and memories, then Yaya started wheezing and put her cup down.

"It's scary when you can't catch your breath," I said.

"Sometimes," said Yaya. "But it's a small price to pay. I have certainly gotten my dollar's worth from this body of mine."

She gazed at her photos, her eyes dreamy. "I've hiked to the peaks of some of the world's highest mountains and snorkeled spectacular coral reefs. I've made love in the moonlight and let my skin drink in the sun dancing in a field of dandelions in my birthday suit."

"Yaya!" I said. "You're crazy!"

"Crazy about life," she said.

"Will you miss it when you—," I couldn't finish the sentence.

"When I die? Dying is just another doorway, honey. A threshold to the next adventure. When it's my time, I'll be ready. Maybe I'll come back as a tree or a pampered Persian cat next time around…something really peaceful for a few years. But I intend to sing and dance right up to the last second, even if I'm just shuffling buffalo from a wheelchair. You've got to love your life, Rocket. Love every single minute of it, even the ones full of pain."

"Now you head home," she told me. "I need to take a nap. Floyd and I are choreographing a flash mob dance—and we've got to practice so we're ready to break into it during bingo night next month. It's set to Viva Las Vegas. Mr. Monahan was supposed to play Elvis, but he just had a hip replacement, and I'm not sure he'll be ready. That Ike Lombard has potential, though—did you see him shaking that pelvis? "

"Um, I wasn't really looking at Mr. Lombard's pelvis, Yaya Sophie," I said.

She giggled.

"The real Elvis visited Mount Helikon a few weeks ago," I confided. "I almost played a 'Love Me Tender' Elvis medley today instead of the Beatles."

"How'd you decide?" she asked.

"I had Elvis arm-wrestle with John Lennon," I said. "John Lennon won."

"Imagine that," said Yaya with a smile. "Just imagine that."

Twenty-seven

BACK AT HOME, MY MOTHER WAS STARING OUT THE WINDOW, TWISTING THE SHEETS INTO knots with her restless hands.

"Knock, knock," I called from the doorway.

"Thank god, you're here," she announced. "I'm bored."

"Only boring people get bored," I replied. From my tote bag, I extracted the golden journals and dropped them onto the bed next to her, right on top of the latest issue of Art Glass. "Here, maybe these will un-bore you. They're dad's journals."

My mother looked shaken. She handled the first book as if it were an ancient and brittle treasure map, hesitating at a page covered with pencil sketches. I caught a brief glimpse of a horse with wings, before she caught me looking and flipped the book shut.

"Wait," I said. "Go back a page. Is that Pegasus? That was Dad's last piece, wasn't it? I read about it in an old copy of Art Glass magazine."

My mother turned back a page, fingering the sketch.

"You were the inspiration for Pegasus, did you know that? Almost as soon as you could talk, you started to make up incredible stories about your adventures with Pegasus—how you tamed him by making up songs for him. You were heartbroken when that piece sold."

"Who bought it?" I asked.

"An anonymous art collector bought it for a ridiculously high amount, and then it vanished out of sight. Funny, someone from the Getty called me about it just a few days ago. A museum curator who was a big fan of your father's has been trying to locate it, so it could be part of some show they're having. But the buyer has kept it completely under the radar."

Her voice seemed suspiciously relieved. She was still flipping through pages of the old sketchbooks. There were some really amazing ideas in there, spectacular vases with wings, a golden mosaic fountain, a bust of a Medusa with a milky white face and fiery red snakes for hair.

After a long minute, she spoke. "I have a confession. These drawings are mine. When I was pregnant with you, I had the most amazing dreams. I would wake up, on fire, and need to sketch. I almost felt possessed by it, like a madwoman. Your father would thrust the journal and pencils into my hand and then lay beside me while I sketched for hours, rubbing my belly and whispering to you. He called you our 'little Muse.' You brought him such joy."

"I wasn't even supposed to be an artist. Your grandmother scrimped and saved to send me off to learn bookkeeping, so I could come home and help her run the family sheep farm. My flatmate and I took the art workshop on a complete lark. Your father was a visiting instructor from the United States. He was much older than I was, almost fifty when we met, but I had never met anyone so alive and vibrant," she continued. "One look into his eyes, and my insides burned as hot as a crucible."

She smiled at the memory. By now, I had settled onto the edge of the bed. I couldn't help wanting to hear more.

"My parents were dead against it, but I went to California when the term ended. For a couple of years, I lived with him and worked with him. He was my mentor and I was his student, and we were in love. We didn't mean to get pregnant. It was a blessing, but it was also a struggle. I was so—" She hesitated, as if there were more to say.

She touched the tip of my nose. "When you were born, I stopped going to the studio. I was so absorbed in mommying you. But when you were about three, Gabriel gave me this book and said it was time to get back on the horse. He insisted that I start working again. I was so out of practice, such a novice, I was too embarrassed to work in the shop during the day. But Gabriel told me I had been given a gift, a talent that I needed to share with the world. We had the most wonderful time. We brought a little playpen into the studio, and you slept or babbled in the corner while we worked all night in secret. None of the other glassworkers who shared the studio knew what we were up to, although I think Nico suspected."

"Probably," I said.

"Gabriel just told them he was working on a special project. In reality, persuading me back into the studio, teaching me all he had learned about the art of glassblowing—that was his legacy to me. To us."

"Why did he do it?" I asked.

She looked across the room at the wall for a moment, as if trying to find the right words.

"Oh honey, years of wondering why never made it any clearer. Was it something I did? Something I didn't do? He had his down moments, but we all do. I just, I never thought…"

She trailed off into sadness deep and thick as a murky pond, then she took a breath and looked me straight in the eyes.

"He loved us, Rocket. He loved us the best he could, for as long as he could. I know that. I finally decided that he was here on this earth for exactly how long he needed to be. That was his path. I'm grateful our paths intersected, but eventually, I had to lay him to rest and start walking forward on my own. "

I was done talking about it for now, so I pointed to the sketches in front of her. "Why didn't you make any of these?"

"I forgot all about these until you showed me the books! I suppose I was sad and angry and didn't have the luxury of art for art's sake after your father's death. I had to make things to sell, to keep us afloat."

She tugged the ends of my hair. "I had some good people around me, like Nico and Megan and Bethie. And you, as little as you were, you kept me going, love. We got each other through it. We survived. Maybe this time around, I'll be one of those proper mothers who remembers to show up with cupcakes for the school bake sale."

"Umm, Mom? No offense, but that's not necessarily a good thing. You burn everything you bake."

"Three hundred and fifty degrees just doesn't seem hot enough when you're used to a crucible."

"Let Rick make his killer peanut butter chocolate chip cookies. You make art. Maybe you forgot me at school once in awhile, but the extra time in the library didn't kill me."

"You're the one cupcake I made just right." She ruffled my hair. "For nine years, I've been making tchotchkes for tourists. Even if I had the time, I doubt I could build these on my own."

Her eyes lingered on the sketch of Medusa. She started musing out loud to herself, feeling around the edges of the hook I'd extended. "Of course, Nico's become very skilled technically, as advanced as your father. If I widened the neck a little here…"

She trailed off, fumbled on the side table with her left hand for a pen.

I pulled a set of colored pencils out of my bag, and she seized them, eager to get down the ideas. I slipped my sunspecs on and took a peek. Yep, her spark had flared up into a nice blaze, red tendrils radiating energetically out into the air around her, as alive as Medusa's slithering snakes. I pulled out my own journal and doodled beside her.

Later that night at Muse School, I practically skipped down the dark trail from the mirror to the meadow. I felt like Charlie when he found a golden ticket in his Wonka Bar. I had inspired someone. Two someones. Ryan had played his guitar again because of me. My mother was back on track to being the artist she was meant to be. I could do this apprentice Muse thing. I danced with the Muses, feeling the power flowing from the crown of my head and into my feet, which felt like they had little wings on them. Brigit, Magdalena and Dani were there, too, and I grabbed their hands and led them whirling and twirling through the meadow for hours that seemed like minutes.

Eventually, we ran out of fizz and found a quiet patch of grass where we could rest. Brigit and Dani went off to the banquet table to get goblets of punch for us to drink. Magdalena, looking exhausted and drawn out, laid down on a chaise lounge.

"Are you okay?" I asked her, concerned.

"Please. This is a place for joy and peace, where I can lay down my troubles and not speak of them. Please."

I fought the urge to pry and picked up a lyre. There were always musical instruments at hand in Mount Helikon, and the Muses encouraged us to use them whenever we felt like it. I began to strum it, enjoying its similarity to the guitar, noting the different qualities of sound that it produced.

Erato flopped down beside us. Well, not exactly flopped. Even in their most casual moments, the Muses moved like ballerinas.

"Are you composing a song?" she asked, in a tone of happy anticipation.

"No, just experimenting."

"I just finished a poem. The title is 'Light is a Feather'," said Erato, beaming. This was nothing new. The Muses were always creating something, spinning out a song or a painting. Erato's specialty was love poetry, and I had heard oodles of her sonnets and haiku. "You strum along while I give it to you."

She stood up and struck a dramatic pose, then recited from memory.

"Light is a Feather"

She looked at me. I hastily strummed a dramatic riff on the lyre.

Satisfied, she continued her recitation, while I improvised along with her words.

"Behind beauty
the same sorrows
the same spirit
the same shifting clouds of confusion

a starving man
shoots an arrow
its straight shaft wings up
it has a point, it is designed
to lodge in soft flesh
it clips feathers
scatters flight
finds its way
into the heart of a white swan

he searches for the fallen
but only finds a feather
in the cranberry bog

he told me he loved me
he told me that evolution
is not survival of the fittest, it is merely
a flow into the path of least resistance

but I have evolved
into a creature who can fly
even after her heart is pierced

through and through again
by wood and words
who can trumpet her song
even after his arrow and gaze
are withdrawn, blood-tipped."

She let the words drift into silence before sinking into an elegant curtsey.

"Beautiful. You're so good at reciting, too," I said. "Must be nice having the Goddess of Memory as your mother."

Erato laughed. "Actually, I have a terrible memory. Erratic, you might say. I've been practicing this poem down by the reflecting pool for three days straight. And I confess, I might have taken a sip or two of Hippocrene spring water to keep my spirits up. What did you think of the poem? Be honest—but remember the first rule of critiquing a tender-hearted poet."

"'We will admire what is admirable'?" I said.

"You memorized that perfectly," she said, smiling. "The poet who coined the phrase would be proud to know you."

She settled back onto a pile of silk cushions and waited for my comments.

"I thought it was beautiful, especially the image of the swan flying away with a pierced heart. But it's so sad. I thought you celebrated love in your poetry," I said.

"Did someone say 'love'?"

A gorgeous goddess paused near us. She was Aphrodite, and she was as blindingly radiant as her portrait in my mythology book.

Erato squealed and hugged her. "Rocket was surprised that my love poem was more on the tragic side of things."

Aphrodite laughed. "All of love's faces have the ability to inspire, not just the tender blush of a first kiss. The green stinging jealousy, the fiery passion, a mother's affection—these are all fruit for the poet to harvest."

Erato looked with pity toward Magdalena, who had curled up on her side and fallen fast asleep, her capable-looking hands tucked under her chin like a child's. "Even the cold mask of betrayal and love's tragic death can inspire."

Aphrodite sighed, extending her silk-draped arms like lovely wings.

Spinning in a slow circle, she exhaled with a loud mmmmmm and wrapped herself in a hug.

Gazing up at the bright stars, she spoke to the sky. "I love being in love. Not just with men or gods, you know, but with everything. Ocean breezes, babies, chocolate, trees, kittens."

Erato jumped up with her and the two of them spun in a circle together. "Oh, and words," said Erato. "I'm especially in love with words, aren't you?"

Brigit and Dani returned at that moment, breathless and laughing, with full goblets.

"Did somebody say 'love'?" asked Brigit in a teasing voice. "Because Dani here just confessed she has her heart set on a boy back home."

"Brigit, hush," Dani said, with an embarrassed look on her usually composed face. "It's nothing. We've only kissed once."

Polyhymnia had drifted in behind them, holding an extra goblet, which she handed to me with a smile. "It's honeyed mead tonight."

"Ah, love is never nothing," said Erato, taking the other glass from Polly's hand and raising it high. "It's the most powerful creative force in the universe. Raise your glasses, my dears, to the intoxicating power of a first kiss. May you have scores of them, each as perfect as the shell-pink blush of sunrise. And someday, but only when you are ripe for it, may those kisses deepen into full radiance and shine you right into the lush-plum midnight of your mortal lives."

Polyhymnia wafted her hand in the air, and a full goblet appeared in it. She spoke next. "And when love flies away, may your parting always be kind and gentle, because love is a blessing, requited or not."

We sipped our mead again, and then I seized my opportunity.

"I have another toast," I said, trying to tamp down my enthusiasm. "I want to toast to inspiring my first client."

Brigit and Dani immediately clinked glasses with me. "Oh, Rocket, that's amazing! How did you figure out who your first client was?" said Brigit.

"And how did you do it? Inspire them?" asked Dani, a little enviously. "I don't even know where to start. I'm going to be a novice apprentice forever."

Erato gave Polly a shake of the head.

"Rocket, let's take a walk, shall we?" suggested Polly, in a very gentle voice. I nodded. Brigit gave me a hug.

I launched into an explanation as soon as we were out of earshot. "I know that probably wasn't the right time to break the news, but I did it! I understand everything now!"

"What is it that you understand?" she asked.

"Well, I learned that my dad was the Muse in my family, not my mother. And I got Ryan to play the guitar again. So I did it, I inspired him!"

"Yes, that is probably true. However, Ryan was not the client assigned to you."

"He's not? Was it my mother, after all? Well, I inspired her, too! She's sketching in her sketchbook again!"

"I'm sorry, Rocket. It's not your mother."

I was so frustrated I couldn't hold myself back. "If you want me to succeed, why don't you just tell me what I'm supposed to do and how I'm supposed to do it?"

"I wish I could, but that's not the way it works," she said, in a voice meant to comfort.

"I wouldn't exactly say this is working so well either! And now I look like an idiot for bragging."

"Great things take time, Rocket," she said. "Be gentle with yourself. If it's any consolation, you're getting warmer."

I didn't feel soothed by her words. I felt angry. If nobody would tell me the rules of the game, how was I ever going to win it?

Twenty-eight

THE NEXT FEW WEEKS PASSED IN A BLUR OF BABYSITTING. AMELIA AND ROBBIE WEREN'T THE ONLY ones demanding my attention. Bed rest was making my mother crazy.

In an attempt to distract her, Rick had coaxed me and my mom into playing cards. I was sitting cross-legged on the bed by her feet slowly getting the hang of Texas Hold'Em.

"Full house!" I said, laying down a pair of aces.

The doorbell rang.

"Indeed," said Rick. "And it looks like the house is about to get even fuller, kind of like your mom's belly."

I popped out a fist. "Rochambeau."

His rock lost out to my paper, and I waved him off to get the door.

"Tell them there's no womb at the inn," my mom quipped. As soon as he was out of sight, my mom pulled a salt shaker from her nightstand drawer and started to shake some onto the bowl of popcorn next to her. I snatched it out of her hand.

"The doctor said NO salt!" I told her.

"Look who's here!" Rick called as he came back down the hallway. Megan, Gillian's mother, poked her head around the partially opened door. Gillian was hanging back behind her. I looked at my mom, wondering if she had masterminded this reunion, too, but she just gave me an innocent look.

"Knock-knock," said Megan. "Remember me, your long-lost neighbor and best friend?"

"Rick is training us to become card sharks," my mother told her by way of a greeting. "Pull up a chair."

"Oh. Well, we don't want to intrude on your family time," said Megan, uncharacteristically shy.

"Don't be silly," my mom said. "You *are* family."

Megan sat down on the bed right next to my mom, gave her a hug, then reached down and rubbed her enormous belly. They leaned into each other, heads touching, like sisters.

Ka-boom. My heart skidded a bit. It was true. Gillian was like my sister. I missed her. But I still didn't know how to get us back on track.

"Learning to play poker was one of the ideas we stuck in the Boredom Buster Box last year, wasn't it?" said Gillian, attempting to make conversation.

I didn't respond. Hope and anger dueled inside my stomach. I felt like I was going to throw up, afraid lava would spew out of me if I tried to answer a simple question.

Rick pulled a couple of chairs up beside the bed, and gestured for Gillian and her mom to sit. "Come on, I'll show you how to do a bridge," he said.

He shuffled the cards, and dealt us all in, but I didn't take the cards laid in front of me. I just sat there, feeling stupid and slow and stuck as the others picked their cards up and began arranging them. Rick was giving Gillian and Megan instructions, I think, but the chatter seemed unintelligible to me, like they were talking in a foreign language. Our friendship seemed so far away.

I ran out of the room, down the hall, and flung myself onto my bed. Moo jumped up beside me and butted his head against my hand, nudging me to pet him. When I ignored him, he settled a few feet away and began grooming his tail. There was a knock at the door. I ignored that, too.

"Go away, whoever it is!"

"I come bearing chocolate," Gillian said, waving a white paper bag through the door like a flag of surrender.

"Brownies?" I asked.

"Nope. Better," said Gillian. "Chocolate pecan turtles from Whipley's."

I groaned. "You may enter."

I peeked down and saw Gillian's huarache sandals and brown legs. She picked up something off my desk.

"Cool do on the BBB box. The monkeys are a nice touch. Remember that time we went to the zoo and got the howler monkeys all riled up?" she said.

"I feel like I have a head full of howler monkeys right now."

"I'm sorry you had to go it alone this summer," she said, opening the bar of chocolate and breaking off a piece. "Josie is going to take a nap. My mom's going to run a few errands for her. So—do you want me to leave or to stay here with you?"

I took the piece of chocolate in her outstretched hand. And she stayed. We spent all day talking, talking while we were sitting in my room, talking while we raided the fridge for Rosa's leftover enchiladas, talking while we floated in the pool, talking as we hiked around the hills. It was kind of like old times, but different. We were different.

She stayed that night, too. The first sleepover since I'd moved. I loaned her a pair of flannel pajamas. She picked up Moo and cuddled him, looking around my room while she got him purring like a race-car engine.

"Still living with white walls, huh?" she commented.

"I'm ready for color," I said. "I just don't know where to start."

"I'm seeing blue paint, maybe? And maybe silvery curtains? You know, Carina's really good with that stuff." There was a wistful tone in Gillian's voice, like she missed Carina.

I tried not to take it personally, but I could feel the brittle, almost bitter edge welling up in me. "So you two have no doubt been living the high life this summer? Swanking it up in Newport Beach and Beverly Hills?"

"Actually, things got kind of weird after the big all-state debate at the end of June. You weren't there."

I wondered if she had a bitter edge of her own. "I wanted to go, but..." I trailed off, not sure what to say.

"I'm not mad. Honestly, I'm glad you didn't witness it. It was a total disaster. Utter humiliation." Gillian shuddered at the memory. "I don't know if I can ever compete in debate again."

"What happened?" I asked, curious. Gillian was usually so confident, but I could see how shaken she was.

"I don't really understand it myself. All I know is that I couldn't come up with any counter-arguments. I just kept repeating what the opposing team said, over and over. It was like I had lost control of my tongue and all I could do was echo." She mocked herself, pitching her voice as it resonated. "Echo, echo, echo."

Echo. Suddenly the dots connected. Carina's weird mood swings, almost like a split personality. The eerie way her face had changed the night of the beach party. The way she repeated everything I said. That shadow I had seen within her.

"Was Carina there? At the debate?" I asked, urgently.

"She had a front-row seat," replied Gillian. "The next day my mom put me on a plane to Houston to spend time with my dad. Why?"

"No reason," I hedged. "We should probably get some sleep now."

I turned off the lamp.

"I've missed you, Rocket," Gillian confided. "You always made me feel like I could do anything."

"Me?" I said in surprise.

"Yes, you. You're going to be a great big sister," she said.

I smiled in the dark. "Thanks."

"I miss doing all the stuff in the Boredom Buster Box," she went on. "Lately, all Carina wants to do is show off her designer clothes and play Rock Gods, over and over and over. She's obsessed. I mean, it's fun, but not for eight hours a day. Get a life, right? You know that friend of yours, Ryan, the one in your cottage? He's just as addicted as she is. Once she got her hooks into him a couple weeks ago, she didn't really care if I was there or not. They spent all day and night at your cottage playing it last weekend."

Ryan was playing virtual guitar eight hours a day? No, no, no! What happened to the real thing?

As soon as Gillian drifted off to sleep, I projected myself toward Carina to do a little spying. Whizzing and whirring, my body entered the psychedelic blur of the astral plane…and got stuck there. I chugged around, feeling like my spirit was stuck in a vast swirling vat of rainbow sludge. I had never been to her house. How to get to Carina without a sensory map? Of course! I could start with the limo, which I had been inside, and which I remembered clearly.

I focused on the limo—the crystal bottles, the buttery leather seats, the tinted windows. Flash. I was there. Only I was in the dark. Inside a garage. I got out of there in a hurry, floating around a bit to survey my surroundings.

Carina lived in a spectacular mansion that rivaled the Getty in size and location, set on a grassy bluff overlooking the Pacific with a staircase leading down to the beach. The garage alone was bigger than our Venice Beach cottage, two stories high and set apart from the main house by a giant circular driveway with an elaborate fountain at the center. I floated through the front door, surveying the interior, which seemed like something out of a movie set—a modern day palace. But it seemed empty and cold. Only one room in the house was occupied, a bedroom so dark it seemed more like a bat cave.

Suffocatingly heavy drapes covered the windows from floor to ceiling. I had to concentrate completely to make out the gaunt old man sleeping in a giant bed, lost among his silk sheets and luxurious linens. He reminded me of Amelia, the first time I had seen her, all tucked in and dreaming. This man was snoring like a sad gorilla with a killer head cold. No way was this Carina's father, a grandfather, maybe?

I was about to try another room when something caught my eye in an alcove adjoining the bedroom. Moonlight spilled through a skylight, bathing a sculpture in unearthly light. It was a figure of a young Pegasus mounted on a simple green marble pedestal. The detailing was exquisite, capturing coltish awkwardness while hinting at the grace and power Pegasus had now. On his back was a little girl, clinging to his mane, her head tipped back in laughter and joy, her hair streaming in the wind.

At first, I thought the statuette was carved from white marble. When I moved in for a closer look and realized that it was crafted from opaque white glass, my heart started beating faster. Thumpity-thump-thump. Could it be my father's last sculpture? I examined it from every angle, looking for my father's distinctive mark. The old man gurgled in his sleep, then rattled out a loud wheeze of air. For a moment, I thought he would stop breathing altogether, but with a jerk, he inhaled noisily. I remembered my mission. The Pegasus sculpture would have to wait for another time. But before I continued my search, I took a few minutes to breathe a little life into that dark room.

Leaning down close to the old man's head, I whispered into his dreams. "It's so stuffy in here! Tomorrow, open the windows and breathe in some sunshine. Go stroll on the beach and feel the salt on your skin."

He smiled a little in his sleep, and his face softened. He looked younger, and I wondered if he was dreaming the dreams of his boyhood. Touching his forehead, I let myself tune in with him for a moment. *A girl he loved. A white horse. A bouquet of daisies with golden centers. Petals pulled off one by one. She loved him. She loved him not. A fist of crushed petals pounding again and again against a stone wall.*

His smile twisted into a grimace, and he moaned in his sleep, clenching the bedcovers. I remembered Polyhymnia's lesson by the river. Gently, I touched his wrinkled knuckles, blanched gray in the grip of remembered pain. I blew softly across his forehead, scattering the petals into the ether creating space for new dreams.

Lights were on in one of the windows in the second story of the enormous garage. Hmmm. I drifted back that way, and I found Carina. She was in a small room, hunched over a sewing machine. Her hair was greasy and limp, her eyes shot through with red. Either she had joined the ranks of the undead or hadn't slept in weeks.

Who's having a bad hair day now?

Photos of designer clothes, ripped from fashion magazines, covered every inch of wall and even the ceiling. The closet door was open, and it was stuffed to overflowing with expensive-looking clothes. The bed, too, spilled over with fabric. Carina top-stitched the pocket on a gorgeous jacket, then pulled it off the machine, inspecting the work with glazed eyes. It looked flawless to me. She took a label from a little box on her desk. Misanthrope, the boutique on Beverly Hills. With a needle and thread, she stitched it inside the collar. She hung the jacket up in her closet then walked over to her photos and marked an "X" across one— an advertising spread featuring some celebrity supermodel wearing an exact replica of the jacket. Actually, I guess the one in the photo was the original. And Carina/Echo was making counterfeits.

Carina looked at the next photo and shambled over to a shelf heaped with fabric. While pulling down a bolt from the shelf, she tipped over her sewing machine and sent it careening to the floor.

'That'll wake up the neighborhood,' I thought to myself. Sure enough, within moments, James the chauffeur burst into the room. In plaid pajamas.

"Carina, sweetheart, are you okay?" he exclaimed. She didn't respond, just picked up the sewing machine and set it back on the table. He grabbed her hands, which were pricked raw and red from too many hours stitching.

"Carina, this has got to stop! Look at you, you're making yourself sick. You're killing yourself with this nonsense. You've already made more clothes than one girl could wear in a lifetime. This whole thing has gone too far."

She pulled her hands away and began re-threading the bobbin, as if she were a robot.

"Why can't you see that you're beautiful without these fancy clothes? I never should have let you pretend we're rich," he said, bitterly. "It seemed like a harmless idea at the time, but I should have known better."

Rocket gasped. I had just been joking about the chauffer being her dad. But it was true.

"And why do you just keep copying these, when you used to have such amazing ideas of your own?" he asked, pointing to the glossy pages torn from magazines. "Like these." He ripped pictures from the wall, exposing another layer—original sketches with Carina's stylish signature in the corner.

Something sparked and glimmered in Carina. 'Yes,' I thought, 'yes.' I moved in closer to her and blew gently on the spark I could see, watched it catch fire and blossom into tendrils of hopeful hot pink. But before it could become a sustained flame, shadow swirled in like a black storm cloud until the light was extinguished. Like a marionette, Carina dropped her father's gaze and returned to her sewing machine. With an exhausted sigh, Carina's dad slumped out of the room, shutting the door behind him not with a slam but with a careful, quiet click that just about broke my heart.

The shadow turned on me next. My astral self recoiled at the waves of pain and frustration, sucking me under like a riptide. It felt something like the sorrow I had felt that one night with Ryan, but bigger. A deep dark well that couldn't be filled no matter how many lights it sucked out of others.

"Echo?" I said, tentatively. The answer came back to me in a loud and clear hiss through Carina's rosebud lips.

"Echo, echo, echo," she raged. "Echo, echo, echo."

I took a deep breath. I could do this. "Get out of Carina, right now!" I demanded in a firm voice. "Do you hear me? Get OUT!"

My anger rebounded on me.

"Out! Out! Out!" screamed Echo, her features contorting into a mask of anger and hate. Carina had disappeared entirely, consumed by a witch. No—a Fury. Echo reached for a pair of scissors on the sewing table and came at me with them, thrusting with all her might into the heart of me. Although the Muses had explained that my astral body could not truly be harmed by objects in the physical plane, Echo's intention was so clear I felt the wounds as if they were real.

My survival instincts kicked in strong. I fled at the speed of light, hurling my spirit into the familiar safety of my physical body. Gillian was sound asleep in a nest of comforters she'd created on the floor, Moo curled into the crook of her knees. When he saw me, he stretched languidly then jumped up on the bed, climbing into my lap and purring in his reassuring way. I clutched him close and huddled under the blankets, shivering.

Combating a crazy, vengeful immortal was not something I'd learned in Inspiration 101. I had some ideas, but I'd need help from the Muses to put them into action. As much as I wanted to stay under the bed and sleep until noon like a regular teen, I needed that help now.

TWENTY-NINE

IT WAS CLOSE TO MIDNIGHT WHEN I STEPPED THROUGH THE MIRROR AT HOME, BUT I LEFT night and starlight behind me. Here on Mount Helikon, it was a gloriously warm afternoon.

I found the sisters gathered on a hillside not far from the meadow. An artist had his easel and canvas set up in front of Apollo's Temple. Calliope and Urania, looking particularly glamorous, were posing for a portrait, while six other sisters fluttered around offering advice.

Polyhymnia was nowhere in sight. I stood back, waiting for an opportunity to interrupt.

"If I might make a suggestion, Monsieur Vouet? Urania is the Muse of Astronomy," said Euterpe in a bossy trill. "Perhaps you might have her lean against a large brass globe?"

"Urania needs a diadem!" said Clio. She pulled a tiara out of the folds of her robes and positioned it carefully on Urania's elaborately curled up-do. "This one, with the silver stars, will be just the thing with that celestial blue satin gown."

Polyhymnia came bustling up, holding Calliope's golden tablet over her head, looking quite pleased with herself.

"I found it up by the stream," she said, all out of breath and flustered. "In that little copse of birch trees. You simply must hold this in the portrait!"

"Yes, yes!" said Calliope, taking it with a look of gratitude. "I shall inscribe the title of Homer's new book on the front. Won't he be pleased?"

"*C'est magnifique!*" said the artist, beaming at them all. "*Merci, merci.* But it needs something more…a background setting…and something in the corner, there up to the right of Calliope…"

"Putti," said Thalia, with a decisive nod. "Sweet little angels carrying laurel wreaths as a tribute to Apollo."

"Genius, Thalia!" agreed Urania. "He will adore it."

Just then Urania turned her head and caught sight of me hovering behind the painter.

"Rocket, is that you?" she said. "What's troubling you, young sister?"

"Don't move! Keep your head just so! Calliope, gaze at Urania!" he commanded, furiously sketching with a pencil on his canvas and muttering to himself. "Yes! That's perfect, yes, yes."

While Urania and Calliope held the pose, Polly and the other Muses flew to me like moths to a candle.

"It's Echo," I told them. "She's got her hooks into Carina somehow, like she's possessed her body. She damps out the creative sparks of anyone who gets close to her. If we don't stop her, she could go global."

"Echo? Are you sure?" asked Clio.

"Positive," I said.

"But what would drive a mountain nymph to do such a thing?" asked Polly in dismay.

"Well, for one thing, she's in love with Narcissus, and he rejected her," I told them. "He found her incredibly annoying, because Echo kept repeating everything he said."

"Why would she do that?" asked Urania, bewildered.

"I looked it up," I said grimly. "Zeus' wife Hera took away Echo's ability to speak."

"Why?" asked Polly, furrowing her forehead in dismay.

"Out of anger and revenge," I explained. "Zeus enlisted Echo to gossip endlessly to Hera and distract her with mindless chatter, so Hera wouldn't notice him philandering with other goddesses. Hera discovered the deception and punished Echo by taking away her voice."

"But Hera is a protectress of women," protested Thalia. "Surely, she wouldn't do such a thing!"

"Rocket is correct," said Calliope, being careful not to move her head and incur the wrath of the artist hard at work capturing her likeness on canvas. "Now Echo is forever powerless to speak her own truth. All she can do is repeat what she hears others say."

"The poor thing," sighed Erato. She strummed a few sad chords on her lyre, a tear coursing down her cheek. "Unrequited love is the most tragic thing in the universe."

"Tragedy wears many disguises, Erato," said Melpomene in a dramatic voice. She waved her solemn mask theatrically in the air and accidentally dislodged her pet fruit bat from his hiding place within the folds of her toga. The poor creature flapped his gangly leathery wings for balance, his eyes glistening with tears as he was exposed to the light. Seeking sanctuary, he hooked his claws onto Erato's gold tasseled belt and began climbing up her, upside down. She shrieked and hopped about, trying to shake him off.

Thalia burst into giggles so infectious that we were all soon laughing with her.

"Erato, stand still. You're terrifying the poor creature," said Clio, calmly plucking the panicked bat off Erato's gown and transferring it to Melpomene with a gentle smile. "And Melpomene, now is not the time for a monologue. Rocket is in trouble, and it sounds as if her friend Carina needs our help, too."

At that moment, Monsieur Vouet stood back from his sketch with a look of satisfaction. "And now I must wake up from this delightful dream and get to work in my studio. Thank you, my lovely Muses, for your sweet inspiration. I shall return soon."

He looked at me. "Do what you must to help this poor nymph. I, too, would become a monster, if I could not be original. That is the true tragedy here, if you ask a humble painter."

Poof. He vanished, along with his easel and paints.

Urania and Calliope set down their props. Released from their pose, the putti began fluttering around the stone pillars in a merry game of hide and seek, giggling and shrieking.

Polly shooed them away with a smile, and the Muses finally focused their attention entirely on the Echo emergency.

"Why would Echo possess one of your classmates?" Polly asked. "And how?"

"I don't know, maybe she followed Narcissus when he was delivering the mirror, and she thinks he likes me?" I said.

Polly gave me a concerned look. "Oh, dear, please tell me that Narcissus hasn't been trying to seduce you."

"What? No! We're totally just friends!" I exclaimed, surprised that she would even think it a possibility.

She continued fretting. "As your godmother, I suppose I should be protecting you from that sort of thing. We immortals tend to get swept away by our passions, you know."

Erato sighed dreamily. "Oh, yes, we do. Isn't it wonderful?"

Calliope was the next one to get all googly-eyed. "Oh, do you remember when I wed King Oeagrus? There was a man among men."

"He certainly was a fitting mate for a Muse, sister," agreed Thalia. "To father a son like Orpheus!"

Like dominoes, the Muses fell into happy reminiscing about their many love affairs. So much for focus.

"Oh my god," I said, exasperated. "The nine of you look like you're about to board bubble boats and float into the magical, mystical River of Love. Any second now, somebody is going to burst into song, dance or an improvised sonnet."

"Oh, yes, please!" said Erato, clapping her hands and jumping up and down on her toes like she was four years old. "I adore the image of love bubbles, floating down the river. It's breathtaking."

"Earth to Erato!" I was practically shouting now. "We've got to stop Miss Crazypants from taking over the material world. She's spreading like a highly contagious virus."

"A DIS-ease," agreed Urania, nodding. "Exactly the opposite of what we Muses want to see happening in the earthly realm. This is serious. Sisters, please, listen to Rocket. I believe she can fix this."

I looked at her in wonder. "You do?"

She nodded. "Oh yes. I have observed you breathe up the most magnificent ideas, Rocket. You're a natural Muse. And when you unite your ideas with action, you are simply unstoppable."

I paused, savoring the unexpected praise. And then I told the Muses my brilliant plan, at least the parts of it I had figured out so far.

There was silence when I finished. The Muses looked at each other, for a few moments. Calliope took a deep breath and was the first to speak.

"I suppose it could work. And, well, this undertaking is fodder for a brilliant epic poem, Rocket. You are very brave," she said, patting me on the shoulder.

Melpomene agreed. "It's true. Even if you don't succeed, your tragic demise at the hands of a jealous nymph—"

"Or an angry God," interjected Euterpe. "You know, Zeus is not going to like her plan one bit."

"Very true," Melpomene agreed. "Either way, your untimely death will provide source material for a truly heartrending three-act play. Brava, Rocket."

"Umm, that's not exactly the reassurance I was hoping for," I said.

"You realize, of course, that until you convince Echo to detach from Carina's body and lure her back to the astral plane, we can't help you," Urania observed, in her practical way. "This is a unique situation. With her current embodiment, I'm not sure what havoc she's capable of wreaking. She seems quite determined."

Remembering Echo's rage, I winced. "I know."

I turned to Polly. "The competition is just a few days away, so I don't have much time to prepare. That's why it's very, very important that you meet me at the Hall of Muses to help me complete my secret weapon when I send you the signal."

Polly nodded. "I've got your neck."

I looked at her in confusion. "'You've got my neck?"

"That's what they say in all those buddy cop movies," she said. "Such fun!"

"I think you mean 'back,'" I told her. "I've got your back."

"That doesn't make sense. Everyone knows the neck is the most vulnerable spot on the body," she said, tilting her head to one side and exposing her lovely bare throat. "Predators always go right here. In fact, jaguars—"

I cut her off. "About the rendezvous…it's going to be tough for me to get there. And I'm not sure how much time I'll have. Promise me you won't get distracted."

"Me? Distracted?" she said innocently.

"You're always wandering off to write a song or stare at clouds or sit under a willow tree to daydream," I pointed out.

"Daydreams are not distractions," she replied indignantly. "You should know by now that dreaming is in our job description! I am quite capable of staying on task if it's essential. Mortals just don't always understand what essential looks like."

"This is essential," I told her. "Critical. A priority."

"Then I will be there," she reassured me, and with that, I had to be satisfied.

As I prepared to leave Mount Helikon, I found myself thinking about Pegasus. Somehow, deep inside me, I knew that he was one of the keys to unlock this whole mess.

I found him grazing in his usual meadow. He looked up at me and tossed his mane by way of greeting but didn't come toward me.

"Hey, Pegasus, how are you this morning? I saw the most amazing sculpture of you," I told him. "I think my father might have made it."

He nickered a little, which sounded a lot like yes to my ears.

"I think I figured something out. You don't want me to sing a song you already know. You only like original music. And it has to be from the heart."

He nickered again, looking gently into my eyes. I knew that I was right.

"I'm not a songwriter, but I want to try. The perfect words haven't come to me yet. Someday, something amazing will just drop down from above, I hope. Melpomene and Calliope seem to think this battle with Echo could be good source material. If I survive, maybe I'll write a song about that. "

Pegasus pawed at the ground with a powerful hoof, scraping aside a big rock. Water gushed out and into the air like the geyser Old Faithful, and showered down upon me, cold and clean.

"Hey!" I said, jumping back.

Pegasus whinnied, and tilted his head up to receive some of the water in his mouth. I did the same, gulping mouthfuls of the sweet water and letting it rain down all over my face, laughing and suddenly, totally, completely carefree. We danced around in the spray and jumped in the puddles, until my white toga and his gleaming coat were drenched and spattered with mud. Pegasus stood still and let the water bathe him clean. He hooved the stone back over the secret font and shook off like a wet dog.

"Good-bye, my friend," I shouted, as he spread his magnificent wings. "I hope you will fly back to me when I write that song for you!"

In response, Pegasus dipped and swooped his wings so close to me he almost lifted me off my feet. As he pivoted and flew away, droplets of water cascaded off his tail, catching the sun, casting a rainbow in the air between us.

Thirty

WHEN I DRIFTED THROUGH THE MIRROR, THE FIRST THING I SAW WAS GILLIAN LEANING over my bed, trying to shake my inert body awake. "Yo, Rocket, are you in there? Wow, you're like a teenage zombie."

I dove my spirit into my sleeping form, just as Gillian scooped Moo off the foot of my bed and dropped him onto my stomach.

"Yeooowww," I screamed, as Moo's claws dug in right through my t-shirt. "Corpus crappy! What did you do that for?"

"Time to get up," she said. "I'm starving."

Over breakfast, Gillian harped on what a sound sleeper I'd become. "I was practically shouting at you, but you didn't even twitch! I actually had to check your pulse and breathing, just to make sure you weren't dead!"

What could I tell her without getting sent off to a nut farm, I wondered? "I was up late last night, worrying about Carina and Ryan."

Gillian nodded. "I'm worried about them, too. Carina used to be nice, but seriously, it's like she's been possessed by demons or something lately."

Yeah, *just* like that, I thought.

When Gillian's mom came to pick her up, I told my parents I'd arranged to work at the hot shop an extra day and bummed a ride to Venice Beach. It was time to move my plan from the ever-blue skies of Mount Helikon into the physical world.

All summer, Nico had been offering to show me how to blow glass. Now, I was ready, I was motivated…and I was terrified. I trusted Nico. He'd instruct me without getting on my case or hovering, just like he'd taught me to play guitar. I wasn't sure I could trust myself, though. I went into the cabinet to find the jar holding the fragments of my original atomizer bottle, pulled it down, and walked over to Nico. I could tell he knew exactly what I was asking when I held the jar up, but I said the words out loud anyway.

"I need to make that new bottle now, but I'm going to need a lot of help," I told him. "I don't think I inherited the glassblowing gene from my parents, you know? And my lungs…my asthma might be a problem…" I trailed off.

Nico held me with that steady gaze of his. "It's just fear."

He fished around in the supply closet and handed me a work apron and a pair of safety goggles.

"Are these so I don't lose an eye?" I slipped the goggles over my head and adjusted them to fit my face. "Fear. Can't go under it, can't go around it, have to go through it."

"Rocket, cara mia, there aren't a lot of accidents in a properly run hot shop," Nico reassured me. "This is a properly run hot shop. Glass doesn't jump at you. And as long as you are mindful, especially when you touch anything metal like the rods or the marver, you aren't going to get burned."

"How long will it take to make a bottle?" I asked.

"We'll start with paperweights and once you've mastered those, we'll use a blowing rod," he told me. "How long it takes is up to you. A few weeks, maybe two months."

"I need it this weekend," I told him.

"Ah. Well, then, we'd better get started right away," he said, as calm as ever.

I knew the name and purpose of every tool, because I had assisted Nico in a million little ways, and I'd watched glassblowing my whole life. My hands didn't seem to care about that though, and I kept fumbling. Rotating the rod with my left hand while wielding calipers to shape the glass with my right was really tricky—the two sides of my brain struggled to play nice. The molten glass kept drooping and hardening into a lopsided blob, which meant trip after trip to the blazing hot glory hole to reheat it to a pliable state.

"Pretend you're playing the guitar," said Nico, when I burst into tears after failing for the eighth time.

"Maybe I should just have you make the bottle for me," I said, defeated. Nico ignored me and switched on the boombox to my Beatles playlist.

Listening to the music calmed my rattled nerves and allowed me to find a rhythm. I tried again, and boom. This time worked. A clear glass paperweight.

"Now can I do a bottle?" I said, after Nico helped me tap my somewhat-mangled masterpiece off the end of the rod and catch it in Kevlar mitts.

Nico shook his head. "Another paperweight, but this time you will add color between gathers. Pick out some frit."

"What colors should I use?" I asked.

"That's up to you. Why don't you do what you did when you were little? Think of the story you want to tell with your art."

I thought of Erato and her swan poem and pulled out frit in opaque white and scarlet red. I added bits of sky blue, spreading them on the metal surface of the marver table. After the first gather, I rolled the tip of the rod into the color bits, which clung like sprinkles on an ice cream cone. I melded it all together in the glory hole, spinning the rod all the while, then sat down at the workbench with the calipers to pinch and twist streaks of color, until they pleased my eyes.

I gathered one final layer of glass from the crucible and returned to the workbench to shape the piece with a wooden tool that looked like a ladle. I kept turning the hot glass bulb inside it, until it conformed to the ladle's bowl-shape, dipping it into the bucket of water at my feet to keep the wood from burning.

"Presto, change-o," I said once Nico helped me rap the paperweight off the rod. "One colored paperweight. Now the bottle?"

Nico shook his head. "One is luck. Two is progress. Three it begins to be truth. Two more colored paperweights. Then, we will practice blowing bubbles."

After an entire day, my arms and back ached from handling the heavy tools. My face felt sunburned, and a river of sweat had stained and stunk up not just my armpits but my entire t-shirt. After mastering the art of puffing air through the rod to create a hollow vessel at the tip, I made three glass ornaments, which met Nico's approval. But now, the work day was over, and he needed to close up the shop.

"Please," I said. "I need to make the bottle this weekend."

"Tomorrow is Sunday, Rocket," he said. "The shop is closed."

After a look at my pleading face, he relented. "Early. Seven o'clock."

I spent the night at Gillian's, to save myself the commute and leave more time for glassblowing the next day. We did yoga in her backyard, so I could stretch out the kinks in my burning shoulder blades and spine. Every so often, I looked across the street at my old house, but Ryan was nowhere to be seen.

Gillian noticed me looking and poked me in the back of the head.

"I knew it—you do like him!" she crowed.

I blushed, but I didn't deny it.

That night, I slept in her trundle bed. She tossed me my favorite quilt, the one her mom had stitched together out of old flannel pajamas and pink satin, the kind they put around the edge of baby blankets. I burrowed under it. We talked in the dark for a little while longer, but my eyes wouldn't stay open.

"I have to get some sleep," I mumbled apologetically. "I told Nico I'd be there at seven."

"Ugh," she said. "You have to work on a Sunday morning? It's summer!"

"It's a special project."

"Wake me up, and I'll come help you," she said, her voice sounding hopeful.

"Oh," I said. "Sure."

But when my alarm buzzed, I slipped into the bathroom to get dressed and then tiptoed away—without telling her. This was something I wanted to do on my own. By the time Nico arrived at the hot shop, I was there waiting with a bag of cinnamon buns from the bakery down the street. Nico smiled as he turned the key and held the door open for me. Boombox first. With my wake-me-up mix blasting, I moved around the studio, preparing materials and laying out tools. Nico heated up the crucible and glory hole.

We checked on the pieces from the previous day, which were slowly cooling in the annealing oven. Everything looked fine, no cracking. I felt a rush of pride looking at all that I had accomplished the day before.

I'd brought a mesh strainer from Gillian's house, because I didn't want any impurities in the new piece. As I carefully rinsed away particles of dust from the shards of my old bottle, though, my confidence ebbed. A bottle—that required a whole new skill level.

"To make a bottle is easier with two people," said Nico. "In order to make the opening at the neck, you must transfer the piece halfway through to a punty rod, so that you can flare out the other end. We will practice the transfer until you are comfortable."

We spent more than two hours on just that. I blew a bubble, shaped it so it had a bit of a neck at the end closest to me, and flattened the outer edge with a wooden paddle. Then, Nico gathered a small amount of glass onto the end of a punty rod, and we made the transfer, "gluing" the bottom of the piece to the punty and breaking the piece off the blowing rod with a sharp rap.

And then we did it again. And again.

On the third pass, I slipped up, sending a piece crashing to the floor. I stood there, staring at the fragments, held by a memory of the day my mom had collapsed and been rushed to the hospital. I hadn't thought about her at all this weekend, I realized.

Nico clapped his hands gently. "Rocket, mia cara, no worrying about what is done. We sweep up the mess, and we move on to the next piece."

By noon, I could manage the punty, and by late afternoon, I had learned how to form an open bottle neck, to narrow it or flare it out into a wider vase opening. Nico even taught me a way to drop larger pieces into a box padded with a fire blanket, in case there wasn't anyone there to catch for me.

After I finished my third bottle, he gestured to my jar. "It's time. If you still want to try."

I laid out the fragments of the bottle my father had made for me, thinking about the night I had shattered it. My anger. My grief. Then I remembered the joy and confidence of mini-me, and I went to choose bits of new color from the jars in the cupboard.

Forging the new bottle, rolling the hot pliable glass in the fragments and frit, I felt like a magician creating a potion, an alchemist, turning base metal into pure gold. I left some of the bottle clear glass veined with a river of colors. Ruby red from the original bottle, layered with streaks of sunny yellow and deep blue, plus a single splotch of opaque Pegasus white that spread across the bottle like an outstretched wing. My bottle was a little lopsided. Its shoulders sloped crookedly from the uneven neck, and there were bubbles galore in the thick glass. Miss Fletcher would definitely call it wabi-sabi.

But it was finished. It was mine. And I loved it. I threw my arms around Nico, giving him a big hug.

"Thank you," I said. I let go of him and spun around the room, hip-hopping and hop-skipping and raising my arms up to heaven. "Thank you, thank you, thank you."

Nico helped me whittle down cork from wine bottles to make snug-fitting bottle stoppers. "Perfecto," he said.

I looked down at my little rainbow bottle. "Do you—," I hesitated then spilled out the words in a rush. "Do you think my father would be proud of me? I know it's just the basics, but—"

"Rocket," said Nico, "your father was proud of you from the moment you took your first breath, and with every breath you've taken since. And I can see that glassblowing…it *is* in your blood. And your hands. And that smart head of yours. But most of all, it is in your heart."

I couldn't wait to show it to Gillian. But when I arrived at her house, she wasn't there.

"Gillian went off with Ryan to Carina's a couple hours ago—something about being a back-up singer for the show," Megan told me apologetically. "She was pretty upset when she woke up this morning and found out you'd left."

Drat. Kapow. Bam. I needed some of those spiky comic book bubbles above my head to express what I was feeling. I'd lost her to Carina again, and this time, it was my own fault. Never mind. I'd save her, too, if my plan went correctly. If it didn't, we were probably all doomed.

There was no time to waste. Now that I had the bottle, I needed godsbreath to fill it. I couldn't take physical objects with me into the astral plane, and that's where Polly came in. I hightailed it to the Getty Museum on the bus, climbed all the steps and found my way to the mercifully empty Hall of Muses. Despite my fears, Polly materialized right on time.

I held my rainbow bottle right in front of her. "Breathe."

Polyhymnia pursed her lips and blew, and wisps of pink goddess breath swirled into the bottle. I quickly replaced the cork.

"It's such a shame we have to do this," Polly said with a sigh. "You know, Zeus might have been wise after all when he punished Prometheus for giving humans fire."

"Why do you say that?" I asked, pulling out Gillian's bottle. I'd brought all my practice models, too, just in case one wasn't enough.

"Well, that started humans on the path to mucking up the air on earth. It all used to be this heavenly," she answered, sending a little puff into my face.

I braced myself, waiting for the impact to send me reeling to the floor like it had the first time. All I felt was happy. More myself. "Into the bottles, Polyhymnia," I told her.

"You can still find pockets of air like this, of course, but so much of it has been contaminated," she reminisced. "Oh, earth was so beautiful once, all green and wild and pure."

"It can be like that again," I replied. "We just need to inspire the right people. Okay, last one."

I held out the bottle, and Polly obediently exhaled into it, in shades of green and gold this time. I was amazed at the range of colors she could produce. I stowed the bottles carefully into a padded case and zipped it up.

"Hopefully, this will do the trick," I said.

"Do you have time to walk around the museum with me?" asked Polly hopefully. "I come here at night sometimes when the place is empty, but it would be nice to stroll around with you."

"When this is over, I'll meet you back here, and we can play tourist. I'll even buy you lunch," I promised her. "They don't have ambrosia, but they make a Greek salad that's to die for."

She smiled and kissed me on the cheek. "You have a sweet heart, Rocket Malone. Goddess be with you." With that, she drifted back into her statue.

I left the museum and took a bus north to Malibu to pick up something else I needed to succeed. It took about a million bus transfers to get back to Hollywood. Rick practically pounced on me when I walked in the front door.

"Where have you been all day?" he asked. "It's almost nine! Your mom's already asleep."

I decided to go with the truth. "After I worked with Nico at the shop, I took a bus up to the Getty Villa. For inspiration."

"You're getting pretty independent."

"Yeah. Tomorrow, Ryan and Gillian and some other friends will be competing in a music event on the pier."

"You want to go support them?" he asked. "That's cool."

"Um, yeah. I can take the bus again. Gillian will be there, too."

Rick didn't interrogate me, unlike my mom. "Cool. I can pick you up, so you don't have to take the bus at night. Just let me know what time."

I nodded. "Thanks. I'm pretty tired…"

"Yeah, get some sleep," he said.

I didn't sleep though. As soon as I was safely in my room, I went through the mirror to consult with Narcissus.

"Here's the plan," I told him. "According to Gillian, Echo is obsessed with Rock Gods."

"Rock Gods?"

"It's a video game where you mimic playing instruments to score points," I explained. "She's hooked in Ryan, and now I'm afraid she's got her claws in Gillian. There's a big play-off at the pier tomorrow afternoon, and they're in it. You and me, we're going to crash this shindig and kick some nymph noogie. Your job is to seduce Echo and persuade her to go back to Mount Helikon with you. Once she's there, the Muses will hold her, until I can deal with her."

Narcissus looked dubious. "Your plan seems quite flawed. Besides the obvious problem that you expect to use me as bait, there are too many variables that could negatively impact the desired outcome. For example, what if Echo no longer finds me appealing?"

"You have no idea how gorgeous you are, do you, Narcissus? It's so ironic," I said. "Don't worry, I have a solid back-up plan. If, for some reason, Echo has lost interest in your pretty face, then I'm gonna unload a bottle of whoop-ass—aka godsbreath—right into hers. Or Carina's, technically. You know what I mean. That should break Echo's hold on Carina long enough for you to grab the little nymph and transport her back to Mount Helikon."

"I don't think it's going to work, and it's simply too risky," he said. "I have to decline."

"What do you mean, 'risky'?" I asked him.

"You remember Artemis, right? Warrior goddess and fierce huntress? Protector of maidens everywhere? She despises me. Last time, I simply ignored Echo, and she turned me into a flower. If she discovers that I'm deliberately toying with Echo's affections, with malice aforethought, she's liable to do to me what she did to Actaeon."

"What was Actaeon's big crime?" I asked.

"He was hunting in the woods one day and saw her bathing naked, so she turned him into a deer. Then, his own hounds savagely ripped him to shreds."

My mouth dropped open. "Seriously? You Greek gods are more immature than middle schoolers," I said. "But too bad. Time to man up, Mr. Fancy Pants! Do you have any idea how expensive it is to get narcissi out of season? They bloom in early spring, and it's almost September. I went all the way to a swanky florist in Malibu that imports them from South America—it took me three bus transfers and half the money I earned babysitting this summer."

I poked him hard in the chest with my pointer finger. "So you *will* get your butt down to earth, mister, and you *will* invite Echo to play Rock Gods with you. This afternoon."

Narcissus rubbed his chest with a wounded frown. "Ouch," he said. "You do realize that I could have come through a mirror, right?"

"There will be mirrors all over the place—I didn't want you popping up in the wrong one. Don't be late, or I'll sic Artemis on you myself. Woof. Woof."

THIRTY-ONE

THE PIER WAS MOBBED WITH THE USUAL SWARM OF TOURISTS, PLUS HUNDREDS OF ROCK God groupies making their way to the performance area. Ducking out of the flow and down the wooden stairs, I found a secluded spot way up under the tar-soaked beams of the boardwalk. I had to crouch, as I pulled the potted narcissus plant out of my backpack. The paper-white flowers with their sunny centers looked pretty bedraggled, but they would have to do.

Holding the pot out in front of me like an offering, I closed my eyes, mentally summoned an image of Narcissus and puffed on the plant. I opened my eyes. Nothing. I blew a little harder. A few bruised petals lost their grip and tumbled to the sand.

"Slow down, Rocket," I said to myself. "You are a warrior now, not a worrier."

Once I had my breathing under control—steady, slow and deep—I tried again, exhaling consciously from my belly. And there he was. In the flesh. Way too much flesh.

"Ouch!" was the first word out of his mouth, as he stood up and crashed his head into the wood pilings right above us. He crouched down, gently patting the spikes of his electric blue mohawk to make sure no damage had been done.

"'Ouch' is right," I said, examining his outfit. "That's what you're wearing?"

Narcissus had paired a short white toga and a black leather jacket dripping with chrome...chains, studs, and oversized zippers. Sandals laced with leather thongs all the way up his bare thighs completed his ensemble.

"Get it? I'm a Rock God," he said. "Classic rock meets Greek classic."

"Whatever works for you, my friend," I said, shoving the poor little flower back into my pack.

"You're just jealous, because I look fabulous, and you look…" he trailed off, shrugging his shoulders.

"What? Boring? Chubby? Let her rip," I said, crossing my arms across my chest. "I can take it."

"You don't look bad. You just look like you're trying to blend in with everyone else," he said. "You're a Muse for goddess' sake. Represent."

"It's too late now," I said. "The show starts in fifteen minutes. Besides, we're in the real world, not on Mount Helikon. I can't just snap my fingers and manifest designer duds. We need to get in there—now. Follow me."

Narcissus stood up quickly, whacking his head on the underside of the pier again. Fortunately the blue spikes on his head cushioned the blow.

"You're kind of clumsy for an immortal," I commented.

"I was immortalized for my extraordinary good looks," he replied. "Not my speed or agility."

"You forgot your legendary vanity," I retorted.

A temporary stage had been erected right on the big pier in the parking lot, between the carousel and the amusement park with its famous solar-powered Ferris wheel. Elaborate scaffolding supported lights, speakers and an intimidating grid of giant viewing screens. A huge crowd was cheering on the first contestants. I could see in the monitors that they weren't our friends.

Narcissus was mesmerized by the video display, particularly the game screen, which was lighting up with every note the contestants were supposed to hit on their mock instruments. The current team was doing okay, until the drummer missed a note. Then, the rest of them tumbled out of sync. Their avatars onscreen slumped over in dejection, just like the actual teens onstage.

"Too bad," I said. "They didn't make it to the bonus round. That's where the real points happen."

"So the goal is to mimic a real song as closely as possible?" he asked.

"Yep," I said. "They get points for every note they hit…the more perfect sequences they get, the higher the score…and if they do the first part without making any mistakes, they enter Hades, the rock underworld, for a bonus round."

I tugged at his black leather sleeve. "Come on, we need to get back stage."

But the sea of people was pushing against us, and I couldn't move forward.

"Allow me," said Narcissus. Shimmering almost imperceptibly, he moved through the crowd so easily, it was as if the Red Seas had parted for us. I followed right behind, clutching one of the choke chains dangling from the back of his jacket. In no time at all, we had reached the stage.

"Being a transcendent immortal walking in the physical plane has its advantages," Narcissus said, a little smugly. "Travel by iridescence is one of them."

"I hate to pop your bubble, but I'm not sure how we're going to get through there," I said.

Red velvet ropes cordoned off the area just in front of the stage. Two beefy dudes stood guard, forbidding expressions on their faces. Tweedle-dum and Tweedle-Dee. Mountain and Man. The Two Towers of Terror. One had a bristly blond crewcut. The other was swarthier and shaved completely bald, except for his face, which sported a bushy black beard.

"Just where do you think you're going?" demanded the blond boulder on the right. He crossed his bulging arms over his chest.

"Our friends are in the competition. We need to see them," I said.

The guard on the left shook his head. "Not going to happen. Only contestants with the proper badges are allowed backstage."

Narcissus nudged me with his 'I've got this covered' look.

"One of the contestants is my girlfriend. I promised I would give her a good luck kiss before she played," he explained, shimmering as hard as he could. "You don't want me to be punished, because I broke my word, do you? Look, I even dressed to impress her."

The guard stared him down. "Nobody gets through. Nobody."

I had a brilliant idea. Or so I thought. "It's really important. Our friend needs her lucky, um, plant to perform."

I fumbled my backpack and was about to pull out the potted narcissus, when the blond bruiser went all commando on me at the first sight of a leaf.

"Drop the bag! Drop the bag!" he boomed.

I dropped it. Before I could blink, he had kicked it away from me and tackled me, expelling every molecule of air out of my lungs with a painful whoosh. From beneath his bulk, I watched helplessly as the narcissus tumbled out in a shower of potting soil. The pot rolled out of the bag and under the velvet ropes toward the stage. As I tried to inhale, gagging on the guard's ripe scent—an eye-watering blend of dirty gym socks and onions—I just prayed that the precious glass bottles inside the pack had remained intact.

A frazzled woman with a clipboard and a walkie-talkie rushed onto the scene. "What's happening here?"

All I could do was wheeze and gag, while the guard saluted her.

"These two were trying to get backstage to bring stuff to their friends," he said in a Very Important Voice.

"So?" she said, sounding confused.

"Our assigned mission is to secure the stage area."

"Your mission?" she said, in an incredulous voice. "This isn't a military operation. It's not like you're protecting actual rock stars from rabid fans. It's a Rock Gods contest! Teenagers playing music video games! Half of them have parents and sibs in the dressing tent with them."

"We're just doing the job you asked us to do," said the guard with the shaved head, in a grumpy voice. Definitely Tweedle-Dum. Duh-Dumb-Dumb-Dumb.

"I didn't tell you to tackle teenage girls. She can't weigh more than a hundred pounds. Get off her, for goodness' sake!" she said. She shoved at him and extended a hand to help me up. I stayed doubled over for a few seconds, gasping for air.

Honestly, sometimes having a human body is just a recipe for pain. Why in the world do football players subject themselves to this kind of abuse on purpose? My conditioning over the summer served me well, though, and I got my breathing under control pretty quickly.

While I was recovering, Narcissus turned his radiant smile up to nuclear fusion strength. The woman blinked.

I smiled at her, too. "Thanks."

She blinked again and took a step backwards. Narcissus gave me a wink. Huh, I thought. Interesting. Maybe my smile had power, too.

I tried to move past her, but she was in a daze. "I, um, just need to get my backpack?"

Although the competition had carried on throughout this whole interlude, we were starting to draw attention from the crowd around us. The emcee threw an annoyed look at the woman, who shook off her bemusement and spoke to the guards in a no-nonsense way.

"They have my authorization to find their friends," she said. "Let them through."

He reluctantly unhooked the barrier rope from its stanchion. "It's on your head, lady. That little girl's packing some kind of unidentified plant material. She claims they're just flowers. And that one—well, look at him. He's a freak."

Narcissus smiled at him. "Thank you! That's the nicest thing anyone has said to me in centuries."

"All the teams are in the big tent behind the stage, getting ready," the woman with the clipboard informed us in a whisper, as she ushered us around the back of the stage, out of view. "What's the name of your friend's band?

"Ummm, I'm not sure," I said. She started to look suspicious. Narcissus stepped up.

"May I?" he said, running a finger down the sheet of names on her clipboard. "Here they are. Echo-Noia."

I nodded. "Yeah, that's them, for sure."

"They're up in a few minutes," she told us. "Better hurry."

The tent was even more chaotic than the area in front of the stage. There must have been thirty or more teams, each with four kids: guitarist, keyboardist, drummer and vocalist. Many of them were sporting even more bizarre costumes than Narcissus. He smugly pointed out that little detail.

"Surely you must concede my superior camouflage skills now?" he said.

"I blend in just as well as you do," I protested, looking down at my worn jeans and black t-shirt.

"Perhaps. But I look much more interesting."

"Stop preening and start scanning the room," I said. "Awk!"

"I get it, Rocket," he said irritably. "You don't have to shriek like a parrot to make your point."

I squawked again. "No, no! Look over there—that's them heading out the back!"

I pushed past a bunch of surprised kids, excusing myself left and right, as I shimmied my way across the tent.

Narcissus followed close behind, grumbling. "Travel by iridescence is so much more professional."

Carina was dressed in a hot pink leather mini dress that made Narcissus look positively prim in comparison. Her glossy black curls had been elaborately teased and styled, and between the big hair and the five-inch black leather boots, she dwarfed me. I gasped when I saw the identically-dressed girl at her side, a black wig covering up her light hair. Gillian.

Bringing up the rear were two boys kitted out in black suits with hot pink skinny ties—Ryan and Gillian's boyfriend Jasper.

"Hey Gillian, look who's here," Jasper said.

Carina spun around. "Who's here?" she snarled.

I knew immediately that Echo was inside her, totally running the show. She locked eyes with Jasper. He paled and went silent.

I looked at Gillian and let out a gasp. Gillian's eyes were blank, unfocused—she didn't even see me. She was like some kind of robot, waiting to follow Echo's lead.

Carina smirked at me in triumph. I stepped forward, wanting to shake the nasty right out of her.

Narcissus stepped in between us.

"Hello, angel," he said, attempting his best seductive voice. I cringed at how phony he sounded.

Echo clenched her lips like she was getting ready to spew venom, but she had no choice but to repeat his words back to him.

"Hello, Angel."

She practically gagged trying to resist speaking. I almost felt sorry for her.

"I've missed you," he said, smiling.

"I've missed you," hissed Echo. "Miss-sssss-ssssed you."

She swiped at him with a hand that was curled into a talon, aiming to carve scars into his flawless face. Narcissus grabbed her wrist with both of his hands, stopping her just before she gouged out an eye.

He looked over at me with a helpless expression. "Maybe we should just forge ahead to Plan B?"

I looked at Ryan, Gillian and Jasper. Angering Echo just made her hold on them stronger, and their faces were as blank as bowls of milk. No surprise, no confusion—no emotion at all. Shadows. Zombies.

Frantic, I put my sunspecs on. I could see nubs of passion and creativity still alive at the core of them, glowing like tiny embers under a bed of gray ash.

I was about to pull the bottle out of my backpack, when the stage manager approached with her clipboard.

"Oh good, you found your friends just in time," she said breathlessly. "Wish them luck—they're up now."

Narcissus brought Echo's hands to his lips. He kissed her knuckles and looked into her eyes with a warning.

"You be careful, baby," he said.

"Careful, baby," she repeated as she ground down on his sandaled foot with one of her pointy boots. Grimacing in pain, he released his hold on her. She smiled maliciously, spun on her heels, and steered her puppets toward the stage, where the emcee awaited her.

Narcissus turned to me. "Surely you agree that seduction is out of the question," he said. "Echo clearly has lost her desire for me. In fact, I think she detests me. She won't be easily manipulated."

He sounded bewildered by the possibility, even a little hurt, but I couldn't deny the truth. I watched Carina, trying to figure out how best to implement plan B.

The emcee was a burly man with hairy arms and a thick black beard he had slicked into a stupid-looking point. He looked familiar. I caught him winking at Carina. She smiled at him, but it wasn't a real smile, just a stiff little upturn of her lips. The emcee slicked back his hair and raised the microphone to his pufferfish lips. As soon as I heard his voice, I remembered him. Mr. Revolto. The creep who had tried to rent my cottage.

"Introducing our local champions, Echo-Noia!" he boomed, as they took up their positions. What was he doing here? Were he and Echo working together? I remembered what YaYa had told me—watch for the synchronicities.

I had to give Echo credit. She had found her game and she played it like a champion, leading the automatons, who had once been my friends, to a punishing victory over all the other teams. Holding the microphone to her lips, she repeated the song scrolling on screen almost simultaneously, the time delay between original and response so brief it was imperceptible. The others under her spell matched precisely on keyboard, drums and guitar.

The crowd cheered them on, clapping and stomping wildly, as Echo hit bonus round after bonus round. I expected frenzied applause when they finished the song with a perfect score. Instead, everyone in the crowd had gone glassy-eyed, swaying back and forth as if hypnotized by a cobra.

Echo dominated the stage, oozing smug satisfaction at the way she had enthralled the audience. She raised her hands above her head and brought them together slowly and deliberately in a loud clap. Jasper, Gillian and Ryan, along with the entire audience, followed her lead and clapped once. She did it again, clapping twice. They copied her. Soon she had everyone applauding after her in a deafening, unified pulse.

She abruptly brought her hands down and the entire pier went silent with her. Revolto came back onstage, a sleazy smile stretching ear to ear—although his hair was so shaggy, it was hard to make out where his ears began. He stood next to Echo and raised his microphone again.

"Wow, that was hypnotic, wasn't it, folks? A perfect score! If Echonoia can repeat that perfect performance in the next round, not only will they land first place, they will set a new Rock Gods record! And—I've got a special announcement."

He pointed to a video crew that had materialized at the back of the crowd. "The final round tonight will be broadcast live around the world, on satellite television! This Rock Gods competition is going global!"

The thought terrified me. Echo zombiefying a world-wide audience, snuffing out creativity all over the planet? We didn't have time to mess around. Fine. On to Plan B. Brute Force. When Echo left the stage, her face triumphant, I was ready for her. Narcissus was holding the flowerpot. I had my sunspecs in place and my trigger finger poised on the atomizer of the bottle of godsbreath.

A tap on my back and a familiar growling voice caught me by surprise. "What do you think you're doing?"

I swirled around, reflexively firing off a spray directly into the face of Tweedle-Dee. And in self-defense, fired again at Tweedle-Dum, who was storming up right behind him.

The guards instantly succumbed to the kaleidoscope mist. Blondie stopped cold, Baldy crashed into his back, and before I knew it, the two of them were giggling and dancing a chorus line together.

"Bobby, buddy, did I ever tell you about the time I serenaded Whitney

Houston? I was on guard detail at the Grammys. *Eye-eee-eye will allllllll-waaaaaayysssss love you...*"

Just as he was really getting into his off-key rendition, Echo rounded the corner. She took in the scene and tried to flee. I spritzed away, praying that one of my shots would land on target. I managed to hit Ryan, Jasper, Gillian. Everyone but Echo.

"Grab her and hold her still!" I yelled at Narcissus. He was busy trying to fend off the guards, who had decided to add him to their impromptu chorus line. Wriggling out of their grasp, he dropped the flower pot and managed to secure Echo. With his arms locked tight around her body, he turned her to face me.

"Sorry, Echo," I said. "You need to go home now."

Squeezing the atomizer bulb over and over as if life depended upon it, I pumped every last drop right at her. Like bellows delivering oxygen to dying coals until they glowed red-hot, the godsbreath nourished the tiny ember of spirit flickering deep inside Carina. As it unfurled and blossomed, Echo's spirit shrunk, until she was huddled into a small cloud of black smoke deep inside Carina's lungs. Carina coughed violently, and Echo shot out of her mouth like a cloudy mess of squid ink.

"What now?" said Narcissus.

"You have to breathe her in, before she takes over another human body," I told him urgently, as we watched the miasma pulsing in the air between us. "You can breathe her out again once you reach Mount Helikon!"

"Then what? How are *you* going to get back?" he said.

Tweedle-Dee and Tweedle-Dum used his moment of hesitation to link their arms over his shoulders for synchronized high kicks. The black cloud was expanding, seeking a new host. I picked up the bedraggled plant and shoved it toward him.

"I'll wrap things up here then follow you to Mount Helikon. The Muses will know what to do with Echo," I told him. "Suck it up, Narcissus!"

He didn't look happy about it, but that's just what he did—he inhaled the inky cloud that was Echo, then dove headlong toward the flowerpot, spiriting her away. The two guards were thrown completely off balance and fell hard, crushing the plant beyond all hope of salvation. It didn't matter—it had served its purpose.

The guards looked befuddled for a second, but they quickly shook it off and resumed dancing. The members of Echo-noia, however, were in various stages of confused euphoria. They didn't have time to get themselves together, however—the emcee ushered them back onstage for the final round.

Bewildered, no longer under Echo's domination, Carina, Gillian, Ryan and Jasper resumed their positions at the instruments. But instead of looking at the video screens, they started looking at each other. At first, they tentatively picked out notes, but soon they were boldly improvising—beating on drums and tra-la-la-ing and having a blast.

The crowd began swaying and dancing, humming and harmonizing. Maybe it was the music, maybe it was the mist of godsbreath wafting over them, but the whole event turned into a hippie love fest after that. The emcee tried to shut down the party, but the guards wouldn't cooperate—they were also under the creative spell of peace, love, music and moonlight.

Me? I just put on my sunspecs and enjoyed the show, dancing my heart out on the sidelines. I was twirling and whirling, when the bottle slipped out of my hand. Dismayed, I watched it arc off of the stage, catching and refracting the spotlights into a million rainbows. I waited for it to shatter—but a miracle happened.

In a moment that seemed almost choreographed, a guy standing at the edge of the crowd reached into the air and caught the bottle in one hand. He looked around and met my gaze.

It took me a moment to recognize him.

"Gary? Gary Grossman?" I said, stunned.

Thirty-two

THERE WAS SOMETHING DIFFERENT ABOUT GARY. HE WAS A FEW INCHES TALLER, FOR ONE thing. His shoulders had gotten broad and muscular. Even his hair seemed thicker. It waved over his collar in a very appealing way.

"Rocket Malone?"

The former whiny quality of his voice was gone entirely, replaced by a deep pitch that did something funny to my belly when he said my name.

"Does this belong to you?"

I nodded and he placed the bottle into my hands, as intact and perfect as it had been the moment I created it. Which is to say, totally flawed…but perfectly able to fulfill its purpose of holding and delivering godsbreath.

"Thanks, Gary," I said, feeling strangely shy.

Gary looked around. "I'm not entirely sure how I got here," he said. "The last thing I remember, I was at the end of the pier, setting up my invention, when Carina showed up. I was telling her how you were the one who inspired me to create it and she went ballistic. After that, everything is kind of a blur. A noisy blur."

"I inspired you to invent something?" I asked, surprised.

"Yeah. When I was at Space Camp this summer, I couldn't stop thinking about what you told me at the graduation party," he said.

"I don't remember," I said.

"You told me that my IQ was off the charts and maybe I should start using my powers for good instead of being a jerk. Like that quote from Spiderman: With great power comes great responsibility."

"I said that?"

He nodded.

"So what's this thing you invented?" I asked.

"It's dark, now. Come to the end of the pier and see for yourself."

We left the music and mayhem behind us and walked, past the Ferris wheel and the boardwalk games, past the food stands with vendors hawking everything from ice cream to souvenirs.

I hesitated and looked at him suspiciously. "This isn't going to be another one of your specialty drink concoctions, is it? The kind that makes me foam at the mouth like a rabid squirrel?"

"No," he said. "Although you'd make a really cute squirrel."

There was something unusual about the way we were communicating. It was like an alien had taken over my voice, made it all coy and girlie. Could this be...flirting? I wasn't trying. It just seemed to be happening on its own.

"Hmmmm. Does the surprise involve launching paper airplanes to the back of my skull?" I said, walking forward again.

"No, although it does involve some sweet aerodynamics," he said, grinning a little. "And maybe it will make up for those other things."

"Huh," I said. "I guess we'll see about that." And so help me God, or Goddess, I giggled.

Gary didn't seem to mind, though. In fact, he seemed very happily mesmerized by me. Bemused.

"I guess we will," he said.

I decided there was definitely an undercurrent of electricity buzzing between us.

When we got to the end of the pier, Gary stopped in front of a big metal chest. He keyed in a combination and opened the lid. I peered in.

"Fireworks?" I asked. "Aren't those illegal in Southern California?"

"I got a special permit from the city to test them off the pier tonight," said Gary, in an excited voice. "These are something I invented in chemistry camp this summer. They're completely eco-friendly. I made the casing out of plastic that's derived from algae, so it's safe for marine life. Instead of potassium perchlorate, I'm using nitrogen, which burns much cleaner. And, the whole thing gets launched with super-compressed air instead of gunpowder."

He reached into the box and pulled out an emerald green cone. "I call this the Green Rocket."

He slid it into a special launcher that had already been mounted onto the railing and handed me a lighter. I lit the fuse that trailed from the bottom. We stepped back and watched as a sizzling, dazzling, dancing shower of green and blue light exploded over the moonlit waves. I even thought I saw a dolphin leaping a little ways off. But it seemed like nothing more than a beautiful backdrop. Center stage in my mind was the boy next to me and the feeling of his arms whispering against mine. When the last spark drifted into the dark, I felt like dancing. So I did, right there in the moonlight.

"You're different," Gary said. "You're all shiny."

I looked at him with a smile and my breath caught at something in his eyes. I felt shivery with promise, a magical tingle of moment that beat in my veins like distant conga drums. It was confusing, because sometimes I felt like that when I looked into Ryan's eyes, too.

But, it made deep sense—it was what Erato meant when she told me she loved being in love…with kittens, with trees, with everything. I suspect she particularly loved this—the giddy feeling deep in your stomach when you're about to be kissed.

That giddy feeling went up like smoke when Gary came at me less like a butterfly and more like a brick, grinding my lips against my teeth.

I pulled back. "Ow."

"Sorry," he said. He looked dazed, too. And really, really bummed.

"Hold on," I said. "Try that again. In slow motion."

I could see the scientist in Gary's eyes, cogs spinning in his enormous brain as he analyzed the problem and formulated a solution. He gently cupped my face with his right hand and used his left to brush back a few strands of hair that had fallen in front of my eyes and tuck them behind my ear. With unbearably exciting meticulousness, he leaned in for the moment of contact, giving those butterflies an opportunity to take wing in my stomach. They danced right up into my chest and began cross-pollinating with the bumblebees that had started a buzzy humming in my blooming heart.

The earth moved. Not metaphorically. No cat sitting on my chest and rumbling.

"Did you feel that?" I asked Gary.

"Mmm-hmm," he said. "A little tremor. Cool, huh? I'd put it at a 3.5 or so on the Richter scale. I wonder where the epicenter was?"

He leaned in for another kiss. Then, the sunspecs started to do something funny. They were pulsing, like the mirror did. And simultaneously, my cellphone went off, ringing and vibrating. Clearly, the universe was trying to send me a message. I was supposed to be back at Mount Helikon by now. Something must have gone wrong.

"Gary," I said. "This is all kinds of amazing. But I have something really important I have to do right now."

He looked hurt. I thought about that quotation. Great power, great responsibility.

I looked into his eyes. "Don't get me wrong, THIS is important to me, too. Very. But I have a job, a job that means the world to me, and I left some things unfinished."

Gary released me. "You'll figure it out, Rocket. You're all kinds of amazing, too."

I headed to the stage. When I looked back, Gary was already setting up for his next launch, showing a group of kids the rocket.

Thirty-three

WHEN I CALLED HOME TO GET A RIDE, MY MOTHER SOUNDED FRANTIC. "ARE YOU SAFE? DID you feel the earthquake??"

"Yeah, it was just a little one, mom. Could you send Rick to get me? I'm still at the pier."

I could hear her panting and suppressing a moan. "Mom? Mom?!"

"The epicenter was right here. I don't want you to worry, but with all the excitement, I'm having what seem to be contractions. I'm sure it's nothing, but—yeowzer, here comes another one." Her phone clattered to the floor.

Rick came on the phone. "Rocket? I'm going to take your mom to the hospital. Can you stay with Gillian?"

Suddenly, Rick's calm efficiency didn't seem quite so annoying.

"I'll find a ride home," I reassured him.

"Oh, and Rocket, some bad news. The mirror in your room fell off the wall during the earthquake. Be careful you don't cut yourself on all the broken glass. I'll help you clean it up later." He ended the call before I had a chance to respond.

Uh-oh.

I thought of Narcissus and his fears about Artemis. I remembered Zeus and his creative punishments. Was it a coincidence that my only passage back to Mount Helikon had been destroyed by an earthquake? Somehow, I doubted it.

If Narcissus could materialize through flowers and the Muses through their statues at the Getty, could I find a medium to travel between the two worlds without the mirror?

Pegasus! I knew just where to find a magical miniature of him. I just hoped Carina would be back to normal, now that I'd expelled Echo.

The crowd was still rocking out to Echo-noia, but that didn't stop me from rushing up to Carina and yelling into her ear. "I need your help!"

She handed her mike to the closest guard, as I pulled her off the stage to a quieter spot. "Where's your limo? Can your dad take me back to your place?"

"My dad?" she asked uneasily, sounding embarrassed. "You mean, James the chauffeur?"

I didn't have time for her to retreat into awkward snobbery, so I blurted out the bare truth.

"I know he's your dad, Carina. And I for one think that is much, much cooler than you being some spoiled rich kid with her own limo and driver. None of that matters right now. What matters is that I need to get your house, right away."

"To my house? Why?" she asked.

How was I supposed to explain that while I was astral projecting, I had visited the bedroom of the old man in the mansion where she lived and seen something I needed?

"Your dad's boss, he collects art, right?" I hedged.

Carina nodded.

"Well, I've, um, done some research, and I think he might be the mysterious man who bought my dad's last masterpiece, the sculpture he did right before he died. And I really, really need to see it."

James was reading a book, sitting on a bench on the pier. Carina sat down next to him, and doffed his chauffeur's hat over his eyes.

"Hi, Daddy," she said.

He looked surprised for a second but recovered quickly, kissing the top of her head. "Hey, little darling. I missed you."

He looked up at me with a shy smile.

Carina nudged him. "Do you remember Rocket? She's looking for a sculpture, and she thinks Mr. Greeley has it in the villa somewhere."

"Oh?" he asked, intrigued. "Well, I've dusted quite a few pieces of art in that house." He shot a quick glance at Carina. "Oops."

"It's okay. She knows you work there, and she doesn't care we're not rich," Carina told him. "Tell us what it looks like, Rocket."

I held my hands an arm's length apart. "It's a statue about this tall, made of white and silvered glass. A winged horse with a little girl riding on his back."

"Pegasus and the Apprentice Muse," replied James promptly. "Sure, I know that one. Gorgeous piece. It's on a pedestal in the master bedroom suite."

"Oh well," Carina sighed. "Mr. Greeley hasn't left that room for years, and he hates to be disturbed."

I wasn't ready to give up. "Do you think he might let me in to see it, just for a moment?" I asked.

James scratched his head. "Well, as a matter of fact, I drove him to the cruise ship terminal this morning for a grand adventure. A round-the-world sailing trip."

The news startled Carina. "What? No way!"

James continued. "He woke up the other morning all spry, saying he'd always wanted to visit places like Bora-Bora and Borneo—and that he was raring to feel the salt air on his cheeks. And just like that, he made it happen."

"That's crazy!" said Carina.

James laughed. "Not as crazy as sitting in your bed for years on end when you have a bazillion dollars to follow your bliss. But it sure was sudden, like someone lit his butt on fire."

I smiled to myself. Score another one for this apprentice muse.

"Not only that," James continued. "He told me he was thinking about donating some of his art to museums."

He winked at us. "So I guess he won't mind if a few people get a sneak preview of his collection. Follow me, ladies. Your chariot awaits."

We wended our way through the mob of dancing teenagers to the stairs leading down to the car, and sank into the cloistered coziness of the limo. James pulled smoothly away from the curb, and within a short time, we were gliding up the long driveway of the mansion in the Palisades.

James eased the car to a stop. Carina and I hopped out of the front seat before he could open the door for us. "Beat you to it, Dad," Carina said.

"You girls go on up," he said. "I'm going to park Miss Delilah here in the garage, and rustle up some dinner."

Carina and I slipped off our shoes and left them in a special cabinet by the front door. We padded up the wide curved stairway, which was swathed in the most luxuriously thick royal blue carpeting. It felt like heaven—or a Muse's meadow—under my bare feet. I followed Carina, trying to stay patient and not reveal that I already knew the way as she led me to the master suite.

She flipped on the light switch, and there he was. Pegasus.

"He's more beautiful than I remembered," I said softly.

Carina looked at me curiously. "You've seen it before?"

"When I was little."

It didn't seem like the right time to go into an explanation of how I'd astrally projected myself through her home a few days ago. "It was sold right after my dad 'checked out and left me with abandonment issues.'"

I tried to say the last line with a casual laugh, but couldn't erase a trace of bitterness.

Carina winced a little. "I'm sorry I said that. I don't know what got into me."

Not what. Who. I thought to myself.

"I'm not mad at *you*," I said out loud. "Besides, maybe you were right. Maybe I do have abandonment issues."

"Maybe we all do," said Carina in a very small voice. She looked so sad all of a sudden, and I realized I didn't know Carina's story. Didn't know how she and her father had come to be here, cleaning house and driving for a rich old man.

I looked back at the statue. "Do you mind if I just sit here alone with him for a moment?"

"Oh, sure. No problem." But she didn't leave—she just sort of hovered a moment, then rushed forward to bestow an awkward little hug on me. Turns out I really needed one of those.

Thirty-four

THINKING OF MY FATHER STIRRED UP A TON OF SLUDGY MEMORIES, MAKING ME FORGET what I was supposed to do. Echo. The Muses. Summon Pegasus. I laid my hand on the smooth white glass. Brushed a finger down the back of the little rider with her mouth wide open in laughter…or was it song? Maybe she could lead the way.

Why was it so hard? Gillian and Ryan were probably still singing their hearts out onstage at the concert. Why couldn't I belt out one little tune? All I had to do was sing. My own song. It didn't have to be perfect, I told myself—it just needed to be mine. What had Ella from choir said? Just open your mouth wide and let sound come out.

"*Ohhhhhhhhhhh-oh-oh-oh,*" I warbled softly. I closed my eyes and let my body sway a bit. "*Mmmm…mmmm…myyyy song…is here, somewhere…*'

And suddenly it came, bubbling up like water from a spring.

> *I'm singing here beneath the moon*
> *Searching for the words and tune*
> *Wishing you could sing with me*
> *Wish we could be in harmony*
> *I'm dancing here in plain sight*
> *Twirling in a pool of light*
> *But you can't see me.*
> *I'm floating in a tranquil sea*
> *Asking you to swim with me*
> *But you can't hear me.*
> *I'm flying through the clear blue sky,*
> *Soaring freely, wheeling high*
> *Above the clouds…*

I felt a change in the room, a deep vibration that shook to the center of me. I opened my eyes. The sculpture had begun to ripple in the moonlight, like waves of heat coming off desert sand, like the glass had suddenly remembered the intense heat of the crucible. I kept singing, kept believing that this could work, despite my tentative voice, thinking of Zeus and what he would do with sweet Polly and mad Echo, if I weren't there to speak for them.

> *Where are your wings? Why can't you sing?*
> *When will you shine? When will you fly?*
> *Why can't you try? I hear your cry*
> *I see your rage, and I see your pain*
> *I see you hiding, filled with shame,*
> *I think you just forgot your name, and*
> *Can't remember why you came*
> *To be on earth, to grow your wings,*
> *To dance and fly and swim and sing*
> *Pegasus, fly over seas and past the dawn,*
> *Please bring me home to Helikon.*

The Pegasus statue pricked his ears in my direction and let out a whinny then tossed its little head with a shimmer and shake. And just like the Muses had emerged from their statues, Pegasus transformed until he was there in his full-sized three-dimensional glory, making even this grand room seem like a cramped closet. His white wings wiggled in anticipation, and he gazed at me intently with his liquid chocolate eyes. I understood his thoughts—he was eager to fly with me, having only been waiting for me to invite him in a language he could accept.

I stroked his beautiful snowy mane. He touched his velvety nose to mine. I saw that his back was empty. He had materialized—but not the little girl.

"Oh," I said aloud, my voice full of wonder. "She's already here. It's me."

Pegasus was tall. Very tall. I patted him on the neck and climbed onto a spindly antique chair near the window. I grasped the shoulders of his wings and pulled myself astride him. He pawed his hoof a couple of times and let out a great whooshing snort. His powerful back and haunches contracted.

I grasped his mane tightly with my right hand, and threw up the other to protect my face as he plunged forward toward the window. Instead of the windows shattering, though, the glass simply dissolved around us as Pegasus swooped up and away. We merged into the sky like starlight.

Flying to Mount Helikon on Pegasus' broad back reminded me of the time Polyhymnia had swooped in and plucked me out of Ryan's room on the night I had found him crying all over his family photo. Swirling through the immensity of space was a relief after the crowds and confusion on the pier. Was this how Amelia Earhart and Icarus felt? 'Something about the wild blue yonder just soothes a body's soul' is how I could imagine my Nana explaining it.

Pegasus reached the rocky landscape of Mount Helikon. He flew past the dense forest and circled over the meadow, but the home of the Muses was silent and dark. No pipes playing. No singing or laughter. I started to get a tight feeling in my lungs and the pit of my stomach.

I laid my hand on one side of Pegasus' neck and urged him forward, hoping to find the Muses gathered somewhere by one of the fountains or in another meadow, working quietly on their various creations or perhaps asleep with their lyres at their feet, dreaming up new music.

In the distance, near the cliffs, I saw a flickering light. "I think someone is standing there, where the paths meet!" I told Pegasus.

He was already wheeling in for a closer look. As we approached, I recognized the bulky cloaked figure. Hekate, maiden-mother-crone, the triple-headed goddess who had welcomed me the first time I entered Mount Helikon.

Apparently, Pegasus knew her, too, because he whinnied a greeting and set down lightly on the ground beside her. A raspy voice issued from inside the shadowy hood.

"Pegasus, son of Medusa, how fare you, old friend?"

That caught my attention. "Son of Medusa? Medusa, the one with snakes for hair who was so hideous just looking at her turned men into stone? How can she possibly be the mother of Pegasus?"

The Crone replied in a weary voice. "There is more to every story than is written in the books of man. I knew Medusa when she was a young and beautiful maiden who helped guard the Temple of Athena.

Poseidon seduced her there in the Temple, and Athena turned Medusa into a Gorgon as punishment. Trapped as a monster, the pain and rage shone out her eyes, turning many men to stone. Glory-seeking Perseus pursued her, used Medusa's own murderous rage against her, and slayed the poor woman. But she was already carrying the Poseidon's babes."

She paused, stroking Pegasus' velvety nose. "Where the blood flowed from Medusa's neck and severed head, this winged beauty Pegasus was born, along with his brother Chrysaor, giant of the Golden Sword."

"Beauty from ugliness, joy from sorrow," added Mother Hekate in a mournful voice. "Destruction and birth—they are two sides to the coin of Life."

The Mother gave a deep, dark sigh, shrugged her shoulders and turned away from me.

Hekate-Maiden threw back her hood and spoke. "You seek Echo and your sister Muses. They are not here because they have been summoned to Mount Olympus to face the consequences of their actions."

She handed me a scroll. I read it aloud.

"To Polyhymnia, my disobedient daughter: I am most displeased to learn that you gave godsbreath to mortals and have taken the nymph Echo into custody. You and your sisters have defied my authority for the last time. I expect you all to report to Mount Olympus immediately, at which time I will pronounce judgment upon you and those who have conspired with you."

Visions of being chained to a rock, doomed to have my liver pecked out over and over, loomed into my head. I shuddered.

The maiden Hekate was oblivious to my fears. She stretched out her arm toward Pegasus, offering him an apple. "I want to ride him!"

"Bound together as we are, it would be difficult, child," said Hekate the mother in a practical voice.

The Crone spoke again. "Rocket, you are at another crossroads. Will you go forward to Mount Olympus? Or back toward the familiar safety of home?"

I pushed my fear down deep. "It was *my* plan that led to this. If the Muses are in trouble, I have to help them. I *want* to help them."

All three mouths opened and spoke the same words in an eerie chorus. "So be it. Pegasus knows the way. He will take you there."

Thirty-five

WITH A WHINNY AND A PARTING BOB OF HIS HEAD, PEGASUS WHEELED BACK UP INTO THE NIGHT sky. His wings beat a steady rhythm, high above the rugged peaks and starlit streams that painted the northward path toward Mount Olympus.

Despite my brave proclamation, I was afraid of what I would find there. Had I failed the Muses? How could I possibly stand up to Zeus, the Father of the Gods?

Mount Olympus was a city dressed to impress—or to intimidate. The monumental columns of white marble could be seen a hundred miles away. The sacred city boasted a vast number of imposing temples and immense formal reflecting pools that made the springs of Mount Helikon seem like birdbaths in comparison. In every direction, I spied bigger-than-life golden statues of Zeus engaged in a multitude of heroic achievements, holding that customary lightning bolt in his fist with a confident smile. Only the highest of the high gods and goddesses dwelled here. Lesser gods were only allowed in by invitation—or command.

In the center of one of the largest pillared shrines, the Muses were huddled together in a golden cage. Echo and Narcissus were trapped in a smaller cage a few meters away from them—she slumped in a corner looking defeated and drained, and he standing as far away from her as their confinement allowed.

Zeus was nowhere in sight, but as Pegasus circled down toward the marble floor, the air began to crackle with static electricity. Roiling clouds gathered, and it felt as if a giant storm was about to unleash its fury upon us. Pegasus set down lightly between the two cages, just as Zeus seated in an elaborately decorated golden throne descended from the midst of the darkness. The throne landed with a thud, shaking the earth and all of us with it.

Pegasus snorted and bowed his head toward Zeus. I had to grip his mane to keep from tumbling over his head. I slid clumsily off his back and stood in front of Zeus' throne, hoping he didn't notice my shaking legs. Zeus glowered at my ride, and waved his arm dismissively.

"Off!" he bellowed.

Pegasus touched his soft nose to my shoulder, pranced a few steps away from me, and then lifted back to the sky. There goes my escape plan, I thought.

Pan appeared out of nowhere and began to prance around the throne on his little goat feet, piping a bawdy little tune. He winked at me obnoxiously. Zeus waved Pan off to one side and glared toward the Muses.

"Polyhymnia, come forward," he boomed.

The cage door swung open, as if it were greased with magic, which I suppose it was. Gentle Polly stepped obediently forward. She was gripping her shawl so tightly that her delicate hands trembled.

"Polyhymnia," said Zeus in a stern voice. "You have destroyed the foundation of trust upon which this family was built."

I stepped up and put my arm around Polly. Her shake was contagious. Breathe, Rocket, breathe.

"F-foundation of t-t-trust?" I asked, looking up at Zeus' stony face. "Are you kidding me? Maybe she thought she could trust *you* to love her and to be there for her even when she makes mistakes. That's what fathers do."

"Who are you?" roared Zeus, glaring at me.

"I'm Rocket Malone," I answered. "Apprentice Muse."

"Apprentice muses. Preposterous idea, as I've been saying since you girls first hatched this half-cracked idea a thousand years ago," growled Zeus, shooting a contemptuous look at his nine daughters. "It was bad enough when you brought on that lily-livered nincompoop Narcissus as a collaborator. Enlisting mortal help was unimaginable. Daughters of mine should be able to handle the job themselves."

Narcissus lost what little was left of his shimmer, when Zeus said his name with such contempt. The Muses stood there, bereft, their faces full of shame and sadness, as he continued to berate us all.

Zeus turned his unforgiving gaze to me. "You humans give me indigestion, breeding like cockroaches, ruining everything you touch. You're destroying a perfectly good planet."

I whispered to Polly. "He means the whole 'indigestion' thing metaphorically, right? He won't actually eat me?"

Polly's lips curved upwards in the tiniest of smiles. That gave me the confidence I needed to keep standing my ground.

"'Lily-livered nincompoop Narcissus'?" I said loudly to Zeus. "You have a talent for alliteration, sir. But you are wrong. Wrong about him. Wrong about the Muses. And wrong about us mortals."

"Wrong?" he thundered. "You dare to contradict me?"

"Well, you are kind of a hypocrite," I commented calmly. "I mean look at this place—talk about rampant overdevelopment. And, let's be honest—you put the "pro" into pro-creation."

Zeus didn't respond. His eyes had shifted away from me and fixated with horror on an enormous peacock strutting arrogantly toward him. Without hesitation or fear, the peacock moved into position just to the right of Zeus' throne then, with a harsh cry, spread its tail in a glorious fan. More static sparks filled the air, and the fine hairs on my arms and the nape of my neck prickled with alarm. As the bird lowered its lush plumage, another golden throne materialized next to Zeus. This one was daintier—and occupied by a very beautiful, very angry Goddess.

Zeus' demeanor went from fierce to flustered faster than the peacock could shake a tail feather. "Hera? What are you doing here? What a lovely surprise, dear."

He leaned over to give her a kiss. She turned her head away from him, and his kiss landed awkwardly on her ear.

"The girl is right, Zeus," she said. "You are quite...prolific."

The peacock hopped onto the arm of her throne. The Goddess stroked his iridescent neck with a languid hand.

"Hera?" I said. "Hera, Zeus' wife? The one who took Echo's voice?"

Hera idly fed her pet peacock grain from the palm of her hand, while she surveyed the scene through suspicious eyes. Her eyes narrowed when she spotted Echo.

"The little sprite was covering up for my husband," Hera replied coldly, turning back to me. "She had it coming."

"I don't understand. Instead of taking it out on Zeus, you took away Echo's voice?"

"Oh, don't be such a goody girl, Rocket. Echo betrayed you, stole your friends and attempted to douse your creative spark," commented Hera. "She's nothing but a shallow, troublesome, talentless girl."

Echo crumpled to the floor of her golden cage. "Talentless girl," she repeated.

Zeus spoke in his most commanding voice. "Yes, Hera. Echo should be punished for all of her meddling."

"Tear her apart! Scatter the pieces of her body into a thousand caves," bleated a hoarse voice from behind the throne. I recognized that voice. Again.

"Revolto?" I asked. "What are you doing here?"

"Not Revolto," said Polyhymnia. "It's Pan!"

Pan sidled out from behind Zeus' throne, a sulky expression on his goateed face. "She spurned my advances, like all the other nymphs. It hurt my feelings."

"Oh, for Pete's sake," I said. "Love hurts sometimes. Get over it. Pick up your pipes and go write a song about it."

"Easy for you to say," sneered Pan. "Ever since the Muses took on apprentices, they've been neglecting their work here on Mount Olympus. That's why Zeus sent me and Echo down in the first pl—"

"Silence, Pan!" Zeus thundered.

But, it was too late. The peacock squawked. In her shock, Hera had clenched her hand around its neck—she released it quickly, patting the peacock absentmindedly on its crown feathers.

The Muses looked stunned.

"Father? Is this true? You were the one who sent Echo to Earth to distract Rocket?" asked Calliope, in a quiet voice that somehow commanded attention just as much as one of Zeus' roars.

Zeus humphed and hawed. Nine muses stared him down.

"I might have brought it to Echo's attention that Narcissus was spending a lot of time down there. And then that girl, Clarita—"

"Carina," I corrected.

"Carina. Yes, she made it easy for me by being so very desperate to fit in. It was quite easy for Echo to take over and wreak havoc."

"Pandemonium," said Pan, slyly. "I helped when I could."

"So, Hera, what shall Echo's punishment be this time?" boomed Zeus from his towering throne.

I rounded on them. "Punishment? Punishment? You blame *her* for this? No, the credit goes to you and Hera, for taking away her voice and driving her senseless with your manipulations."

"Who sings for Echo? Who sings for the Muses?" I demanded of Zeus. "You expect your daughters to write hymns of praise every time you knock down a mountain or stab someone with a lightning bolt or murder a monster to keep your throne!"

Zeus blinked, no doubt surprised by my attack, like a mouse had just turned on an elephant.

"If you're so all-powerful, why don't *you* try singing to *them*? You think it's so easy, doing what your daughters do? It takes talent and courage to turn yourself inside out like they do, to dive into your feelings and set them to music. Muses have mastered the art of making meaning out of things that don't make sense. What do you do? Besides fight all day long and chase women who aren't interested in you? I dare you to write a song or a poem half as good as one of theirs."

By now I was right up in Zeus' face, my finger practically poking him in the nose. He shrank back from me, losing his swagger for a second.

"I've never written a song before," he whispered, looking more like an insecure teenager than the god of gods. "I wouldn't know where to begin. I'm completely lost when it comes to poetry."

As soon as he uttered the word 'lost,' he disappeared. His throne remained behind, empty. Pan dropped his pipes and bleated in dismay.

"Where has he gone?" asked Hera, alarmed. "Where is my husband?"

I had a hunch about Zeus' whereabouts, but he wasn't my first priority.

"Who's got the key to Echo's cage?" I asked the Muses. "She deserves a second chance."

Polyhymnia shook her head and held out empty hands. I ran over to the cage.

"I'm going to get you out of there," I reassured Echo through the bars. "You'll find there are much better ways than copycatting to make friends."

"Friends, friends," wailed Echo.

Narcissus stood behind her, helplessly. "I'm lost here. I don't know what to say to her," he said. "I don't know what to do!"

And with those words, he disappeared, just like Zeus. Zap.

"What to do?" repeated Echo with a sigh, so deep in her pain that she was oblivious to Narcissus' disappearance.

I searched for words that would get through to Echo and give her hope.

"Some of the most beautiful music in the world wouldn't exist unless people had the ability to repeat what they hear," I offered. "Polyhymnia is the muse of choral music. She can tell you."

Polyhymnia took the cue. "It's true. You would be a glorious back-up singer, Echo. You're a natural for call and response choral music."

"Your ability to mimic can be a strength, not a weakness," I went on, in my most encouraging voice. "Some animals—like dolphins or Melpomene's bat—use something called echolocation. It helps them navigate."

Echo pulled a face that made it pretty clear what she was thinking.

"If you don't like that, then develop some talents that don't require you to use your voice at all," I said, pulling other Muses forward. "Terpsichore here can teach you how to dance. Or, you could learn about science from Urania—she's a total genius when it comes to astronomy and stuff. You could learn a musical instrument or write epic poetry like Calliope inspired Homer and Virgil and Milton to do. Find what makes you happy."

I rattled the cage door, and to my surprise, the lock fell away. But Echo, in stubbornness or terror, was clutching the bars of her cage door so tightly I couldn't pull it open. Still slumped on the ground, she banged her head against the bars in frustration.

I crouched down to her. "You don't have to be perfect, Echo. Yes, you will do stupid things, and you'll feel like you don't fit in, and people in your life will leave sometimes. I know you want friends, Echo. I know you want to be loved, but you'll only find shadows of love, echoes—until you learn how to love the most important person in your life. Yourself."

"Yourself, yourself, yourself," she sang back to me.

Oh. Oh! I finally understood who my first and most important client was meant to be. Who it always would be. Me.

I paused for a moment to take in that revelation. But by this time, Hera was squawking and sobbing more loudly than her peacock. I helped Echo stand up and step out of the cage.

"Where is Zeus? Tell me what you've done with him," pleaded Hera. "Please, help me—I'm lost without him." And poof…she vanished, too.

Echo looked at me, her mouth an open O of surprise.

"Don't worry. I know where they are," I said. And I did.

Thirty-six

GETTING BACK TO MOUNT HELIKON PROVED SURPRISINGLY SIMPLE. BEFORE I FINISHED humming the very first note of a new song, I felt the air flutter. Pegasus swooped to my side, followed by Apollo.

Thalia greeted them with a grin. "Divine timing, boys," she exclaimed, giving Pegasus a fond pat on the neck.

The Muses hastened into Apollo's golden chariot, and I gave Echo a knee up onto Pegasus' lofty back. She extended a hand and tugged me on in front of her. In a breath, we ascended into the night sky. Another breath, and the pillars and pavilions of Mount Olympus gave way to starlight, as we hurtled at a dizzying pace toward the natural beauty of the Muses' sanctuary.

Before we could even set down in the meadow, Narcissus rushed up.

"Zeus and Hera are at the pond. They haven't spoken to each other," he said. "They're just sitting there looking miserable. The good news, though, is they seem to have forgotten all about *us*."

"We don't want anyone to be sad," said Thalia, as she scrambled out of the chariot. "Let's get them smiling again."

Melpomene took her time stepping down and rearranging the drape of her gown. "Nonsense," she said. "A little sorrow is good for them. Cathartic. Give them some time to reflect and remember."

"Did I hear you say 'remember'?" came a lilting voice.

"Mother!" exclaimed Calliope. "What are you doing here?"

So this was Mnemosyne, the Goddess of Memory, mother of Muses. Tall and slender, elegantly draped in a shade of deep blue that exactly matched her wise eyes. Her hair fell gently in silvery waves, held loosely back by two long narrow braids circling around her face at her temples.

"I heard about the hullaballoo between Zeus and Hera and thought you might need a little support," said Mnemosyne to her daughters. "Come, let us go find them."

Zeus sat hunched over near a weeping willow tree, a shrunken shadow of the domineering deity he had seemed on Mount Olympus. Just a man.

"Who am I, stripped of my glittering throne, my pillared city," he moaned. "Forsaken by wife and daughters."

"I can see where Melpomene gets her flair for melodrama," I whispered to Polyhymnia.

But when Polyhymnia saw how miserable Zeus was, her eyes welled up with tears.

"Never mind, Father," she said softly, kneeling beside him. "Writing poems of praise and gratitude is our job."

"It's everyone's job," I countered. "Yours, mine, Echo's, Hera's."

Hera's head snapped up at this. "I hardly think it's my responsibility to write jolly sonnets and hymns when I have been so abused," she commented in a snippy voice.

Mnemosyne stepped forward quietly, her hands opened in supplication to Hera and Zeus.

"It is indeed up to you, great ones. What will you choose to remember? The music, or the misery?" she asked, her voice soft and strong. "The losses? Or the loving?"

"I wouldn't know where to begin," huffed Zeus. "I'm not a poet."

Hera looked at Zeus. "That's not true. Once, when we were new, you wrote love poems to me all the time. I believe you composed a new verse every day of our honeymoon."

Zeus looked at her, his eyes brightening. "I remember!" he said. "Odes to your loveliness! Sonnets about your fingers and toes! Verse after verse about dancing with you in the meadow. It's why I went to so much trouble to preserve this place as a creative sanctuary. Only seekers sincere of heart can find this oasis."

He looked around and sighed. "I didn't realize it would take me so long to find it again."

"You've been busy," said Hera. "Creating—and populating—an empire. I thought you had forgotten me."

"Perhaps it's time to retire and enjoy the fruits of all our labors," Zeus reflected. "How can I convince you that you will always be my one true Queen?"

"Your children can help you find your way," said Mnemosyne, smiling.

The Muses, delighted by the idea, danced to Zeus' side and began peppering him with advice. Apollo and Artemis joined them. The God of Gods and his Queen—lost and found together on Mount Helikon. I was beginning to think they had a shot at a second honeymoon of three hundred years.

Mnemosyne approached me. "Granddaughter, you have done well, and I have a gift for you. Close your eyes, hold out your hands."

Curious, I did as she told me. Mnemosyne laid her hands over my upturned palms.

"This memory has been waiting for you," she said. "But you had to heal enough to receive it."

Unbidden, the memories bubbled up from deep inside me.

A sparkling pond surrounded by tree-covered hillsides. A small white horse with wings. Pegasus as a colt. Me, astride him, barefoot in a simple white dress. A giant bear of a man led us through the meadow. My father. All around us tiny fairy lights blinked and twinkled—from the air, the grass, the leaves on the trees. My father lifted me down and patiently showed me how to catch fireflies, how to cup my hands around them one by one and transfer them into a beautiful blown glass jar. Once we had gathered what seemed like a million delicate winged beauties, my father tipped the entire lot over my head. Fireflies caught in the strands of my hair. I resisted the impulse to shriek and giggle and stood very still.

"Just look at yourself, Rocket girl," he said. He picked me up as if I were made of nothing but a spring breeze and set me down at the edge of the reflecting pool. In the glassy stillness, I saw a golden child shimmering there, wearing a crown made of dancing light.

"Queen of the Fireflies!" he said, setting his hands gently on my shoulders. "Look how you shine! So wise, so strong, so loving!"

On the still surface of the reflecting pool, his eyes smiled into mine.

I sighed, and a breeze blew up. My child face rippled away, replaced by modern me. His face stayed the same.

"I miss you," I said to his image in the water. "Why couldn't you stay?"

But I already knew it was something he could never put into words. Life on the earthly plane can be hard, even for people who seem strong. The world is always spinning, spinning, spinning. Some people get dizzy and stop seeing things straight. They forget how to breathe and balance, and sometimes, they just fall down so hard and so fast that nobody on earth could ever catch them.

For a brief moment, my father materialized beside me, as real as the Muses. He kissed me on the forehead then gently scooped a firefly from my hair with one finger and plopped it onto my nose.

"Give your mother a hug from me," he said. "Tell her she needs to start doing her art again. The world needs more pieces like Pegasus."

He turned and dissolved into the night like mist.

Mnemosyne moved to my side and clasped my right hand in her left. "He will always be here for you," she said. "Here, on Mount Helikon."

Polyhymnia stepped in and took my other hand. I looked at her—and she looked at me—and we began to sing. Echo promptly followed, her repetition adding resonance. One by one, others joined us, lifting voices, lyres, drums. The Muses, of course, and all of my sister apprentices, but also Zeus with his thundering bass rumble, tentative then providing a strong and sure counterpoint to Hera's rich contralto. Narcissus and Apollo added their bright and clear baritones, while Artemis and her warriors halloo-ed like trumpets.

Mnemosyne lovingly conducted the putti who had fluttered in on their cherub wings when they saw the gathering sparkle. At the edge of the meadow, Icarus and Daedalus swooped in on their handcrafted wings. Emily Dickinson, flushed and giggling, made a graceful land-ing right between them. All three entered the circle and joined in the singing.

Harmony reigned on Mount Helikon. Muse or Mortal, Apsara, Faery, Spirit, Goddesses and Gods…it did not matter how you labeled us. We were pure energy, pillars of light and sound and love. A tribe of fireflies. Together, we illuminated the night—rivaling even the sun's radiance.

We sang and danced into the dawn, until spent, I sprawled on a grassy slope where I could watch the revelries.

"I wonder if earth is having a solar eclipse?" I said to Polly, watch-ing Apollo weaving ribbons around the Ever-May pole with his sister and his father Zeus. "It's way past time he was supposed to drive that chariot across the heavens."

And once I remembered the concept of time…I realized that it was time for me to go home.

"I don't want to leave this place," I said.

The Muses gathered around me.

"Sister," Calliope said to me gently. "The first level of your apprenticeship is complete. You see what you are, and you know your purpose. You are needed on earth, but you will return here to the source of inspiration to dance and dream and sing with us whenever your soul needs to be fed with joy and re-creation."

Narcissus stood beside her. "You don't need the mirror anymore, Rocket. You can travel here through any vehicle your imagination can conceive. A ray of sunlight, a still pool of water, the dream of a breeze riffling through leaves—whatever transports your spirit."

"So I could just say 'Beam me up, Zeus,' and I'd be here?" I said.

He laughed. "Whatever works, baby."

Baby. Baby. The word tickled my mind, until suddenly, I remembered something so important I couldn't believe I had ever forgotten. "My mother! The babies."

"Let's have a look, shall we?" said Zeus. He snapped his fingers. "Apollo, fetch your priestess, Pythia, from the Oracle at Delphi."

"I think I just have to do it the old-fashioned way," I told him. "By returning to my body and seeing for myself."

I reached out to give Polly a good-bye hug, and she drew me under her shawl, like it was a tent for the two of us.

"Every song that sounds—and resounds in your heart—has a message for you," she whispered. "The songs that you hear and the songs that you sing. Listen to them. Follow the music."

THIRTY-SEVEN

THEY WISHED ME WELL AND I WAS ON MY WAY, LUNGING THROUGH SPINNING STARS WITH no mirror on the other end to guide me home. I summoned the memory of the old man's bedroom, where I had climbed astride Pegasus—but my body wasn't there.

I started to panic. How long had I been away? Minutes? Or was it weeks? Years? Time had no meaning in the astral plane. What if my body was just walking around zombie-style and I never found it?

The little wave of fear began to spiral out of control, until I realized that I didn't need a mirror to remember my self. Ten toes with chipped nail polish, adorning two strong feet, which enabled me to dance and run and squish through mud puddles. Legs that had become long and strong this summer.

Those hands of mine and what they could do—wield a pen, strum a lyre or a guitar, spin a glassblowing rod. Hard-working lungs and heart and brain, working together all the time without me even having to try to keep the blood pumping, that body jumping. I saw myself clearly, and called myself home to my body.

And, oh, ahh, big sighs of relief, it worked! There I was, sitting in one of my lovely old wicker chairs on the front porch of the Venice Beach cottage, rocking back and forth to the beat of my pulsing heart. Ba-bum, ba-bum, ba-bum.

For a moment, I just took it all in, the sights and sounds and smells of this amazing planet. It was hot outside, the sun blazing down on the flowers in the front yard. A skateboarder rolled along the sidewalk, intent on getting to the beach, his wheels clicking over the cracks. The Cecile Brunner climbing rose on the side of the porch smelled as sweet as the perfumed air of Mount Helikon.

I reached out to pluck a pale pink blossom and brought it to my nose.

"Ahh, she wakes," said a voice behind me. "Welcome back."

It was Bethie. She limped over to the empty rocker beside me and eased herself down.

"Where is it that I've been?" I asked, curious to find out what people thought when I vanished to Mount Helikon. "And how long was I gone?"

"Technically, you've been here the whole time. At least your body has been present enough to eat and drink and move around. But the part of you that twinkles through your eyes, well, that's been missing since the night before last when your friend Carina and her father brought you to me. Some folks call it 'shock.' I call it wandering. They thought about taking you to the hospital with your mom, but I told them I could take care of you here."

"I've met Evie," I told her. "She has a beautiful voice."

Bethie didn't look surprised. She just kept rocking and smiled a little. "Evie's beautiful all the way through. Was."

"Is," I said. "It's way too soon for the babies to be born, isn't it?"

Bethie stopped rocking. "I just got off the phone with Rick," she said. "He has been ringing it off the hook checking on you."

"How's my mom?"

"Well, the doctors tried to keep those babies in longer, but your brothers were in a hurry to be born. Congratulations, Rocket, you're a big sister now."

We went as soon as I could get shoes on my feet. Rick met us in the hospital lobby. He looked tired, but happy. My mom was sleeping off the anesthesia, so he took us up to the neonatal intensive care unit to peek through the observation window. Twin boys, each weighing just a couple of pounds. It hurt so much to look at them, those impossibly teeny fingers and toes, their blue skin. I wanted to pull them out of their little plastic bubbles and hold them, but Rick explained that they needed the incubators to get extra oxygen and stay safe from germs, until they could breathe on their own.

"They gave the twins a special medicine called surfactant to help develop their lungs quickly, but it will still be weeks before they can come home. Going home without them will drive your mom even nuttier than bed rest!" he said.

After that, Rick took me to my mom and left so we could have some privacy. I curled up in a chair next to her bed and waited for her to wake.

"Why didn't you tell everyone that *you* created 'Pegasus'?" I said, as soon as her eyes fluttered open. Maybe it wasn't fair to exploit her wooziness, but I needed an answer.

"Hello, Rocket," she said in a groggy voice. "Did I? I just forgot, I guess. I don't know how that happened."

She closed her eyes again. I remembered what Polyhymnia had said, way back when. She had given my mother Lethe water to ease the sadness, not realizing that she was also taking away memories that my mother would need.

"Wait, I *do* remember," she said, her eyes opening in surprise. "Gabriel guided me every step of the way. Without him, 'Pegasus' would have remained a sketch, just another idea of mine scribbled on a piece of paper."

She spoke again. "Your father was an amazing artist, but he wasn't a very good businessman. We didn't have insurance, didn't have any money saved—what I had was a child to raise and bills to pay. It was a hard time. Selling Pegasus helped get us through."

"He passed off your work as his own?"

"Oh, Rocket, no, you're getting it backwards," my mother corrected. "He was planning a big debut show for me—but then he…" She trailed off, and her face went all weary again.

I suddenly realized. "Then he died. You sold it after he died."

We sat there in silence for a few moments.

"Mom?" I said, in a quiet voice. "Rick wants to adopt me."

She looked up at that. "Oh, Rocket, of course he does. He loves you."

"But it's okay if you're not ready," chimed in Rick from the doorway. "I don't need a written contract to know that we're a family. I've got it here."

I turned to see Rick behind me patting his heart with his right hand. In his left hand, he was holding a bag of Stan's Doughnuts. "Whatever you want, Rocket, is fine by me," he said.

I knew he meant it. Something settled in me, like the last tile in a mosaic. I didn't have to chase after love or inspiration. They were always there waiting for me to let them in. To say yes.

So, I said it. "You know what? Let's make it official."

Rick handed us each a doughnut and we raised them up.

I expected one of his longwinded, schmaltzy Irish blessings, but instead he just said one word. "Toast."

My mom and I sang back our response. "Wishes it were a doughnut."

It might be a silly tradition, but it's ours.

EP·I·LOGUE /ˈɛpɛˌlôg/ N.

1. the final section of a literary work, often added by way of explanation, comment, etc. 2. a closing speech in a play, often delivered after the completion of the main action—etymology: from Greek epi- "in addition" + logos "word"

IT'S TIME FOR ME TO WRAP UP THIS STORY, TAKE ALL THE LOOSE ENDS AND FASHION THEM into an elegant bow. But that's impossible, since I don't believe in endings anymore, happy or otherwise. Every moment is a new beginning.

Today is Thanksgiving and we are having a party, Muse-style. So much has happened in just a couple of months. So much to celebrate. Last week, Bethie and Ryan moved out of the cottage and back onto their property in Sun Valley, and today we are going to visit them. It's the twins' first real outing, and I'm scrunched in between the two infant seats. Not that I mind. Looking into their dreaming faces, while they curl their tiny fists around one of my fingers, one baby on each hand, brings me this sweet sort of peace. I didn't tell Rick and my mom that, of course, just griped that it was the only way to keep them from screaming the whole way there. They gave each other those smirky little smiles.

Strangely, I don't find that quite so annoying these days. Rick's turned out to be an amazing dad. He took an extended paternity leave, so he could help with feeding and diapering and dishes and all that grunt work. Baby socks and preemie onesies look impossibly small, but they stack up to a gigantic mountain of dirty laundry faster than one of the twins can regurgitate. You know that story about Sisyphus and the boulder? It's like that—the work never stops.

We turned a corner of the hot shop into a safe zone for the twins, squeezing in a crib and a proper changing table, so frit doesn't land in their diapers. The old sofa's still there, for my mom to catnap. She claims it's not just for sleep deprivation; it's part of her creative process. She's on fire these days, ideas streaming out of her like sparks from an Olympic torch. Sometimes I assist, learning techniques for my own projects. Sometimes, Rick and I sit in the rocking chairs we brought over from the old cottage porch, holding up the twins so they can watch their mother transforming handfuls of sand into miracles. Rick suggested we turn the front shop into a sort of observation deck. Tear down some walls and replace them with windows. He thinks if people could see the glass being made, they'd understand why it's worth spending a few extra dollars.

I see signs of life everywhere as we wind our way up the hill to Bethie and Ryan. Carpenters are at work, hammering together fresh wooden frames that rise up pale and clean against a powder blue sky. Mother Nature has also been rebuilding, painting a soft wash of green over the scorched earth. Everyone panics during the first rain after a fire in the hills, but our autumn storms have been gentle, allowing the grasses to grow and the chaparral to begin its job of sinking roots down into the fragile soil.

I was expecting the Mathews' new home to be a trailer park kind of place, one of those tin boxes that seem to be magnets for tornadoes to twist and trash, but instead, I see a funky little modular house trimmed with horizontal wood siding.

"Did you put those in?" I ask Rick, pointing to an array of solar panels on a shade structure near the house.

He nods. "The Mathews family is officially off grid. The solar panels provide all their power, and it creates shade for a nice outdoor entertaining space."

Rick keeps talking in a nonchalant voice after he parks the car and comes to help unlatch the carseats. "I'm thinking of adapting this model for an urban setting. Say remodeling an old beach cottage into an efficient smart house, fit for a hip family of five."

When my mom sees my shocked face, she laughs. "Just something we're pondering. I know you miss your old home."

"Actually," I tell her, "I've realized it's not about where I live, it's about *how* I live." Once people discover they can be happy wherever they are, joy drops in to visit all the time.

Bethie oohs and coos over the twins as we carry them in, the universal response. Adam continues sleeping peacefully, but Zach—who likes to be in perpetual motion—starts wailing when Rick sets him down on the living room floor. I expertly free him from his restraints and scoop him out, patting him on the back.

Rick turns to Bethie. "It's a good thing Mother Nature makes babies so cute, because otherwise all the crying and sleepless nights would make you want to drop them off at the nearest orphanage."

I know it's just one of his lame jokes, but I give him a warning scowl anyway and he holds up his hands in mock surrender.

Near the living room window, several wind chimes dangle from hooks on the ceiling. I carry Zach over. Bright tinkling music fills the air, and the sunlight streaming through the glass beads casts rainbows of dancing color on the walls. Zach stops crying instantly, his liquid eyes fixing on the chimes. I wonder if he, too, can see the shimmery outline of Evie, blowing him a kiss.

Bethie comes to stand beside me, gesturing to the kitchen table, where fragments of china are arrayed next to tidy trays of glass beads and metal tubes. "Those bits are what your mom salvaged here, after the fire. I call them Memory Chimes. I've already had a few custom orders."

She picks up a twisted spoon, half melted by heat. "This one's from an apartment fire in Arkansas."

Ryan comes through from the back. "Jeff's here."

Jeff Jamieson, that bearded park ranger guy, has come bearing dozens of flats of native plants. Ryan and I are doing a homeschooling study unit with him, on eco-systems and sustainable forestry, and today we're getting a hands-on lesson before dinner.

This year, I'm doing some of my classes online, plus some mini-apprenticeships in things that interest me. Last week, I worked with a pastry chef at a bakery in Venice Beach. The last day, a few of my friends showed up to support me (and sample cupcakes), including Gary Grossman. Gary and I have entered this fuzzy twilight zone between friends and dating. We kissed that one time on the beach, in the moonlight, with the fireworks, but since then, not much sizzle. I'm not really sure which way I want it to go. I don't think Gary is, either. He's been spending lots of time fiddling with his fireworks, improving them so that they actually wash pollutants from the air. I've written a lot of poetry about it, trying to figure out how I feel.

There's this one little haiku that's sticking with me:

in the torpid mud
the lotus dreams of the sun
time to reach and bloom

I'm still fiddling with it, but isn't torpid an awesome word? I'm really into lotus flowers these days, ever since Dani led me on an astral tour of her favorite spots in Bali. I'd like to go there in the flesh someday. Maybe bring my brothers along when they're old enough.

Jeff shows us how to prepare the holes and sink sprigs of manzanita, sage, coyote brush.

"I read that some pine trees only release their seeds during a fire," says Ryan. "The heat pops open their cones so the seeds can be released,".

Jeff nods. "We used to try to stop forest fires from happening at all—then we realized that they were a vital part of healthy forests. New saplings grow fast in ash-rich soil, tall and straight without any tangled overgrowth blocking their light."

He points out a blackened oak tree on the slope, showing us the new green shoots around its base.

"Look—some of the live oaks are already coming back. See the buds ringed at the base of their trunk? They sprout after the brush is blazed away."

Maybe hearts are like oak trees.

We finish with just enough time to scrub our hands before sitting down to the feast my mom and Bethie have spread out on a battered wooden table under the solar awning. They've made it beautiful with colorful fabric and platters heaped with food. After the meal, Ryan disappears while I am burping one of the twins. I know where to find him, though—I can hear the guitar music wafting up from the grotto.

I hand Zach into Bethie's willing arms and pick my way down the old stone-edged path, until I spot Ryan sitting cross-legged on the flat top of a massive boulder, guitar in his lap. I pause out of sight, behind one of the burnt oak trees and reach for my specs, until I realize I don't need magical devices to see the spark inside Ryan. He cocks his head to one side, trying different combinations of chords, plucking a pencil from behind his ear to scribble into the notebook opened next to him. It's a beautiful sight…watching music being born.

Someday, Ryan and I might be more than just friends. For now, we are here, and I am happy. That's enough. No matter how long I study, I'll never know all the answers of this world…but not knowing what's around the corner doesn't scare me anymore.

I find a boulder of my own and climb aboard. There's comfort in its rough surface, the weathered bulk that has sat on this hillside bearing witness to thousands of fires and floods, absorbing and reflecting the music of the universe. A million billion stars singing above, a million billion voices thrumming below. Once I heard a scientist on the news say that after a major earthquake, the entire planet vibrates a little—like a big bell ringing. Inspiration is like that, too. Every single creation makes the world shiver with delight. As I sit and stare at the horizon, words come knocking at my brain like guests arriving at a party, and I reach for the journal I carry with me.

The muses and I can't be everywhere all at once, you know. Don't just sit around waiting for us to show up on your doorstep. You have to do your part. Learn from the bright stars, the heroes of art and science and adventure that the Muses praise in their song and dance. Study them, fly with them, let yourself get a little lost with them. Sooner or later, though, you need to reach inside and show the world the divine spark that is all yours. I see that flame in you. Give it some oxygen…feed it, fan it, fire it up. Do the things you love, the things that light you up from the inside. Huff and puff and burn those walls of yours down until there's nothing left between you and the universe. Then, there's only one thing to do.

Shine, firefly, shine.

ACKNOWLEDGMENTS

SOMETIMES, A BOOK JUST SLIPS OUT OF YOU IN A GREAT BIG RUSH AND EASILY FINDS ITS WAY in the world. This is not one of those books. In 1994, I woke up dreaming about Muses and a girl named Rocket. I embarked on a very, very long journey of taking that thread and weaving it into a book. Many people helped me dance through the hard parts.

Extra special thanks to my book doula and editor, the gifted Kara Masters, for her boundless patience and gentle guidance through the years of revision! At times, it seemed I might never be able to finish this book...nevertheless, she persisted! She believed in the book, and in me, and that made it possible.

Many wonderful 'apprentice muses' gave me feedback along the way, which was of great value to me: special thanks to my sister Holly, my nieces Eliza and Anna, Brooke and Sophia Ali, and to Aimee, Taylor, Suzie, Katya, Riley, Rowan, Rory, Macallan, Aurora, Georgina, Carleigh, Shorty, Carmen and Joanne. Much love to the women of my remarkable writers group, who've been here from the beginning—Jenny, Tari, Carolyn, Lisa, Ingrid, Amanda and Rena. I am ever grateful for my cherished circle of mommy friends who show up at every poetry reading, celebrate every book launch and pull out tissues or cake on an as-needed basis. Amy, Lisa, Debra, Suzie, Danielle...what would I do without you? Ditto to Carrie, Becky, Gia and Joyce!

In a time of darkness, Elaine Alghani and Kristin Davis brought me back to clay, paint and my self. Jo Cobbett keeps expanding my creative horizons, from dancing in Bali to losing ourselves in a multitude of museums. So many teachers have inspired my love of reading, writing, history, and art—most especially Jules Tanzer, who passed away last year. I miss you terribly, Jules. Thank you for taking me on my first field trip to the sumptuous Getty Villa, which clearly sparked my imagination! Like Rocket, I had some very good friends as a teen, friends who amaze and encourage me to this day…thanks to my middle school bestie Jenni and my "decorous, demure and definitely divine" high school posse, April, Laura and Michele.

I am grateful to librarians everywhere for their warm welcome and the magical work they do to connect readers and books. I especially want to thank Wendy Westgate and Catherine Royalty of Los Angeles Public Library for their support of indie authors, and the amazing staff at my local branch library in Sherman Oaks.

Much gratitude to Elizabeth Nicholson and Karen Levine of Getty Publications for their consideration, and to Terri Bryson for her support and kindness. Thank you for the music, Shannon Curtis, especially your song #ForBeth. Beth Caldwell shines forever in our hearts. Gratitude to Valerie Bellamy for her gorgeous interior book design. And hey out there to my Facebook, IG and Twitter friends—thanks for the votes on book covers, the words of wisdom on all things writerly, and for lifting me up whenever I sing the blues.

To my partner-in-rhyme and illustrator Courtenay Fletcher—working with you is a joy (and thanks for the beautiful book cover, my super cool, sneaker-sporting friend!). I am also indebted to my parents Frank and Noeleen Schaefer, who instilled my love of travel and adventure, and to my sons Brendan and Charlie, who fill me with wonder and are the best adventure of all. Lastly, this book might never have been released without my partner Kevin Polk, who patiently read the entire final draft aloud to me and helped me polish all those last little bits. Thank you for holding my hands and my heart with such sweetness.

The list is infinite—to those I have not named on this page, you are here in spirit! I am blessed to be surrounded by so many muses.

NOTES

NOTES

NOTES

About the Author:

SUSAN SCHAEFER BERNARDO IS A PUBLISHED POET AND THE AUTHOR OF several award-winning picture books, including *Sun Kisses, Moon Hugs*, *The Big Adventures of Tiny House*, and *The Rhino Who Swallowed a Storm* (a collaboration with LeVar Burton that was sent via rocket to the International Space Station for Storytime from Space!).  This is her first novel. She loves school, and has collected her B.A. from UCLA, a master's degree in English Literature from Yale, and teaching credentials from Pepperdine University. She lives in Los Angeles with her family and an always-entertaining assortment of cats, dog, chickens and creative clutter. When she's not writing, you might find her gardening, sculpting, tidepooling, painting, wandering through a museum or jetting off somewhere exotic in search of inspiration. You can also find her online at **www.susanbernardo.com**.